At the Quiet Edge

"The plot's many twists and turns will stun and surprise readers. Suspense fans will get their money's worth."

—*Publishers Weekly*

"Sharp and sophisticated, *At the Quiet Edge* commanded my attention from the captivating first chapter to the electrifying ending."

—Minka Kent, *Washington Post* bestselling author

"An utterly compelling blend of family drama and suspense, *At the Quiet Edge* pulled me in and didn't let go. I read this riveting, twisty book in one sitting. Not to be missed."

—A. J. Banner, #1 Amazon, *USA Today*, and *Publishers Weekly* bestselling author

"I raced through the pages of *At the Quiet Edge*. This propulsive story places you inside a world of secrets, and locks you inside. And like our heroine Lily and her son Everett, it's hard to know who to trust. This is taut, heart-pounding suspense."

—Kaira Rouda, *USA Today* and Amazon Charts bestselling author of *The Next Wife* and *Somebody's Home*

"As a single mom, I couldn't help but identify with the complex dynamics between mother and son as each protected the other in this gripping thriller. It is a thrilling game of cat and mouse that kept me guessing all the way up to the jaw-dropping conclusion."

—Lucinda Berry, bestselling author of *The Best of Friends* and *The Perfect Child*

Evelyn, After

"Hands down, the best book I've read this year. Brilliant, compelling, and haunting."

—Suzanne Brockmann, *New York Times* bestselling author

"Readers will cheer on Evelyn when the power dynamic with her lying, cheating husband shifts, even while they watch her flirting with disaster in her steamy affair with Noah. A solid choice for Liane Moriarty readers."

—*Library Journal*

"Stone (a nom de plume of romance writer Victoria Dahl) . . . ably switches to darker suspense in a compelling story exploring what lurks behind a seemingly perfect life."

—*Booklist*

"Stone pens a great story that will have readers wondering what will happen next to the characters involved in this mysterious tale . . . Fascinating tale told by a talented storyteller!"

—*RT Book Reviews*

"Victoria Helen Stone renders the obsessions and weaknesses of her characters with scorching insight. Her sterling prose creates a seamless atmosphere of anticipation and dread, while delivering devastating truths about the nature of sex, relationships, and lies, often with a humor that's rapier-sharp. *Evelyn, After* reads like *Gone Girl* with a bigger heart and a stronger moral core."

—Christopher Rice, *New York Times* bestselling author

Half Past

"A gripping, haunting exploration of the lengths to which we'll go to belong, *Half Past* will hold you in its thrall until the very last page. Stone's expert storytelling, vivid characterizations, and tantalizing dropping of clues left me utterly breathless, longing for more—and a newly minted Victoria Helen Stone fan!"

—Emily Carpenter, bestselling author of *Burying the Honeysuckle Girls* and *The Weight of Lies*

"A captivating, suspenseful tale of love and lies, mystery and self-discovery, *Half Past* kept me flipping the pages through the final, startling twist."

—A. J. Banner, #1 Amazon and *USA Today* bestselling author of *The Good Neighbor* and *The Twilight Wife*

"What would you do if you found out that your mother wasn't your biological mother? Would you go looking for the answer to how that happened if she couldn't provide an explanation? That's the intriguing question at the heart of *Half Past*, Stone's strong follow-up to *Evelyn, After*. [It's] both a mystery and an exploration of what family really means. Fans of Jodi Picoult will race through this."

—Catherine McKenzie, bestselling author of *Hidden* and *The Good Liar*

Jane Doe

"Stone does a masterful job of creating in Jane a complex character, making her both scary and more than a little appealing . . . This beautifully balanced thriller will keep readers tense, surprised, pleased, and surprised again as a master manipulator unfolds her plan of revenge."

—Kirkus Reviews (starred review)

"Revenge drives this fascinating thriller . . . Stone keeps the suspense high throughout. Readers will relish Jane's Machiavellian maneuvers to even the score with the unlikable Steven."

—Publishers Weekly

"Crafty, interesting, and vengeful."

—NovelGossip

"Crazy great book!"

—Good Life Family Magazine

"Stone skillfully, deviously, and gleefully leads the reader down a garden path to a knockout WHAM-O of an ending. *Jane Doe* will not disappoint."

—New York Journal of Books

"*Jane Doe* is a riveting, engrossing story about a man who screws over the wrong woman, with a picture-perfect ending that's the equivalent of a big red bow on a shiny new car. It's that good. Ladies, we finally have the revenge story we've always deserved."

—Criminal Element

"Jane, the self-described sociopath at the center of Victoria Helen Stone's novel, [is] filling a hole in storytelling that we've long been waiting for."

—Bitch Media

"We loved being propelled into the complicated mind of Jane, intrigued as she bobbed and weaved her way through life with the knowledge she's just a little bit different. You'll be debating whether to make Jane your new best friend or lock your door and hide from her in fear. Both incredibly insightful and tautly suspenseful, *Jane Doe* is a must-read!"

—Liz Fenton and Lisa Steinke, bestselling authors of *The Good Widow*

"With biting wit and a complete disregard for societal double standards, Victoria Helen Stone's antihero will slice a path through your expectations and leave you begging for more. Make room in the darkest corner of your heart for Jane Doe."

—Eliza Maxwell, bestselling author of *The Unremembered Girl*

"If revenge is a dish best served cold, Jane Doe is Julia Child. Though Jane's a heroine who claims to be a sociopath, Jane's heart and soul shine through in this addicting, suspenseful tale of love, loss, and justice."

—Wendy Webb, bestselling author of *The End of Temperance Dare*

"One word: wow. This novel is compelling from the first sentence. An emotional ride with a deliciously vengeful narrator, Jane's tale keeps readers on the edge without the security of knowing who the good guy really is. Honest, cutting, and at times even humorous, this is one powerhouse of a read!"

—Brandi Reeds, bestselling author of *Trespassing*

False Step

"[A] cleverly plotted thriller . . . Danger and savage emotions surface as [Veronica] discovers that she's not the only one whose life is built on secrets and lies. Stone keeps the reader guessing to the end."
—*Publishers Weekly*

"Intense and chilling, *False Step* wickedly rewards thriller fans with a compulsive read that'll leave readers wondering how well they know their loved ones. I was riveted!"
—Kerry Lonsdale, Amazon Charts and *Wall Street Journal* bestselling author

Problem Child

"Outstanding . . . Readers will find vicarious joy in Jane's petty vengeances and unabashed meanness to anyone who tries to take advantage of her. Stone turns some very dark material into an upbeat tale."
—*Publishers Weekly* (starred review)

"This installment is highly recommended for fans of edgier psychological fiction."
—*Library Journal*

The Last One Home

"Stone gradually reveals her multifaceted characters' secrets as the intricate, fast-paced plot builds to a surprising conclusion. Fans of dark, twisted tales of dysfunctional families will be satisfied."
—*Publishers Weekly*

"The story gives just enough detail each chapter to keep the reader intrigued about where it is going to go next . . . family secrets will never be looked at the same."

—*The Parkersburg News and Sentinel*

"A slow burner . . . *The Last One Home* takes its time to set the scene for the twists and revelations that will come in the last chapters of the book."

—*Mystery & Suspense Magazine*

"*The Last One Home* is elegant and chilling, an indelible novel of family secrets. I couldn't put it down until I learned the truth about these finely drawn characters—the ending left me absolutely shocked and amazed, and I can't stop thinking about it."

Luanne Rice, *New York Times* bestselling author of *The Shadow Box*

"Gripping and relentless, *The Last One Home* stalks you like the serial killer within its pages: you know danger is right around the corner, but you don't know when it'll strike. And just when you think you have the story figured out, Victoria Helen Stone rips the rug right out from under your feet. Highly recommended!"

—Avery Bishop, author of *Girl Gone Mad*

"In *The Last One Home*, Victoria Helen Stone weaves another sure-handed story, this one about mothers, the fierce love they have for their children, and just how far they will go to protect their progeny. This is a suspense novel that's in part a love story, as well as a chilling mystery. But it's the kind of tale that sneaks up on you, revealing discoveries in the last scorching chapters that flip the whole narrative on its head. Full of shifting family loyalties and recollections of the past, and creepy, alone-in-the-countryside vibes, this book held me, start to finish, in its mesmerizing thrall."

—Emily Carpenter, author of *Reviving the Hawthorn Sisters*

THE
HOOK

ALSO BY
VICTORIA HELEN STONE

THE HOOK

A NOVEL

VICTORIA HELEN STONE

LAKE UNION
PUBLISHING

Text copyright © 2023 by Victoria Helen Stone
All rights reserved.

Published by Lake Union Publishing, Seattle

www.apub.com

Amazon, the Amazon logo, and Lake Union Publishing are trademarks of Amazon.com, Inc., or its affiliates.

ISBN-13: 9781662507786 (paperback)
ISBN-13: 9781662507793 (digital)

Cover design by Caroline Teagle Johnson
Cover image: © Ebru Sidar / ArcAngel; © Luis Molinero / Shutterstock

Printed in the United States of America

THE
HOOK

CHAPTER 1

KATHERINE

Katherine Rye turned a fork in her fingers as she watched her husband's boss through the dancing flames of the fireplace. The huge gas monstrosity—the fireplace, not the boss—squatted on the boundary of the dining room and formal living room. It was glassed in on both sides, yet people never seemed aware that others could see through it.

It had been a plus during her daughter's playdates years ago. Katherine could sit in the dining room with a book and a glass of wine and observe Charlotte and her school friends from a comfortable distance, a bubble of silence around her.

Now that Charlotte was in college, these rooms went mostly unused. They were quiet. Dim. Occasionally employed for a book-club meeting or a one-off burst of interest in an online exercise class. But tonight the house was studded with groups of party guests, and for Katherine it felt a bit like watching a television show play out on the square of glass.

She took a bite of one of the chocolate cream-cheese tarts the caterer had laid out next to the birthday cake. The cake itself was German chocolate, Peter's favorite, and a birthday special since Katherine hated coconut. She'd requested the tarts for herself and tried not to feel gratified that they seemed more popular than his beautiful three-layer cake.

The delicately painted plates had come from her great-grandmother, and Katherine remembered reading that most old china was decorated with leaded paint that leached into food through microscopic cracks in the finish. She took another bite, wondering if leached lead had made her a bit duller over the years. Maybe that was a good thing, though, not to feel everything so intently as the decades trudged by. To be worn down like an old pencil.

As she watched, Monroe Daley placed his hand on a woman's arm and leaned closer, flirting. He was allowed. His wife had died two years earlier. Cancer. A man needed a helpmeet, didn't he?

Still, the woman had come here with someone. One of Peter's friends? Not a wife, though. No ring on the hand she swatted playfully in Monroe's direction. Katherine couldn't remember the woman's name or if she even knew it. She'd always had a good memory for useless facts but not for useful names. They floated past her as she moved through the world, little leaves on the wind.

Men floated past too. They'd never flirted with her, really, not even when she was young. And that was fine. She'd been married since graduating from college, locked in tight partnership for twenty-three years with her upright and devout husband. Katherine was a mother, a wife, a daughter, a homemaker. Nothing exciting, but certainly nothing pitiable.

And she could have been pitiable. That was the key fact of her life and always had been. She knew it deep in her bones.

Her hand went briefly to the fabric patch that covered her left eye. It added a little something, at least. Memorability. A story. And this patch was new, bought for the special occasion. Not functional black or nude, but a pretty dark-gold linen that flattered her brown hair. Peter had smiled indulgently at it. She'd added a touch of gold highlighter to the inside corner of her right eye to play up the festive look and even swept a tiny hint of that dust over her cheekbones. Sparkle and shine for his birthday.

She was smiling at the thought when a dark shape swooped in from the kitchen. "Katherine! There you are!"

She set down the ornate fork with a soft, controlled click. "Mom?"

"We're out of red wine!"

Katherine winced a little at that, aware of her own contribution to the problem. She'd had one glass before the guests had arrived and then somehow worked her way through four more over the course of the evening. She felt weighted to her chair as everyone flitted and socialized around her, and when her mom turned up the dining-room chandelier with an irritated flick of her hand, Katherine realized she'd been hiding in near dark, the light set low to keep others away.

Now the blazing crystals seared her vision. "I was enjoying the fire," she explained quickly. When her mother only stared, she sighed. "Okay, I'll grab a few more bottles. Have you seen Peter? Charlotte is going to FaceTime at nine o'clock sharp."

"We should have waited until then for the cake and candles!"

Katherine shrugged. There was a spring snowstorm heading through, and people would be itching to leave soon. Maybe some of them were starting to edge toward the foyer already. Even in Denver, no one wanted to deal with driving through a storm in the dark. She glanced out the window and saw the first drips of fat, melting flakes slide down the glass. "I'll track him down, and then I'll grab some wine from the case in the garage."

Her mom didn't offer to get the wine herself, but she was appeased enough to move back into the kitchen to futz around, bothering the caterer. Their kitchen needed updating, and Katherine wondered if the caterer had been scornful when she'd entered, used to fancier clients.

There was no glass-tile backsplash, no six-burner stove, no updated cabinets, just the same maple wood and gray granite they'd always had. Everything still worked, though, and it felt wrong to spend thirty thousand dollars replacing a perfectly good kitchen, especially when it was just her and Peter.

The place was already too big for them, bought when they'd imagined four or five kids filling it up. Instead it had just been the three of them rattling around on more and more disparate schedules as Charlotte grew older. Katherine and Peter would sell it one day, and the new owners could put in their own dream kitchen, wrinkling their noses at the water-stained cabinet doors beneath the kitchen sink.

If she judged herself by those home-buying shows, Katherine was living in a hell house with her outdated appliances and huge red-brick fireplace. Her dining room was fully carpeted, for God's sake, not a cute throw rug in sight.

As she forced her heavy limbs to push her up from the chair, Katherine fantasized about the airy little condos she'd been perusing online for the past year or two. She knew her type now. A two-bedroom place with floor-to-ceiling windows and a water view. A bay or the ocean, even a lake. Stone floors, a small fireplace, cool colors, but not too modern. The sound of waves and gulls on the breeze. She couldn't wait.

Finally floating into the heart of the party, she looked around for her husband. "Have you seen Peter?" she asked Monroe. The seat next to him was empty now, but a purse perched against the leg of the chair as if the woman meant to return.

"Not for a good while. What a great party, Katherine." He grinned as if he meant it.

"Thank you. I'm so glad you came. We should catch up after I find Peter. Charlotte is going to surprise him with a call at nine."

"Is Peter's princess still liking Gonzaga?"

"She loves it!"

She circulated through the front hallway with careful steps to hide her tipsiness, checking on guests and asking each and every person if they'd seen Peter. Nervousness slipped into her voice despite her best attempts to sound normal.

When she finally made it into the family room after one more careful check of the time, she spotted Father Carlo in his conspicuous collar and black suit. He'd been their priest for only the past two years, and she truly liked him. He was a genuine and warm man, unlike his predecessor.

"Father, I didn't know you'd arrived! When did you sneak in?" She rushed forward to give a hug to the middle-aged man, keeping her body carefully crouched so that his face wasn't straight in line with her breasts. She was five ten, and the priest was definitively shorter.

"My apologies, Katherine, a visit at the hospital ran longer than I expected."

"It's fine. Please be sure to get some cake. Should I have the caterer put together a plate for you?" She gestured toward the wide table set up in the breakfast nook of the kitchen. "The main buffet was already cleared."

He waved her off with a half-empty glass of wine. "Don't worry about me. I'm wonderful."

"Have you seen Peter yet? Charlotte is surprising him with a call."

"He took my coat about fifteen minutes ago when I came in."

Smiling, she swung back toward the front hall, though she paused to chat with another guest before checking her phone again. Four minutes to nine. Almost time.

The door of the guest bathroom was closed. No surprise there with twenty people in the house. A glance down the long hallway of her ranch home revealed the dark rectangle of the open door of their master bedroom. The hall bathroom that had once been Charlotte's exclusive domain was open too, dark and obviously empty.

Katherine swung back to eye the closed door of her husband's office, right next to the front entry. It was a small sunroom they'd once imagined they could turn into a fifth bedroom if needed, but tonight she'd thrown in a few extra jackets that wouldn't fit in the overflowing coat closet. She was taking a step toward it when the door of the guest bath squeaked open an inch.

Katherine frowned. "Peter?" she asked as she spun back.

"Katherine?" a woman whispered. "It's me."

For one strange moment, Katherine's neck prickled, someone walking over her grave. She felt the hair on her arms rise, her nipples tighten; then for one swelling heartbeat, pure calm descended over her as a premonition began to play out right in front of her. Peter was missing, and a woman was calling to her from behind the bathroom door. But he couldn't be in there. Could he?

The strange fever broke when a man's voice boomed from the family room, "I'm here! I got your message!"

The wave receded, leaving something as flat as disappointment in its wake as she twisted her head toward the voice. It wasn't Peter. His younger brother, James, charged across the hall, holding his phone up. He called out, "To the rescue!" as the door opened inward to admit him inside.

Thirty seconds of giggling later, James and his very pregnant wife emerged, her face pink with laughter and his wide with a pleased grin. She laughed aloud when she met Katherine's gaze. "I knew wearing this stupid jumpsuit was a mistake. I couldn't get it zipped past the middle of my back. I had to send out an SOS."

"It's beautiful, though!" Katherine surveyed the floor-length aubergine jumpsuit with envy, knowing she'd look like she'd dressed in an eggplant costume if she tried it. But Rachel looked stylish despite her huge belly and the chunky knit sweater she wore over it. She was a younger generation, somehow, even though at thirty-five she was only ten years Katherine's junior.

Katherine's smile tried to twitch, but she forced it wider. "Hold on, I want to get a pic with you two, but I'm still trying to find Peter. Wait right there. Don't move."

Determined now, she marched straight toward the office door. The knob turned, but her toe and elbow banged into the unmoving wood. A shush of movement shifted against the other side. Fabric sliding. A muffled grunt. A hiss. Katherine shoved harder. Too hard. She felt that the force was too strong, nearly violent, but she'd already barged ahead, the movement beyond her control. A man bit off a cry of pain. Weight hit the wood floor.

"Peter?" she yelled, reaching for the light switch. She spotted his gape-mouthed face near the floor when the light bloomed and asked, "Are you okay?" in an overly loud rush of words even as her brain noted that the light had been off. What a strange circumstance. Why would he be in the office in the dark?

He scrambled to his knees.

"Pete?" his brother asked from behind her. "You all right, man?" The murmur of guests in the family room grew louder as people began to notice the scene in the foyer.

There was a hard click of a boot heel on wood, but it came from inside the office, not from behind Katherine, where her stylish sister-in-law stood in cute brown half-boots.

She pushed the door open farther.

"It's not . . . ," her husband said, his blue eyes wide, his sharp cheekbones flushed. For once, his friendly, easy smile didn't slide into place for the crowd beginning to gather. Instead his upper lip curled high and in, showing his gums in an ugly display of aggression or distress. His gaze touched on Katherine, then on the people behind her before sliding in a half moon of wide-eyed white toward the space beside him. Another person stood there, the door swinging slowly inward to reveal her like a suspenseful shot from a TV movie.

She was beautiful, of course. *Of course.* A stunning stranger. Her short blond hair was cut close to flawless medium-brown skin, the style setting off cheekbones that were somehow sculpted even beneath cheeks still plump with youth. The woman's lips were full, and her

eyes—two working, beautiful eyes—were so green they offered promises of cool grass and poetry. She was petite, and her cropped sweater
revealed a stomach taut enough that even her tight jeans didn't create
a bulge of fat.

Had Katherine ever been that smooth and perfect? If so she couldn't
remember. She was thin but still sagging somehow, her skin looser than
it had been. And she'd certainly never been a tiny feminine ideal.

The rumble of whispers behind them increased when Peter finally
stood straight and his friends and family could see that his belt was
unbuckled, his shirt untucked. Mercifully his pants were still zipped,
though, no little Peter craning its head for all to see.

The girl—a woman, of course, but not yet thirty—was fully
dressed, thank God. Still, her burgundy lipstick had smeared a bit,
pulled toward her chin as if Peter had slid right down her like a cartoon
character hitting a tree, like he'd been that eager to smash himself into
her. She looked even smaller now that he was standing, the top of her
head barely passing his shoulder.

"Peter," Katherine said, her voice still loud and strong as if nothing
bad were happening. She lifted her phone, nodded, her head a little
loose on her neck. "Charlotte is going to call for your birthday," she
explained.

"Katherine," he responded, his voice too loud like hers, but not
strong, not confident; instead it squeaked at the edges. "This isn't . . ."
His eyes shifted away again, out to his people, his real audience. There
was a straight line of sight to the family room from here, though she
assumed most of them had trickled into the entry hall by now. "I'm
not . . . ," he tried again.

Katherine spun on her heel, not a delicate heel, but a solid square
of clunky wood, conspicuous in its lack of sex appeal. The room spun
too, and her stomach followed suit, reminding her of the wine she'd
told herself to stop drinking even as she finished glass after glass. She
shouldn't have had so much. But now she thought she should have had

8

more. She should have had so much that she had crawled to her room and passed out, a woman who could feel nothing and certainly couldn't track down a hiding husband.

She lurched toward the guest bath, desperate, but the door was closed again. Hadn't it been open? James and Rachel had only just emerged, laughing.

As everything spun, a hand touched her elbow, and she jerked away, lunging for the knob. It wouldn't twist, wouldn't give. Unlike the office door, this one had a lock to protect the privacy of whoever hid behind it.

She managed to swing toward the family room and the group of friends blocking the hallway beyond it that led to another toilet, but it was too late now, everything too sour, and her stomach squeezed hard, determined to fix this problem the only way it could. Get the poison out, stop the sickness, purge the betrayal.

Katherine clenched her eyes shut, bent over, and vomited up a hot torrent of her guts. The splash and the smell reached her despite her fervent wish that it wouldn't. The buzz of the guests deepened and peaked at the same time, no one bothering to whisper anymore, because it was all out in the open. The blood-red wine, the scandal, the surprise, the bile. Why bother pretending? Why speak in hushed tones when there was nothing left to hide?

A hand touched her back. "Katherine, oh my God," Rachel whispered.

"Let me help," James said as another palm touched her shoulder.

But Katherine twisted away, pressing her spine to the wall. When she opened her one good eye, everyone was looking at her, staring aghast at what she'd done. Her mother, his boss, the caterer, their life-long friends, their priest, the neighbors. Even Peter stared, his mouth open in an amoeba of cartoonish dismay.

The only one not looking was the woman. The beautiful, baby-skinned woman who'd just embraced Katherine's husband was moving, head ducked, eyes on the floor. She stepped past Peter, glided through the entry, and slipped outside into the dark. She didn't look back at Katherine; she didn't even close the door.

Katherine watched fat globs of snow appear like magic from the dark and blaze through the glow of the porch light. The snow that blew inside hit the wood floor and immediately dissolved into a mess she'd have to clean up later when the guests were gone and she was all alone.

"Party's over, everyone," she said before she let her woozy head fall back against the wall and began to laugh with giddy surprise. It was the perfect party, really—they'd be talking about it for years—and she couldn't believe she'd actually pulled it off.

CHAPTER 2

GENEVA

Once upon a time, Geneva Worther had left the blinds open so the sun would wake her at dawn. In darker months, when dawn came too late, she'd leave them open just for a glimpse of pink sunrise as she rushed around her kitchen. Now she kept the blinds closed tight so she could sleep through the day unless some obligation tugged her up to pull on joggers and a hoodie.

For three months there had been no rising with the sun, no backup alarm, no quick shower and professional dress and packaged carb-loaded breakfast before she greeted dozens of tiny faces that smiled at the sight of her. It was only the dark now, barely cut by the weak gleam of day through blinds, the light grayed out and ugly.

Grayed out and ugly was what she could accept, which was why all she wanted was sleep. More sleep. Then more after that until she might be able to drift away into a better world somewhere.

But she'd eventually wake up to this.

This, her childhood bed, narrow and squeaking, the same cheap mattress she'd peed on when she was four. The bedroom she'd moved out of at nineteen after her first year at a local college. The home her mom had bought during her parents' divorce two decades earlier. She should be happy she'd had a soft place to land. And she *was* thankful for that. Thankful that her mom had opened her door wide when Geneva had come limping home, hauling the ash of all her incinerated dreams with her. But she still lay in bed and stared at the narrow slants of dust motes until her nose stuffed with snot and her tear-wet hair made her shiver.

But today she actually did have a reason to get out of bed and tug on a hoodie, and when she heard the garage door rising, she knew it was time to get up. If her mom found her still in bed this late in the afternoon, she'd ask too many questions Geneva didn't want to answer.

Despite that she was only twenty-six and certainly hadn't done anything strenuous yesterday, her joints protested when she sat up, urging her to tunnel back into her den and hide from the cold that radiated from the latest storm front. A perfect idea, really, except that she needed to pee.

Groaning, she pushed up from the warmth into the chilly air and hurried out to the pink-tiled cave of their bathroom. It was the only bathroom in the tiny house and would have horrified any modern buyer, but her mom had cheerfully insisted it was "full retro" when they'd moved in. And it was. Pepto-pink tiles marched up the walls to chin height except in the tiny shower stall, where they paved every surface, including the ceiling. "A perfect bathroom for two girls on their own," her mom had declared. Maybe it had been, but it was pretty tight for two adult women.

She closed the door behind her before her mom even made it into the house, desperate to avoid her. After last night's shenanigans, she'd fallen into bed with a full face of makeup and now felt filthy and grimy. Her eyeballs were raw from the dried-out contacts she should have removed. Once she caught sight of her red-rimmed, smoke-shadowed eyes in the mirror, she desperately wanted to be clean.

Clean. The idea made her laugh as she flushed the toilet and started the shower. As if. She felt dirtier than ever after that little excursion.

Once the water was going, the small bathroom warmed quickly, and she almost felt human. She tossed the contacts, brushed her black hair into a tight bun so she could shelter it beneath a shower cap, stripped down, and stepped into the steam.

For a long moment she let the water stream over her face like a bubbling hot spring, parting her lips just enough that she could breathe past the flow. Every once in a while she drew in a bit of water with the air, and she imagined herself sinking beneath a still surface, disappearing forever. Her skin tightened from the heat, but she didn't move, barely breathed.

The children brought her back. The sound of them squealing, laughing, shouting. She clenched her eyes further shut and turned away from the little frosted window, wishing she could close her ears as well. It should have been safe by the evening, but there was an aftercare program that ran until six.

Her mom had been so proud of finding this house that backed up to the elementary school. So excited that Geneva would be near other kids and a playground and be able to walk safely home from school while her mother was working. Geneva had even mentioned it in job interviews, claiming it had been her destiny to teach: She'd grown up right next to a school like a flower leaning toward the sun. "I went to school all day, then took a few leaps home and played teacher with my stuffed animals."

That had all been true. Every moment of the dream, every promotion of her skill, every step she'd taken fighting to make her career happen.

She washed up quickly, humming frantically to herself to cover the bittersweet ring of tiny voices shrieking just beyond their fence. As soon as her foot hit the fuzzy white bathroom rug, she reached forward to snap on the ancient fan. The thing probably used as much electricity as a modern fridge, based on the roar of the rotors, but today she was thankful for the ear-stuffing noise.

After drying her face of shower spray and tears, she smoothed on moisturizer, ignoring the tubes of makeup she'd used last night. She couldn't imagine when she'd need them again. Never, maybe. When the hell would she be ready to put herself out there?

She snorted at the very idea, avoiding her own eyes in the mirror as the exhaust fan pulled steam from the air and exposed gradual inches of her reflection.

Frank had ruined her. Stupid, evil Frank, who hadn't meant enough to her to even hurt her feelings. And that had been her biggest mistake, hadn't it? Letting him know he meant nothing? That had really pissed him off.

His revenge had worked perfectly, though. She thought about him every day now, when before he'd been nothing but a blip on her screen when she felt restless.

Towel still wrapped tight around her, she slipped into the hallway. "Hi, Mom!" she called out even as she darted for the safety of her room.

"Getting ready for the gym?" her mom shouted back from somewhere in the vicinity of the kitchen.

"Yep!"

"Can you stop at the store on your way home?"

She shouted agreement before closing her door and pressing her back to it. The least she could do was buy a few groceries. She should have been up hours ago to vacuum or wash towels or something. But the simplest tasks felt impossible from the depths of her mattress.

She quickly tugged on underwear and was digging through her stuffed dresser drawers for a clean exercise bra when her phone rang. The unidentified number wasn't familiar, but it was local, and for the briefest moment Geneva wondered if a cop was calling about her complaint. Maybe they'd finally decided to help her.

Just as she admitted to herself that would never happen, she remembered she was waiting for a call from someone who'd actually *promised* to do something, and she snatched up the phone. Crossing an arm over her chest for a play at modesty, she offered a tentative "Hello?"

"Ms. Worther?"

She winced at the male voice. Not the call she'd been hoping for then, but *maybe* a cop? "Yes?" she said even more softly.

"Oh hi! Hello. This is Tom Sanders!"

Tom Sanders? For a few heartbeats, the name meant nothing at all, but then she remembered a little smiling face. Tommy Sanders had been one of her first-grade students. "Are you Tommy's dad?" she ventured.

"Exactly. I'm so glad I reached you."

"Oh." She frowned until the muscles between her eyebrows began to ache, then snatched up her damp towel to cover herself more completely. Her body recalled that awful vulnerability of being exposed when she was supposed to be safe and secure at work, and it wanted a shield. "Is something wrong? Is Tommy okay?"

"Everything's fine. He misses you, of course."

She swallowed so loudly she was sure this man must have heard it. "I miss him too. Of course." Tommy was kind and funny, a boy who loved facts about birds and pointed them out whenever they appeared near a window. He'd once painted all of his fingernails orange during art hour and called himself an eagle. "He's a sweet boy."

"So I was calling because I've been wondering if we could get together sometime."

Cold flashed through her. Goose bumps erupted. "With Tommy?"

"No, I meant . . . I'd love to grab a drink with you. Catch up. You know."

Her frown smoothed out. In fact, her entire face went slack and waxy, lips parting in something that wasn't quite shock. Nothing terrible was actually a surprise to her anymore, after all. Still, the air of her room felt suddenly too humid, too thick, as if she'd never left the steam of the bathroom. "That wouldn't be appropriate," she said numbly. "As your son's teacher—"

"But you're not," he interrupted. "You're not my son's teacher anymore. So . . . a little drink wouldn't hurt anything, would it? Maybe that's a silver lining?"

"No," she whispered, not meaning to answer his question, meaning only to protest, to deny, to reject everything about this.

His voice dropped as she stared at her open dresser drawer, at the mess of old clothes and wrinkled fabric. All her work outfits hung useless in the closet, packed in too tightly to access, because when would she need them again? Next term? Next year?

"Listen," he said on a low, husky breath. "That video didn't bother me. I wasn't one of those parents. I never said a word to the school. In fact I . . . Ha. I've watched it quite a few times. You're a beautiful woman, and no one should tell you—"

Her limbs finally obeyed her. One hand pulled the phone from her ear while the other reached to hit the red button that would make him disappear. But that was the extent of her strength. She stared at the glowing screen past tears that smeared and twisted the words. Everything was smeared and twisted. Everything.

Breath shuddering out of her, she raised the towel to wipe her eyes clear, motivated now by a fizzing anger that rose to bubble beneath her skin until her knee began to bounce, her hands shake.

Tom Sanders. She had a vague memory of meeting him—fit, White, handsome—at the start of the school year. Tom and his wife—Brook, maybe?—had stood arm in arm, gazing dotingly on their towheaded little boy as he found his desk. A beautiful couple. Young and crisply dressed and successful enough to afford tuition at the expensive private academy where Geneva had landed her first teaching job.

She drew in a deep breath at the memory of the happy little family they presented. How dare he call her? How *dare* he?

But of course Geneva knew exactly how he dared. She was a young Black woman who'd been devastated by scandal. A vulnerable target Tom could set his sights on. An object of fantasy who was probably a little desperate, a little low.

Fuck that guy. She should send a screenshot of his recent call to his wife. Let her know exactly what handsome Tom Sanders was up to.

She wanted to. She really did. But the phone trembled in her hand at the idea. No one would consider her a victim in this, least of all Brook Sanders or Brooklyn or whatever her damn name was.

She snapped the screenshot just in case, then blocked his number, hating herself for cowering away from the idea of getting revenge.

She deleted her recent call history, just to get it out of her head; then she considered deleting everything, wiping her phone clean and tossing it in the trash.

Yet she couldn't. She needed it. Because this tiny revenge might be beyond her, but it wasn't her only path. She'd done her work, played her part in a new system, and it would be her turn soon.

But class wasn't for nearly another hour. Desperate, she sent a frantic text. Can I meet you early before class? I'm crawling out of my skin.

When the answer came, she sagged with relief. Sure. Meet you there in 30?

Geneva yanked on the last of her workout clothes, grabbed her water bottle and her bag, and pushed out the door and down the hall. Her mom was just stepping out of the kitchen, her round face a worried frown before she brightened it into a smile for Geneva. Her cheeks were beginning to sag a little at fifty-one, but her skin was as smooth and glowing as ever. Geneva could see herself there, what she'd look like as a mature woman. The loves and the heartbreaks all gathered up and taken in.

Her heart twisted at the bittersweet thought, at the hopelessness that she'd ever trust anyone enough to feel love again. She tried to rush by. "Sorry, Mom. I'm late."

"Give me a kiss, at least."

Geneva darted in, shoving her seething anger down for a moment to press a kiss to her mother's temple. "Text me a shopping list," she said as an apology for her hurry. "I love you."

"You feeling good?"

Geneva's face twisted at the fear in the question as she fled toward the front door. "Yeah," she lied, her pulse pounding harder as she stepped outside and removed the stifling grip from her heart to let her anger free.

She growled as she slammed her car door, then threw the car into reverse. She zipped into the little street where she'd played throughout her childhood, learning to ride a bike and skip rope. Learning to dream about boys and girls and the warm and sparkling life she'd meant to live.

Until Frank.

She cursed him for the entire ten-minute drive to the Hook but kept her jaw clenched tight and quiet as she hurried in and dropped her bag on the ground to wrap her hands and begin her warm-up.

When Maggie walked in, Geneva didn't rush to her the way she wanted to. Several men were still working out with private trainers, and Geneva knew she needed to maintain a casual air. But she was hyper-aware of Maggie's presence in the room, aware of her movement as she stopped to say hi to another instructor and then pointed at the jump ropes and raised her eyebrows at Geneva.

Geneva hurried to begin jumping rope as Maggie walked toward the office, and the anger began to shake free and fill her veins as her heart galloped hard. Three minutes, then four and five, but she kept going.

Finally Maggie emerged, head cocked in question as she gestured Geneva toward a speed bag.

This was what she'd been waiting for. The violence, the punching, the bob and weave as she pictured Frank's face in the bag and hit it over and over and over again.

Maggie was close enough to talk to now, but Geneva couldn't speak; she was too busy trying to purge the shame of trusting Frank with her intimacy and with Omi's too. The shame all women were meant to feel for wanting pleasure when that had been men's purview for millennia.

Revenge porn. The term made it sound like some kind of action movie instead of the dark, quiet poison it truly was, a seeping, caustic acid that crept on and on and couldn't be cleaned up.

"Geneva." The voice cut into her thoughts, and she realized her face was wet with tears again. Maggie moved over to a heavy bag and braced it to wait for Geneva.

"Ready?" Despite the gray strands in the short coils of her natural hair, Maggie looked young and powerful in her sleeveless workout top. Like Geneva's mom's, her dark-brown skin was still wrinkle free. Unlike her mom's, Maggie's arms were strong and firm with muscle, though when her biceps weren't exposed, her petite body looked chubby instead of muscular.

Though she looked like she could be one of Geneva's gentle aunts, she projected herself like a motivational speaker, a woman who could take on the world and rule over it as a benevolent leader.

"You having second thoughts?" Maggie asked as Geneva squared up in front of the bag.

"Not in the least."

Maggie smiled, her cheeks bunching. Her eyes drilled straight into Geneva, paring away her exterior and focusing on the soul beneath. "I thought I detected regret, but now I see it's fury."

"It is." She threw two hard jabs and followed with a left hook. Maggie nodded approvingly. "Your time will come."

"Soon?" Geneva pressed, grunting a little with the next blow.

"Have patience."

Geneva nodded. "I know. Sorry."

"Don't apologize. This is for you. This is for all of us. And there's nothing sorry about that, is there? We're strong together."

Geneva panted as some of the anger burned itself into reassuring warmth. "We're strong together."

"We work the system," Maggie said in a voice soft enough to be a whisper.

"And make the system work for us," Geneva responded just as softly, her words an answering hiss of breath past the hard smile that came to her face.

"That's right." Maggie nodded proudly. "How did it all go?"

"Fine, I think."

"That was a complex plan."

"He was predictable, though."

Maggie laughed. "Aren't they always? But I'm proud of you. A lot of things could have gone wrong, and now the hardest part is already done." After a few more minutes, Maggie waved her off the bag. "Do you want to talk about anything else? You okay? I was worried about you after that text."

She'd come here to talk, but the violence was what she'd needed, and she felt better now. Not wanting Maggie to think she was sliding backward, she shook her head. "I'm okay. Just restless, I guess."

"All right, then. Keep warmed up. I need to make a few calls before class. But you've got this, woman. You've got this."

She was right. She was always right. Geneva had done the hard part, and now she only had to wait.

Afterward she could move on and reconstruct something for herself. She'd change up her looks, move to another state, get a gig at some unregulated charter school that hired teachers who couldn't get past public school boards. A few years of keeping her head down, and then she'd be back on track.

But first, she would make Frank pay. Everything else was a meaningless distraction.

CHAPTER 3

KATHERINE

"It's only been a week," her mother snapped, her barely there patience finally cracking open into shrill words. "*One week*, Katherine. None of this makes any sense. You have a home."

"It makes perfect sense." Katherine paced back toward the row of living-room windows. The two-bedroom apartment didn't overlook water but did have a great view of the mountains and a new street she hadn't been staring at for twenty years. It wasn't a fancy condo, but it was something. "Peter cheated on me. He's cheated on me before; I just never had proof, and no one believed me. Charlotte is at college, starting a new life, and I'm simply done with all of it."

"*Done* with it? With your marriage and your child and the vows you took? It's that *simple* for you?"

Smiling, Katherine watched the white flash of her teeth in the glass before schooling her face back into a mask of hurt. "I didn't betray my vows, Mother. Peter did, so that's between him and Father Carlo and God. And I still have a child, regardless of how faithless her father was. I didn't forsake my right to her by signing a six-month lease."

"You can't just—"

"I won't ever get married again, so if that's what you're worried about, my soul will remain unsullied by cleaving myself to another outside the church."

She was shocked when her mother grabbed her shoulders and shook her. "I'm worried about you running from your problems like a coward! Do you think any marriage is perfect? Do you think it's all easy? Instead of talking to Peter, you put your time into finding *this* . . ." She let Katherine go to wave a disgusted hand at the furnished apartment. Katherine would never admit it to anyone, but it looked more like a midclass hotel suite than a comfortable home. Still, it was hers.

"Peter might have his flaws—" her mother continued.

"*Might* have his flaws? I knew he was cheating, Mom. I told you over and over. You said I was insecure and not to ruin a good thing. Do you remember that? Ha!" Her hard bark of laughter made her mom flinch away. "We'd only been married four years the first time I told you! I was pregnant with Charlotte!"

"And do you think that didn't drive him away? Your constant doubt? That sour face waiting for him after every business trip? Of course he cheated; you practically drove him to it!"

"For God's sake, Mom." She tried to laugh, but tears rushed to her eyes and spilled over before she had time to even swipe a hand over her cheek. "You really do love him more than me, don't you?"

"Don't be ridiculous. You're both my children."

"No! No, we're not! *I'm* your child, Mom! Becca is your child. Vivian is. You have three children to love, but what a disappointment we've all been since the moment Prince Peter walked into your life."

She chuckled past her own tears at that, because it was true. Mary Whittle had three daughters, and all of them paled in comparison to her precious son-in-law. Becca and Vivian were easy to explain away in her mom's heart. They'd rejected the church early in their adolescence, humiliating their devout mother and both getting suspended from Catholic school for various and varied transgressions. They'd betrayed her.

But Katherine, she'd been the good daughter. The rule follower and nice girl. She'd done everything her mother had expected of her, including marrying a lovely Catholic boy in an age when hardly anyone worried about marrying in the church.

She'd truly cemented her place as the best daughter with that. Peter was a deeply, *truly* Catholic man who'd been a lay minister in the church for the past twenty years, even devoting free time to Catholic retreats and counseling. People loved Peter. People looked up to him.

But he was a lying asshole golden boy who'd fooled everyone completely. Everyone except his wife.

No, even that wasn't true. She couldn't absolve herself. He'd fooled her too for quite a while, and he'd had to keep her miserable and low in order to do that. Through all her suspicions and the miscarriages and the demeaning counseling from their old priest, she'd kept the public lie going for the security of her own position, an actor in their family play.

Plain Katherine with her ugly, useless eye and her straight-as-a-stick figure and her failure of a uterus. She'd been so lucky to land a man like him.

But perfect Peter wasn't so perfect anymore, was he? He was tarnished and cracked, and now Mary Whittle was silently crying, wiping tears from her face as she grieved. She desperately wanted to choose Peter over her daughter in this fight; she'd even tried for a few days, but Father Carlo had counseled her to give Katherine the space to deal with this devastating betrayal.

Even Charlotte, who'd inherited her love of sticking to the rules from her mother, had given up her natural inclination for compromise and unity and had condemned her father's awful behavior. The momentary allegiance might not last long, but Katherine needed to feel Charlotte's love right now. She'd soak it up until the puddle dried, because Peter would worm his way back into the center soon enough.

He worked people, and Katherine had to act quickly to make sure the truth stuck in their minds. She might be walking away from the world they'd built, but she wanted the stain on his image to be permanent. She *needed* that. It felt as if her own truth wasn't real unless others saw it too.

"I need to finish unpacking," she said flatly as her mother continued to weep. When her mom didn't respond, Katherine lied. "I have my class tonight."

That perked her up. "Boxing? I keep telling you you're going to lose your one good eye playing around with something like that."

"We box heavy bags, Mom, not each other. No one is going to hit me."

"Ridiculous," she hissed, but she marched over to grab her handbag. She'd invited herself here, and she could see herself out. "He's sorry, you know," she said, hand on the lever of the front door. "Peter is *sorry*, and you won't even acknowledge that."

"He'd be more sorry if you stopped going over to fix him dinner every night."

"Well, someone has to do it!"

What the hell was she supposed to say to that? To the idea that a grown man couldn't prepare or arrange his own meals? That fending for his own basic needs would somehow demean and destroy him? Yet did Katherine ever get credit for the monumental task of keeping the man fed and clothed for almost his entire adult life? "Bye, Mom."

"I'll see you on Sunday," she said, as if Katherine actually planned on going back to church again. She'd mostly kept up on Sunday mass even after she'd stopped believing, because it was easier than arguing with Peter. She'd stayed in bed until noon last Sunday, stubbornly determined to sleep in even though she'd awoken at eight.

A little laugh escaped her as she told herself she'd go buy a vibrator, her very first sex toy, and use it on Sunday in her husband's honor. But that would never actually happen. She couldn't walk into one of those stores. She'd have a panic attack. And she couldn't order one online either, because what if it went to the wrong mailbox? She'd just moved in, and she'd be trapped for six months in this building, wearing scarves and sunglasses every time she snuck through the lobby.

The door banged closed behind her mom, the solid metal thunk of it another reminder that this place was more like a hotel than a home. But she loved hotels, and she desperately needed a vacation from her entire existence. For the first six months of her new life, this place would be perfect.

My God, she'd done it. After twenty-five years together, she'd left him. And she was never, ever going back.

Boxes and suitcases littered the living room and tiny dining area. She'd piled packing paper so high in one corner it threatened to bury her in an avalanche. She needed to clean, organize, settle in, but she dropped onto the couch instead.

She didn't actually have boxing class until Thursday, but she'd driven by the Hook earlier to glance through the windows. The studio was only a mile away from this apartment, and Katherine felt drawn to it as if it were a church that could help her get through this. In some ways it was.

The second class Maggie taught was tonight, and she desperately wanted to try that one too, but she didn't want to upset Maggie. Katherine might be obsessed, but she couldn't let anyone else see that. That wasn't part of the agreement, and she couldn't be involved if they couldn't count on her. Maggie had told her that explicitly.

"Stay cool," she murmured to herself as she opened Facebook to see if Peter had posted any inspirational sayings today, some scripture or hypocritical pablum to feed his friends and colleagues.

Yes. There it was, as expected as his regular daily bowel movement. Today he'd posted an unattributed quote in flourished calligraphy about God offering comfort and growth through dark days. She clicked to read the four supportive comments, knowing before she even looked that one would be from her mom.

Still, there were far fewer than the two dozen he'd normally have racked up, and one comment was a reassurance about the fallibility of all sinners. Ha. That part was true enough.

Her mother had left a glowing heart emoji bracketed by two pairs of praying hands and followed that up with the words "WE LOVE YOU" in all caps.

What must their friends and family think, seeing that? Did they feel sorry for Katherine, or did they assume she must deserve what she'd gotten if her own mother took Peter's side? A wave of weariness flowed over her at the thought. She'd kept up appearances for so long and thrown up so much fake window dressing that her reality had disappeared for the rest of the world.

She'd refrained from any posts or comments on her own page, though several people had been kind enough to offer their own praying hands or pink hearts. She felt dignified silence was her best look in the face of such public betrayal, and all of their oldest friends belonged to Peter, anyway. They always had. Screw him and his gang of buddies who'd passed the test of being perfectly devout on paper. He could have them.

It was all so odd, though. The realization over the years that she'd somehow been born into a 1950s family despite her actual birth date. And then she'd married into a 1960s household. Not the kind with moms in microminis, but the kind that carried signs protesting sinners. Whatever. It had taken her so, so long, but she had finally joined the ranks of the dreaded lapsed.

She'd realized that an entire lifetime of praying and going to mass and believing deeply in sin and order and God had been nothing more than affirmation. An assurance that if she followed all the rules, the people in charge would approve and keep loving her. Her mom, her teachers, her church, her husband. She'd get the gold star and be the best daughter, the best girl.

Her sisters had never needed that. Perhaps because they'd been normal. Because they hadn't been in that car and smelled their own hot blood when they reached for their face and felt glass and bone. Or maybe because their father hadn't ignored their cries, staring straight ahead, not even bothering to look when Katherine had begged him for help. She hadn't realized he was dead. She'd thought he was still mad that she hadn't followed the rules.

Even her mother didn't know that part. *Don't turn on the light, your father can't see to drive.* With three kids, how many times had her mom repeated that? Katherine had blinded him, and she'd been blinded in turn, and that had been justice. That had been penance. The perfection of that had only pushed her deeper into her beliefs.

She'd been thirty-five and driving her own daughter in her car when the sudden realization had slapped her full force in the chest. The tiny dome light in the back seat hadn't killed her father. It had been his overwhelming irritation that she'd broken the rules.

Jesus, the memory of that epiphany still made her break out in shivers. He hadn't been blinded; he'd been swinging around to yell at her for disobedience. *That* was what had caused the crash.

Desperate to shove the thought back to the past, Katherine quickly clicked away from Peter's Facebook messages and navigated to the Hook's page to check for any new pictures. She'd already scrolled carefully through all ninety-three of the previous media posts from her boxing gym, checking each photo for a certain young and beautiful Black woman, but her efforts had been fruitless. She had spotted herself in one, sweating and rumpled while the other women somehow looked strong and determined, but most of her face was obscured by the bobbing head of a woman in front of her.

Thank God. The less exposure the better.

When her phone vibrated in her grip, flashing an incoming call, Katherine jumped as if she'd been caught with her hand in the cookie jar. The caller wasn't identified, but she answered it quickly anyway.

"Are you ready?" a voice asked, and Katherine's entire body went rigid with a bolt of alarm as she wondered if the Facebook page was monitored somehow. Could everyone see what she was looking at? Who she was stalking?

"Maggie?" she whispered.

"It's me. You remember what we need from you?"

We. Yes. Katherine was part of a group now. A group fighting for the greater good that *she* had chosen to join. She nodded. "I remember. Of course."

"Okay. His username is BrightLife01. If you need to write it down, do it on paper, not on your phone. Burn it when you're done."

Katherine surged to her feet and looked frantically around at the chaos of her half-unpacked apartment. "Hold on. Wait. I just moved in. Everything's crazy."

"Hey! Congratulations on that."

Her muscles relaxed a little at the audible pleasure in her friend's voice. "Thanks, Maggie. It's been chaotic, but I made it." She smiled suddenly and straightened, pushing her shoulders back the way Maggie had taught her. "I did it!"

"You worked the system, girl."

"I actually did!"

Maggie's soothing, deep chuckle smoothed over Katherine, and she closed her eyes and inhaled, trying to settle her nerves.

"You doing okay?" Maggie asked.

"Yeah."

"Good. I hope that means you're ready to pay it forward. Or"—she laughed that amazing, contagious, head-thrown-back laugh she had—"ready to pay it back, I suppose. Your problem was complicated, but it was quite a triumph in the end."

Grinning, Katherine grabbed her purse and dug around for a pen, then snatched a crumpled piece of packing paper from the floor. "Ready as I'll ever be! Give me the username again." She wrote down "BrightLife01," then underlined it as Maggie repeated the letters and numbers.

"We need video," Maggie reminded her. "And we need to see his face to truly expose him."

"I know."

"Listen, I understand that this is outside your comfort zone, but that's what will make it work. It makes you authentic. And once you're through this, you'll be stronger. We'll all be stronger. *Together.*"

She nodded to herself again. "Right. We make the system work for us."

"That's it exactly."

"Maggie? I . . ." Katherine cleared her throat. "I'm sure I shouldn't, but maybe I could come to tonight's class? I just feel like I need a little extra time right now. I've got all this nervous energy to get out."

"Not a good idea," Maggie said, the words crisp and stern.

"No. Of course not. I figured."

"Go for a run. It'll feel good to get out in the world. You have a whole new life to build."

She did. She really did. "That's a great suggestion."

"You could also channel your nerves into the assignment. Men have a way of sensing vulnerability."

"Right." She hiccuped a nervous laugh.

"And let me know when this is done." When Katherine didn't respond right away, Maggie pressed. "I know this part is a lot to ask, but so was your request. That's why we're helping each other. We've got your back. Work the system. Stay strong."

"I will."

Maggie hung up without a goodbye, and Katherine dropped her phone on the generic blue cushions of the couch so she could scrub her hands over her face.

"You can do this!" she ordered herself. She was sure she could. Hell, she'd volunteered for it even though Maggie had eyed her doubtfully. Or was it *because* she had eyed her doubtfully? In that moment when Maggie's expression had morphed from speculation to careful approval, Katherine had stood straighter, bolstered by the older woman's gaze.

She could do this because she wanted to be the type of woman who could. It was as simple as that. After all, she'd been terrified to try the boxing class too, hadn't she? She'd been intimidated by Maggie, stuttering whenever the instructor tried to engage her in conversation.

She'd discovered the class when she'd searched for women's support groups in Denver almost a year earlier. After yet another confrontation with Peter, she'd been desperate for support, for someone outside her own world to hear her and confirm that she wasn't crazy or selfish or hysterical.

She'd tried one therapist, but they hadn't clicked, and Katherine had felt even less sure of her own thoughts. When she'd gotten back online to search for more help, an ad for the Hook had popped up, promising "fitness, self-defense, and esteem-boosting magic for women of all ages and sizes!" It had sounded unintimidating and accessible, but when she'd first walked in, she'd almost walked right back out.

Maggie had looked so powerful and confident, nothing like Katherine. She was strong in body and mind, strong in her beliefs and convictions. But then . . . then she'd smiled at Katherine and welcomed her so warmly that she'd stayed. She'd soon discovered that Maggie was strong enough to teach Katherine to be strong too.

She wouldn't let Maggie down.

Katherine grabbed a tumbler she'd unwrapped that morning, filled it with filtered water from her near-empty fridge, then sat down with her laptop to open the private browser she'd already been instructed to use.

Unlike her usual browser, this one apparently filtered identification through a dozen sites across the world, and it seemed to take forever to load. When it finally stopped grinding away, Katherine opened an anonymous email account that couldn't be traced back to her. Then she typed in the name of the site she'd been too afraid to visit until today: LordsLink.com.

A row of beaming, perfect faces smiled at her when the site appeared, and she winced away from the idea of cozying up to any of them. She had no experience with the evangelical world, but she was way too wise to Peter's righteous smile to fall for that kind of nonsense. No thank you.

She hadn't lied when she'd told her mom she wouldn't marry again. She couldn't even imagine dating. The idea of taking care of another man, of subsuming her opinions and desires for the greater good, in the name of compromise or family or ego . . .

No.

But this? Katherine cleared her throat and swallowed hard, unable to even peptalk her way into saying, *This I can do!* because she still wasn't sure. She'd barely dated before she'd married Peter, had been a virgin, though she'd had a few sexual experiences. Maybe this wouldn't be so different after all.

Her hands were trembling too hard to even click the SIGN UP button, so she set the laptop down and stood to shake out her arms.

When she noticed a box marked *Pantry—Fragile*, Katherine checked the time. It was nearly six o'clock, and she had nowhere to be. She wasn't in the suburbs anymore, so she could walk to pick up dinner or even groceries. Seizing on the idea, she dove toward the box and ripped off the tape with one long pull.

She'd hastily wrapped up spice bottles and pickles and even a jar of capers, for some reason, but right now she needed something else: wine. White wine, though. Her mouth went a little dry at the thought of drinking red after Peter's party.

After dumping the water from her tumbler, she poured a couple of inches of room-temperature chardonnay and took a big gulp to settle her nerves. Liquid courage, and she desperately needed it. After all, she'd rarely done anything dangerous before and she was about to jump straight into the deep end. It was past time for her to be brave.

She signed up, and then downloaded the app to her phone.

CHAPTER 4

Luz

"Can you get your hands on some drugs?"

Luz Molina hadn't thrown one punch yet, she hadn't even gotten out of her car, but her heart was suddenly galloping at top speed. "What?" she whispered into the phone. "No. Why would you ask that? Are you . . . ?"

"I'm trying to find a way around any sex stuff, that's all. I think I have a solution for your plan."

That didn't slow her heart rate, but it did perk her up. "Really? But you said maybe it would be too hard with my situation."

"Yes," Maggie confirmed, "your circumstances will be a little more complex since it's not personal. Personal mess is so much easier."

"It's personal to me," Luz snapped, then winced. Maggie was trying to help her. "Sorry."

"No, I get it," Maggie said. "If someone did that to my partner . . . Woo. That's as personal as it gets, so I'm sorry for phrasing it that way. I meant . . . hands-on. Intimate. How is Sveta doing?"

Luz peered through the huge glass window of the Hook, trying to get her eyes on Maggie as she spoke to her, but she saw only a couple of other clients stretching. Maggie was probably in the tiny gym office, feet up on the desk, since class didn't start for another five minutes.

Luz was early for class because she was early for everything. Dependable Luz, always striving to prove she was worthy in a world where people looked at her and assumed she was nothing at all. Her anger was a stone inside her, pushed down and hidden until she could work it out on the heavy bag.

She tugged nervously at her braid.

"Sveta's okay," she finally answered quietly. "She's living with family, and I'm able to send some money." All true, but tears still burned her eyes. "She'll be all right." The words sounded doubtful even to Luz's ears.

"I'm so sorry," Maggie said, making the tears spill over onto Luz's cheeks. Why did kindness always make her cry harder? She could deal with cruel comments dry-eyed and unaffected, but a little bit of caring sent her into a tailspin.

"I can't believe it's only been three months," Maggie said softly. "It feels like a lifetime ago I'd see her waiting outside after class with your puppy."

Luz had started the class only a month before ICE had knocked on their door. Her brother had boxed a little in high school, and Luz had always been curious about it. But she'd been too shy to try. When she'd driven past the Hook and seen a big banner about a women's class, she'd mentioned it to her girlfriend, who'd pushed her to do it.

And thank God she had. Luz wasn't sure how she would have dealt with Sveta's deportation without Maggie's support and the fury she allowed Luz to purge.

"Thank you again for reaching out when I stopped showing up," Luz said. They hadn't talked much about it. "I wouldn't . . . I mean, I don't really know how to ask for help."

"Me neither. That's why I get you. And that's why I'm here to help."

"Thanks. This has been the best therapy I could get. The boxing and . . . everything else."

"Speaking of everything else . . . do you have access to any drugs?"

"I don't know anything about that stuff." Luz felt the stiffness return to her words, and obviously Maggie picked up on it.

"I'm not asking because you're Hispanic, Luz. I just need to determine if we can make this scenario work. That's all. I think this will be a good match for you."

"Right. I get it. Well, I could get weed, obviously, since it's legal. And I have a friend who sells Ritalin, or he used to, anyway."

"Yeah, we're going to need something a little harder for this."

Luz cleared her throat, hesitant to let Maggie down when this was all on Luz's behalf. "Am I supposed to drug someone? Because I'm not comfortable with that."

"I told you from the start this wouldn't involve physical danger for you or anyone, and I meant it. That's not who I am, and that's not who you are either. I know that. We're stronger together, which means we don't have to get in the gutter with them. This scenario would only involve the *presence* of said drugs, not the use."

"And you're sure this person deserves something like that?"

Silence met her question, and her face heated with embarrassment. She knew she wasn't supposed to ask. But a story told over coffee wasn't the same thing as real life. It had just been shooting the shit with Maggie, her friend, her instructor. It had felt like brainstorming, nothing more than casual talk, but now she was apparently going to plant drugs on someone. "Sorry," she muttered. "I know I'm not supposed to ask."

"Listen, if you want out, we don't ever need to discuss this again. Absolutely no hard feelings and no regrets. I'm not here to talk you into anything. You know yourself and you know your life, Luz. That's why we get along."

Luz scooted down in her seat and glanced around the parking lot, already imagining someone watching, gathering evidence. As far as she knew, her own request for help had already been set into motion. She couldn't abandon the others now. "Don't *you* have access to drugs?" she asked. "Surely with what you do . . ."

Maggie sighed. "Yeah, I guess I could make that happen. We'll talk after class, all right?"

"Maggie, I'm sorry. I didn't mean . . . I'm not trying to back out or anything. I can get drugs if you need me to. I think." Surely some of those guys in sales did coke. Hell, maybe even some of the other software engineers did, though she'd never noticed anything. Her team was pretty quiet, and a lot of people worked from home these days. If they were partying, they sure weren't involving her in it, and that was the way she wanted it. Plus she was their boss now, technically.

"Don't worry," Maggie said, her words a soothing rasp, back to conveying cool confidence and all the reassurance Luz needed. "We will figure this out, and I'll hook you up with a task that doesn't involve sex. I know it's not your thing."

Luz had to laugh, because it really wasn't. She loved her girlfriend to death, but the reason it worked for both of them was because they were honest about what they wanted—and didn't need—from a relationship.

When she was young she'd attributed her nonexistent sex drive to being gay in a straight culture. But even in her college years, nothing had ever really bloomed for her aside from vaguely romantic love and a desire for emotional intimacy. She'd been on first dates with different genders and felt nothing like desire.

But she did love the more comforting side of physical touch, and so did Sveta, and once they'd truly bonded, some of the other stuff had opened up for them too.

Thank God for online forums and digital honesty. It was how they'd found each other, both of them adrift in a society that seemed to pulse with sex, sex, sex twenty-four hours a day. They'd made a home together.

"Don't worry!" Maggie crowed. "I love a challenge!"

Luz had to smile. "Good, because that's what I am."

"I'll make you pay during class. You already here?"

"You know me."

"All right, I'll see you in five."

Five minutes. Not quite enough time to call Sveta and hear her voice, but she opened a text and sent a quick message. I love you so much. I'll call tonight. Stay strong!

Aware that Sveta had worked late and probably not woken up yet, Luz opened her doggy daycare app to check the camera for Ballyhoo, their shaggy little mutt.

Mutt or not, when the live feed finished loading, Bally looked to be ruling over the big group of excited pups with his usual quiet dignity. He was patient but arrogant with other dogs, though he fully enjoyed their presence, and his tail wagged nonstop as he herded them toward a wooden ramp.

She sighed and watched him for a few minutes. She knew he missed Sveta as much as she did. It was why she'd enrolled him in daycare. He'd been so miserable without his constant companion.

After seven years in the US, Sveta had been deported back to Russia. ICE had banged on their door at 3:00 p.m. on a quiet Saturday, throwing their peaceful little world into chaos. "Following an anonymous tip," they'd said.

Anonymous. Her lip curled at the memory.

A suspect had popped into Luz's mind immediately, even before the tears and frantic instructions had quieted. Tanner. Tanner, who'd thought himself a shoo-in for the promotion last year. Tanner, who'd made snide comments about tokenism and affirmative action, pretending he didn't think Luz could hear him from two desks away. Tanner, who'd seemed so damn nice and helpful the first year she'd worked with him.

They'd been friends. Truly. They'd shared lunch in the break room a couple of times a week and bonded over a mutual love for flying drones. They'd even met at the park once to show off their skills to each other. But that had all stopped when Luz had risen above him at work. Then Tanner had declared war. That bastard.

She would never, ever forget the email she'd gotten the day after Sveta had been hauled away: Hey, Luz, did I mention my brother works for ICE???

Her poor girlfriend was the collateral damage of Luz showing him up at work, and she would never be able to quiet the burrowing, gnawing guilt of that. Sveta had planned to stay here forever, doing programming work online with no need to flaunt her presence in the US by taking an office job. Now with Russia under so many international restrictions and Sveta facing monitoring at home, she was lying low and working for cash at her aunt's store.

When her muscles began to burn from the tight stress, Luz finally grabbed her bag and got out of the car. Even after wasting all that time, she was still the third woman to arrive for the class. Ever the introvert, she headed to a far corner to unzip her bag and retrieve her wraps to start getting ready.

She checked her messages again for any response from Sveta. Nothing. They were living in different worlds, at different times, Sveta waking up just as Luz was entering her evening habits.

She nervously tugged at her long braid, checked one more time, then tucked her phone away with a heavy sigh.

She knew she hadn't done anything wrong in accepting that promotion at work. But exposing Sveta? That had been her fault.

She'd thought she was speaking to a friend when she'd told Tanner about Sveta's tenuous status in the US after overstaying a student visa. She hadn't realized she was handing the man a weapon. How could she have? Still, her soul gladly clasped the burden of guilt tight, and it would always live there inside her.

But the rage? That was something she could purge. That she could learn how to work with.

Dependable Luz, always on time and *over*time and picking up other people's slack . . . She'd trained her whole life to be good at everything she tried, and she was determined to be good at revenge too.

CHAPTER 5

KATHERINE

The wine buzz had faded, but it had served its purpose. She'd signed up for a profile and given herself a new name: Katy. It felt close enough to her own that she wouldn't stumble over it, but somehow felt entirely different. Katy. A bold woman full of happy brightness. It would be a nice costume to slip into.

She entered a zip code smack dab in the middle of Denver and identified herself as a married evangelical. Surely she could fake her way through that.

LordsLink wasn't a dating site. People used it to organize prayer gatherings, fundraisers, hobby groups, and local Bible studies. It was more like a heavily moderated mash-up of Facebook and Craigslist, though it did host personal ads with stern admonishments about using them only in keeping with Christian values. She was immediately fed topics like "volunteer hub" and "requesting prayers," but she tagged "faithful friends" on her list of interests.

This BrightLife guy was apparently using the site as a hookup app, so she approached with the same idea, bumping her age down a few years and giving herself new hobbies that she wished she had: mountain biking, pottery, dancing. In reality, she was terrified of heights due to her limited depth perception, had no artistic skills, and had been far too self-conscious about her height as an adolescent to learn any sense of movement.

But what did the truth matter? She could be anyone she liked online, and the stats for lying obviously went way up when people were looking for sex.

She wondered why this guy didn't just use a hookup site. Was it the deception that turned him on? Or maybe it was the transgression of doing it with a woman who knew it was wrong. Maybe it felt extra dirty with a nice Christian girl who hadn't even been looking for an affair but had been seduced into it.

When it came time to post a picture, Katherine froze again. Somehow she hadn't thought of that. In the past her online profile pictures had been cutesy photos with her family, whatever stage of self-doubt or resentment or depression she'd reached measurable by the age of the photo.

Now she needed something decidedly un-mom-like and veering toward sexy. But it couldn't be identifiable either. After scrolling through a few profiles, she decided to show only half her face. The bottom half. No one would recognize her mouth and chin. The only thing people ever noticed about her was the eye patch. They saw it and looked away or saw it and stared. It was her one solid identifier.

Still, for a split second she considered posing as a sexy pirate and giggle-snorted before getting to her feet to march to her closet. How was she going to pull this off?

After a half hour of scowling her way through her hanging clothes and the suitcases still stuffed with other options, she finally realized she had one garment that looked absolutely sexy to her when she put it on: her little workout top with the spaghetti straps. The dark teal blue set off the paleness of her skin, and since she'd begun boxing classes, her thin arms and shoulders looked defined instead of weak.

Before she could lose her nerve, she tugged on the top, smoothed on red lipstick, tousled her hair, and took a dozen quick selfies around her apartment, searching for a light source that didn't make her neck creases look worse than they were. Forty-five wasn't old, but it certainly wasn't young and dewy.

The final result was . . . actually kind of hot? She cropped the picture into a square that showed her smiling mouth, sharp chin, defined shoulders, and delicate collarbone. Then she covered her mouth and laughed with genuine delight. She looked dateable as hell. How funny was that?

Once she'd posted the photo to the app, she burned with restlessness. Her head felt floaty, untethered. After a few uncomfortable minutes of trying to talk herself into sending BrightLife01 a private message, she yanked on a lightweight sweatshirt and jacket and pulled a fuzzy knit cap down to her eyebrows before setting off.

When she got close to the Hook, she slipped on a pair of oversized sunglasses so no one would notice the beige eye patch. Between the glasses and the red lipstick, she looked nothing like herself. Still, she moved swiftly past the front window of the Hook, hoping for a chance to note Maggie's location. The instructor was at her normal spot at the front of the class, not yet roaming around to check form.

Katherine hurried all the way past the Hook and didn't stop until she reached the window to the hair salon next door. Then she carefully edged back until she could see most of the boxers, but not Maggie.

She looked from one woman to another, searching for a blond pixie cut against medium-brown skin. The woman should be easy to pick out, but Katherine didn't find her. After her first quick scan of the room, she tried to look again, but Maggie strode suddenly into view, reaching for a boxer's elbow to position it closer to her body.

Katherine spun and race-walked away, past the salon and the Greek food place and the wig store. It wasn't that she wanted contact with the woman who'd seduced her husband into recklessness. She knew that

43

couldn't happen. But starting her own plan of seduction had churned up a boiling curiosity in her veins.

How had it all happened? What had the woman said and done? How many times had she screwed Peter? Once or twice or more?

Katherine had given Maggie as much information as she could, telling her about her husband's schedule, his hobbies, his likes and dislikes, even the actresses he clearly found attractive.

She'd eagerly offered up a birthday party for the cause. That had been a one-in-a-million shot. Her ultimate revenge fantasy. And she'd gotten it.

During the initial planning stages, she'd searched his phone for a dating app, knowing it wouldn't be Tinder this time. The man had a hundred apps on his phone, at least. He loved gadgets and tech, and not one prayer session or exercise routine happened without some assistance from an app or at least a brief digital log of his work.

But a year before, as he'd been scrolling through his screens, she'd seen the icon she recognized from a news story: Tinder. Such a simple little square with a pretty neon flame to indicate how hot it all was.

She'd frozen in shock next to him, stunned to finally see proof of what she'd known in her heart for so many years. What she'd accused him of, what he'd denied, what he'd thrown in her face to prove how hysterical and insecure she was every second of every day.

He hadn't actually been wrong about the insecurity, had he? Because when she'd seen the proof, she'd just sat there next to him on the couch, watching a baseball game, heart thumping and vision blurring, and she'd said nothing. *Grab his phone,* she'd told herself. *Take it. Open the app. Shove it in his smarmy, lying face.*

Because there was only one reason for a married man to have Tinder on his phone, and it couldn't be explained away by meetings or assistants or business trips. She'd sat through three goddamn innings of that stupid game, the Rockies against the Astros, her paperback open to the same two pages, unread.

He'd finally checked something on his phone and stood up, muttering, "I need to respond to this."

Peter had been halfway out of the room before she'd pulled free of her panicked freeze and blurted out, "Is it a date?"

"What?" His dismissive annoyance had snapped out like a whip.

"On Tinder? Is that what you need to respond to?"

"What in the world are you talking about?"

"I saw it!" She'd suddenly pushed to her feet, leaping free of her safely cushioned hiding spot. "I saw it on your phone!" She'd pointed furiously. "I saw it!"

But her trap had been too weak. He'd rolled his eyes, stormed off to his office, and then returned a few minutes later, calm as a cucumber. "You want to tell me what that outburst was about?"

Of course he'd shown her his phone. Of course the app had been gone, replaced by something similar. "This one?" he'd suggested, touching the orange flame to open a program that tracked wildfires. "I got it last year after that huge grass fire a few miles from here."

It was then that she'd descended into her lowest trough of hopelessness. She'd already been so low after losing her part-time PR gig during the pandemic closures and then concentrating all her energies on helping guide her daughter toward college. An empty, unhappy nest was a hell of an end goal for any project, and she'd been dreading the success of sending Charlotte far away from home.

She'd known she'd need therapy or at least some support. Instead, she'd found Maggie.

But that girl, that woman, the one who'd played Peter so skillfully . . . what was her story? Why had she come to Maggie? Katherine felt connected to her. After all, she was about to do the same thing, wasn't she?

She wanted to look again, but she was too scared of getting caught and disappointing Maggie, who'd specifically told her to stay away. Impulsive. That was what Peter had called her. Of course, when they'd dated he'd called her spontaneous. But what was fun in a girlfriend became an irritation in a wife.

Impulsive because she knew if she thought too much about any action, she'd lose her nerve. Just like she had now.

Katherine was stepping off the curb to cross the lot and head home when she looked over her shoulder and stutter-stepped to a halt.

A *wig* store. That was what she'd had her back pressed to. She'd seen it before, of course, but today it meant something else to her. She'd never set foot in one, but she turned and moved slowly back toward it, eyeing the beautiful wigs set on mannequin heads in the window.

She touched her cap, thinking of the hair beneath it. Light brown, wavy, and long enough that she pulled it into a thin ponytail on most days. A deep-brown wig caught her eye. It was a long, straight bob with a blunt fringe, and she could picture herself in it. Picture herself as Uma Thurman in *Pulp Fiction*, a tall, thin badass who could dance and screw.

The thought popped a bubble of shocked laughter from her chest.

Blond would be a better color, surely, if she wanted a disguise or even just a fantasy. But her eye skimmed over the long blond wig in the window just as it skipped past the short bobbed red one and the many braids of the black wig that had scarlet highlights.

Hadn't someone told her she looked like Uma Thurman once back in high school? She'd hated the comment at the time, too aware of her long, gangly legs and the height that left her nearly a head taller than most boys in tenth grade. But now? If she could pull off Uma Thurman now, she would take it and run.

A little metal bell jangled when she opened the door of the shop. The owner spoke hesitant English, but she guided Katherine through every step, offering a wig cap and a booklet, pointing to the URL at the bottom that linked to YouTube videos. The wig was more expensive than she'd expected, but she didn't care. Her pulse raced as she paid the extravagant bill and clutched the bag tightly in her sweaty hand.

Katherine nearly jogged her way home, giddy and almost paranoid about the nondescript paper bag that banged into her leg with every step. This was the solution to her self-doubt. She would pretend to be someone else. She would *be* someone else, not just the costume she'd thought to assume, but a whole new attitude.

A different sensation overtook her as she rode the elevator to her third-floor apartment. Her heart was still beating hard, her skin still buzzing with something like fear, but for the first time in ages, Katherine felt distinctly . . . aroused. By the time she locked her apartment door behind her, she was nearly panting.

It all felt so deliciously wrong in the best way. She'd felt wrong at her husband's birthday party too, but that wrongness had been twisted up with guilt and regret and an awful terror. This was a different feeling. Something pleasurable. Probably the same way Mr. BrightLife felt when he logged on to a Christian website to search for forbidden fruit.

Was this how people became supervillains? They got away with one bad act, and that freed them up to enjoy the next and then the next?

Maybe. Maybe she'd been destined to be a villain all along, with her eye patch and her childhood trauma. Too bad she wouldn't be able to wear her patch for her date with her target. She'd have to don the custom scleral contact that made her milky, sightless eye look normal. Because of her eyelid scarring, she could wear it for only a few hours at a time before the irritation turned to pain, but it was the only way to truly stay incognito, to blend in.

She'd worn one for her wedding, as her last, best effort to prod her handsome fiancé into marrying her. By the end of the reception all those hours later, her eye had been watering in a constant stream of pain, but she'd considered it worth it. This time she wouldn't have to wear it for nearly as long.

She whipped off her eye patch and raced to the bathroom with her new purchase. First she pulled the wig cap on, making a sloppy mess of it; then she tugged the wig into place. It took less than thirty seconds to retrieve her eye prosthetic from the solution and nudge it carefully in. She then shucked her fleece jacket, touched up her red lipstick, and took a step back.

"Oh my God," she murmured, her body flashing hot. She looked like an assassin. Or a spy, at least. Yes. She should have been a spy. Because hot damn, she was good at this. Unassuming Katherine, the good daughter, the helpful wife, she was actually really good at role-playing.

That made sense, though, didn't it? Hadn't she jumped with gusto into every role she'd ever been given? So it was hardly a surprise that she'd be worthy of a gold star sticker for pretending to be a seductive adulterer. Another perfect fit into the box she'd been assigned. At least this time she was faking it for herself.

She retreated to the bottle of wine again, but that was okay. Stage fright was normal, and the wine gave her the strength to take another picture showing nearly her whole face above the long, sexy line of her shoulder. She loaded it to the app, making it private, visible only to people she connected with. It wasn't a nude or anything, but it still felt dirty and hot with her fake hair and her fake eye and the fake scarlet confidence of her smirking mouth.

It was finally time. She couldn't busy herself with administrative tasks anymore. She needed to channel her nervous energy into bravery and take the leap.

She searched for his username, took a deep breath, and messaged him with a friendly hello and a note that she liked his smile. It was her sole gambit, since his smile was all she could see.

Like her, he'd included only part of his face, less than she'd shown, even, and he'd written a very sincere note that he was happily married and merely looking for connections with new Christian friends in the area. Interests: classic movies, snowmobiling, volunteering, water-skiing. He claimed his name was Brad. A fake name like hers?

She didn't know the whole story, but she did know he was some kind of local politician with a serious problem keeping it in his pants. That was good enough for her. Someone had helped with her hypocrite, so after decades of watching Peter ooze through the world like the slimy shit-snail he was, Katherine was happy to return the favor for another woman.

If it was his real picture, the guy looked cute enough in his partial photo. In his late forties maybe, square jaw, a little heavier than Peter, but that intrigued her. She'd been a virgin when she'd married. Not inexperienced in every way, but not exactly a connoisseur of men's bodies. A change felt fun and naughty.

She spent a whole hour checking and rechecking the app for a message from him. Then another. She even added a few other men to her contact list, worried he'd be able to see she'd targeted him alone.

After all that work, she was left with disappointment. Mr. BrightLife was the only one who didn't respond in some way, and now she had a bunch of unwanted messages from random men. One called her a beautiful soul, one addressed her as "my love," and all of them contained prayer-hand emojis. She felt like she was in the pew at Saint Cecilia's, trolling for a strange man while Father Carlo frowned from the nave.

Yuck.

She made herself dinner and watched a movie, then tossed the phone on the bed in disgust and retreated to the bathroom for a long shower. That was the key, of course. That was the magic. A watched pot never boiled, and after not checking for forty-five minutes, there it was waiting for her. A happy little icon that revealed a happy little message from Mr. BrightLife.

Hi there! You've got a pretty nice picture yourself! Are you new to the site? I'm on the road a lot for work so it's nice to have quality people to chat with. Are you looking for company too?

Katherine laughed. She wore no makeup now, no wig, no patch to hide her milky eye, and she wasn't anywhere approaching sexy in her ratty green terry-cloth robe, but in that moment she felt more powerful than she had in years.

Yes, she was definitely looking for company too, and apparently this was the right place to find it.

CHAPTER 6

GENEVA

Sweat poured down Geneva's neck, and her legs shook, nearly ready to collapse beneath her, but the physical exhaustion from her extended workout somehow felt completely different from her panic attacks. It was the one time every week she felt alive. Triumphant, even.

But no amount of exercise could cast out her current anxiety of *when, when, when?* It shivered beneath her skin, an electric current of impatience.

Still, as she tugged off one glove, the firmness of her biceps caught her eye, and she raised her chin with pride at her new strength. Sometimes she fantasized about passing her school's principal on the street and punching him right in the throat with a hard cross. But it was Frank's face she pictured on the bag with every blow. She imagined his nose pulpy with gore, his mouth begging her to stop before his eyes finally rolled back in his head. She wished she had it in her to actually do it.

Finally free of gloves and wrap, Geneva watched through her lashes as a few women chatted with Maggie at the front of the class. Their instructor exuded something that pulled others toward her. Confidence, yes, but she cared too. Her charisma wrapped around everyone like an enchanted hug, and Geneva imagined that if Maggie didn't already have a busy career, she could fill this class every night of the week.

When she'd first started coming to this women's class, Geneva had chatted with the other boxers, the first steps in the start of possible friendships. But eventually she'd only found them irritating. The other women were distractions pulling Maggie's attention away from Geneva, when all she wanted to do was talk to Maggie, listen to her, learn, and absorb.

Despite their session before class, she still desperately wanted Maggie all to herself today, but Geneva refused to act like she was that needy. She could be strong and patient if she wanted to be. She just didn't want to be.

As Maggie patted a woman's shoulder and turned away, she caught Geneva watching and gave her a wink. Geneva ducked her head to look at her bag and pretend she wasn't straining for a signal like a dog begging for scraps. Maggie had already reassured her. She couldn't let her know how desperate she still felt.

Dropping into a crouch, she dared another glance up and saw her slip into the office and close the door. *Don't follow her,* she ordered herself. *Don't follow her.*

It was only that she missed the buoyancy of spending one-on-one time with her. Now that the plans had started coming to fruition, they'd ended their occasional coffee-shop chats. It wouldn't do for Maggie to be openly seen as her mentor until all the risk had passed.

But God, she missed their nascent friendship, missed the warm confidence that a successful Black woman was looking out for her, helping her along. Another drag on her patience. But Geneva knew they'd get back to it once the need for discretion passed.

As she watched, another boxer tapped on the door. She was a short, curvy Latina with a thick braid that hung down her back. Luz? Geneva had spoken with her a couple of times in the parking lot before class.

When the woman slipped into the office and closed the door behind her, Geneva stood up and unabashedly stared at the little papered-over window as if she could see through it.

Was Luz part of the system too? Another woman in need of help?

She seemed perfectly serene and nearly shy when Geneva spoke with her, but now she recalled a moment of surprise when she'd glanced over to see Luz driving blinding punches into a heavy bag halfway through a workout. That serene mouth had twisted into contorted snarls, teeth showing as if she were ready to rip flesh from her opponent.

For a moment Geneva considered remaining in the studio, maybe even staying close to the office door. She could walk out with Luz and chat her up, probe a bit, and see if she was involved.

But that was a terrible idea, not worth the risk before Geneva got what she needed. Upsetting the system instead of making it work for her? That was a betrayal of the plan. But afterward . . . afterward maybe they could talk, compare notes, sympathize.

Yeah, still a terrible idea. They weren't supposed to be friends or even acquaintances. That was the point.

With a deep sigh, Geneva had to admit to herself she was only lingering because the Hook was the one place she felt alive these days. She could experience her body here, feel her energy flame back to brief life. It would all vanish when she got back home to her current reality.

Admitting defeat, she hoisted her workout bag over her shoulder and headed out into the crisp spring evening. The chill felt amazing on her skin. Even though she'd be shivering halfway through her drive home, she luxuriated in the brilliant sensation, hoping she could hold on to it for a while.

The studio door hadn't even closed behind her when a male voice called her name. "Gennie!"

Nearly tripping over her own feet, she frantically scanned the lot even as her brain told her exactly who it was. Her heart clenched, torn between joy and grief. "Daddy," she said as she picked him out heading toward her on a path between two cars. "What are you doing here?"

"Well, you don't answer your phone, and your mom told me this was your new Tuesday hangout, so . . ." He shrugged, his normally serious mouth flashing a sheepish smile.

Geneva swallowed a huge lump in her throat as he jogged the last few feet to give her a hug. His smell swallowed her up, sending her straight back to childhood. The leather of his coat and the spice of his aftershave, even a faint hint of paint from his work as a contractor. "I'm sorry, Daddy," she said into the smooth brown leather of the bomber jacket he'd worn for thirty years. "I've been really busy with the new customer-service gig."

"Mm." He somehow conveyed forgiveness and doubt with that one syllable.

"I'm sorry," she whispered again, closing her eyes. She was sorry. She hadn't done anything wrong, but she was so, so sorry.

"Nonsense." He pressed a kiss to the top of her head and pulled away. "Let's grab dinner."

"Dad, I'm all sweaty. I need a shower." She tried not to notice the way his face fell. She'd been avoiding him for so long that now she could barely meet his eyes, but his face looked so precious to her. She'd once created constellations from the small black freckles that were scattered across his cheeks from his beard to his smile lines. His bald head was a smooth expanse that picked up the orange of the setting sun.

"Come on. There's a taco place right there," he said.

She followed his gesture to the restaurant even though she'd passed it many times. She couldn't say no again. Her dad hadn't done anything wrong, and he didn't deserve this. It felt impossible to process that her father knew she'd been fired for a sex tape, so . . . she simply hadn't processed it.

Unable to bring herself to say yes to him, she tipped her chin up in a faint nod.

"That's my girl."

Geneva followed him past the Hook toward the taco joint, though she craned her neck over her shoulder when she realized Luz was opening the door of the studio. Her head stayed straight ahead, and she hurried toward her car, removing herself from Geneva's orbit.

"So are you really fine?" her father asked as he swept his arm wide for her to precede him into the restaurant. "You keep telling me you are, but I want to know for sure."

"I am fine," she said, then laughed at his narrow look. "Taking it slow. Working online. I'll get things figured out."

"I don't doubt that."

"In a few months I'll have some money saved up, and then I'll probably move. I have a friend down in Florida."

"Florida?" he barked.

"You can come visit in the winter. You always complain about the snow."

He went silent as they peered up at the menu board. She was more than grateful for the chance to change the subject and order a meal. She didn't want to have to explain that Florida had some of the loosest rules for private-school teachers. She didn't have a record, so she could withstand the bare minimum of scrutiny if she could save up money to pay an online clean-up firm.

Whatever happened, she wouldn't stay in Colorado, where it felt like everyone in the elementary teaching community would recognize her name right away: Geneva Worther, the first-grade teacher with the hottest sex tape. Imagine how many group texts and Reddit posts featured her name, and maybe screenshots too.

She pretended to concentrate completely on choosing one of the eight empty booths so she wouldn't have to look at her father until after the thought faded.

Surely he'd never seen it. She *knew* he hadn't. But he'd heard the description. He'd been determined she should file a lawsuit against the school. He'd marched her into the police station himself to demand that they do *something*. Posting a video like that was illegal, and Frank had sent it to the school board simply because she hadn't wanted to see him anymore.

But Frank had denied everything and told the police she must have posted it herself. It had been recorded on her phone, after all. *She'd* made the thirty-second video and never even sent it to him, and she hadn't been able to deny that. Her burning hatred for her own decision felt as though it would eat her alive sometimes.

It had been nothing more sordid than a drunken birthday night with Frank, a man she saw on occasion, and Omi, her ex-girlfriend from college, who'd been staying with her for the week. They'd all been drunk and horny, and Geneva had decided to treat herself to some birthday fun just a few weeks before she started her first real job as a teacher. One last summer before she truly settled into the burdens of adulthood.

Her generation held no shame about sex, about sexuality, about consenting adults making their own choices. But she'd been fooled by her peers, lulled into a false sense of bodily rights and sex positivity, convinced she could choose to live any life she wanted. She'd forgotten that others would hate her for that, that they'd want to destroy her for being herself and controlling her own body.

She had no idea why she'd recorded part of it. She had only vague memories of being caught up in the beauty of their pleasure and their limbs, all contrasting with each other in tone and texture and strength. She'd thought she was recording art instead of porn. A tiny snippet of her own beautiful youth.

So stupid. So fucking stupid.

She'd been forced to explain the complications to her father because of Frank's claims. He said she did it herself, the police had explained, hardly bothering to hold back their smirks as they pretended to take her seriously. Hadn't she recorded the whole thing? Hadn't it all been her idea? Where would he have gotten the video?

As if he hadn't been near her phone on other nights when he'd slept over.

She hadn't fought much harder after that. The school had already fired her, the parents of the community already knew, and if it went to court, the whole damn country would be digging up illicit files to watch her most intimate moments after reading a headline about a first-grade teacher and her sex tape.

She'd managed to get it pulled from the major sites, at least. The "online reputation" firm claimed it would do a deeper scrub, though it would likely remain out there on the dark web.

She told herself she'd get her career back and put it behind her, write off that first job, and pray no one asked questions when checking her license. But at night when she couldn't sleep, she knew it would always be out there waiting to resurface. She wouldn't be able to be a school principal or a city councilmember or, hell, a congressperson.

She'd never dreamed of going into politics, but lately the idea bubbled up constantly, until she pictured it as one of those deadly pools her parents had pulled her away from at Yellowstone. *Don't touch. It'll burn you right up. That's not safe for you.*

She could recover from this, get out of her current depression, start a job search, pay enough of her late bills to get her own place. But her larger dreams were limited now, forever.

Fucking Frank, that selfish asshole. Her only consolation was that her gut feeling about him had been correct. They'd had good chemistry, but the hard edge of his humor and his leering remarks about women had eventually turned her off. She'd told him it wasn't going to work out, and he'd sent a lot of shitty texts and posted a few insults to her social media accounts before she'd blocked him. That had been the last she'd thought of him until she'd gotten the weekend text from her principal with that singularly terrifying message: We need to talk.

After her dad grabbed their drinks, he joined Geneva at the booth she'd so carefully chosen. "Florida is too far," he declared.

57

"I won't stay here. Not if I want to teach."

"Somewhere closer, then. New Mexico, maybe."

She gave in with a smile as a server approached with their plates. "I'll check out New Mexico too, okay?"

"You know you love the mountains."

"True."

The silence felt nearly comfortable as they dug into their food, and it didn't hurt that she was starving after that workout. Every bite tasted like the best thing she'd ever eaten. But even this nice moment with her dad made her blink back tears, because the pleasure of seeing him sharpened the guilt for pushing him away for all these weeks.

Despite the divorce, she'd always been close to him, and her mom and dad had worked hard to be good coparents. There had been tension between them for a couple of years, but it had long since dissipated.

"I really don't like Florida," he muttered. "Too dangerous."

"Everywhere is dangerous," she said, knowing exactly what he meant.

"I'm aware, Gennie."

They'd had this conversation many times. How he'd moved to Colorado from Arkansas, expecting a mountain paradise and finding that the state was beautiful but many things were the same as the crap he'd left behind in Arkansas. Still, the construction market In Denver had been booming, and he'd made a great living for a man with only a high school diploma, starting his own contracting company. He'd married, bought a fixer-upper, raised a child, and grown his thriving business since then.

He'd made her so proud, and she'd managed to return the favor for a few years. But only a few.

Did his friends know about her? What about his brothers and sisters back in Arkansas?

She had only the vaguest memories of a family reunion there when she was seven, a sea of faces ebbing and flowing past in the backyard of a farmhouse, falling asleep in a pile of sleeping bags with cousins she'd just met. Had they all seen the video too? She'd made it for herself, only for herself, and none of this was fair. But life was never fair. Not unless you forced a little fairness out of it. Maggie had taught her that. And who would know better than Maggie?

Geneva finished her second taco, then stretched her neck, already tightening after the workout. "Thanks for dinner, Dad."

He reached out to cover her hand, obviously aware that she was beginning the process of extricating herself. "You have nothing to be ashamed of," he said quietly.

"Dad," she managed before her throat clogged with such heaviness she could barely draw a breath. Her mouth tried to twist into grief, so she pressed her lips hard against her teeth to hold them still.

"You're a teacher, not a nun. You didn't promise anyone your personal life or your passions. That was your business, not the school's, not the parents', and not mine. And I love you more than anything in the world."

She breathed through her nose, exhaling in shaky huffs, trying to shut down all the screaming parts of her heart so she wouldn't have a wailing breakdown in front of the other diners.

The hard grip around her throat finally eased. She swallowed, coughed, raised her gaze to the ceiling to blink back tears. "I miss the kids," she said.

"I'm sorry."

"And I miss you. But when I see anyone I know, but especially you, it's all I can think about, so I just . . . try not to see you."

"We've had twenty-six whole years together, and that's what you're thinking about?"

"I just need time, Daddy. That's all."

His lips pressed into a hard, straight line, but he finally nodded. "All right. But at least answer your damn phone."

"Okay."

"Promise?"

"I promise. Thanks for dinner."

She left him there still eating his meal, ashamed that she would do that to him, ashamed that she couldn't love him well enough to set her own feelings aside to make him happy. But she worried that if she let the grief out, everything would come with it. All the rage and anger and violation would pour out in a violent fit of snot and screams and fists.

She'd isolated herself from everyone. She'd pushed Omi away, too guilty about dragging her into it to accept the comfort she offered. She'd practically cut off her best friend, Jess, who heaped so much fiery rage on Frank that Geneva felt small and stupid for dating him. Even all her time with her mother consisted of Geneva pretending everything was fine so they wouldn't have to talk about any of it. She'd be hiding from her mom too if she had any choice in the matter.

She felt exploited and exposed, as if everyone who looked at that video had put their hands on her, wiped open mouths across her body, had laughed, jeered, jerked off.

Why couldn't she just go back to that night and make a different decision? Or even go back a few weeks more to when she'd met Frank at a concert and taken him back to her place? Or hell, all the way to college when she'd met Omi and they'd dated on and off for a couple of years? She'd give all that up. One tiny step placed in a different spot and she wouldn't be here.

Jesus, she needed therapy, but that was yet another expense. Between her student loans and her car payments, her new gig barely allowed her to contribute to the grocery bill, much less spend money on therapy.

Eyes on the ground, she marched to her car and opened the door to drop quickly into the driver's seat. The cold had finally soaked in, so she started her car and turned the heat to high, switching on the seat heater for extra warmth. At least the shivering distracted her from the churn of feelings inside her. After grabbing groceries, she'd drive home, take a very hot shower with no distracting sound effects from the school; then she'd take the time to do her hair. Or maybe she'd just wash it, work in a deep conditioner, and twist it into a bun like she'd done for the past eight weeks.

It wasn't until she was looking side to side as she reversed out that she caught sight of Luz again. The woman was sitting behind the wheel two cars over, her phone to her ear, talking to someone as she wiped tears from her cheeks. She managed a smile and a laugh, but then covered her eyes with a hand for a long moment.

When Geneva hit the brakes, the jerk of her car drew Luz's attention, and she looked up and over, eyes going huge when she saw Geneva watching.

Geneva swung her head to the front and almost hit the gas in a panic, horrified to be caught spying, but then she stuffed her first impulse down. Luz had to be part of this. She looked almost as broken as Geneva felt.

Before she could turn back, offer a wave, mouth, *You okay?* Luz's car pulled out and sped from the lot.

Geneva took a moment to calm her nerves, then left in the other direction and tried to pretend she didn't see her dad still at the booth where she'd abandoned him. She couldn't make anything right today. But soon.

CHAPTER 7

KATHERINE

Good morning! I'm glad you wrote back. Are you up? I'm an
early riser. How bout you? I wake up ready to go!

Ready to go? Was that sexual? Or did this BrightLife guy whistle
through his morning chores like Ned Flanders?

She stared at the phrase *early riser* and wondered if this was a
Rorschach test. A good Christian woman would respond with something chipper and not up for interpretation. But a bad Christian woman
would know exactly what was rising. Hm.

Katherine curled back into the covers, her fingers grasping her
phone. She'd opened her eyes only sixty seconds earlier, but she was
wide awake now despite the early hour. At 7:00 a.m. she was already
on a stranger's mind. How odd. How exciting.

She truly was reshaping her whole life with a swiftness that should
have been alarming. But didn't all those years of fantasizing about her
escape count toward the change too? Really, she was just catching up to
where she should have been.

She pictured herself in the wig and makeup, her skin bared in an
off-the-shoulder sweater. What would Katy say to him? Something that

plain old Katherine would never dare. She glanced at the time of his message and grinned. It had arrived only twenty minutes earlier.

Hmm, she typed back. I guess it depends. Right now I'm still in bed and I really don't want to get up. It's too warm and cozy. She hit SEND without even rereading it. Better to appear sloppy and desperate than wise.

Katherine laughed into her dark room, grateful for the west-facing window. The dimness made her feel like she was in a movie, a hard-drinking woman who kept the blinds closed and lit a cigarette before getting out of bed. But the good girl in her won out at even the thought, her nose wrinkling as she pictured the next scene's title: *Katherine with a sinus infection!*

All right, no morning cigarette for her, just some so-mild-it-might-not-be-sexting sexting.

She glanced at the app again, enjoying the tight, winding squeeze of anticipation, a boa constrictor of adrenaline. She'd spent so long thinking about Peter every day, her every misery, his every betrayal, but this was the first time her husband had popped into her head in twelve hours, maybe even more.

It wasn't much, but she'd claim it as a tiny victory and pin it to her chest. She'd left him, and she was raring to move on already. Easy peasy.

When her phone gave a tiny, eager ping, Katherine snatched it up and hit the app icon with a trembling finger.

Still in bed??? That's a little naughty. ☺

Squealing, she tossed the phone aside so she could smother a quiet scream. This was crazy. Just pure madness.

Were men always this easy? Was that the kernel of truth she'd never understood about her husband?

She'd spent the first years of her marriage jealous, angry at every pretty woman in their orbit, viewing them as birds who flashed their feathers and tried to lure her mate away. But now she wondered if her mate could have been lured by a mildew-ridden stuffed pigeon propped up with popsicle sticks and glue. Or maybe just lured by the same fake feathers Katherine had donned for her mission. Scarlet lipstick and an eagerness to please.

She responded with a quick laughing face. Naughty, huh?

We'll see! What are your plans today? All alone?

She scrunched up her face at that, aware of the role she was supposed to be playing. Lonely wife and mother. Not yet.

I got it. So tell me about yourself.

She fed him her cover story in bits and pieces. Married, proud mom, #blessed, looking for new friends and exciting conversation. He asked a few leading questions about her beliefs, and she confirmed for him that she believed in marriage for life.

She'd been told that this was the gig. She was married but available, interested but not clingy. Send signs that she wouldn't cause him any trouble. Then when he proposed video sex, his standard MO, get a recording of him that showed his face. This was a man who deserved to be exposed for his lies. And she believed that. He hunted women for sex on a site meant for pure-minded connection. Lonely women who just wanted a friendly shoulder. He enjoyed the chase, which made her the prey.

I saw your other picture, he typed. Then he left her hanging.

Katherine sat up to rest her back against the headboard. Oh? she prompted, pretending she was only playing along, but she found herself holding her breath while she waited. As if she *needed* this. She shut her eyes tight, then peeked her good eye open when a message dinged.

It's super hot.

"Ha!" she yelped, shot through with a jolt of joy that thrilled her with the surprise of it. This wasn't supposed to be so arousing. But no one had ever found her super hot before.

When Peter had taken her on their first few dates, she'd thought he was perfect. A real gentleman, the kind of boy she'd always been promised would be her reward for being a nice girl.

They'd met at a youth event organized by the diocese when she was twenty and he was twenty-five, both of them chaperoning teenagers and representing the hip young adults of the church. So she'd understood his slow approach to even kissing her. It felt as if Bishop Mannon were watching them. He'd introduced them, after all.

Even after their engagement, Peter had never tried to talk her into sex or even a little oral sodomy, though they'd made out often enough in the junior-high sense. She'd loved him madly and wanted more.

As a girl who always felt too tall and awkward, she'd been wild for Peter, who was six two and made her feel petite for the first time in her life. But he'd wanted to wait. Wanted to preserve her precious virginity until their wedding night. My God, she'd felt aglow with superiority that he'd held her in such high respect.

She'd never asked him about his virginity, of course. Bastard.

But this man online—this stranger—could barely wait for introductions before calling her hot. Why shouldn't she enjoy it if she could?

A new message popped up. Sorry, was that too forward?

Her lungs emptied on a rush of relief and slightly hysterical amusement.

No! Thank you for the compliment.

He backed off a little and asked a few innocuous questions. Favorite pizza toppings, favorite movie. Shallow topics, as if he needed nothing from her heart. She returned the favor, and he eventually affirmed his own selfish explanations about his situation. He and his wife had problems, but he was dedicated and would never break up his family. He was a hero, really, if you nodded hard enough at his excuses.

What's your church? he asked her a few minutes later.

Katherine frowned at that. Even if she were an eager evangelical, she wouldn't brag about her church in this situation, would she? It's in Wheat Ridge, she finally lied.

Ah. I'm in Aurora.

I guess we'll never run into each other then! 😞

True but . . . maybe we can chat?

That made her heart stop despite that she'd come here for exactly this. Chat? she typed carefully.

I could call you at lunchtime if you're not busy.

A call. Just a regular phone call, probably, but she'd need to be ready for video just in case. She'd need to be in costume and ready to go. Goose bumps erupted over her skin. She shivered or shuddered—surely that was nervousness and not excitement?

That would be great. Noon?

Noon.

They said their goodbyes, and Katherine hopped out of bed. The apartment already sparked with the scent of the coffee she brewed on a timer, and she had half a cup before setting it down with a decisive click. She had too much energy pulsing through her already. She should go for a run while she was in the mood and feeling good.

She smiled stupidly through her jog. The next time she saw Maggie, she'd have good news. Maggie didn't exactly hand out gold stars, but she had a way of beaming with pride, adding in a little smugness that she'd chosen the right student. The first time she'd singled out Katherine, the exhilaration had left her even more light-headed than the boxing routine normally did.

Katherine, can you stay for a moment after class? I'd like to get your opinion on something.

The something had been a little advice about PR. As if they were equals. That advice had turned into a glass of wine at a tapas bar down the block, and then they'd had tapas too, along with a discussion about Maggie's career.

That was when Katherine had spilled her guts about Peter. She'd laid it all out. The miscarriages, the disappointments, the infidelity. And strong, successful Maggie hadn't brushed any of her pain aside or made her feel small. Instead she'd pointed out that Katherine didn't have to keep living a life just because she'd chosen it once. She could make a new choice to burn it all down and start over with the support she deserved.

And so she'd burned it. And she was still burning, though now with a different fire licking at a different man. Her smile turned into a grin as she picked up her pace.

At this rate, her scheme wouldn't take long. A few days at most. Her fish was already tugging at the line. She veered away from the thought that the line was tugging at something inside her as well. This was a task, and no one had ever claimed a task couldn't be fun as long as you got the job done.

Once she'd held up her side of the bargain, she'd get back to . . . Well. She wasn't sure. Being boring? Her steps slowed a bit from a run to a jog, then even slower than that.

For the past few months, Katherine had been so focused on setting up Peter and finding a new place to live that she'd forgotten the next part. Charlotte was off at college and texted only once or twice a week.

Her daughter had already applied for internships in California, hoping for a beachy summer, and after her first couple of years at school, she likely wouldn't come home at all.

Katherine needed other connections in her life. Other goals. She was an independent woman now, and she needed to find a new job. A new career, even, if it wasn't too late.

She'd done part-time PR work for a local theater company for years, but it had closed down at the start of the pandemic and never reopened. Then she'd just . . . wallowed. Stayed in pajamas. Worked through her depression by fantasizing about revenge.

But now, in the interest of positive thinking . . . If she could do anything, what would she do? Could she go back to school?

The idea hit her hard, and suddenly she wasn't moving at all. She stood at the end of someone's driveway, panting and staring at an untrimmed blue spruce that pushed out over half the sidewalk. Her breath misted around her in the crisp morning air.

Back to *school*?

She already had a bachelor's in English, and she'd managed to find a job at an ad agency doing grunt work before Charlotte had come along. Then she'd gotten the PR gig because the theater had been run by a friend. But creativity wasn't really her thing. She liked detail work. She liked nitpicking. She liked quiet.

She burst out laughing at the job she'd secretly fantasized about all these years. The people she'd asked too many questions of during her appointments: *What is your day like? Do you enjoy the work? Did you always know?*

Dental hygienist. Dental hygienist! What a strange thing to call a fantasy. It wasn't big enough to count as a dream, surely. And she already had a degree from a good school. She couldn't start a totally new education at age forty-five. How much could she even make?

Ridiculous. But when she took off at a run again, the idea turned in her mind.

Peter would owe her half of everything in the divorce, including the retirement accounts. She'd stayed home full time for fifteen years to raise their daughter and nurse herself through the miscarriages she'd had after Charlotte. The house was paid for and worth quite a bit. She'd get half of that too, more than enough to get herself a modest little condo here or somewhere by a lake. Anywhere, really.

And wasn't that all she wanted? A few rooms of her own? Some peace and quiet? And not one husband anywhere around to be seen or heard or obeyed? Paradise.

She smiled grimly through the last mile of her run, thinking of the small amounts she'd shuffled into a secret savings account over the past years, feathering a nest that he wouldn't be able to track, trace, or spy on. She didn't trust Peter not to play dirty, although she had him hemmed in now that he'd screwed up so publicly.

She thought she'd be okay financially even with a modest income. Maybe she'd look into school when she got home. As for her personal life . . . Well, she wasn't interested in love, and if she wanted sex, it was easy to get these days. She'd go to the same place that cheating husbands went and take what she needed from the world like they did. When she stepped into the elevator, she checked her LordsLink account for messages. There were two waiting for her, but they were from other thirsty fellows, not Mr. BrightLife.

"Married, seeking friendship," she muttered as she shed her workout clothes and headed for the shower. An hour later, she was clean, dry, and bewigged, and sporting more eye makeup than she'd worn since her last trip to the ballet with Peter. Just in case.

At eleven thirty her phone rang, and she jumped in shock, nearly spilling the strawberry smoothie she'd grabbed from the fridge. Was he early? Did a Skype call alert with the normal ringtone?

She lunged toward the table where she'd set her phone, then cursed when she spied the caller. Charlotte? No way. Not now. She clicked the button to reject the call. This was not the time for parenting.

But a text came through a few seconds later. *Mom, did you just send me to voicemail? What's up? You ok?*

She cursed a little more loudly this time and shook her head frantically. No, no, no. She couldn't be thinking about her child when she was about to do something dirty. She paced for a few moments, but when the phone buzzed again, she couldn't ignore it. Face twisting into horrified embarrassment, she answered.

"Mom?"

"Hey," she croaked.

"Are you okay?"

"Of course, I'm just . . ." Her mind spun through all the options, reasonable options, because despite what children thought, their parents had actual lives. Normal lives doing normal things that weren't necessarily sexual. "Peeing," she finally muttered.

"Oh."

"I mean, I'm done now."

"Sure, okay."

She glanced at the clock on the microwave. "Everything all right?" she prompted.

"I guess. We haven't talked in a few days, so I thought I'd call. Dad says . . . He says you're all moved out? Because you didn't tell me anything about it." Before Katherine could explain why, Charlotte launched into the exact reason and got it right on the first try. "Are you just walking away from Dad? You're not going to try at all?"

"I need space, Charlotte. This isn't all about what happened at your dad's party. We haven't been happy for years."

"Dad was happy! I know he was! He says he loves you!"

Something primal rose up inside Katherine, roaring to get out. She bit down so hard on it that her jaw creaked with sharp pain. *Of course he was happy, he had me as a maid and a cook and a babysitter while he did anything he wanted with whomever he wanted. I was nothing but boring drudgery and parenting. Do your homework, eat your vegetables, comb your hair, pick up your clothes. I was a smear of poop on the bottom of his shiny shoe.*

But she didn't say any of it. This was her child. She loved Charlotte to death. So she breathed in and out and fought the tears.

"I'm sorry, Mom," Charlotte said, and that made her blink with surprise.

"What?" she whispered.

"I shouldn't have said that. I just really want you two to work it out, you know? I'm worried about both of you. I know this is hard."

Katherine cleared her throat and wiggled her jaw a bit to loosen it. Of course Charlotte was traumatized by this. She'd gone to Catholic school from preschool on up and had happily headed to a Catholic college too. "Charlotte, I'm sorry it happened this way, but I have to focus on what I need. I can worry about you, but I can't worry about your father. Not now."

"I know," her daughter whispered, sounding miserable and broken.

Katherine squared her shoulders. She needed to watch out for herself *and* her daughter. She could do both. "And you shouldn't be worrying about either of us. That's not your job, sweetie. You enjoy college. Your dad and I are adults, and we're responsible for the consequences of our actions. We're both going to be fine no matter what happens. Heck, Grandma is probably over there prepping something for his dinner right now."

Her daughter managed a laugh.

"And I'm good," Katherine insisted. "This apartment is temporary, but it's nice."

"But why do you need it?"

"Need what?"

"The apartment. Why can't you just move into the guest room? Just in case you decide to . . . Wait a minute. Mom, you're not, like, dating or anything, are you?"

Like your father? she wanted to snap. She managed not to, but she didn't know what else to say. She didn't truly want a new relationship, but she had a right to it, despite the guilt creeping over her at Charlotte's question.

When she took too long to answer, Charlotte groaned. "Mom, tell me you're not dating! It's only been a week! And Dad . . . he . . ."

"I'm sorry, baby, but I'm not discussing any of this with you. It's not appropriate. Your father and I both love you more than anything, and that's all you need to know. We'll work this out one way or another, and we'll be here for you. And hey, when you come home for break this time, I've got a cool new apartment with a bedroom for you. We can walk to dinner from here. Go to the movies. Whatever you want."

"What I want is for none of this to have happened!" she wailed.

"Well, me too!" Katherine snapped. She meant it, despite that she'd brought it all to a head.

What she'd wanted from the start was a simple, stupid dream of being a wife, being a mom, being *good.* Then the miscarriages had started, little bombs going off in her body, her heart getting shredded by shrapnel. Then the jealousies, the small cruelties, the hints from her husband that she was defective, his snide, shitty remarks about the failures of her uterus.

God, she hated him.

"Mom, don't cry! I'm sorry."

Crap, her makeup. She hadn't even realized she was blubbering. "No, I'm fine. Really." She swiped a finger under one eye, then the other. At least her contact was more comfortable with all the tears. "I'm fine, I'm just trying to find my way. I'm trying, baby."

"You're right. I'm sorry. We'll have a fun girls' night when I'm home, okay?"

A girls' night. They'd never done anything like that. Not since afternoon matinees at Disney movies until Charlotte had outgrown them and her. She'd gotten so involved with being an altar girl and leading her Catholic youth group that any time not with her friends involved hitching a ride with Peter. "That would be really nice, sweetie."

"I love you, Mom."

"I love you too. Please try not to worry."

When they hung up, Katherine grabbed a tissue and dabbed at her eyes. After she'd calmed herself, she smoothed down her wig and checked her eye makeup. Not totally ruined. And the guy was only calling, probably.

Still, the cocky anticipation she'd been nursing all morning had deflated. Her guts and courage pooled in her belly like limp carcasses.

She wasn't ready for this. Not at all. Would she have to get naked? Would she have to perform? What if he recorded it too? Oh my God, would he—

The ten-minute reminder she'd set on her phone trilled its alert.

Her fears didn't matter. She didn't have a choice. She had to repay her debt to the other women in the system.

Grimly determined now, she gulped down her water, then used the bathroom while she had the chance.

At five to noon she checked all the settings on Skype, making sure she was logged in with the anonymous email address she'd set up. She felt almost like crying again as she snuck one more look around her apartment to check for any identifying features.

But when the call came, she made a fist, took a deep breath, and dared to answer.

CHAPTER 8

Luz

Luz had bundled up way beyond the layers required for a fifty-degree evening, but she needed the comfort of the chunky knit hat pulled down past her eyebrows. Ballyhoo was utterly unbothered by the cold in his favorite bright-red sweater. He was as sophisticated as Sveta, and on any other day his posing would brighten Luz's mood. But today was hardly a day for snapping a dozen Instagram pictures.

Sveta had been Ballyhoo's primary caregiver, since she'd worked from home and had been passionate about adorable dog paraphernalia. But it was all up to Luz now, and she felt entirely inadequate.

Ballyhoo had the attitude of a confident professor or perhaps a distinguished playwright, so Luz sometimes felt as awkward around him as she did around anyone with a tendency toward a dry sense of humor and a haughtily raised eyebrow.

He'd gotten more cuddly since Sveta's disappearance, snuggling into Luz at night the way he'd once snuggled into Sveta. They were bonding over their loss of her, Luz wearing Sveta's fuzzy slippers around, and Ballyhoo sleeping on them all day until he was picked up for his afternoon fun. He also slept on them half the time Luz was wearing them, and the warm comfort sometimes made her cry. She missed touch. She missed her girlfriend. She wasn't sure what shape she'd be in if Ballyhoo weren't always there.

Most of the time Luz was able to keep Sveta's worries in the forefront of her mind. Sveta was stuck. No way out. There was zero chance the Russian government would return her passport anytime soon since she'd gone no-contact after getting her degree at the University of Colorado.

Sveta's job prospects didn't look great these days either, though she picked up a quick online gig here and there. But she wasn't on anyone's honor roll at home, and she likely never would be.

Her family expected her to marry, of course, and she'd be fighting that for the rest of her life in a country so hostile toward gays and lesbians that she could be fined for even mentioning her sexual identity to her niece. She couldn't count on securing a good job in that environment, so her family desperately wanted her to lie low and blend in. They wanted her to marry a man and shut up. Luz couldn't imagine the pressure and stress and deep unhappiness of having all her choices stolen from her while she was told to keep quiet.

But despite her urgent sympathy for the woman she loved, sometimes all Luz could think about was her own loneliness. It felt like Sveta had been her one chance at happiness and she'd been stolen away. But that was only misery, not danger.

She just wanted her here so much, wanted her safe and cozy, snuggled on the couch to watch cooking shows together. Neither of them cooked, but Luz could order a hell of a take-out meal. Now whenever she walked into one of their regular spots, it felt like getting too close to a fire. Maybe she'd suffer a momentary sting or maybe the wound would burn for days.

"Bally," she said, "that's enough sniffing. Pee already."

Ballyhoo shot her a black-eyed glance of scorn, but he finally lifted his leg and watered the bush. She hoped it was a satisfactory location.

"We've got another mile to go," she said. "The long walk of your dreams. So many things to sniff." He tipped his head away from her but trotted happily along as soon as she started moving down the walk. She slipped in one of her AirPods and hit PLAY on Karol G before opening her rideshare app.

Her driver, Frank, was two miles away, probably taking a break at the Sonic Drive-In, if she was reading the map correctly. He was scheduled to pick her up in fifteen minutes, and she'd singled him out as the only driver in the area who was pet friendly.

They weren't easy to come by, but Frank had picked up her request right away. It was her one point of access to him. She'd been told he liked dogs a lot more than he liked people and kept a bag of doggy treats in his glove compartment for any pup he encountered. Strangely, he seemed like he could be a nice guy. None of the other drivers wanted dog hair or wet paws in their cars, but he allegedly went out of his way to take dog owners where they wanted to go.

Ballyhoo pranced along, either not noticing or not caring that Luz's blood pressure rose with every step toward the meeting spot. Her head began to sweat beneath the hat, and she tugged incessantly at her braid with her free hand. She alternated between watching the sidewalk and watching the screen. Frank hadn't moved yet.

She was halfway hoping he'd cancel the request and disappear, but he was still hanging in there. Shit.

This was her last chance to back out. She trusted Maggie, trusted that this guy had done something just as awful as Tanner had. Something that was utterly immoral but not quite illegal. Or not prosecutable, anyway. But she'd feel so much better if she just *knew*.

That wasn't the way their system worked, though. It wasn't the way *any* system worked. Not for people like her. Maggie knew that truth up close and personal, and that was why Luz trusted her. She understood the injustices, the risks, the outcomes.

And the truth was that no one besides Maggie was going to help her. Everyone else would shrug and say, *Your girlfriend was breaking the law, right? An illegal alien?* as if there were something wrong with wanting to stay in the US the way everyone else's ancestors had stayed here. Before there was ICE, before there were passports and visas and immigration authorities, if you made it here alive, you got to stay.

But no. Not for Sveta. Not for Luz's dad either.

She and Sveta had just been living normal lives. They hadn't done anything cruel or mean or damaging. But Tanner had. He was an evil, selfish piece of shit who deserved to have a little pain of his own. No official government system would enforce that. It was up to *them*. And it was up to Luz to help with this Frank guy.

What if he'd done something like Tanner had? What if he'd done something worse?

She clenched her teeth and walked a little faster. Ballyhoo wasn't tiny. He was schnauzer size and could easily keep up. His little paws danced in a blur beside her, perfectly trained to heel by Sveta. My God, her whole world was just a space formerly occupied and improved by Sveta.

When tears burned her eyes, she blamed it on the crisp evening air and angled her gaze high at the purpling sky to try to cut off her tear ducts.

She finally let go of her braid to touch the envelope in her pocket. She'd met Maggie on her lunch hour in a library parking lot to pick it up. *Gloves on when you open this,* she'd said before repeating the very specific instructions she'd already given over the phone.

Through the thick white paper, it felt like the envelope held a small plastic bag with some kind of substance inside it. Barely enough to make a bulge. Was it cocaine? Heroin? Did heroin come in a powder? She had no idea.

It could be some drug she'd never even heard of, because the hardest thing she'd ever tried was alcohol. Or maybe a weed gummy. She couldn't decide which had made her feel more out of control, but she didn't like either feeling, mild as they were. But this? She winced at the idea of it being one of those drugs that news anchors breathlessly claimed could kill you with one touch.

What if it did kill him?

"No," she whispered to herself as she led Ballyhoo across another intersection. Maggie wouldn't do that. "Probably just cocaine." As if that were a comforting thought.

A pair of police officers emerged suddenly from a doorway, and Luz yelped at the sight of them, which could have been a truly disastrous response when she was carrying drugs. But the cops ignored her and her thundering heart. Maybe they'd thought Ballyhoo had made the noise.

Good God. She wasn't cut out for this.

The sneakiest thing Luz ever did these days was play a little Candy Crush during work meetings. Every once in a while, she dealt with the guilt of calling in sick with cramps that weren't *quite* debilitating. That was it. But this? She wasn't sure she'd be able to face her mom over their next family dinner with this burden on her shoulders.

Despite that she hadn't set foot in a church in five years, when she passed a mountain of steps that led up to the doors of a cathedral, a bolt of need slashed through her, a nearly violent urge to sprint up the stairs and go to confession. She snorted at her own ridiculousness. Drugs weren't even in the Bible, but there were a host of other things they'd love for her to confess while she was there.

Luz walked on. Screw all that. Shitty ideas about women and their place in this world were exactly why she and the others were doing this. After all, hadn't these bad things happened because she was a woman?

Her career progression wouldn't have surprised Tanner one bit if she'd been a man. Hell, she would have bypassed him months earlier if she hadn't had to prove her work every step of the way to an industry that rarely saw a woman succeed, especially a Mexican American woman.

Tanner had completely lost his head about her promotion. He'd started off merely exasperated and rolling his eyes when she spoke. Then he'd progressed to downright insubordination, as if the very sight of her in the office had been a daily dose of poison. He'd finally been "encouraged to seek new opportunities" after an episode in the break room that had devolved into him shouting about affirmative action while his coworkers—and Luz—backed away in horror.

Jesus, the humiliation of that. All she'd ever wanted was to be good at what she did. No, she'd wanted to be *great* at it. First at programming, then coding. Eventually she'd started classes in software engineering, and it had all clicked into place like a perfectly shaped puzzle piece.

She loved coding, but it felt claustrophobic to her, so narrow she'd get sucked in and shrivel up in the dark. But the project side of engineering felt open and challenging in the best way. She'd gotten her first engineering job straight out of college, and she'd thrived. But now instead of being known as a hot new engineer at her current company, she was eyed as some token employee. The one who'd driven poor Tanner to madness.

Infuriating. And heartbreaking on the days she let herself really feel it.

In the end, Tanner had been fine, shucked off onto some other corporation and all the unsuspecting brown folks and women who worked there. He should have been thankful for the chance to calm down and start over. But no. Of course not.

He'd hated her even more after that, posting bullshit about her on social media. Luz had been left to block him wherever she could and muddle through her own mortification and the uncomfortable silence he'd left behind in her office.

She'd felt mildly betrayed after their short friendship, but these days she was left wondering if he'd been nice to her at first because of a *personal* interest. She grimaced at the thought.

Luz had never been very good at those kinds of signals, and men in her industry were so often allowed to be awkward in ways she grew to ignore. Maybe that was what had set him off on such a cruel course. He'd seen her as a sexual opportunity, and suddenly she'd transformed into a workplace superior, like a reverse Scooby-Doo villain, yanking off her harmless little lady mask to reveal the terrifying testosterone-sucking demon beneath.

"Heh," she huffed to herself as she stepped off another curb. She wished she could have swiped some big, scary claws at him.

The thought pumped her up with just enough anger that she marched the last quarter mile without guilt. When she reached her pickup spot, she still had a few minutes of leeway, so she pulled on her fleece gloves and watched the dot of Frank's car, now on the move, draw closer on the grid.

She took the envelope from her pocket and ripped it open, then plucked out the tiny baggie, which contained a teaspoon or so of white powder, just as she'd suspected. She dropped the envelope in a nearby trash can, then shoved the baggie quickly into her coat pocket, trying not to imagine all her stray DNA clinging to it.

She knew they weren't going to bring DNA into a drug case, but her skin still crawled, all her little cells reminding her of their tenuous hold on her body. Some of them were falling off *right now*. Some were—

"We're going to spring for a ride home," she rushed to tell Ballyhoo. "Want to go for a ride?" Her high pitch sounded like normal pet-talking mode instead of the terror it actually was, and Ballyhoo yipped in answer, winding around her legs until she had to turn twice to untangle the leash. He did that when she was anxious, and she was starting to wonder if he meant to give her a hug. Or maybe he was trying to stop her from doing something stupid?

Oh God, was this really, really stupid?

When she looked up from fixing his leash, a shiny black sedan awaited. Her heart lurched with such alarm that she worried she might throw up.

The window rolled down. "Luz? Hey, I'm your driver, Frank."

He was a White guy with black hair buzzed down to stubble, the short cut offset by a thick beard. A tattoo wound down the arm he'd perched on the steering wheel, and another one colored his right forearm, though she didn't stare long enough to make out any details. Honestly, he looked a little scary, and he didn't smile at all until she reached down and picked up Ballyhoo.

"Hey there, buddy," he said, eyes lighting up at the sight of the dog as his grim mouth bloomed into delight.

Luz reached for the handle of the front passenger door, something she'd never do on a normal trip. No, she usually hid in the back and kept busy on her phone so she didn't have to make awkward conversation. Not today.

"Thanks for accepting pets," she said as she climbed in and shut the door.

"It's no problem. I absolutely love dogs."

"Speak," she said to Ballyhoo, who gave a happy yelp that seemed to enchant the man.

"He does tricks! Beautiful. There's really nothing better than good obedience training. You know?" He winked at that, and Luz wondered if it was some kind of double entendre. Ew.

"I've got treats," Frank added, "if that's okay." He leaned forward, his hand already reaching past her toward the glove compartment.

"Oh!" she yelped, making him jerk back in surprise. She was on a sharp edge, teetering toward panic, but in the blink of an eye, her well-honed ability to function under pressure kicked in. Blood rushed in her veins, but everything inside her slowed to a manageable pace. This stress response had saved her so many times in the past, and today it saved her again.

Luz curled her hand around the baggie in her pocket and smiled. "Be sure to make him do a trick," she suggested. "Several, even." Her voice echoed in her own ears, as if she were standing just around a corner. "He gets spoiled if he doesn't have to work for it, you know?"

"Absolutely. I totally agree. A good dog loves to work. I can tell you're great with him."

He reached past her again and popped open the glove compartment to withdraw a bag of sausage-shaped treats. Ballyhoo went tight with attention and looked intently from Frank's hand to his face, then back to his hand. His little haunches shook against her, and his mouth opened to a pant. Luz eased him farther forward on her lap until he was perched directly over the open hatch. Then she slid her own treat bag free of her pocket.

"Speak," Frank said, prompting a sharp bark from Ballyhoo. He happily handed over one treat.

"Try 'sing,'" she suggested. Her dog glanced at her, but Frank jumped in with the command, easing Ballyhoo's confusion. He braced his body and let out a beautiful, warbling howl.

Frank threw his head back with a delighted laugh, eyes squinting shut. This was her best chance. Instead of just dropping it in, Luz smoothed her hand down Bally's side and slid the baggy next to the car's instruction manual in one quick motion. She could see it, but she was sure Frank wouldn't spy it from his angle.

She wished she'd been able to put it underneath the manual, but she was too scared to try. That little packet of powder had already shaved a few minutes off her lifespan, judging by the way her heart shook with the force of her pulse.

By the time Frank said, "He's the best!" she was scratching Bally's neck.

"Good boy! Aren't you the best boy? Give him a high-five," she suggested, and Frank and Ballyhoo both obeyed.

"You get two treats," Frank gushed, and the dog gobbled them both up happily with hardly any chewing. Frank offered one more with a wink. "All right, we'd better get going or my stats will be way off. Ready?" He stashed the treats and shut the compartment door.

Luz stared out the windshield as they pulled away to head toward the address she'd given him, a big-box pet store two blocks from her place. "Yes," she said softly. "Let's do this."

CHAPTER 9

KATHERINE

"Jesus, that was great," Brad said in a pleased growl as Katherine tugged the blanket up to hide her naked breasts. The phone shook a bit in her hand until she could rest it on her leg again.

She couldn't believe she'd done it. Too nervous to let her guard down, she hadn't had an orgasm, but he sure had.

But she'd loved that. Loved watching him do something she'd never watched a man do before. The way he'd filmed himself shamelessly, utterly thrilled that she wanted to be his audience.

She'd been thrilled too. Truly. It had been absolutely filthy and wrong, both of them showing their bodies and hiding their faces, and my God, she felt disgusting in the best possible way. A goddamn trollop. A slut. A cam girl!

She laughed with delicious shame. "Maybe we should try that with more lights next time."

"Damn, I'll do anything," he moaned. Moaned for *her*. She laughed again, high on arousal. And utterly fearless for once in her life. "Did you come?" he asked.

"Yes," she lied. She didn't care. She liked the lying. Liked filing secret after secret away in a compartment she'd used only for her saddest untruths before. That first early miscarriage she'd hidden from Peter, too aware of his eagerness to start a family to dare such disappointment. His dumb confusion about their long bout of infertility after the fourth pregnancy she'd lost. The dry heat of her hatred for the man she'd married.

Now she was filling that compartment of secrets with fabulous lies. Spectacular deceptions covered in sequins and masked in stage fog and strobing lights. Her secrets had become absolutely delightful.

Their phone call the day before had started out friendly and platonic until he'd told her she had a sexy voice. She'd responded truthfully that no one had ever said that before.

"Not even your husband?" he'd asked. That had led to confessions of their difficult marriages and the pressures of making a lifelong commitment work. Then of their loneliness. Their shuttered needs. Their hungers.

Aware that he'd never actually know her, that he was merely a mark in this con, she'd let her guard down and been honest. Her husband had been her first and only. She'd dated but had never sown her oats, and she wondered now what sex was like with someone else. Was she even capable of it? Was she sexy enough?

"Oh, you're sexy enough," he'd growled, and Katherine had glowed with the power of that. Because desire was power, and that had been one way Peter had kept her contained. After the novelty of the honeymoon period had worn off, she'd been constantly off kilter, worried that they only had sex once a week. Then it had drifted to once or twice a month when she was ovulating. Then hardly ever. Her whole life had been a question of how she didn't please him.

But this guy? This guy she could make groan with just a word or two, the horny bastard.

He'd said he was a pharmaceutical rep and traveled a lot and would be staying in a hotel the next night. She'd said her husband was usually out late. Her lies, and maybe his, had led them to this 7:00 p.m. appointment and the video call she'd been so scared of.

She wasn't scared anymore. "So does that mean you want to do this again?" she asked eagerly.

"Yes, I very much do," he said, lying back in his hotel bed, one hand splayed over his bare chest.

She grinned at the dim outline of his face in the partially darkened room. He'd suggested the idea of a dark room to her—almost as if he'd done this before—and she'd jumped on it, reluctant to expose herself in harsh lighting even if she did need video of his face. This was just an introduction, after all. If they did it once, they could do it again. And again after that.

Even in the dimness, they could see enough of each other on their phones in indirect light from distant lamps. Enough for sex, if not for her actual filming purposes. She'd had a screen-capture app recording his video call the whole time, but he hadn't revealed enough. Not of his face, anyway. He'd revealed more than enough of other parts.

As she'd suspected, Brad was a little husky, and she liked his broad chest and slightly thick belly. The intrusion of it on her screen. She wondered how tall he was but didn't bother asking. She'd gotten tired of looking up at Peter for all those years, and it hardly mattered on video.

He had either a very short beard or two days' worth of scruff, and she appreciated the outdoorsy look it gave him, enjoying the dangerous flash of white teeth when he smiled.

She was just settling back to watch him in repose for a while—was his hair dark blond or brown?—when he yawned. "I'd better sign off," he said abruptly. "This was really great, though."

"Oh. Okay." She didn't want to let him go, and how stupid was that? This wasn't a relationship; it was revenge. "Thanks . . ." She faded into silence after that awkward word. What was she thanking him for?

"See you online?" He waved, and then his dim image disappeared like a genie returning to a bottle.

Katherine frowned, feeling a little used. She turned off the screen record and turned on her bedside light, then caught herself in the bedroom mirror. The sight of her unhappy glare snapped her out of her mood and sent her into laughter again. Did she really feel *used* by a man she was setting up for a downfall? Was she really that sensitive? No.

"Good Lord," she said before giggling. "Welcome back from fantasyland, you idiot."

It had been a good ride, though. She'd alternated between turned on and terrified all day, and had even skipped boxing for the first time ever so she could shower and shave and exfoliate before spending an hour fussing over her makeup and wig.

After all that worrying, in the end it had been easy. Brad had done most of the work, jumping right off the bat into how hard he was, what he was doing to himself, what he wanted her to show or touch. Really, all he'd needed was her viewership.

Easy peasy. Now she'd draw a hot bath and maybe continue her own party there. She might even watch the video again for her own personal enjoyment.

She'd touched herself over the years, of course, even as a teenager. But over time even her own body had frozen up in the coldness of her marital home. Not anymore. There wasn't a flake of ice in her tonight. She was all warm liquid.

Her wicked grin was yanked off her face by a knock on the apartment door. Katherine whipped her legs off the bed and stared out into the cavern of the living area. Who the hell could it be? There wasn't a single person she'd welcome at this moment and no one in the building who knew her.

She reached for her robe, then remembered the wig. "Shit," she whispered as she yanked the robe on. No, it didn't matter. She wasn't opening that door. That wasn't her mom's knock; it was way too strong and booming. Whoever it was could go away.

Oh my God, was she already being stalked because of an online profile?

After another three bangs on the door, she heard a muffled voice through the metal. "Katherine?"

"No." It couldn't be. She knotted the tie tightly around her waist and crept out into the living room to tiptoe toward the entrance.

"Katherine!"

Shit. There was no doubt that was her husband's voice. She looked through the peephole and saw him standing rigid, fists on his hips, head bowed to glare at the floor. He shouldn't be here. Not ever, but especially not *now*.

"What do you want?" she asked tightly.

Peter's head whipped up at the words. "I want to talk."

"I can't. I'm not dressed."

"We've been married for twenty-three years. How could that possibly matter to anyone?"

She watched through the peephole as the door across the hall opened and a gray-haired woman stuck her head out to frown at him. Peter raised a friendly hand. "Sorry," he offered, and she glared at him for a moment before closing the door again. Crap.

Damn him. She'd just moved in. She didn't want a reputation here. Didn't want any trouble at all. She growled in frustration, panic beginning to grip her as guilt snuck its way into her first sexual foray in decades. "Fine. Hold on. I'll be right back."

Katherine dashed to the bathroom, cursing with every step she took. This was not how she'd wanted this evening to end. The scandal was supposed to be all *hers*, not some round robin of dirty sex with a stranger and irritating divorce negotiations with her husband. Maybe her mom would drop by later and really add insult to the injury of the whole ordeal.

"Damn it!" she growled as she yanked off the wig and nylon cap. She tried her best to fluff her sweaty hair with her fingers, but it still looked damp and matted. After scrubbing a makeup wipe over her face, she snapped her eye patch on over her contact and tugged the collar of her robe higher.

Good enough. She looked like a sweaty mess, but she didn't owe him an airtight explanation, and she certainly didn't owe him good looks.

When she opened the door, she swept it wide so Peter could see the modern furnished apartment she'd chosen for herself. No more of her grandma's china and his dead mom's crystal and the massive cabinet his grandfather had sanded and stained with his own two hands.

She was a new woman who'd chosen a whole new world all her own, and she wanted Peter to see no space for himself even as she waved him in. He could stand between her cute LED chandelier and the modern blue couch and wait forever for an invitation to sit that she was never going to issue.

"Well?" she demanded, keeping her voice steady even as she noticed that he looked like shit. No wonder her mom was worried. Circles nearly as dark as bruises stained the skin beneath his bloodshot eyes, and he looked like he'd been wearing the same orange polo shirt for days. His hair, kept short and always neat like a 1950s businessman, looked a bit mussed today.

"What's going on with you?" he snapped.

She held up both hands in a baffled shrug. "Nothing? I'm getting ready to take a bath."

"How long have you been planning this?"

"My bath?" she responded sarcastically, but then her bravery dried up along with all her spit. She might have a new willingness to push him, but what if he hadn't been talking about the divorce? What if he knew something about the girl at the party?

He looked around and grimaced at the open bottle of wine on the kitchen counter as she tried to calm her nerves. There was no way he could know about the system, but her skin still prickled.

"Don't think I didn't notice," he sneered as if he'd heard all her silent fears. "You rented this place without using our checking account or credit cards. So how did you do it?"

Crap. Had that been a misstep? She'd just wanted the ability to move without him watching every step on their credit card account. "I . . . I used my savings."

"What savings?"

She shrugged at the barked question because it wasn't his business. Not anymore.

"I knew it," he snarled. "I knew something wasn't right. You were planning all this."

The familiar nasty bite in his voice fired up her anger and pulled her free of the fear. Her mouth opened and filth spilled out. "No, Peter. Something definitely wasn't right, but I wasn't planning on you fucking someone at the fucking birthday party I threw for you in our family's home!"

"Really? Wow. Nice language, Katherine."

"Are you serious? You're chastising *me*? I didn't *do* the fucking, Peter, I just *said* it. Which do you think is more foul? The dirty sex or the naming it?"

He shook his head, a tight little jerk of his chin as his lips curled into hostility. "What the hell's gotten into you?"

She stood straighter, proud of her new ugly vocabulary. "To answer your previous question, I opened a savings account a few years ago because I figured at some point I'd have proof of what I've always known about you. I thought it would come in the form of an STD, so that little scene in the foyer was good news for me, I guess. I got away free and clear."

"Are you wearing makeup?" he growled. "Charlotte says you're dating. Is that what this is all about? A midlife crisis after you missed out on your chance to slut it up in college? Pitiful."

Of course their daughter had run right back to him. She'd always been a daddy's girl, and Katherine had known his cheating wouldn't put an end to that. She'd just wanted to carve a bigger place for herself.

"You've got some nerve, Peter. What I do now is none of your business."

"You're still my wife."

She scoffed. "I'm sorry, are only husbands allowed to date during the marriage? I guess I wasn't so clear on that. Is that part of the catechism? Let's call Father Carlo and ask what the church says."

His sneer faded a little as the red umbrage of his cheeks paled. Their priest for the first twenty years of their marriage had been Father Donnelly, and he and Peter had been two peas in a pod. Donnelly had even performed the traditional Latin mass at 7:00 a.m. on Sundays with Peter right there at his side. They'd teamed up time and time again in "marriage counseling" sessions in Donnelly's office as well.

Father Carlo, on the other hand, believed in modernizing the gospel. He believed in kindness and equality, neither of which was Peter's strong suit.

Her husband cleared his throat. "I don't know what happened that night, Katherine. I obviously had too much to drink, and that woman . . . She was . . ."

When he frowned like a puzzling thought had just occurred to him, Katherine jumped in with a question she knew she was supposed to ask. "Who the hell was she? Some little girlfriend? And you invited her to our *home*? How dare you?"

"I don't . . . Yeah, I don't want to discuss that. I came to ask what you're planning. Charlotte is extremely upset. You've thrown everything away because of a misstep, and she can see that."

"First of all, a *misstep*? Second, are you seriously standing here explaining that our *daughter* wants me to come home? Not you?" When he stared at her, she laughed. "No, you don't care about me, do you? You just care that you're a laughingstock in your community."

"Don't be ridiculous. You're my wife. Of course I love you."

She looked at him. Looked at his tired blue eyes and the deep lines bracketing his mouth. The brown hair that was just as thick as ever, though turning gray at the edges. The proud nose he'd broken in a hockey game in high school. The hollows of his temples, and the way they'd always looked so delicate to her. She'd stroked that part of his head so gently in the beginning. Eventually she'd transitioned to imagining how susceptible the thin bone would be to a blow.

"You don't love someone because you're married to them, Peter. Those two things are completely separate. I'm not sure if you ever loved me."

"Of course I did. What the hell are you talking about? We had a good partnership."

"I think you loved the idea of me. The virgin bride, the Catholic homemaker, the stay-at-home mom. And most important, the scarred charity case to polish up your image and make you shine brighter. You never loved *me*, Katherine, the person."

His eyes glinted with scorn. "You're insane. This is some kind of embarrassing menopausal crisis."

"Funny, my cycle is still regular. Not that you would have noticed."

"You really think you're going to find someone new? You're forty-five."

"You're fifty, and look at you playing the field."

"Good God." He sighed as if he were trying to reason with a child. As if she were a supremely irrational creature. "You're clearly having some kind of breakdown."

"I'm not having a breakdown, you asshole." The words ripped from her in a spray of spittle. "You're having the breakdown. Who are you if you're not the perfect altar boy, huh? Do you even *know*? Who the hell are you if Father Carlo and my mom and all the ministry look at you and see a man with his dick out in the entryway of his own home? Huh?"

His face twisted between anger and horror as she watched, like an android whose wiring was beginning to glitch. "That's not what happened," he rasped, face turning red and ugly again.

"They know what you were doing in your own home with your family a few steps away. They know how cruel and stupid it was, and now they can't deny how cruel and stupid you've *always* been." She poked a finger at his chest, thrilling when he startled and stepped back. "Should I tell them how you mocked my eye? How you said, 'Thank God she has two,' after Charlotte was born? How you asked if the accident might have ruined my womb too? What did you mean by that, Peter? The way it ruined my *face*?"

He recovered enough to draw himself tall and snarl down at her. "You're out of your goddamn mind. Either that or you've found someone else to take care of you. Or are you going to pretend after all these years you finally grew a spine?"

He actually dared to move past her then, barreling toward her bedroom door as if he had a right to be there. He slapped on the overhead light and marched over to her bed.

"Get the hell out!" she screamed. "Get out of my house! You don't belong here!"

"You're disgusting," he snapped, the words a terrible echo to the worst thing he'd ever said to her.

Stunned, she screamed, "Screw you, you monster!" and he returned, abandoning whatever search he'd started. In fact, he passed her in a blur, already reaching toward the door handle before he was anywhere near the front door, suddenly eager to escape her.

Good.

"You need mental help," he spat.

"Oh, I'm fine. No thanks to you, you self-righteous asshole."

When the door slammed behind him, her rage began to drip away. She became slowly aware of her clenched fists, her twisted snarl, her legs tense and ready to pounce.

She'd never spoken to him that way. She could see now that he'd trained her not to. His little gasps of horror when she'd let out an occasional curse when they were dating. His stunned disbelief when she raised her voice during the early years of their marriage.

Whatever transgression he'd committed, her reaction to it was always the worse violation. Katherine was out of control, unnatural, immodest, unchristian. She was so much to *deal* with, so much to suffer, so unbearably emotional and overwrought. If she couldn't give him children, the least she could do was be ladylike and grateful. Father Donnelly had practically said those exact words to her once.

And of course, her mom had been there the whole time, reinforcing Peter's every dig, standing with him before he even asked for reinforcements.

Her eye patch felt icy cold against her cheek, pooling her tears on her skin. She ripped it off, swiped the tears away, and marched to her phone. I want to do that again, she typed to Brad. Soon.

Tonight, tomorrow, she didn't care. She'd burn the whole world down and enjoy every lick of flame.

CHAPTER 10

GENEVA

Geneva clocked out of her customer-service gig for a fifteen-minute break and reopened the message she'd received from Jess a moment earlier. Hey, girl, she typed. Sorry, on break now!

Her phone rang immediately, and she answered with a tentative smile as she headed to the kitchen to refill her water. "Hi."

"Hi yourself," her best friend said, sounding angry and friendly at the same time. "Does this mean you've stopped avoiding me?"

"No."

"Oh my God, grow up," Jess ordered. "So you did the wrong guy on camera. Show me someone who hasn't."

"You!" Geneva yelled, but she was laughing over the roar of the ice cubes dropping into her bottle.

"I'm too uptight for all that."

"Yeah, that's why I'm still avoiding you. You really let loose with the *I told you so*s."

"I just didn't like that guy. That's all. He seemed like an ass."

"Well, you were right about him. Is that what you called to hear for the fifth time? You were right? I get it." She regretted the cutting words as soon as they were out. She wasn't truly angry at Jess. Or not so angry she wanted to start a fight. Mostly she just resented knowing Jess would never have left herself vulnerable like that. She wasn't great at trusting people.

In the past, Geneva had felt her own enthusiasm for openness and trust was a gift. Being positive and free. Not so much anymore.

"I'm sorry," Jess said, her voice dropping. "I said the wrong things and made it worse. I was angry for you. And scared. I really am sorry."

"I know." She did know, but it still hurt that Jess had reinforced the judgmental things Geneva had been saying to herself. *I should've been more careful. I shouldn't have trusted him.* Yes. She was very clear on that.

Jess lived way up north of Boulder, so it had been easy to avoid her in person, but Geneva was starting to miss her now, and she was tired of holding herself back from everyone who loved her. Did that mean she was healing? "What do you want? I need a potty break before I get back on the clock."

"Potty break? Jesus, you elementary teachers are unbearable."

"Shut up." But she smiled because in that moment her best friend was no longer tiptoeing around her. They'd gotten back to their habit of casual insults and the standard old jokes they'd quickly perfected after meeting in college. "Oh, like you're so damn edgy with your eighth graders."

"I am!" Jess insisted. "I'm cool. We make history memes. The kids love it."

"My God, you should be ashamed of yourself for bragging about that. They make fun of you when you leave the room, you know."

"Shit, they don't bother waiting for me to leave."

"Good. I wouldn't either."

"Whatever, Miss Pleated Skirts and Rainbow Sweaters. Anyway . . ." Jess's voice had suddenly gone chirpy the way it did when she had a secret. "The thing I was calling you about . . ."

"What?"

"Please listen first and don't say no."

Geneva went immediately rigid. "No. I'm saying no."

"Just listen, okay? I think I can get you a teaching job."

Her mind stayed blank for one gracious moment because that wasn't at all what she expected to hear. She thought Jess had met yet another cute lesbian and decided she'd be perfect for her friend. Jess was as straight as they came and thought every chick with an asymmetrical haircut and clipped voice was going to be Geneva's type. She was right only about seventy-five percent of the time.

But a teaching job? That was a whole different kind of third rail these days, and she was way too scared to touch it. "What are you talking about?"

"Our morning kindergarten teacher was just ordered to bed rest in the sixth month of her pregnancy. They need a long-term sub."

"I can't—"

"It's only half days, but still. You always say kindergarten is different, but the kids are practically first graders already, so they're ready for you."

"No."

"It could really work out. We have a lot of turnover here because the parents are demanding, and you know how I feel about that shitwad CEO." Jess bit out the CEO part.

She worked at a K–8 school that claimed to "prepare kids for the future!" and handed out titles like CEO and CTO instead of principal and librarian. The parents and the school were one hundred percent invested in capitalism and the American way, and Geneva winced at what that might mean for a kindergarten class.

"They'll know about me," she said, starting to frown as anger began to bubble up. Anger that Jess had planted a tiny seed of hope in her. "I haven't saved enough to clean up my name online. They'll know why I got fired, or they'll find out."

"They won't. You only had that job for five months, so leave it off your résumé. That's not a crime. Just say you took time off after school to care for a family member or something."

"That's unethical."

"The American School of Excellence believes in pulling yourself up by your bootstraps, and that's all you'd be doing. You're a good teacher. The kids deserve that. Heck, you don't even have to be licensed for long-term subbing. They'll be thrilled to have someone with your education."

"No." Geneva shook her head, the phone trembling in her hand. "I don't want to."

"Yes, you do. Come on. You'd have to get up at the ass crack of dawn for the drive, but this will be a gig you can put on your résumé to get you back in the game. You need this. It'll be a great buffer between that last school and the rest of your career."

"I can't risk it, Jess. I can't risk everyone finding out and looking at me that way again. Like I'm dangerous around the kids. Like I'm disgusting. They'll Google me and—If I have to go through that again . . ."

Jess interrupted. "But you're not dangerous, and you're not disgusting, and you deserve to start over now. And no, I am not going to let you keep pushing me away. You didn't do anything wrong, Gennie. And you're such a goddamn good teacher. You know you are!"

"No," she groaned, terrified by the prospect of coming out of hiding. "I just need a few more months," she said. "I have a plan. I need to ease back in."

"It's only going to get harder the longer you put it off. This isn't good for you."

She knew that was right. She knew she was sinking deeper into depression, and every suffocating inch was another mile she'd have to climb out of later. The high point of her every day was imagining Frank getting arrested and sent to prison, and it couldn't be healthy to be so focused on revenge.

She wasn't a fan of the justice system or incarceration by any means, but she'd gouged out a big exception for this man who'd so deliberately ruined her. He hadn't only posted the video; he'd sent a link to the whole school board, pretending to be a parent concerned about "the welfare of our children." He'd used a burner account, but she knew exactly who'd done it, and she needed him to pay. For ruining her career and for making her feel shame for her own joyful sexuality.

Did that make her a monster too? The way she delighted in how he'd have to start over? Back at square one, exactly where he'd put her? Frank was still on probation for a long-ago drug violation. It wouldn't even be difficult to make him pay.

God, she hated herself. She'd never, ever hated herself before this. She'd thought most people were good deep down, and now all she could think about was the way they'd all seemed to revel in her violation.

"I know you're scared, Gennie," Jess said softly. "Just do it quick. Say yes and I'll text Principal CEO right this minute and tell him I have the perfect solution to his problem. Substitutes are scarce, and they're bringing in parents to cover the class. They need you. I bet he'd call first thing next week."

Her heart hurt. Not like the ache of emotion, but as if it were cramping up, ready to leap into a heart attack. Anxiety, probably. Or her soul trying to leave her body by any means necessary?

"I can't," she said.

"You can," Jess insisted, and Geneva could hear the love in those two syllables, the hope for her that she couldn't bear to feel for herself. "Just say yes. Leave the rest to me. I'll set it up."

"Jess?" she whispered, with no idea what she was asking.

"Yes?"

The seconds ticked by. She needed to get back to her desk, clock in, take complaints and abuse via chat from people whose flower orders had gone awry. "Okay," she finally whispered, the word dragging from her throat and leaving rawness behind.

"*Okay?*" Jess yelled back.

"Sure."

"I'll text him right now. I love you. I love you!"

Geneva hung up and took a few steps toward the bathroom, worried she might be sick. The feeling rose up and crested, but she slowed her rush, took a deep breath, then let the panic wash through her and recede. She turned toward the wall to press her hot forehead to the cool paint. She breathed slowly, counting it out, until finally her heartbeat stopped its frantic gallop and let go of that gripping pain.

Panic attacks were another new indignity she'd learned to live with since the video had gone off like a bomb in her life. The crushing feeling that something was wrong, something was coming to destroy her, even if she couldn't see it.

"I'm okay," she whispered. "I'm okay." And after a few long moments, she actually was okay. She counted down. She didn't keep spiraling. Didn't curl into a ball and wrap her arms over her head.

Because honestly, what was the worst that could happen? She'd already suffered that worst, hadn't she?

She was still living through it, but she was *living*, and she'd even worked toward a plan to get back in the game. This job possibility didn't change any of that. If Principal CEO recognized her name or even Googled her and hunted down the video, she'd know right away before she got called in for an interview. No harm and . . . only a little foul?

Talking to Jess and feeling normal again for those few brief moments had given her a bit of bravery, but regret followed close on its heels, chewing her nerves alive.

But she no longer needed the potty break. The job prospect had frozen up her whole system, apparently, shut everything down. So Geneva sat, logged back on the clock, and concentrated on the menial work of her job, trying her best not to imagine that this might be one of her last shifts.

A tiny balloon of hope inside her trembled. It seemed she wanted more than revenge for herself after all.

CHAPTER 11

KATHERINE

The sound of ripping tape echoed through her bedroom until Katherine finally paused to catch her breath and wipe sweat off her upper lip. What the hell was she going to wear tonight?

A workout top wasn't going to cut it this time. She pulled open yet another moving box and dove in to yank out more clothes, as if sexy underwear would suddenly jump into view from the pile of sweatpants and the dozens of pairs of cotton undies she'd accumulated. When was the last time she'd bought sexy underwear? Before Charlotte was born?

This was insane. It was madness. It was really, really stupid.

But she wanted it so much.

She'd found a black pencil skirt and a beautiful blue sweater that she could pass off as sexy, but she still needed heels. Not blocky heels, but something impractical that she'd never wear in everyday life, something naughty.

Because what the hell had being the good girl gotten her in life? She'd done everything right. Everything. And she'd lost so much because of it. She'd lost any hint of closeness with her sisters, she'd lost passion, she'd lost four pregnancies and all her hope. But being bad? That was bringing her hope back, so she planned to embrace it.

Okay. She still had four hours to prepare. Maybe—

Her phone rang, cutting off her low-grade panic and tossing her into a new fear. What now? She'd already ignored a call from her divorce lawyer, knowing she couldn't take any more stress.

It was the unlisted number Maggie had called on last time.

"No video yet?" the woman asked without even a hello.

Katherine winced so hard she saw stars against her right eyelid. "Maggie! Hi! No, actually. I'm sorry. No, no video yet."

Maggie's sigh was long and loud. "Nothing?" The weary tone suggested maybe Katherine wasn't cut out for this seduction, which wasn't true. It wasn't even close to true. But she was in no position to defend herself because she was being bad again. "You've made no progress at all?"

"No, it's not that," she answered quickly. "We texted. On two different days! But he seems super busy. He said something about a sick kid? So I'm thinking maybe this is just bad timing for his personal life. I still feel confident. He seems to want contact."

"I see. Okay, not your fault, then. The best-laid plans and all that. But he's not being a perfect gentleman, I hope?"

"Definitely not. We've chatted a bit, and he sent a dick pic."

"Well, all right! That's promising!"

She giggled before she could stifle it, but Maggie laughed along with her. "Still," Katherine continued, "he seems careful. He didn't show his face." Another lie, though it had been true at the beginning. He'd definitely gotten more careless on the second video call.

"It's much easier to avoid giving yourself away in a still photo. Once you get him on video, there should be something we can work with. You still feel up for it? It's not too much?"

It definitely wasn't too much. "I'm good. It's been easier than I thought. Kind of fun, even?" She covered her face, suddenly panicked that she'd voiced it.

But then Maggie said, "No reason it shouldn't be!" and Katherine was laughing again, happy surprise bursting from her.

"Hey," Maggie said, "you're a vibrant woman with half of your life still ahead of you. There are so many new experiences and feelings waiting out there."

For the first time, the truth of that really hit her. That she was only halfway through living. "Yeah. Yeah, that's right."

"You're in your prime, Katherine. Sometimes we look at younger women as our competition, and who can compete with the beauty of youth? But would you want to be your twenty-year-old self again? I wouldn't. Jesus, the *confidence* I have now."

That was exactly what Katherine wanted. "You are so right. Twenty-year-old me had no idea who she was. All she knew was what others expected of her."

"Exactly. Now you get to be whoever *you* want. I figured that out a couple of years after my divorce. You've got a head start, ma'am."

A strange, sweet peace fell over her. She nodded. "I've got this. I'll get in touch as soon as I have something. You don't have to worry."

"All right. We're not on a deadline, so better to let him set his own pace. You've got good instincts."

"Thanks. Thank you. I mean . . . Yeah. I'll keep trying."

"Got it. I'll see you on Thursday, then?"

Katherine felt so much better when she got off the phone, her treasure box of secrets glowing fiercely inside her. She'd felt this exact thing long ago, and she couldn't believe she'd forgotten the sensation so completely. At age sixteen that dirty complicity had been an ember in her chest, warming her when she'd otherwise felt cold and unseen. It had burned, yes, but it was the same good kind of burn she felt today.

Her mother hadn't understood, of course. Neither had the school. Even the boy had been completely dense about her motivation. The secrets had all turned to shame and fear eventually, but at first . . . at first they had felt exactly like power.

At five ten, Katherine had been taller than most boys in her class in junior high. By high school a few of them had caught up, but by then it was too late. Her identity had solidified into the shy girl with the eye patch who had towered over them for so many years, and she didn't even have the good grace to have breasts worth noticing.

There hadn't been a lot of outright bullying or anything, but there also hadn't been any positive attention from the boys in her class, though she'd nurtured several painfully secret crushes.

And then one day, one of those boys, a boy she'd always thought so cute, had told her he'd take her to the winter formal if she'd give him a blow job. It had been a joke, of course. A nasty, winking joke, said in a low voice so no one else would hear, because his friends would tease him about wanting to screw the one-eyed wonder. At the time it hadn't even felt mean, just commonplace, though she recognized now that his vulgarity must have been motivated by at least a hint of cruelty.

But in that moment when she should have felt horror . . . in that moment something strange had come over her. The power behind the crude jab had transferred itself, whipping from the boy to her, and Katherine had looked him straight in the eyes and said, *Sure.*

For one heartbeat the long, bony lines of his adolescent face had twitched into a spasm of fear. He'd looked away then, trying to laugh it off, the tips of his pale ears turning red. But she'd waited him out, staring until he finally met her gaze again. His ears had turned even redder then. He'd suggested a meeting spot, as if goading her to back down, but she'd only stared harder.

That afternoon, she'd watched him lie to his friends, telling them he had to stay behind and make up a test. Instead he'd met Katherine in a storage room for the theater department—he'd played one of the leads in *Our Town*—and she'd done it. She'd crouched in front of him like some kind of feasting animal, and she'd made him squeak and moan and shiver. He'd lost control so quickly she'd almost been disappointed with the brevity of the act. Was that all it was?

Even now she couldn't say why she'd done it. Or why she'd done it again, the second time or the third or fourth time. Why she'd kept meeting him and servicing him and walking out of that room with her chin held high like she was the one using him. It was almost as if she'd grown impatient with the mean uncertainty of adolescence. As if she'd wanted to violate herself before they violated her.

The boy hadn't even taken her to the winter formal. She hadn't even *asked*. But once every couple of weeks, she'd catch him staring at her, and she'd raise her unscarred eyebrow in question, and his cheeks would flush as red as his ratty spiral notebook. He'd blink, with a stutter of his eyelashes and nervous chewing of his raw bottom lip, and without a word of conversation between them, she would meet him after school.

Somehow . . . somehow in that moment of debasement, Katherine had felt special. Not special like he loved her; she hadn't been a stupid girl or even a particularly romantic one. But special like she could control that boy with a tiny glance from her one good eye, and he'd cower and shudder and obey. Like she was a puppet master and he was just a stupid little twitching marionette.

The best part was that she only had to confess later, and it was all over, washed away. She was still a good girl. She'd finally figured out the system.

The most amazing thing—the most amazing thing to her *still*—was that he'd never told his friends. Even after they'd been caught by the drama teacher, after he'd been sent to after-school detention and she'd been suspended for a week, because she was a girl, after all, the arbiter of decency. Even then that boy had never bragged. Maybe because she hadn't been worth bragging about. But maybe because she truly had been the one in power.

In the end she'd paid dearly for that brief, sordid high. Her mother had exploded into a sobbing temper that had lasted two full days. She'd first locked Katherine in her room; then she'd thrown things at the door, her fists, her shoes, every item in Katherine's backpack that she'd pulled out to inspect for contraband.

After Katherine spent those long hours crying in her room, there had been no secret confession in the dark to cleanse her sins. Her mom had dragged her to the church office and insisted on a lecture on sex and hell and disease and sin from their priest right there in the full light of day.

She'd been grounded for the rest of the semester. She'd always been kind of shy, with only two or three friends at school, but after she'd stopped seeing anyone outside of class, even those friends had dropped away. She'd had no one, and she'd never dared to do anything like that again.

Until this. But *now* . . . now this seduction returned all those old feelings for her. The power. The boldness.

She was taking what she wanted, letting Brad think it was his idea, that he'd landed a live one. But it was hers. Her idea, her decision, and she was lying to everyone so that she could do what she *should not* do. Lying even to Maggie, the powerful woman in their friendship, the mentor. Katherine seemed weak, maybe she even was weak, but she was the only one who knew the truth of what was happening.

It was a deep, dark joy.

After the call with Maggie, she felt surprisingly calm. She didn't need sexy underwear to meet Brad in person. She didn't need any underwear at all. All she had to do was look straight into his eyes, and he'd meet her in whatever closet she wanted.

Katherine tipped back her head and laughed. She didn't need heels either. She suspected she'd be taller than him, even in bare feet. She could wear the cute sparkly sandals she'd bought for vacation last year. It wasn't as if he'd close the door on her if she didn't choose the right footwear.

This was nothing. This was just one horny man. And if Katherine wanted the same dirty act he did, wanting it didn't make her desperate; it made her powerful.

She'd forgotten that power after so many years with Peter, and the realization flew through her on an icy gust, as if someone had walked over her grave.

She'd been so timid and cowed and passive all these decades because her husband hadn't truly wanted her. Not in the sense that he'd been *hungry*. No, what he'd wanted most of all was the symbolism of her. Of course he'd also been eager to plant babies inside her; he'd tilled that soil over and over, and then he'd hated her as much as any man would hate a field that refused to fruit.

Damn him. Damn all of them. Tonight she was going to be *filthy*.

Instead of rooting around in more stacks of clothing, Katherine sat down, crossed her legs, and returned her divorce attorney's call, pulling new confidence around her like a cape. She confirmed to him that the call from Peter's lawyer had been correct. She did have her own savings account, and at the moment it totaled a hefty $3,028. She wasn't hiding assets from anyone. There was no conspiracy.

After the conversation with her attorney, she texted Charlotte with a few cheerful thoughts, just to keep the line of communication open. In the past, they'd mostly communicated via group text with Peter included.

Hi, Mom! Charlotte texted back. Hey, I looked up your new place online. There's a great breakfast spot a couple of blocks over. Let's plan brunch when I'm back in town.

"Oh," Katherine said out loud, pressing her palm to her chest. Charlotte had been thinking about her, planning a visit, trying to be positive. That would be really, really nice, sweetie. There's a bedroom ready for you!

I checked out the tour from the property place. It's cute, Mom.

Tears rushed to her eyes. All those years of staying with him, of enduring, knowing if she left her marriage she'd leave some of Charlotte's love behind too . . . All those years had been worth it because she'd threaded the needle just the way she'd hoped.

Charlotte wasn't happy about the split, but she understood it, at least, felt sympathy and understanding because of what her father had done. That was all Katherine had wanted. A little light shining on that darkness Peter kept so well hidden from the world.

She'd done it.

They signed off with *I love you*s, Katherine forcing herself not to gush or overwhelm Charlotte with these emotions that made her want to cling. If she acted normal about this with her daughter, it would become normal, and then their relationship would get closer in new ways.

She couldn't wait.

This was a great omen. A great promise. A great start to what she hoped would be a fantastic evening.

After a long bath, she smoothed on lotion and took special care with her wig. After she inserted her contact, she took a long time with her makeup to distract from the differences in her two eyes and slopped on thick concealer to hide the pink tugs of scars on her eyelid and brow. The last step was penciling in the two narrow scars that cut her eyebrow into three mismatched pieces. Hopefully Brad would be focused on other things and not notice.

She stocked a few extras in her purse—wipes and mouthwash and the red lipstick—then left for the hotel early. It was a classic name-brand hotel in downtown Denver that was nice enough not to feel seedy, but not quite high end.

The bar was more crowded than she'd expected at 6:00 p.m. on a Monday, full of men in crisp button-downs or wrinkled suits. A few signs around the lobby indicated there was a political convention going on. Ah. That made sense. He'd said he was in pharmaceutical sales, and maybe he was, but she knew he was involved in state politics as well.

The hotel room in Denver had been a slipup on his part. He'd already claimed to live in Aurora, so why would he need to be here? After she got a good look at him in person, she'd probably be able to find him online and figure out who he really was.

Whatever. Her persona was that she was too horny to care, and apparently she was. She no longer cared what he'd done to some other woman. He certainly hadn't promised Katherine anything except sex. Instead he'd made it very clear that he was married and intended to stay married. But that other woman must have fallen in love with him, and maybe he'd let her. Maybe he'd promised things and ruined her heart and her life.

She stopped in her tracks when she realized she'd been thinking of only her own role with Brad. Because there was a good chance that the one who'd set him up was his wife, just as Katherine had set up Peter. For a moment she stood frozen in the hotel lobby, her neck prickling at the thought that she might be doing something very wrong. She wasn't supposed to have actual sex with him, his wife wouldn't have intended that, but Katherine had rushed into this without thinking of anyone else.

She already had the evidence she needed to expose Brad in whatever way Maggie saw fit. There were two videos now, and she'd watched them both carefully. There was enough light in the second that his profile was obvious. The slightly large nose, the round brow, the beard that turned out to be blond enough to look like scruff in the first video.

He had a birthmark too, a pale splotch of beige high on his thigh and very prominently featured thanks to his camerawork.

No, she decided, this wasn't something wrong, or not too wrong to forgive. How could private sex be a worse transgression than posting a video of the man pleasuring himself for all the world to see?

Katherine squeezed her thighs tight together at the memory. After Peter's surprise visit on Thursday, she'd messaged Brad and asked when they could connect again. He'd quickly proposed Saturday at five.

She'd been dirty and shameless that second time, doing everything he'd instructed her to do. She blushed hard thinking of what her own camera had shown him, yet she planned to do the same thing tonight. It felt strangely freeing, following his commands, as if she didn't have a choice and therefore didn't have responsibility.

That was how she'd agreed to this terrible idea. He'd messaged on the app just hours ago and said, I'm here in Denver, I'll send you my room number, meet me there. She'd felt almost drugged when she'd agreed. She was just doing what she was told, after all. None of this was her fault.

She ordered a glass of white wine to bolster her courage and thought of her two sisters and what they'd learned from their mother's deep devotion to the church. Rebecca, two years older than Katherine, had struck out for college on a scholarship to a liberal-arts school that had welcomed her after a scathing essay she'd written about the patriarchy of the church. She was bold and loud and confident and had been that way from the start as far as Katherine could tell. She was now a tenured professor of women's studies at a small school in Oregon.

Vivian, on the other hand . . . only a year younger than Katherine, she'd rebelled in a different way. Drinking, smoking weed, running away to go to concerts with her friends. She'd also come out as an atheist at her thirteenth birthday party, and their mom had nearly had a breakdown. Viv, after battling their mom in screaming fights nearly every day, moved out of the family home the day she turned eighteen. She'd worked her way through culinary school, and lived a far more nomadic life than her two sisters.

In fact, Katherine couldn't honestly say where Viv was living at the moment. Somewhere exciting, probably. Maybe she was even back in Europe. They hadn't seen each other in over ten years. Vivian could walk right by and she wouldn't even recognize Katherine.

Then again, who would? She was Katy, not Katherine. In fact, maybe she really was a Katy. Her mom had despised nicknames, and

Katherine had hated the name Kathy so much that her sisters had tormented her with it in their youth. But Katy? That was something to consider.

She caught herself smiling in the mirror behind the bar. She definitely didn't look like the good Catholic girl tonight. She looked like a dirty girl who needed to get upstairs, where Brad would tell her what to do.

After digging through her purse for cash, she slipped off the stool to head upstairs. Her sandals slapped loudly against the shiny tile of the hotel lobby. The elevator smelled like stale cigar smoke, but it floated her up to the sixth floor like a gentle cloud. Once the doors opened she floated herself down the brown-and-gray swirls of carpet to room 614. She could barely feel anything when she raised a hand to knock.

When Brad opened the door, she stepped in with no hesitation at all.

CHAPTER 12

LUZ

Another Tuesday meant another early arrival at the Hook for Luz. She was so early this time that the space looked empty through the windows, so she relaxed back in her seat and called Sveta to see if she was up.

"Hello, my moon," Sveta answered, her voice still a little husky with sleep on the other side of the world.

"Sveta," she sighed, her body loosening at just those brief words from her girlfriend's mouth. "Did you finally get some rest?"

"Finally."

She smiled at the sound of Sveta's yawn, picturing the way her skinny feet would form taut points when she stretched hard in bed. She never wore fingernail polish, but her toenails were always brightly colored in whatever jewel tone suited her mood that week.

"I'm sorry," Luz murmured into the phone. "I shouldn't have called so early." Sveta struggled with insomnia, and it had only gotten worse since the deportation.

"No, no, I need to get up. I'm walking my cousin to school and then helping my aunt with some work at the shop today."

"Maybe we can play some games online this weekend if you're off work," Luz suggested. "Something soft. No shooting."

"No shooting," Sveta promised. "You going boxing?"

"Yeah."

"I can't believe I never got to see you punch someone."

"Don't say that. You'll see it someday. I mean, I've never punched an actual person, but I'll do it for you if that's what your dark Russian heart craves."

Sveta laughed.

"As soon as you get back!" Luz promised.

"Luz."

She closed her eyes. "I know."

"It's impossible."

"No, we'll figure it out. It's not impossible. I'm saving already. We'll fight this. We've both been feeling hopeless, but you are going to get back here."

"What's gotten into you?" Sveta asked, a puzzled smile in her voice.

"I miss you. And I've been so angry and scared for you and just . . . I've been really overwhelmed. But now I'm settling down, you know? I'm determined. And you understand how goddamn stubborn I am, right? Don't you want to come back?"

"You know I want to," Sveta said without hesitation. "I feel like I'm dying here. Like no one even sees me, and . . . and like if they did see me, that would be worse."

"Then we'll figure it out. I'm not going to settle for sad and helpless anymore." She almost mentioned Tanner and the system. Almost finally spilled the truth. But she knew Sveta would try to stop her, and Luz didn't want to be stopped. She'd done the scary part already.

"Look," she said, "we were going to buy our own place after my promotion, right? I don't need to save for a down payment now, so that money is just gravy. I'm sitting at home too mad to go spend it on anything good, so that's a big savings too. I'll hire an attorney."

"Okay. We'll see."

Luz could tell by Sveta's voice that she was only humoring her. "Don't do that," she countered, frustration rising.

"Do what?"

She wanted to push back, wanted to argue, start a fight just so she had somewhere to put these feelings, but she stopped herself. "Nothing." She couldn't add to Sveta's worry.

"My moon, if you're lonely, you need to make some new friends."

"I don't want new friends. I want you."

"Okay, but you can have me *and* friends."

"I have the gym. And work."

"Right. Yeah."

Luz watched as another boxer walked toward the front door, and she felt her shoulders tighten with the fear that she'd be late. It was a good excuse to end this conversation, anyway. She wasn't as social as Sveta. For Luz, the boxing class was more than enough exposure to people. She liked being around the other women without the pressure of navigating conversations.

"I should go."

"Okay. Kick some ass for me."

"I love you," Luz said. "And don't forget to check in on Ballyhoo."

Sveta laughed. "You know his daycare feed is the first thing I look at in the morning. Even before I check for your texts."

"I know," Luz said, trying to get back to their light-hearted teasing. "I'm sure you miss him more than me."

"Never. Though he doesn't kick as much in his sleep." Sveta yawned again, then groaned as if she were struggling to move. Luz pictured her sitting up and stretching, getting ready to start her day.

"We'll talk more later," Luz promised. "We'll figure this out. I love you, babe. Don't give up."

She knew Sveta thought she was only offering reassurance, but they weren't platitudes. Luz had lived through a vivid dream the night before. A dream of being older, old enough to have gray waves in her hair, and she'd been telling someone about Sveta, about her incredible brain and heart and her amazing laugh, but it had all been in the past tense. As if Sveta were dead or lost forever. The ache of grief in her bones had felt old and familiar, like she'd lived with it for a long time.

When she'd woken up, she hadn't felt sad. She hadn't even cried. Instead she'd glared at the three rectangles of light glowing through her bedroom curtains, the moon too bright to be kept out by mere fabric.

Moonlight, that was what Sveta called her. Luz, my light, my moonlight, my moon. The glow in the window had been a sign, and she'd heeded it. The tides had shifted for her. She needed revenge against Tanner in order to move on. But she would move on somehow. She'd stay positive and she'd fight to get Sveta back.

As she emerged from her car and walked toward the Hook, Luz felt quiet inside. She felt solid and strong.

A young Black woman waited at the door. "Hey!" she said, pointing toward the glass. "Apparently Maggie isn't here tonight." A handwritten sign had been taped to the adjacent window: *Maggie called away. No class. Free use of the bags until 6:50.*

"Oh," Luz said. That had never happened before, though Maggie had once gotten a call from work and left class early. "I guess . . . Should we go in and practice?"

The other woman looked doubtful. "Maybe? I'm not so great at self-motivation these days. Hey, you're Luz, right?"

"Yes." Luz racked her brain, trying to find a name for this woman she knew she'd chatted with a few weeks before. "Geneva?"

The woman smiled. "That's me." She looked inside again, raising a hand to her mouth to nibble at her thumbnail. The other nails all looked thoroughly chewed down. Luz felt a surge of sympathy at that physical manifestation of anxiety. Then she remembered Sveta's orders to find new friends.

"We could work out together," she suggested.

A twanging melody suddenly sounded behind the glass, and the two women inside gave each other a high-five as pop country began blaring.

Geneva winced.

Luz took a deep breath and put herself out there. "Or we could just grab dinner? I've been meaning to try the place next door."

"I had it last week. It's good."

She cleared her throat, fighting the urge to say, *Never mind,* and head for home. Spontaneity wasn't her favorite thing. She liked to plan vacations for months and had spent years working on her life goals and endlessly mapping out plans. Something like this sudden dinner decision made her squirm. But with the class canceled, she couldn't use it as an example for Sveta that she honestly wasn't becoming an antisocial hermit.

But then Geneva made the decision for her. "Okay, let's go. That music would give me a headache today, anyway. And tacos are always the right choice."

They hiked their bags up and walked to the taco place, while Luz mentally composed her text to Sveta to brag that she was putting herself out there. Planning those messages got her through the ordering, though her nervousness returned as she and Geneva grabbed a table. Now she'd have to do small talk.

"I hope Maggie's okay," Geneva said.

"Just a work thing, I'd guess."

"Yeah, she has big responsibilities, obviously. And to be honest, I was really tired tonight," Geneva said as they sat down. "I'm grateful for the break."

She looked a few years younger than Luz. She was almost as short as Luz was, with a round, pretty face and shoulder-length hair she'd plaited into two pigtails today. Her widely spaced eyes watched Luz with open curiosity.

God, she hoped this wasn't flirtation. She was terrible at picking up on that and even worse at responding. Since she'd met Sveta she always played it safe by discussing her girlfriend early on to make sure she sent out the signal that she was taken.

"This is really my only regular outing anymore," Geneva continued when Luz didn't pick up the conversation. "I work from home, and I get more and more entrenched, you know?"

"Yeah."

"What do you do?"

"I'm a software engineer," Luz offered, still too stuck in her own mind to engage more.

"Whoa. A software engineer? That's so impressive. Well, I think it's impressive. I'm not even sure what it means. Is it something like programming?"

Luz smiled. "It's kind of like programming but with a broader view and more meetings. It's a client-facing job, if that makes sense."

"None at all, but I'm going to nod like it does because I don't think a longer explanation will do it. The hard sciences are *not* my thing."

"What do you do from home?"

"Customer service, but . . ." She hesitated a moment before finishing her sentence. "I'm going into teaching."

"Now I'm impressed. You mean teaching little kids?"

"Yep."

"That's seriously terrifying," Luz said.

Geneva smiled. "They're fun once you get inside their little minds and learn how they think. No one has forced them into a standard form of logic yet. Their minds are so free flowing. It's honestly fascinating."

"Yeah, I'm a huge fan of logic, so I think I've identified why I find kids scary. Look, I've got goose bumps."

Geneva snorted out a laugh. "Makes sense for what you do. If you didn't like logic, you wouldn't like your job much." She checked her phone, then raised her nail to her teeth again before cringing and folding her hands together. After a long moment she cleared her throat, then cleared her throat again. "So can I ask . . . how do you know Maggie?"

Luz stiffened at the question and suddenly wondered if she had made a bad mistake. Geneva tipped her head a bit, studying Luz's face, which made the skin of her cheeks heat with self-consciousness. "I just know her through the class," she said quickly.

"Me too. Yeah." Geneva's smile flashed, then disappeared, then flashed again. "I saw you talking to her after the last class, and I thought maybe you were close."

"No!" Luz said too loudly.

"Oh. Okay." Geneva still watched her too carefully, but then she shrugged. "It's nice to get to know someone else in there. Some of the other women come with friends, but I don't really know anyone."

"Me neither."

"I've been kind of working through some damage with the boxing, and I guess that's why I've kept my head down."

Luz nodded, her skin prickling. There was no reason to think Geneva was part of the system. There were at least fifteen other women in the class, so the chances were low. Probably most of them were working through some kind of damage, after all. Maggie gave lots of inspirational advice in there.

The server finally brought their orders, which broke the odd tension that had fallen over the table, thank God. Luz mentioned her girlfriend as they chatted more about their jobs over the food, just in case. Geneva didn't respond as if she cared much either way, which put Luz more at ease.

Until Geneva spoke again. "Maggie's great, huh? She's really helped me get through a rough time."

The last bite of Luz's taco went gummy in her suddenly dry mouth. She chewed and chewed until she was finally able to swallow. "Yeah," she said before covering her mouth to cough. "Sorry."

"She's a great coach."

"Sure, the boxing is fun."

Geneva stared at her intently. Her lips parted once, then closed again. Luz felt sweat break out at her hairline. If Geneva was part of the system, they shouldn't be here together, and they definitely shouldn't talk about it.

She grabbed a chip, dipped it in salsa, then stuffed it into her mouth before she was saved by the bell. Her phone rang as she swallowed some water to wash down the food.

"It's my girlfriend," she said, holding up a finger. "I've got to get this." Thank God. "Hello?" she asked. "Sveta?"

"Hey. Sorry, I thought I'd get your voicemail." Her words came thick with tears. "Aren't you still boxing?"

"What's wrong?" Luz pushed back from the table and stepped out the door so she could hear better. "Sveta, what happened?"

"It's nothing," Sveta replied, telling the lie with a loud sniff.

"Are you okay?"

"I'm fine. I just . . . I walked Nadia to school, and she asked me to leave her at the corner and not come into the yard."

"Why?"

"Because . . . because I was wearing short sleeves, and she was afraid someone would see my tattoo."

Luz stopped and let her head fall. "Oh, baby. I'm so sorry."

Sveta had been so damn proud of the rainbow flag she'd had tattooed on her bicep last year. Proud specifically because she'd been brave enough to show off something she'd been told to hide her whole life.

"She doesn't understand," Luz said on a rough whisper. "She's only nine."

"Right. Except that she understands perfectly. It's not okay here. I could be fined. Maybe arrested. Especially if they see my tattoo at a grammar school. Fuck!" She sobbed, then blew her nose. "I'm just hurt. It's no big deal."

But of course it was. This was going to be her life until she could get out of there. She couldn't afford to move to Moscow or Saint Petersburg, where she could at least find more liberal groups of friends.

"What if I helped you move?" Luz asked. "To a bigger city? Or out of Omsk at least! Would that help?" But as soon as she spoke the idea, a better one popped into her head. "Or what about Poland? You could go to Poland, and I could move there too!"

"No. They'll never give me another passport. And you can't leave your mother. I wouldn't even want you to."

"But anyone can get across the border if you bribe the right person, right? It's not like the old days. And at least I could come visit anytime."

"Luz, neither of us speaks Polish, anyway."

But Luz rushed on. "My mom has Leon. And she could visit us as much as she wanted. I could get a job in tech over there. Everyone speaks English in tech. We could . . ." Her heart leapt into a gallop in panic at the idea of proposing this with no planning, but she pressed her palm to her chest and ignored it. "Can you find out how much it would cost to leave? To go somewhere you'll be safe?"

"I don't know."

"I don't have to move there, Sveta. We can talk about that another time. But I could visit. I hate the idea of you being so alone and so . . ."

"Scared?" Sveta offered.

"Yes. Scared."

Her girlfriend sighed. "I'd have to be careful asking. I don't want to get in more trouble."

"I know."

"But I'll think about it."

When she hung up and went back inside, Luz was grateful to have an excuse to escape.

"Is everything okay?" Geneva asked.

"She's okay. Just some trouble at home. I'd better get going. Thanks for grabbing dinner with me."

"Here," Geneva said, pushing a torn bit of napkin at her. "Here's my number. Just in case you hear the class is canceled again, or even if you ever want to hang out. Can I get yours?"

She waited so hopefully, pen poised over the other half of the napkin, that Luz rattled off the number without even thinking. "I'm sorry, I have to go."

"Stay safe out there!" Geneva called, but Luz didn't even bother to wonder what that meant. Her own safety was nothing compared to Sveta's.

CHAPTER 13

KATHERINE

Answer your phone. Now.

Okay, that was weird. Katherine sat up straighter in the bathtub and frowned at the screen. She'd silenced a call from a strange number just a minute before, and now that strange person was texting her.

A shiver of alarm crept through her at the thought that it could be Brad, but the alarm was generously spiked with a jab of excitement. Had he tracked her down somehow? She wasn't sure she'd mind if he did.

No, that was wrong. She couldn't want that. It was important that there be no traceable web in this game. She was just going soft-minded over the sex.

It had been filthy, empty, meaningless, and deeply satisfying. Occasional glimpses of her husband's disapproving glare had flashed into Katherine's head like snapshots as she had sex with a near stranger on a hotel bed. And on the floor. On that dirty, abused carpet that smelled sharply of cheap cleaner and old cigarette smoke. She'd gotten on her knees like an animal, her fingers spread wide on the ugly green pattern. And when she'd thought of Peter, she'd smiled down at the floor.

He hadn't wanted her dark and dirty. Ever.

On one hand she'd been raised to believe a wife was meant to be treated respectfully at all times, even in bed. The sin of lust was made pure in God's eyes by marriage. On the other hand that quiet sex in the dark hadn't felt at all like respect. It had felt like being overlooked and utterly lacking. Like Peter had needed a shroud of darkness to make her appealing, to make her disappear beneath him. And she had disappeared every single time. In the beginning she'd tried to introduce more passion into the act, tried to act as if it all felt better than it did, but eventually the trying had been just another secret humiliation.

Was it Peter trying to get a hold of her? Trying to control her still? She'd blocked their home number and his cell phone after he'd called her at 10:00 p.m. the night before about God knew what. She'd refused to answer and let him intrude on her special, sparkling night the way he'd intruded after that first call with Brad.

She didn't need one damn thing from Peter that she couldn't get through her divorce lawyer. She had Brad now for fun stuff, for a little while, at least. And she could sign up for Tinder later if she wanted to. She'd also promised herself she'd make some regular friends, women she could hang out with just for fun.

And of course she had Maggie for advice and pep talks. Screw Peter. Her new life was already full enough to burst.

Her phone shook with another call. "Fine," she muttered, picking it up to hit the green button. "Hello?" she drawled slowly. If it was Peter, she wanted him to hear slutty satisfaction in her voice.

"Where were you last night?" The curt, low voice cracked through the phone, and Katherine jerked so hard that water splashed up and over the edge of the tub.

"W-what?"

"Where were you?"

She blinked, her eyelids stuttering in shock as she placed Maggie's voice. The recognition only added to her confusion. "Maggie? Is this a new number? What's wrong?"

"Were you with him? Your target?"

"No. No! What are you talking about?" Katherine's lungs seized up with panic. How could Maggie know that? No one knew. She hadn't recorded anything last night, hadn't tried to set a trap. Was Maggie *watching* her? She could be. She was trained in that sort of thing.

"Listen to me," her voice snapped. "Do you have any recordings? Any pictures? *Anything?*"

"I . . . I . . . Maggie, what's going on?"

"Did you ever get video?"

"I did," she answered, too afraid to keep lying about that. "Yes. I got it."

"Delete it. Wipe everything off your phone. Then take enough random video to rewrite everything on the fucking memory. Delete that too. Then do it again. Do *not* ditch your phone. That's the last thing we need. Understand?"

Her heart thundered so loudly in her ears she could hardly think. "Okay, but—"

"You used a throwaway account, right? On that Christian site? Get rid of that too. Delete everything. Close it all out. Anything else I haven't thought of, delete that also. All of it."

"Maggie!" she shouted, her voice throwing itself back at her in the tiled space. "What's going on? You're scaring me half to death."

"Brandon Johanssen is dead."

The words were startling. Frightening. But they meant nothing to her, just a nonsense phrase. "Brandon who? I don't even know who that is."

"Your target's real name is Brandon, and he was found dead in a downtown hotel room this afternoon by housekeeping."

The bright white of the tiled wall went splotchy with black holes and flashing stars as Katherine's vision receded. "What? What are you *saying?*"

"He's dead, so needless to say, your task is done. Keep your head down. Don't breathe a word to anyone."

"Brad?" she rasped, barely able to speak past the desert of her tongue.

"You don't have the goddamn cloud, do you?"

"No. You said to turn it off. I . . . I just don't understand what's happening. How did he die? A heart attack? Drugs? He was—" She caught the words in her throat at the last minute and held them back.

"No. It looks like it could be homicide at first glance."

Katherine's body lost traction on the bottom of the tub with a loud squeal. She sank low in the water and had to throw her free hand out to the side to save herself, banging her wrist hard against the edge. The pain sang through those delicate bones, numbing her fingers. She was suddenly freezing even though half her body was submerged in hot water.

"Someone *killed* Brad?"

"Yes."

"Was it . . . ? Oh my God, Maggie, was it the woman who wanted help with him? *Was it one of us?*"

"I have no idea. Don't mention our system to anyone. Understand? Come to class this week like you normally would, no matter what is happening. None of us can change our routines. Got it?"

"Yes. Yes, of course." But she was talking to a blank line. Maggie had hung up.

Shivering, Katherine stayed where she was, wrist aching, phone pressed to her damp face, both feet braced against the end of the tub. She couldn't move. If she moved, something would happen, the world would snap into action, the police would break down her door, everyone would know.

Ripples traveled through the bathwater from her shaking knees toward the edge of the tub, then doubled back, breaking their own pattern, shattering against her skin. Teeth clicking, she stared at the wavelets and trembled.

Brad was dead. He was dead, and she'd been there. She'd been there with him, he'd been *inside* her, and then he'd been murdered.

Oh God. Oh no.

No.

She hadn't done anything wrong. She really hadn't. She hadn't killed him, and she was allowed to have sex. She was even allowed to hook up with someone under a fake name. She hadn't hurt him at all.

But if they found out about her, the police wouldn't know that she hadn't hurt him. She'd be the main suspect, especially if she'd been the last person known to see him.

She tried to set her phone down, but it slipped to the floor with a clatter, bouncing between the tub and the wall. Ignoring it, she lurched to her knees and used the towel rack to steady herself as she climbed out, still shaking hard.

She had to get dry, get warm; she couldn't think with her muscles cramping with the shivering shock of what she'd heard. Less than twenty-four hours ago, that man had been in her body, and now he was cold and dead. How was that even possible?

She dropped her towel on the floor, wrapped herself in her robe, and retrieved the phone, vaguely aware that any other day she'd be cringing and rubbing the surface with sanitizer. Germs certainly seemed a laughable worry when her fingerprints were all over a murder scene.

"No, no, no," she droned as she rushed to turn up the heat and open her laptop.

Fingerprints, DNA, security feeds, messages, all of it would point right at her. Which didn't make any sense because she *hadn't done anything.*

Had she?

For a moment she had a terrible fear that she'd murdered him. People did awful things and then blacked out. Their brains tried to protect them from the horror. What if he'd gotten rough with her and she'd lashed out in defense and accidentally hurt him?

But she could remember the whole evening. She hadn't been drunk. She'd had a glass of wine at the bar, then a little Scotch with Brad in his room. (More DNA, more fingerprints, more evidence that a woman wearing scarlet lipstick had been there that night.) There hadn't been much conversation, and she'd remained for only an hour or so. (She'd touched the glass, the bedside table, the headboard, the bathroom door handle, the toilet, the faucet.) They'd had sex for so long she suspected he might have taken something to prolong it. (His body must be covered with her DNA, absolutely soaked in it.) Maybe some little blue pill had killed him and Maggie was wrong.

Or maybe he'd put something in her drink and she couldn't remember the violent struggle that followed because she'd blacked out?

No. Good God, she was losing it. He'd been *fine* when she'd left. She couldn't have blacked anything out, because he'd escorted her out of the room, getting the door for her, promising he'd be in touch again soon. He'd only been wearing briefs, and when he'd started opening the door, he'd spotted someone in the hall and pushed it partway shut with a smothered laugh.

She remembered all that. Remembered thinking that he was shorter than she was when they stood side by side. Remembered walking down the hall, slightly dazed and a little sore, but smiling that she could still smell his cologne on her skin. She normally didn't like cologne, but it had seemed the perfect fit on him, a seedy man for seedy sex.

He'd been alive. So had he gone back out?

When the elevator had opened at the lobby floor, the bar had roared with conversation, and she'd thought to herself that Brad would be in there soon. That was why he hadn't wanted her staying, not even for another round of sex. There was more fun to be had with his buddies. He'd ticked her box, so to speak, and was moving on with the evening. She remembered all of that clearly, so she definitely hadn't murdered him during a drunken blackout.

Her shivering stopped. For a few seconds she was warm and dry and trying to stay calm, but as soon as she opened the private browsing app on her laptop, she swung straight into sweating.

She first logged in to her LordsLink account. The secret half-profile picture of Brad's face was right there in her messages from yesterday evening. He'd sent her his room number, then a happy emoji. She'd sent him a thumbs-up and a little champagne icon.

Then they'd had sex and now he was dead.

She shook her head hard and swallowed a sticky lump in her throat. She'd messaged him on the app that morning and had never heard back. I don't suppose you're alone again tonight? she'd asked. Pitiful and embarrassing and so, so stupid because she couldn't take back the message. It was sitting right there in his inbox, waiting to be discovered.

Then again, maybe it absolved her. If the police saw it, they'd say to themselves that the murderer wasn't that woman he'd had sex with; it was someone else.

"Oh Christ," she said on a sob as she deleted every message on her end that she'd sent or received from Brad and everyone else. She deleted her pictures, her fake bio, unclicked every interest, and then deleted her account. It was all she could do on that front.

Picking up her phone again, she tried to catch her breath. It was too warm now, the air too dry and thin as the heater blew over her like wind, desiccating her skin, her throat, her eyes.

It was only then that she realized deleting her whole account would make her look more suspicious. Fuck. It was too late.

She trashed the LordsLink app on her phone first thing, then turned to the more important task of getting rid of the videos. But when she opened her phone gallery, she stared at the freeze-frame of the second video she'd captured, at the faint view of Brad's face. No. At *Brandon's* face. Brandon. He'd been a real person, not just a fantasy she'd lived out. She stared at him until her good eye stung.

This was all wrong. Katherine felt grief at the sight of him, but it *couldn't* be grief. She barely knew the man. He'd been a body to her, an indulgence. He had a wife and children and probably a whole big family of parents and grandparents and cousins who knew and loved him. *That* was grief. All she was filled with was sickness and regret.

She deleted the video she'd captured from their last Skype session, then deleted the first one too. She deleted the three dozen photos she'd taken of herself, trying to show off without revealing anything, then remembered to dump the dick pic he'd sent via the app as well. After that, she opened the folder of recently deleted files and wiped them clean.

"Please, please," she prayed breathlessly, trying to think.

The whole Skype app had to go too, just in case. What else? Her fitness tracker? Was that mapping her steps? She trashed it too to be safe. Thank God she hadn't used her phone's map to find the hotel. She'd been smart enough to look it up on her secure browser before leaving. But had she been smart enough to think of everything? It didn't seem possible.

She started to delete the secure browser on her laptop too, then remembered the throwaway email account and groaned. What else was she forgetting? After wiping her sweaty hands on her robe, she logged in, deleted every email, then closed that account as well.

"What else?" she muttered to herself as she tossed the browser app and emptied her digital trash again on both devices.

That was good enough for now, surely. She'd have hours and hours of lying in bed in paranoid terror to think of a thousand other details. How the hell would she ever sleep again?

After plugging in her phone, she faced it toward the wall and hit the RECORD button. How long would it take to fill up the memory? An hour? Two? She'd save a video every fifteen minutes until it stopped saving them.

She stood there helpless for a long moment, staring down at her phone; then she looked at her laptop, then the phone again. Finally she turned in a slow circle, searching for anything that might betray her.

"It's going to be okay," she croaked. He must have gone to the bar, gotten drunk, started an argument. Someone had followed him back and killed him, and it would all be on the security tapes—

The security tapes.

The guttural moan that wrested itself from her mouth was so deep and primal it scared her, her own body warning her she was in serious danger. She sucked in air and tried to exhale normally, wrapping her arms around herself, but it was still there, a groan at the edges of her breath, leaking her fear out into the world.

When she moved toward the kitchen, her sweating feet were too slick on the floor, so she had to move stiffly to avoid slipping. Once there, she gulped water until her gut was full and taut, and still her mouth felt parched. But at least she could breathe again.

Okay. Any security footage was a good thing because she looked nothing like herself. This was easy. She just had to get rid of the wig. "Easy peasy," she whispered, insisting to her wildly beating heart that this must be true. "You got this. Everything's fine. It's okay. You're okay."

She wasn't. She was sure she never would be again.

A few minutes later she was dressed and bundled up against the wind and carrying the crumpled paper bag tight against her body. After walking two blocks, she headed straight for the parking lot of a burger joint. The scent of fat and grill smoke turned her stomach as she crossed the lot and dropped the bag into a half-full bin before going inside. The grease enveloped her, and she held her breath as she stood still, gazing up at the menu board as people moved around her. A toddler brushed her legs. Her gut clenched.

Katherine spun and walked out. She'd meant to buy something, at least for show, but the scents were too overwhelming, the people too loud, so she immediately turned toward home instead.

Still, with the wig disposed of, the walk home worked a bit like meditation. She felt better by the time she hit the small lobby of her apartment building. If there was video of her going into Brad's hotel room, there was video of what had happened after. She'd left and someone else had gone in. There'd be proof of whoever had killed him. Someone would be identified.

She was fine.

And then she wasn't in any way fine because when the elevator doors slid open, she stepped out to find someone bent over and fiddling with the handle of her apartment door. Katherine gasped in shock, giving herself away, and the wide swath of black shifted and rose.

"Mom?" she yelped.

Her mother, who never seemed shamed by anything, actually looked a little embarrassed as she poked a finger toward the door. "I could hear your phone ringing! I thought something was wrong!"

Well, something was very wrong, it just wasn't anything her mom could imagine. "I ran out for a second and forgot my phone." She'd actually left it at home purposefully so no one could retrace her steps to the burger place and find the wig. All those years of watching network crime shows had finally paid off.

"Where were you?" her mom demanded.

Katherine surrendered with a sigh and moved forward to unlock her apartment. "What do you want?"

"That's a rude question. I'm your mother."

"I just . . . I'm exhausted, Mom. That's all." Katherine considered slipping in quickly and closing the door behind her to leave her unwanted guest in the hallway. But she didn't, of course, and her mom followed just inches behind, hot on her heels and unwilling to wait for an invitation.

"Katherine," she intoned with the graveness of someone announcing a terrible accident, "we need to talk. Your husband has been drinking."

"Oh. I see. He's certainly allowed to drink if he wants to."

"Don't brush that aside like it means nothing. He's *never* been a big drinker."

"Well, Mom, his actions have never caught up with him publicly before, so I guess he's finding new ways to self-soothe."

"I didn't raise you to behave this way!" she snapped. "Peter is your husband. You can't just turn your back on him. He's very upset. He's heartbroken!"

Katherine drew in a deep breath, her shoulders rising toward her ears, jaw tight and heart pounding. How did it still hurt so much? Why did it still burn through her like acid every time she wasn't good enough for her mom? She'd tried so damn hard for so many years. Couldn't she just grow a permanent callus over her heart and be done with the pain?

"Do you know what I would have given to have your father back?" her mother continued, settling into her never-ending disappointment. "To have our family whole again? And you're choosing to throw yours away over a temporary hiccup! It's shameful and selfish."

Katherine wanted to yell, but she let her breath out on a long sigh instead of a scream. That old question came back, the ghost that had haunted her childhood. "Did you wish it was me, Mom?"

There. She'd finally asked it. She'd set it free, and maybe it would fly away now, to roost somewhere harmless and strange. To purge her of the horrible belief that she'd deserved to die and her mother knew it too. They'd needed their father. No one had ever needed Katherine. Not her sisters or her mom or her husband or even her daughter. She was a void sucking space away from someone else.

Her mother missed the import of the question completely and shook her head, eyes rolling with impatience. "What are you talking about?"

"The accident," Katherine explained dully. "The *crash*. Did you want it to be me who died instead of Dad?"

"Oh, good Lord." Her mother's face twisted with ugly scorn. "Here comes the melodrama."

"I'm serious," Katherine said on the barest breath. "It would have been easier, right? Never in a million years did you think you'd end up a single mom with three mouths to feed. Medical bills to pay. You had to work. Live in a shitty apartment. If I'd died, your life would have mostly carried on as normal, just with one less daughter. But you had two more. A husband is much harder to come by." Vivian, the youngest, had been only five. They could have had more kids and replaced her easily.

"I wasn't a single mother, I was a *widow*."

Katherine shot an exasperated look at the ceiling. Her mom always dreaded anyone thinking she might be divorced. Or worse, never married at all. Out of everything she'd just said, that was the part that upset her mother, that others would think she'd lost her grip on a man when he was the one who'd dared to die.

It hurt. It still hurt, but she was stronger. "Whatever, Mom. But you certainly latched on to Peter like he'd come to shepherd us safely back to the bosom of patriarchy."

"Sweet mercy, Katherine, you sound like your crazy sister."

"Which one?"

"Have you been talking to her? Is that what this is about?"

She obviously meant Rebecca, who taught feminist theory and believed marriage was an outdated tool of societal control. Or something. "No, we haven't spoken in a very long time." Katherine was too embarrassed to talk to Rebecca, actually. She'd been embarrassed for years.

During her most passionate days post–graduate school, Becca had often mocked Katherine's traditional beliefs, but eventually she'd matured into knowing looks and eye rolls about her sister's devotion to the church and marriage and all the other Catholic trappings.

So Katherine had returned the scorn, amping it up in the hope that it would hurt. But if it left any marks at all, Rebecca had never revealed them. She'd just gone on living her independent, scholarly life in Oregon, gliding high above Katherine's small orbit in Denver. She'd been too busy, too accomplished to think much of anything about Katherine unless they were forced into close contact over a holiday meal. Those meals had come less and less often over time.

The truth was that Katherine had spent the past decade coming around to her sister's point of view, but that had only made her more self-conscious and less likely to reach out. She'd slowly stopped believing and started feeling trapped, but who wanted to call their older sister and say, "You told me so and you were right the whole time! My entire life is a lie"?

"Can you just stop by the house?" her mom continued. "Talk to him. He's sorry. He's really sorry. And what kind of woman can't find forgiveness in her heart for a husband after all those years together?"

"I don't know, Mom," she said wearily. "I don't know. I'm just . . ." Her throat thickened, and tears sprang to her eyes. "I'm just really tired."

"Katherine," her mother said on a hushed breath.

For a painfully long moment, she thought her mom would pull her close. That she would wrap her up in arms gone soft with age, and Katherine could just cry out all her fears and worries and regrets. It would feel so good to lean on her and give up for a few grinding sobs. To be held. Comforted.

It hadn't been right to set her husband up for a public fall, but it hadn't been so wrong, had it? Had she done something awful enough to deserve this twisting terror in her heart? She'd tried so fucking hard for so fucking long. She just wanted one simple moment of uncomplicated love.

But her mother didn't reach out and she didn't hold her. She clicked her tongue in disgust and shook her head. "You promised to love him in good times and bad, sickness and health. You promised that to God and to the church."

"*I did all that!*" Katherine screamed, her voice so loud it shocked her. "I was sick, and I loved him! All those bad times . . . Mom, I lost four babies, and I tried so hard, so damn hard, to keep everything going. I was just . . . *I* was hurting! Why couldn't *he* have tried harder for *me*? What about *my* sickness? *My* bad times?"

"God never gives us more than we can handle, Katherine."

"Oh, for Christ's sake. He truly overestimated me, then, because I sure as shit couldn't handle all that, and it's his fault if he thought I could."

"Katherine Faith, you shut your mouth right now!"

"Why? I kept it shut for all those years and look where we are."

"Disgusting blasphemy and disrespect. You've missed too many masses, and when was the last time you confessed, because you surely have a lot to atone for. You should see Father Carlo right now, young lady."

"Oh God, Mom." Instead of more anger, a wave of exhaustion plowed through her. Katherine dropped onto the couch, bouncing slightly on the new cushions. "I'm not a young lady. Look at me. I'm old and tired, and I just want to be alone. I'm not going to church anymore. Ever. You can't make me, Peter can't make me, and I don't even believe in God anymore, so what would be the point?"

That whitened her mother's face more than any of the honest pain Katherine had torn open and shown her. "Don't you say that."

"Fine. I don't need to say it; it's the truth even if I never say it out loud."

"I've lost in my life too," her mother ground out past a tight jaw. "I lost so much, and I was able to handle it all."

"I *am* handling it," Katherine said, "whether you like my technique or not, *I'm handling it.*"

"How? You've broken Peter's heart and you've crushed your own daughter."

"No. You've got me mixed up with the real villain, Mom. He's the one you fix dinner for every night, playacting at being his wife. Isn't that what you've always wanted?"

She hadn't touched her mother, but she could practically hear the crack of the slap as her mom reared back and pressed a hand to her pale mouth. "How dare you?" she whispered past her fingers.

"I don't know. But I wish I'd dared it sooner."

"I'm not putting up with this," she hissed before spinning for the door.

"I'll also be drinking heavily tonight," Katherine called after her. "In case you find it in your heart to worry about me too."

The door slammed hard behind her. She stared at it, stunned and drained.

Now what?

As devastating as it was to be so easily dismissed by her own mom, now that she was gone, Katherine had to worry about a murder. She almost got up to call her mother back, pretend to apologize, play at contrition. Instead she let her head fall against the cushions with a groan of defeat.

It felt like it'd been a year since Peter's birthday, and a whole decade since she'd walked into the Hook with that coupon for a free class and met a woman who somehow tapped into Katherine's long-dormant pool of bravery and daring. Maggie had changed everything for her, and Katherine had repaid her by screwing things up completely.

She'd done what she could to cover her tracks, hadn't she? All that was left was to obsessively check the news for any hints of the story, but she couldn't even do that. She'd only risk leaving more bread crumbs back to her involvement in Brad's life.

So . . . maybe she'd get drunk after all.

CHAPTER 14

GENEVA

Her mother had suffered a broken leg, Geneva had decided, sending up a quick prayer for forgiveness for the awful lie. That was why she hadn't gotten a job straight out of school. Instead, she'd moved back home to assist her mom, and then she'd done a little traveling.

But if the children of this school needed help, Geneva would cut short her imaginary gap year and jump into the fray. She'd do it for the children!

Her heart clenched at the idea of a classroom full of kids again, their sweet faces and messy hands and the way they lit up from inside when they learned something new. They were so beautiful, and even their raucous moments kept her energy high, her mind ready for any zig or zag the day might take.

All she had to do was stay calm through this interview and keep this man's antennae from perking up. As Jess had promised, he'd so far been too desperate in his search for a substitute to question anything about her story. She just needed to pull off this interview, and the job was hers, with no suspicion about what she'd been doing in the months since graduation.

She'd stayed up late the night before to wash and twist her hair. She'd awoken at dawn to let out her perfect twists, giving her roots a bit less volume than normal for the interview. Then she'd ironed a black skirt and pink shirt, and added a cardigan, flats, and tiny hoop earrings for the perfect conservative style that any CEO would fall for, surely.

Jess had been right. She felt better after being shoved forward by her friend. Less terrified, somehow, now that she was actually putting herself out there and taking a risk, her inertia interrupted. With the mountains to her left and her car pointed toward the north, she put on a positivity playlist that leaned heavily on Arrested Development, her dad's favorite group. Being from the South originally, he didn't care about East Coast versus West Coast sound. He believed in the sound of Atlanta.

And he believed in her too. Surely that meant she could do this.

As she drove, as the music washed over her, she began to realize she'd been working through grief and all those stages of it everyone talked about. Grief for her job, of course, but also grief for her own confidence in herself and her choices. She'd lost that during these awful months too.

So there'd been denial at first, though it had passed quickly. Then anger and bargaining had tangled up tight together between her fury at Frank and the promise to herself that she could work through it if she could only get revenge. Depression was a huge red check mark, of course. She was still right smack in the middle of it.

Did all that mean she could get to the final step of acceptance? It felt like she might be climbing closer, though she couldn't pretend that one step toward healing meant she was free of the depression. She could feel it waiting for her in her room, a stretched line tugging her back toward bed, back to that hole that sucked her hope dry. She could only do her best to outrun it for the day, and then tomorrow she'd try again. And again. Maybe one day it would snap.

By the time she made it to Longmont, the music had enveloped her in her father's love and she could wear his confidence like armor as she pulled onto the school property. The building did look a little like a corporate headquarters, with its silver reflective windows and gleaming white tile, but she could be a cog in this capitalist wheel if it helped her rebuild.

She parked in a visitor space, but just as she set one foot out onto the asphalt, her phone rang. A glance at the screen told her she had a full eleven minutes before her interview appointment. It also told her the call was from the Hook.

Maggie. *Finally.*

"Hi!" she answered as she pulled her foot back into the warmth of the car.

"Geneva Worther?" a man's voice asked.

She sagged in disappointment. "Yeah."

"Just calling to let you know your three-month pass expired and you'll need to get another at your next visit. However, if you sign up for a year—"

"Will Maggie be back on Thursday?"

"Uh. Yeah. I believe so. Yes."

"Okay, great. I'll take care of it then."

She'd been so excited to tell Maggie about the job interview, to tell her she was ready to climb out of this awful stage and start taking chances again. She'd texted her after the missed class, but had gotten no response. That was okay. She could reach out with some really great news if she landed the gig.

Inspired by that imaginary scene, she grabbed her bag, got out of the car, and marched toward the building. When she reached the front door, she was surprised that it opened on its own, and even more surprised to find Jess standing there, giving her a tiny, excited wave. "Eeee!" she squealed quietly.

Geneva gasped. "What in the world? Are you interviewing me? Because if so, I'm feeling pretty good about this."

"No, I'm just escorting you in. I personally vouched for you, so I'm going to present you like the princess of education you are."

Geneva froze, pulling Jess back before she could open the second door and lead them out of the relative privacy of the entryway. She didn't want to linger in the smell of years of mud and rain tracked into the rubber grips of the rugs, but she couldn't risk anyone overhearing this. "Jess, no. You can't put your own reputation on the line for mine."

"Of course I can. Don't be ridiculous."

"Absolutely not! This isn't—"

But Jess leaned forward and grabbed the door handle, cutting off Geneva's frantic argument. Smiling, she tipped her head in encouragement. "Let's go, killer. Knock 'em dead."

"You watch too many old movies," Geneva whispered, but her chest glowed with warm gratitude as she followed her friend inside. She couldn't cry now, but she'd cry about it later. Despite Geneva's best efforts, Jess hadn't let her push her away.

She'd chosen her wardrobe well, at least. Jess was also wearing a skirt and flats, though her striped flowy skirt went nearly to her ankles, and she'd topped it off with a bright-blue top beneath a black blazer. The place hadn't struck her as a yoga-pants-and-sweatshirt kind of school, though the thought did hit Geneva with a pang of envy.

Jess's presence did a lot to calm Geneva's nerves, despite that she still wished her friend hadn't taken such a chance. Recommending an unemployed teacher was one thing; walking a scandal right into the office with a big smile was another, but that was exactly what Jess did, her cheeks dimpling with delight.

Geneva was extra happy to have Jess at her side as another Black teacher. She was, at the very least, a comfort, but also proof that the school was open to hiring women of color.

"Mr. Yemich," she said confidently, holding out her hand. "Thank you for the invitation."

Despite her nervousness, it all went well. Really well. Principal CEO not only offered her the job after just fifteen minutes of conversation, he also volunteered to give her a tour of the school and let her see the class. When she accepted the offer over a handshake, he asked if she could start Monday. She was terrified when she said yes, but she said yes, reminding herself that bravery wasn't a lack of fear, it was rising above it.

In the hopes of smothering her worst worries, she'd also asked to be introduced as Jennie instead of Geneva in any notices or directories. Jennie with a *J* in hopes that a slightly fake name would help separate her from her past. Surely "Jennie Worther" wouldn't reveal much in a casual online query.

The interior of the school looked like any other, aside from the inordinate number of framed inspirational posters on the walls and the **TECH CENTER** sign above the library entrance.

When he gestured toward one classroom at the end of the hall, Geneva's throat tightened and her pulse raced. She approached quietly to peer through the long window next to the door. The kids were seated in a circle on a colorful rug, sunlight slanting in from the windows behind them. A few hands shot up at a question from the substitute, and when one boy stood, the rest of them clapped in encouragement. Geneva felt a surge of love so bright she even felt a moment of generosity for Principal CEO as she turned back toward him.

"I can't wait," she said honestly. "Thank you so much for the opportunity."

After retrieving a packet of the school's rules and regulations and a link for all the documents she'd need to sign, Geneva walked out. Just like that, she was a teacher again.

She called her dad first, but it went directly to voicemail, so she texted him to get in touch when he was done with work. Then she tried her mom, who worked at a desk at an insurance company and rarely missed a call.

"I did it!" she yelled, and her mom yelled back, no doubt startling everyone in her office.

"I'm so proud of you!"

"I start Monday. Can you believe that?"

"Yes, I can. They'd be foolish not to snatch you up. We'll go shopping this weekend for anything you need And we'll grill up some steaks tonight to celebrate."

"Can I invite Daddy?"

"Absolutely. We'll all toast to putting this horrible nonsense behind us. You are back on track, Gennie. I love you so much."

She *was* back on track, and she would put this awful episode behind her. She'd also stop and pick up groceries for their dinner tonight. It was the least she could do for her mom.

But she'd barely buckled into her seat when an icy thought chased across her mind and her smile dropped away. She'd had nothing to lose when she'd plotted revenge against Frank. He'd already taken everything valuable with his cruel stunt. But now . . .

Crap. She hadn't expected to be teaching again when he finally got the trouble he deserved. He wouldn't know that she was the one who got him thrown back in prison, but he might suspect. And it wasn't as if he'd hesitate to make things worse for her, given any nudge in that direction.

She should call a stop to it. Unless it had already happened. Oh God, what if it had already happened? What if he was already in jail?

She picked her phone back up to check Frank's Instagram account for an abrupt silence. It took forever to load, so she held the phone higher in the car in that modern superstition that she'd suddenly go from two bars to three if she raised her arm nine inches. It worked. His feed loaded. And there was a new picture of him and his pit bull from that morning.

Whew. Okay.

She didn't have all the details, but she knew the overall plan. The first time she and Maggie had spoken about Frank, Geneva had been the one to bring up revenge. She'd told Maggie the whole story, then let drop that she knew Frank was using his brother's identity to drive for a rideshare. He wasn't eligible to work as a driver because he was on probation after being busted for dealing ecstasy four years before.

He'd volunteered the information one night when he was drunk. Giggling, he'd told her that his name was Francis Biago, named after their grandfather, but his brother's name was Michael Francis Biago, named after their dad. He'd shown her his brother's picture, and damned if the two didn't look exactly the same, aside from variations in their tattoos. He'd shrugged, grinning with pride. *I just told them I go by Frank, and voilà, it's barely even a lie.*

So she'd planned to turn him in to the company, get him fired for faking his identity. But Maggie had been thinking much bigger than that. *Not quite equivalent to what he did to you, is it?* she'd asked.

Not even close.

I bet he's making plans for his life.

Yes. His probation is set to drop off next year, and he's already petitioned to have his record expunged. He'll be squeaky clean after that.

While you have to live with your past hanging over you forever.

Geneva had been deep in her spiral at that point. And it was true that the video would always be out there on some corner of the internet. It was even true that she'd never be able to run for school board or get into administration . . . but she'd never planned to do those things, had she?

And maybe, just maybe, she was starting to see a way out, starting to feel a little hope?

If so, this darker revenge, this plan to report him for dealing out of his car and get him back into legal trouble, didn't feel like the right thing anymore. If it wasn't already in motion, she might still have a chance to stop it in its tracks.

She tried calling Maggie again and got a message that her voicemail box was full. Shit. Her only option was to drop by the other women's class on Thursday and ask Maggie to pull the plug if it wasn't too late.

Yes, she'd take a safer route even if that meant abandoning vengeance. Didn't everyone say that living well was the best revenge? Maybe she could put all her efforts into that.

Denial. Anger. Bargaining. Depression. And perhaps at long last she had nearly reached the final step: acceptance.

In fact, she thought she might already be there.

CHAPTER 15

KATHERINE

She drove to the Hook instead of walking, unable to bear the suspense of a slow approach. Maggie had told her she had to attend, had to keep everything normal, but her brain had been spiraling like a top in the two days since she'd heard the awful news. She felt as if one more added ounce of stress would break her, and she couldn't handle the idea of walking into class without an easy and quick escape route.

She was sure the car still smelled faintly of the cologne that had clung to her when she'd left the hotel. Brad's cologne. *Brandon's* cologne. It darted in and out at the far reach of her sense of smell, a ghost of him, a haunting. The scent tapped into deep fear, like catching a hint of smoke in the air during wildfire season. Warning. Danger. *Run.*

Unlike drivers with full vision, Katherine had to concentrate on distance and depth as she drove. On a short drive the task didn't usually add to her stress level, but today her tension was already sky high, and the cologne only made it worse.

The sight of the wig shop as she pulled in evoked more memories, adding substance to the ghost that rode with her, so Katherine parked at the other end of the shopping center. She stared into the busy little restaurant and shook out her tense hands, trying out a few moments of deep breathing.

She had to get through fifty minutes under Maggie's watchful eye without hyperventilating. She could do that. Probably. But knowing she'd lied to Maggie about so many things, it felt a little like she was about to sit down in church after she'd been caught with that boy. All those long Sundays of Jesus staring down at her from the cross, his big, beautiful eyes full of liquid sadness and disgusted love.

She'd lain low for forty-eight hours, thinking over and over again what her story should be if there were any questions. The truth, she supposed, though only a limited version of it.

She'd wanted revenge on her cheating husband (true), so she'd created an online account with a fake name (true). She'd engaged in some sexting and then met the man at a hotel (still true). The morning after, she'd sent him an embarrassingly eager message, and when he hadn't responded, shame had overwhelmed her and she'd deleted everything (close to true in its own way).

The plan felt simple enough, but she still wanted to run back home and hide, turning the details over and over again.

Her mom hadn't returned to the apartment, at least, and Peter hadn't dropped by again. Even Charlotte was busy cramming for midterms and mostly sending emoji responses to any texts. She'd almost gotten straight As her first semester, and she was determined to beat her record with this round of grades. She was a typical only child in that way, mature beyond her years, but also maybe a little selfish.

Left with a few minutes to waste, Katherine navigated to a local news website, her new obsessive hobby. She didn't dare search for Brad's real name online, so this was her only option. News had broken the day before that Brandon Johanssen had died while attending a local political convention, but there had been no details.

But today a headline on the first local news site she visited stopped her heart for far too many seconds.

The Hook

Colorado State Senator Brandon Johanssen Dead from Undetermined Cause at Convention Hotel

She needed to click on the story. She had to or she'd lose her tenuous hold on reason and descend into screaming.

After a guilty glance out both sides of her car, she hunched lower in her seat and clicked first on an unrelated headline, hoping to paint a forensic picture of a local interested in any local news. She let it sit open for a moment, then moved back to click on the story about Brandon Johanssen.

There it was, a picture of Brad, dressed in a dark suit and red tie, dimples showing with his smile. Her eyes scanned the rest of the screen, coming quickly to the end of two paragraphs before running into a promise for more details as they became available.

She slowed down and reread the brief story. "Found by housekeeping . . . Suspicious circumstances . . . No cause of death given by police."

"Forty-eight years old," she whispered aloud before her throat dried up and closed. She took in the last two lines in silence: "He is survived by his wife and two children. His family is asking for privacy at this time."

Her vision went blurry from staring at the rectangle of damning words until she noticed that Brandon's name was highlighted with a link. She touched it and held her breath as the story loaded. It was a feel-good local article from the year before about a pastor receiving a service award. The person presenting it was State Senator Brandon Johanssen and his wife, Lee Johanssen.

Katherine leaned in closer to her phone, curling herself around the screen to hide it. His wife didn't look familiar. Katherine was almost sure she'd never seen her at the Hook or anywhere else. She was a White woman with a face that was neither pretty nor ugly, and she was average height and build, but Katherine would have remembered her pale-blue

147

eyes paired with wild blond curls. Perhaps she was in Tuesday's class. It was possible.

She clicked back and read the original story once more before closing it. Suspicious circumstances. What the hell did that mean? They hadn't declared it a homicide. So had it been drugs, as she'd wondered before? Or maybe he'd gotten drunk and hit his head on the bathroom counter?

She wanted to wish for that, wanted to hope it was some tragic accident instead of someone hurting him, but that would mean the worst for Katherine: that she had been the last person in his room.

She wiped sweat off her forehead and glanced toward the gym. She couldn't just leave even if she felt like she would faint if she tried to stand. Maggie had told her specifically not to skip the class.

And this didn't change anything. It was what Maggie had already told her about his death. Except now it was laid out for everyone to see, crumbs for the entire world to follow right back to Katherine, so it was even more important to behave normally.

But after reading it she couldn't dodge reality anymore. *He is survived by his wife and two children.* She'd been able to shove that thought away through this entire scheme. The wife. The kids. The safe snow globe of a life they'd been living in with absolutely no idea of what forces might kick up a storm at any moment.

She wasn't the world's worst hypocrite, at least. She hadn't performed decades of self-righteousness before sleeping with someone else's husband. After those first few years of jealousy, she had never blamed the unknown women. Her hatred, her blame, had all landed squarely on the man who'd promised her love, safety, and loyalty. But if Brandon's wife was an innocent bystander, she'd blame Katherine as the villain, the homewrecker, the last woman to touch her husband before he died. Katherine would be the cause of either his actual death or the death of their marriage.

Then again . . . maybe Mrs. Johanssen had already blamed her husband. Maybe she'd blamed him so enthusiastically that she'd murdered him herself. Katherine had spent years imagining a heart attack or car accident for Peter to end her suffering; was it a huge step to imagine a wife deciding to play a more active role? Men killed their cheating spouses all the time.

Surely that was who the police would look at first. His wife certainly made a lot more sense as a suspect than some random hookup.

Slightly reassured, Katherine tugged up the hood of her sweatshirt and forced herself out of the car. A warm front had blown through overnight, waking her every hour or so with strange noises she wasn't used to in the new place, but it was beautiful now. Nearly balmy for a Denver spring. Maybe she could have a glass of wine or three on the balcony she'd yet to use. Watch the world go by.

Or watch for police cars to arrive.

"Shit," she whispered, cursing her stupid imagination.

When she reached the windows of the Hook, she paused to take inventory of the situation. Three women were already inside, though one of them seemed unhappy to be there. She looked almost as bad as Katherine felt, so she scooted back out a few inches to watch.

The woman was tall, nearly as tall as Katherine, though much heavier. She could definitely take Katherine in a fight. She'd seen her in class before, though they'd never spoken.

She was White with a smooth brown bob she wore in a headband on most days, though she'd pulled it into a stubby ponytail today. Despite the thickness around her waist, the woman had a thin face with cheekbones that pressed up beneath her skin, as if they might cut their way through.

Her wide smile usually mitigated the severity of her face, but today that happy grin was nowhere to be seen. Her full lips were tightly compressed, and her red-rimmed gaze stayed on the floor as she paced and stretched her arms.

Could that be the woman who'd used the system to target Brandon Johanssen? She certainly looked distressed and maybe even in shock.

When someone walked up behind Katherine, she startled, but the woman brushed past without noticing and walked into the Hook. She was a young Black woman, and instead of being dressed for the gym, she wore a maxi dress. Katherine didn't recognize her, but she seemed familiar with the place, moving straight toward the office door with purpose.

When Katherine was about to turn her eye back to the distraught woman, the office door opened, and her gaze returned, looking desperately for Maggie inside the office like a guilty person drawn back to her bad deed. But that was a man's tanned shoulder settling against the door frame, not Maggie's.

She craned her neck, moving forward a step to see past a hanging bag. A very muscular guy stood in the office door, shaking his head at the young woman who'd just walked in. He gestured toward the room, his face impassive. The class started in five minutes. Did that mean Maggie wouldn't be here to lead it?

Relief washed over her, relaxing her shoulders. But the moment of grace lasted less than a minute, because the woman at the office turned to walk back toward the front door, and the sight of her face hit Katherine with a ruthless blow.

It was her. *Her.* The woman who'd been with Peter at his birthday party. Except her hair was no longer short and blond. It was black and long enough to brush her shoulders. But there was no mistaking the sweetly pretty face and wide-spaced eyes.

Katherine raised a trembling hand to her own hair, thinking of the wig and wondering why she imagined she'd be the only clever woman in the group. This one had obviously worn a wig too, and though her eyes were recognizable, they were no longer a startling green but a dark brown.

As the woman neared the door, her narrowed gaze slid over to rest on Katherine for a brief moment that didn't blossom into recognition. Katherine stepped back.

This woman looked upset too. Her eyes weren't red and downcast, but her face was tight with worry. Did she know something? Was she also connected to Brandon?

She pushed out the door, her stride long and fast, her skirt swinging. Instead of freezing with fear, Katherine's body lurched, chasing after her, drawn forward as if the woman had promised her answers. "Hi," she said, hoping for a conversational tone and landing on a yelp.

The woman stopped next to a small blue car, her hand reaching for the door as she threw a stiff glance toward Katherine. "Hi?" she said, the question obvious in her voice.

"Do you . . . ? Um . . . Is Maggie not here?"

"No. Second night she's missed."

"You're in the other class?" she asked, then moved forward in three quick steps as the woman angled herself to slide into the driver's seat. "On Tuesdays?"

She ignored Katherine, which prompted a twist of anger that this person had been sleeping with her husband, had been in her *home*, and Katherine still meant nothing to her. Stupid, of course. And utterly unfair in every obvious way. It was the whole point of Maggie's system.

But when the warm wind gusted and shoved Katherine's hood back an inch, the woman looked up and focused on her eye patch. A heartbeat later, her expression shut down, flattening into ice-cold anger. "No," she bit out. "Do not do this."

She closed the door before Katherine could move.

"Wait!" She was at the car's window now, both hands pressed to the glass, but the other woman stared straight ahead, knuckles pale with her grip on the steering wheel. "Please! I'm sorry! I'm not . . . I'm not trying to do anything wrong."

She only shook her head tightly in response.

"I just want to know if you knew Brandon."

Her eyebrows jerked down harder, her gaze darting toward Katherine. "Who?" she asked, the word muffled by the glass.

"Brandon? Or maybe Brad?"

She started the car, and Katherine backed away until her hip hit the cold metal of the vehicle behind her. She'd already given up on any answers and waited for the crunch of tires turning, but then she was greeted with the faint whir of the window rolling down an inch.

"I don't know who that is. Please leave me alone. We can't do this. It's not cool."

Nodding, Katherine pressed tighter against the vehicle at her back. "Okay, I'm sorry. I just thought . . ." But the car was already pulling out, and then she was gone, and all Katherine could do was stand there and tremble.

The woman had obviously recognized the eye patch from that brief encounter at the party, but she hadn't reacted at all to Brad's name. Which made sense, of course. They wouldn't have been assigned to each other, because that would make a link, a connection. Like the one Katherine had just impulsively created.

She spun on her heel and jogged toward the gym, regretting that she'd spoken up at all. She shouldn't have done it, but she was sinking, drowning, and desperately grabbing at any limb she could reach. *Help me, help me.* If she wasn't careful, she'd drag them all down into the terrifying depths.

She rushed through the door of the Hook and straight into a class that was maybe half full instead of packed. After dumping her backpack against a wall, she tied back her hair, so much adrenaline pumping through her veins that she felt like she could easily make it through any workout.

Wanting to be as hidden as possible, she chose a spot at the back row of bags, then watched as a couple of women moved toward the front when they saw their substitute instructor. The muscular arm she'd glimpsed was connected to a very muscular body clothed in tight Lycra.

Still, one woman headed straight for the back row as Katherine had. It was the brunette with the troubled face.

Katherine watched from the corner of her eye as she began her own warm-up, bouncing up on her toes, rocking back and forth, but the woman next to her barely moved. Her hands were raised in the traditional sparring stance, but she merely shifted, face still tucked down to look at the floor. After a few heartbeats passed, a tear rolled down her cheek.

"Hey," Katherine said softly. "Are you okay?"

She nodded but didn't speak, didn't raise her head at all, though she did swipe a sleeve across her face and begin bouncing a bit more in time with the music.

Swallowing hard, Katherine grimaced and faced straight ahead. Something bad was happening to that woman, and maybe it was a coincidence but maybe it wasn't. Maybe she was grieving. Possibly she was regretting a murder and waiting for the police to show up?

Shit.

Katherine tried to concentrate on the routine they did before every workout, tried to ignore the possibility of a ticking time bomb next to her, but she was more than relieved when it was time to move away and grab the jump ropes. She'd have to concentrate on the rope, have to keep her rhythm and her breath steady. Have to focus all her being on staying strong and not giving out even when her body wanted to stop.

After five minutes, her racing heart had cleared the drag from her mind a little, but then the instructor called out that it was time for sparring. Sparring meant a partner. And only the two of them were standing at the back of the class.

Cursing inside, she tugged on her gloves as she desperately scanned the rest of the room, hoping for contact with someone else. But when she had finally turned a full 360 degrees, the teary-eyed woman was waiting in front of her with the sparring pads. She held them listlessly up and tipped her chin in the tiniest acknowledgment.

"Introduce yourselves," the guy at the front instructed. "You should always know who you're fighting and why you're fighting."

Katherine winced. There was no getting out of this. "I'm Katherine. I'm just here for exercise, not really for fighting."

"Nicole" was her only response. They faced each other and found the rhythm of the dodge-and-punch dance. It wasn't truly like a battle, more like a strenuous performance.

Nicole seemed to have gotten herself together, as if the jump rope had settled her a bit too. Her olive-toned complexion hadn't turned bright pink from exertion the way Katherine's had, but those sharp cheekbones were now slashes of reddened skin. Still, her black-brown eyes stared through Katherine as if she were trying to forget the whole thing, as if none of them were there and she were far away.

When the instructor called out, they switched places. The punches that fell on Katherine's hands were weak and halfhearted, which was better than being filled with rage, at least for her own peace of mind. The woman didn't seem to have murder in her heart, not at that moment, anyway.

But she definitely didn't want to be here. She was barely working out and clearly didn't want to socialize. So why the hell would anyone come to boxing class in that state? Unless she'd been told she had to.

After what seemed an endless time, they moved on to take turns on the heavy bag. Neither spoke again, but Katherine tried to take in as much about her as she could. Had this woman had an affair with Brandon Johanssen too? Had she loved him and been so broken by that she'd called for vengeance? And now was she grieving . . . or drowning in guilt?

By the time the core workout period rolled around and she dropped to the floor, Katherine's shoulders were so tense she was guarding against a charley horse as she did her crunches. The final cool-down stretches didn't make a dent in her clenched muscles no matter how much she tried to relax them.

Nicole. Her name was Nicole.

Before Katherine had even picked herself up from the cooldown, Nicole was snatching up her bag and headed for the door as if she'd been counting the seconds toward being released.

Come to class this week . . . None of us can change our routine.

Katherine watched her disappear into the parking lot. A moment later a large white SUV with a blue logo on the side pulled out. The lettering was a blur in the graying light of dusk.

"All good?" the instructor asked from above, offering her a hand. He tugged Katherine up as if she were a dried leaf.

"I'm good. Thanks." He turned away, already done with her, but a lie suddenly sprang to her mouth and set itself free. "The young woman who came in before class? I think I dinged her car with my door. Is her name, um . . . Tessa?" She spit out the first name she could think of.

"Which woman?" He looked completely puzzled as he glanced toward a redhead in tiny gray shorts.

"She was wearing a dress?" Katherine pressed. "Came to the office?"

"Oh. Right. I wrote down a message for Maggie, but it wasn't Tessa. Geneva? Genoa? Something like that. Name of a city."

"I see. Did you take a number? I could call her about fixing the dent."

"Sure. Hold on a sec."

Geneva or Genoa. And Nicole, she repeated to herself.

"It's Geneva," he said before reading the number from the note. Katherine entered it into her phone with shaking hands, then spun and hurried out of the Hook. She race-walked to her car and jumped in to huddle in the seat.

After opening her mail, she searched for emails from the Hook, then scrolled down until she saw a visible cc line. She'd remembered it clearly because at least a dozen people had sent chirpy responses to the entire list after the gym had cc'd everyone instead of blind copying the group.

After opening the list, she checked it carefully. No Geneva, though there was someone listed as GennieW. Could that be her? She copied the email address to her notepad and then returned to look for a Nicole. There. Right there. NicolePark@HTRealtyCO.com. "Nicole Park," she murmured.

Katherine searched for "HTRealtyCO," and the page popped right up, stamped at the top with a blue logo with the same general shape as the sign on that SUV. "Holy crap," she whispered as she clicked on the ABOUT US link and glanced over the roster of realtors.

And there she was, Nicole Park, nearly unrecognizable in the picture with her blindingly white smile and perfectly symmetrical bob, her skin glowing bronze against what looked to be an expensive white cashmere sweater. This woman looked like she'd never cried a day in her life and popped uppers for breakfast.

> I have lived my whole life in the Denver area—born and bred!—and am familiar with every nook and cranny the Front Range has to offer in your search for the perfect home! Urban, suburban, mountain, or ranch, I've lived in or sold all of them! I currently reside in Englewood with my wonderful husband and our three beautiful children, a great central location to meet you wherever you are. Call with your questions today! The market might be crazy, but it's no match for me!

In another picture at the bottom of her bio, she wasn't alone. It was a family portrait, everyone dressed in summer whites and khakis. Her husband looked to be of Asian descent, and they stood with three adorable children, the youngest girl just a toddler in this picture, her hair in a perfect high ponytail topped with a white bow.

Katherine stared at them for a long time, hoping to somehow absorb the story of what had happened. The husband with the kind smile, the kids all beaming . . . but nothing came to her. She knew better, being well acquainted with the false happiness of family portraits. No one ever seemed to glean any hints from hers.

Clicking back, Katherine saw that Nicole's realty office was in Littleton, not too far of a drive. She didn't know why she needed any of this information, but it felt important, if only for her own safety.

It didn't seem possible that Nicole Park of HT Realty of Colorado could be a murderer. But those men who were featured on crime shows for killing their families never looked like murderers in old pictures either. And if this woman had killed a man she'd once loved, she could kill Katherine too. Why not?

The market might be crazy, but it's no match for me! What the hell did that mean? It felt like a warning.

Setting down her phone to start the car, Katherine decided to skip the wine tonight. She had too much research to do.

CHAPTER 16

Luz

Luuuuuuz! Did you hear Tanner got fired from his new gig???

Luz straightened from a slump over her desk and glanced around to be sure none of her colleagues were watching her check her phone. A silly reaction, of course. It was leftover guilt from when she'd been lower on the ladder, and that was amplified by her permanent curse of being a perfectionist.

The text had come from Eddie on the second floor. He worked in accounting but was stationed very close to the door of their HR manager, and that woman did not have an indoor voice. Loud talking was quite a quality in an HR professional. Luz shuddered to think what might have been said about her own situation behind that thin door.

What??? she texted back. What happened? Then she stared for an eternity, waiting for him to see her question and respond, but the message stayed unread.

Her knees bounced with nervousness as she waited. She'd had absolutely no indication her plan in the system was moving forward.

Was it possible Tanner had been fired for being an asshole and not because she'd set him up? The odds did seem decent. The guy *was* a huge asshole, after all. Maybe he'd messed with the wrong person at his new company.

She knew only the barest possibilities of Maggie's plan for him. She'd asked Luz many weeks ago where Tanner lived, where he worked now, what his hobbies were, anything else that might help.

Luz hadn't known everything. The name of his new employer, sure, that had come to her through the grapevine. She knew his ex-wife's name and where she might be living. And she knew Tanner owned his own home in Highlands Ranch and was pretty passionate about lawn maintenance and home improvement, if his preferred topics of conversation were any indication. If poisoning his beautiful lawn would have brought Luz any solace, she'd have taken care of the revenge herself. It had been her backup plan if everything else fell through.

She and Tanner were close in age, but he'd married young and had a teenage daughter. His ex-wife was permanently out of the picture. He'd called her a skank and a druggie who couldn't hold down a job, and he'd fought hard to keep her visitation so restricted that she'd eventually stopped trying to see their daughter. Now that she knew how vengeful he was, Luz had no idea if any of that had been exaggerated to get revenge on his ex.

In the end she hadn't felt she'd had much to pass along to Maggie, but now . . . now Tanner had lost his second job in a year. That had been Luz's favored goal, the only revenge she could think up that didn't involve violence. After all, his career had been his motivation for ruining Luz's life. The punishment fit the crime in a way that pleased her perfectionist soul.

Hyperaware of how long she'd been staring at her phone, she finally set it down and looked back to the email she'd been composing. Of course her phone buzzed as soon as she started typing.

From what I overheard, someone sent his new company screenshots of a totally racist conversation he had. On Nextdoor,

I think? Or maybe there are other neighborhood apps? It was something like that.

Nextdoor? That was weird. You couldn't just join from anywhere; you had to have a verified invitation for your address. Luz had joined right after they moved into their rented condo, but she'd quickly noped out after reading too many posts about health conspiracies and "suspicious" youth in the area.

So how could it be connected to the system? Had Maggie found someone at the Hook who lived in his neighborhood? That didn't even make any sense. Highlands Ranch was thirty minutes away, a huge suburb with dozens and dozens of neighborhoods.

Was it possible Maggie's professional tentacles went so deep that she could find a random neighbor near his street to help get him fired? It was possible for someone in Maggie's position, and just imagining that scared Luz.

Grab a coffee? Eddie asked, and she responded nervously with a thumbs-up.

Feeling more guilty than ever—slipping out for a midmorning coffee while also gossiping about a former coworker whom she'd possibly, maybe set up—Luz pretended to check around her desk for something before slipping her debit card into her pocket and striding authoritatively toward the door. This is totally work related, she tried to project with a very stern look down the hall.

Once she was out of sight, she raced down three flights of steps and beelined for Eddie, who was waiting outside the front door of their building. Though they performed totally different work for the company, they'd bonded over being the only two Latinos there, and it didn't hurt that he was queer too. The world of software engineering could be pretty damn homogeneous. She often wondered if her coworkers felt the same way about her that Tanner had.

"Oh my God!" Eddie said before she even made it all the way out.

"What the hell happened?" she asked as they set off toward the Starbucks two blocks away.

"I couldn't believe it. She called one of the executives, I don't know who, and told him they'd really dodged a bullet getting rid of Tanner, because it was worse than they thought."

"How did she hear about it?"

"Some recruiter friend? Software engineering is a small world in Denver, I guess. Anyway, apparently he was ranting to some neighbor on Nextdoor about Black people in the area. Like, he was messaging her that he was upset about 'hoodlums' moving in and affecting property values. Said they didn't belong there. The neighbor sent the screenshots to his new boss yesterday and—" He dragged a thumb across his neck like a knife. "He got the cut, baby."

"But . . . why would a neighbor do that?"

"I don't know. They hate racists, I guess? That's a good neighbor, right there."

"It's just . . . Wow. Insane."

Eddie shrugged and tucked his shoulder-length hair behind his ears. "Is it insane? It seems like the exact right thing to me. And fuck if he didn't deserve it after what he did to Sveta. Karma is a bitch."

Karma was a bitch. Or maybe it was just Luz who was a bitch, but she'd wear the mantle proudly.

She ducked her head to smile at that lie. It wasn't true. She didn't want anyone to know she was a mean bitch even if she was. But was it really possible she'd done this? She couldn't wrap her head around the logistics of it.

She desperately wanted to call Maggie and ask, but that wasn't the deal. Surely there would be some confirmation or something. A signal? A mysterious white rose laid on her doorstep?

When she laughed, Eddie laughed along with her, assuming she was just reveling in the news.

"He'll just get another job, I suppose," she said, trying to talk herself down from giddiness to common sense.

"He can try. But with two jobs lost in quick succession, his résumé is going to look bad."

"Yeah, but he'll leave the last one off."

"I bet the whisper network will get him. People are already talking, after all. Apparently the recruiters know."

Luz grinned. "Wow. Maybe you're right." The idea filled her up with a warmth that might have been a glow of hatred but still felt nice and toasty. "What do you want to drink?" she asked as they approached the corner Starbucks. "I'll treat. Today's a special day."

"Mm. This feels like you're buying illicit information, and I love it."

"Just be sure to pass on any other illicit tidbits you hear. I will reward you."

"Deal."

She got her first iced latte of the season in honor of the seventy-degree day, though Eddie reacted with horror as he always did. He was the type to order any drink extra hot. Meanwhile Luz lived in terror of burning her tongue, and her hot drinks were usually lukewarm by the time she felt safe enough to sip them. She truly didn't understand how he could immediately take a gulp of near-boiling coffee.

She'd almost finished her latte by the time they got back to the building—all the better to ditch the cup before she returned to her desk for her last few hours of work before the weekend—when Eddie stopped in his tracks and put a hand on her arm to drag her to a halt too.

"Wait," he murmured. "Is that . . . ? No."

"What?" Luz asked, running her gaze over the cars parked in front of their building.

She spotted nothing, but Eddie gasped. "It's fucking Tanner!"

"No," she insisted, even as her eyes whipped back and forth trying to spot whatever Eddie was seeing. He stepped backward and pulled Luz with him.

"I'm calling HR right now."

"He's allowed to be on a public street," she said, the words too quick and high. "Don't call." She didn't want all this to start up again. Didn't want any more trouble when she was just trying to do her damn job. She knew how the world worked. The company probably already saw her as a problem.

"Luz, there's no decent reason for him to be here!"

"Let's just go around back and avoid him, then."

"No. I'm going to ask him what the hell he thinks he's doing."

"What if he has a gun?" she cried. "What if he's totally lost it?"

"If you're worried about that, then let me call HR."

"No," she ordered, poking her head past the doorway they'd stopped in, trying to place Tanner. "Where is he? In a car?"

When Eddie didn't answer, she twisted around to check on him, and that was when she realized he'd left her and was already five feet ahead on the sidewalk. "Eddie!" she called, but he held up a finger, signaling her to stay there.

A few things happened as she watched him walk away. Her vague alarm sharpened into real fear for Eddie. Then her grace-under-pressure stress response fell over her like a cloak, slowing her racing brain down as her nerves leveled out. She had a few seconds to think, to evaluate. And that evaluation made her remarkably, overwhelmingly furious.

How dare that shameless shit come here after what he'd done? To appear at *her* place of employment when he should be hiding his face from the world? Was he stalking her? Hoping to surprise her and scream out his blame and frustration over the career he'd ruined for himself? Did he think she'd be *scared*?

No. He'd taken enough from her already. He'd deserved what he'd gotten, and in that moment Luz wanted him to know who'd done it to him. Who'd used his own stupid, ugly hate against him.

She jumped from her hiding place and rocketed after Eddie. She could see the vehicle he was headed toward, a huge black pickup, of course, because what else would a man like Tanner drive to his cushy desk job?

What an overcompensating dick.

Eddie drew even with the truck and knocked on the passenger-side window. As the window lowered, Luz could hear Eddie asking what he wanted. She could see Tanner now, his face turned toward Eddie, his mouth moving as he answered. Eddie said something else, and Tanner began to argue, rolling his eyes, but then those eyes got stuck like they'd stumbled onto a glue trap. The trap was Luz, barreling toward him, yelling, and his eyes were widening with alarm.

"Get out of here!" she screamed "Get out!"

Eddie spun toward her. "Luz!"

"Don't you ever show your face here again, you racist asshole!"

The window began to roll up.

"You hear me? Go away. Disappear!" she yelled. "You thought you ruined my life, but I ruined yours! And you deserved it!"

"Luz!" Eddie tugged her back as the engine of the truck roared and the tires twisted. She was just opening her mouth again when the pickup lurched away. "Luz, what are you doing?"

"I wish he was dead!"

"I know, I know. It's okay. He was here to pick up his profit sharing."

Luz panted, heart hammering as Eddie smoothed calming circles onto her back. "His what?"

"It was only partially vested, so he had to sign something before he could get the money."

"Huh?" she huffed.

"Woman." Eddie pressed a hand to his mouth, then doubled over to laugh. The laugh turned into a cackle. "What the hell was that?"

"I just . . . I thought he was here to . . . I don't know."

"Well, you put the fear of God in him! Told him you would ruin his life! You Hulked out."

"I guess I did." She glanced self-consciously around, but if people had been watching, they'd already moved on. Thank God her company didn't have any offices on the first floor.

"Remind me never to piss you off!"

"I . . . I've never done that before."

"Shit, maybe you just don't remember. It came pretty naturally." Eddie was still laughing, tears leaking out of his eyes. "That was amazing. I'll definitely treat you to coffee next time because that was worth the price of admission."

"Must've been the caffeine," she said faintly, realizing she could have easily outed herself and the whole system if she'd kept shouting. Then again, she didn't even know if it had been her doing.

Because how could it have been?

"I'd better get back up," she murmured, dropping her cup in a trash can, too wired to finish the last few sips.

Eddie walked her inside, grinning the whole time. When they reached his floor, he winked and told her to behave herself. "And believe me, I *will* be in touch with any more gossip."

On the stairwell between the second and third floors, Luz stopped and got out her phone. There were no messages. No emails. And there weren't supposed to be. She opened her contacts and tapped Maggie's name, then stared for a very long time at her phone number.

She knew the rules, knew she couldn't ask what had happened, but she still needed a confirmation. She opened a text box and typed, Missed you at class on Tuesday. Hope all is well. I just had a very strange encounter with a former coworker. Wondering if something is up.

After hitting SEND, she took a deep, calming breath, closed her eyes, and let herself smile. She hoped that shitty excuse for a human being never got another job again. Hoped he was miserable and poor and deeply unhappy for the rest of his stupid life.

Yeah. Maybe she wasn't so perfect after all.

CHAPTER 17

KATHERINE

"An A plus?" Katherine screamed into the phone. "How did you get your grade back so quickly?"

"She's always a quick grader," Charlotte gushed. "Oh my God, I can't believe it. That was the only class I was worried about. If I keep my grades up until May, I'm going to make the dean's list!"

"You're amazing. You got your feet under you so quickly. I felt lost at college my freshman year. I'm incredibly proud of you."

"Thanks, Mom."

"It doesn't even matter if you make the dean's list. I'm just thrilled it feels like the right place to you."

"I like it a lot. But I miss home."

Katherine smiled through the stab of guilt. "I'm sorry everything has been weird and stressful. I know this is hard for you, but I can't wait to see you."

Charlotte's little sigh didn't escape her, but when she spoke again her voice sounded upbeat. "Dad's going to pick me up, and I'll stay with him for two days; then I'll stay with you before I head back."

Her daughter was probably the only person who could distract her from the mess she'd made for herself, and Katherine couldn't wait to see her. But she'd have to wait, apparently. It would be better for Charlotte if Katherine didn't join Peter at the airport even for a quick hello. It was all strange enough without that added tension.

"Sounds great to me. Have fun at the show tonight." Charlotte had driven to Seattle with a friend for a concert and then a camping trip before flying home. It sounded exhausting to Katherine, but youth was for the young.

"Thanks, I need the escape." Katherine could hear the edge behind the words, but Charlotte had done her best to make them sound chipper, so she let her get away with the effort.

"Well, your bedroom here is all ready for you. You pick a movie you want to see, and I'll make brunch reservations. Sound good? If you need any duplicate supplies here, we'll go shopping for them."

"Perfect."

Katherine told her again how proud she was, trying not to get choked up. Maybe all those years she'd stayed with Peter had been worth it. Her daughter was happy, healthy, and ready to take on the world. And they'd already communicated one-on-one more in the past two weeks than they had during her first semester at school. It seemed as if they were both growing up and finding their way. She tried to wrap the positivity of that around her, tried to hold it tight.

Her attempt worked. When they hung up, Katherine's little bubble of dreamy happiness stayed with her. She looked around at the messy nest she'd built and decided that instead of spending her Sunday morning hiding under blankets, she'd clean her apartment. She couldn't keep wallowing in worry and regret. She hadn't killed that man. It was time to stop acting like a guilty person.

She'd wasted too many days obsessively looking for new information about Brandon Johanssen while trying her best not to leave a trail, downloading and deleting a secure browser app over and over. Eventually she'd given up on that. If she was leaving some digital trail, the repeated deletion of an app would raise eyebrows too.

But she couldn't win. The information simply wasn't there. Not one new detail had appeared on any of the news sites. Maybe it actually had been some kind of tragic accident.

As for Nicole Park . . . Well, her online presence was a never-ending pep rally. A thousand photos of her kids on Facebook interspersed with pictures of the latest property she'd sold.

There were a few pictures of her husband here and there, though there'd been many more five years earlier. Katherine could assume what that must mean. They'd been juggling kids and busy careers, and they'd grown apart.

She couldn't ferret out much more because he didn't maintain his own online presence, not one that was linked in any of Nicole's posts, at least. And she only ever referred to him as "the hubs," so Katherine didn't even have a name. What seemed more important was that Nicole didn't mention him often.

But Katherine couldn't keep thinking about all that when she had more important things to consider: Charlotte and her upcoming visit.

She climbed out of the pile of pillows and cushions she'd amassed on the couch, then carried last night's empty pizza box and wine bottle to the trash. Her daughter would be at her place in a few days. She had to get her shit together and make it a home for both of them.

After gathering the rest of the trash and returning all the throw pillows to their correct places, Katherine surveyed the last few moving boxes. They'd each been opened and abandoned at various points during her unpacking process, and she knew one of them held cleaning supplies.

Her phone buzzed against her hip, signaling a text. Smiling that Charlotte would be reaching out again so quickly, she tugged it from her pocket.

Don't panic. Follow my lead. Delete this.

"What?" she muttered, wondering what the hell Charlotte was talking about. But it wasn't Charlotte. It was yet another unknown number, and the sight of it raised goose bumps on her arms.

She jerked her head up, whipping it first toward the door, then toward the wide-open curtains of the patio, as if someone might be waiting and watching. *Don't panic?* What the hell did that mean?

A distant rumble became the bass thump of footsteps coming down the hall toward her apartment. They were firm. Heavy. Authoritative.

Follow my lead.

Oh holy hell, no, no, no. It couldn't be. Charlotte was coming to visit soon. What if she arrived to find Katherine had been taken away? What if everything spiraled and she never returned to her apartment, her daughter, her life?

The footsteps stopped.

Katherine held her breath. Her heart felt as though it were crawling around inside her chest, looking for a way out, reaching, writhing, ready to abandon its owner and escape on its own.

The silence ticked by, and when the sudden booming of the knock sounded, Katherine knew it wasn't her husband. It was too loud. Not angry, merely strong.

And she knew then she had no choice but to answer.

Stupidly, she smoothed a hand over her hair to tidy it. She swiped the sleeve of her sweater across her forehead to wipe off any shine.

Did the place still smell like old wine? Did it matter?

She deleted the text, then shuffled across the tile, quieting her movement. When she looked out the peephole, she found a man, his face distorted by the lens. He looked White, middle-aged but trim. His eyes had been focused somewhere near the door handle, but they suddenly narrowed and rose to look right at her like he knew she was there. Perhaps she'd blocked the light or—

"Mrs. Rye? It's Denver PD." Just like in the hundreds of television episodes and movies she'd seen over her lifetime, the man held up a badge so she could view it. In the pale white light of the hallway, the gold metal didn't shine so much as ooze out an ugly plop of reflected light.

He cocked his chin and raised his eyebrows. "We'd like to speak with you for a moment."

"Okay," she squeaked, her throat a near-solid mass that cut off most of her breath. A lump, yes, like she needed to cry, but it was pushed even higher in her throat by the rising gorge in her stomach. Perhaps this would play out like the birthday party, with her vomiting on her own floor again.

Shaking, she reached for the lock. The dead bolt clacked so loudly when she turned it that Katherine jerked in shock, fearing a bullet fired through the door, but that made no sense. When she pulled on the handle to reveal herself, the man—the *cop*—opened his mouth to speak, but his words trailed off, his gaze shifting to her eye.

"Oh," Katherine croaked, reaching to cover the milky-white damage with her palm. "Sorry," she apologized, as if her blind eye and scarring were an insult to him. "I forgot my patch."

He ignored her misplaced regret and held up the badge again. "I'm Detective Koval with the Denver Police Department. This is my partner, Detective Hamilton. We'd like to ask you a few questions about a man you might know."

Katherine stared at him as another set of footsteps moved closer from a few feet away. She kept her gaze straight ahead, refusing to give in to the danger of seeing the other detective. Refusing to imagine how her own face might react to seeing her. Then she heard a click and whoosh of another door opening.

It was the gray-haired woman across the hall, who never seemed interested in Katherine unless something untoward was happening. She hadn't once looked out during Katherine's move in. Never said *hi* or *welcome* or even *shut the hell up out there*. She poked out her wild gray curls to frown only when Katherine's least welcome guests appeared.

"Come in," Katherine murmured, her voice still reedy. Detective Koval dipped his head in thanks and moved inside when she opened the door wider. When the other detective approached, Katherine lowered her gaze to the handle. The sickly white fingers of her own hand were wrapped so tightly around the lever that her bones hurt, fighting against the edge of the metal bite.

An awkward moment passed of her still holding the door, the woman across the hall still blatantly spying, the detectives hovering there, barely inside, waiting for her to behave normally so the interview could begin. But her hand only tightened, tightened until she thought her fingers might snap against the unwavering strength of the handle.

With a defiance that was sparked by her desperation to avoid what happened next, Katherine stared at her neighbor until the woman gave in and closed her door first. She was left with nothing to do then but force her body to move in slow degrees.

She shut the door and uncurled the fist of her hand. Pain sparked through her knuckles, and she waited even longer to let that pass before finally turning to her guests.

Her eyes rose, traveling over black slacks, strong thighs, tight hips, all the way up to the torso wrapped in a spruce-green blouse, and then, finally, to the familiar round face of Maggie Hamilton, her mentor, her coach, her inspiration. And now, her investigator.

Funny that it had felt so safe to scheme and plan with Maggie before, because if she was in law enforcement, how bad could any of it be? It didn't feel safe now.

"What's happened?" Katherine asked from very far away, telling herself that's what Maggie would want her to ask. "Is something wrong?"

Yes, of course something was very, very wrong; the police were here; what kind of idiotic, ridiculous question was that?

"Is it my husband?" she tried, hoping that was the right thing to say. Maggie's expression stayed closed to her, offering silence.

"No," the man answered, "it's nothing to do with your husband. I need to ask if you know someone named Brandon Johanssen."

She shook her head, because of course she wouldn't—couldn't—know that name. "Johanssen? No. Should I?"

"Well, that's what we're here to find out. Could we have a seat?" He gestured toward the dining table, but Katherine lurched to the living room before she noticed his hand.

"Yes. Here. Yes." Babbling. She was a babbling idiot moving like a broken puppet, first toward the couch, then the table, then back toward the couch again. "I can make coffee," she offered.

He didn't respond, and both of them followed her to the living room. Maggie moved quickly to the far side of the couch, gesturing Katherine to the solitary chair. Detective Koval sat on the side of the couch closer to her. Now she faced them both, Maggie just past her partner and staring hard at her.

Katherine stood dumbly, terrified to take her seat and hear their questions.

"I'm sorry," she said again. "I need . . ." With an awkward gesture toward her eye, she hurried to the bathroom and snatched her patch from the counter. She pulled it on too quickly, snapping the elastic against her forehead, struggling to position the patch into the right spot. It never quite settled, and dug into her skin as she rushed back to the armchair.

"Sorry. I'm a little . . ." Another awkward gesture, this time at the kitchen, pointing them toward nothing at all. Neither of them fell for it, and both pairs of eyes stayed right on her, one pair intensely familiar, one completely unknown.

When she was finally seated and frozen like a terrified rabbit, Detective Koval reached into the breast pocket of his blazer and withdrew his phone. "Do you recognize this man?"

He turned the screen to reveal a picture of Brad. He was smiling into the sun, the hint of his bare shoulders implying he was at the beach or pool. Maybe on a boat? Had he mentioned a boat? Her mind churned through nonsense as she pulled her gaze away to touch on first Koval, then Maggie. Maggie's chin dipped in the tiniest nod, her expression still cool and neutral.

"Oh." Katherine swallowed hard, the sound a cartoonish gulp in the quiet room. "I think that's Brad. Maybe. I don't know his last name. Just . . . Brad."

"Brad," he repeated. "And how do you know Brad?"

"I, uh . . ." That tiny head tilt from Maggie again, her brow lowering in stern warning. "I don't really know him. I just met him recently."

"Okay." He glanced at Maggie, and she withdrew a notepad from her back pocket and jotted something down. "Met him how?" he pressed.

"Online?" she squeaked as if it were a test. And it was a test, because he must already have the answer if he'd tracked her down. He wasn't asking idle questions of a chance bystander. They'd found her. What did that mean? A high-pitched whine began somewhere inside her head, like her nerves had set off an internal alarm.

"Dating app?" he suggested.

"Not really. Not a dating app. Just an app for church kind of stuff."

"So you were just doing some church stuff when you met him?"

This time Maggie's chin made a minuscule side-to-side movement. Katherine echoed it, terror turning her into a mimic.

"Not really?" she answered.

"All right. When did you meet him online?"

"Last week. I think."

"A week ago?" he pressed.

"Yes. Or more? Things have been hectic. I'm going through a divorce; my life is a bit upside down."

"Ah. And that's how you met Brad? Or *why* you met him, perhaps? The divorce?"

Tears suddenly pushed at her eyes, her throat turning nearly solid again, but she had the presence of mind to ask the right questions instead of the wrong ones. Years of hiding her real feelings had trained her to fight through them. "What's wrong? Did he do something? I don't understand. Is he a criminal?"

"Let's just slow down," Koval said calmly. "Let's discuss a bit more how you two met. So you were on this site, what did you say it was called?" She hadn't said the name before, of course, but Maggie scratched down LordsLink.com when Katherine spoke it. Her pen sounded like a claw.

"And then what happened?"

"We started chatting about our lives. Marriage. Movies. Just regular stuff."

"Okay. Just casual chitchat? Or was it more flirtatious than that?"

She swallowed again, squirming under his steady stare, his eyes such a pale green they looked gray. "I guess it got flirtatious, yes. We flirted."

The skin around his eyes tightened at that. He shifted forward the tiniest bit. "How flirtatious did it get?"

Another faint dip of Maggie's chin.

Embarrassment flooded over Katherine at what she was about to speak aloud. Not just embarrassment, but fiery shame.

Despite all her pep talks to herself, she'd been taught that sex was a dirty thing. *Something disgusting to be shared only with the man you love.* The phrase popped into her head so suddenly that she coughed out a shocked laugh she had to cover with a hand. She did her best to turn the noise into a tiny sob.

"I'm sorry," she said. "You have to understand. I found out my husband was cheating on me. Has *been* cheating on me. Maybe I was lashing out. Or not lashing out, but just . . ."

"Getting revenge?" Koval pressed.

Her vision went spotty at that word, and her heart thumped fast and hard, a drumbeat of warning. "I was in a very weird place, and when Brad started flirting with me, it felt like a sign. Or affirmation? It made me feel better about myself, honestly. So I flirted back. And maybe it moved too quickly."

Maggie finally spoke. "Moved to what?" she asked. "You met him in person?" Her face spoke of challenge now, a demand for answers for the lie she'd been told.

"Yes," Katherine said softly. "I've been with my husband for almost twenty-five years. It's not like me to . . . I've never . . . I don't know why I did it, but when Brad said he was at a hotel in town, I just went there without even thinking about it."

"I see. So you met him in person. When was that?"

She knew she had to be honest about this part, because there were likely cameras everywhere. And she was telling the truth. Surely the truth was the safest route. "It was last Monday."

Maggie's pen scratched away.

Koval nodded. "I see. Tell me what happened when you got to the hotel."

"I went to the bar. Had a glass of wine to calm my nerves. Then I went up to his room."

"You'd arranged that in advance?"

"Yes."

"And then what happened?"

Her face burned as her tongue went clumsy and numb. "We h-had sex. That's all it was. Not a date or anything. We barely spoke. We had sex, and then I left and came home. Here. To my apartment."

"How long were you there with him?"

"An hour or so. A little more."

Maggie jumped in with a question. "Was anyone else there in the room?"

Katherine gasped as she tossed a look of betrayal at her friend. "What? You mean . . . ? No! No one else was there!"

"And when you left," Maggie continued, "was this man in the shower? Getting dressed to go out? Passed out in bed?"

This man. Reminding her that he was a complete stranger. A helpful suggestion if she were keeping Katherine on the path of her fake story. Or it might just as well have been a dig. "He walked me to the door. We said goodbye. He was awake but not dressed. Just wearing briefs, actually."

Koval picked up the interrogation. "And you left the hotel immediately? There was no additional contact after that?"

"I left, yes. And we didn't message or speak afterward. Or, I mean, I messaged him."

"When?"

"The morning after. Tuesday. I asked if I could see him again. When he didn't respond, I . . . You have to understand, I've never done anything like that, and I felt ashamed. Stupid. I thought he'd been using me and was ignoring me. I got mad and deleted everything so he couldn't contact me again or track me down."

"So you were angry with him?" he pressed.

"Embarrassed!" she corrected. "It sort of all hit me at once, and I regretted that I'd done it. I don't even know him." She swallowed hard, her mind scrambling to pluck the best thing to say from her racing thoughts. But she'd had years of practice at pretending to feel one thing when she was feeling another. Years of hiding her truest emotions. "What happened? Is he okay? Did he do something?"

Koval ignored that. "You looked different."

"I'm sorry?"

"In the surveillance video. You looked very different than you do today."

She felt her eyes go wide. Felt him watching closely, still leaning toward her, perched at the edge of the couch. Was her face sending signals? Were they the wrong ones?

"Oh. Yes. I wore my prosthetic contact. And my hair was different."
His gaze slipped doubtfully over her messy ponytail. "I was afraid I'd see
someone I knew or he'd somehow recognize me. I told him my name
was Katy. This is all very new to me, and you hear stories. Crazy men
online. Murderers. Is he a murderer? Is that what this is about?"

He pretended again not to hear her question, or not to care about
answering, at least. After relaxing back into the deep cushions of the
couch, he took in the apartment. "Just moved in?"

"Yes."

"Running from something?"

She flushed hot again. "I'm making some changes in my life. Like
I said, I found out my husband was cheating. And maybe I rushed too
quickly to stretch my wings."

"Did you speak to anyone else at the hotel? See anyone as you were
leaving?"

"No. Oh!" She touched her fingers to her lips, thinking. "I didn't
see anyone, but when he first opened the door to walk me out, Brad
laughed and shut the door, as if he was startled. There was no one there
when I went out, though."

Eyes narrowing, Maggie wrote that down.

"Do you think—?"

Koval cut off Katherine's question. "Did you stay at the hotel? Go
to the bar?"

"I didn't linger. I didn't want to seem like I was . . . No, I just left
the hotel, came home, and showered."

"And you were alone here, right? No one to back that up?"

"Yes. No."

"Right. Well, Mrs. Rye. We'll be in contact with more questions,
I'm sure. If you could refrain from leaving the area for at least a few
days, I'd appreciate it."

"Detective," she began, pleading, "I don't understand what's going
on. What happened?"

"Brandon Johanssen—the man you knew as Brad—is dead. He died in his hotel room around the time of your encounter."

"Uh." All the air in her lungs fell out of her body on a grunt. She didn't have to fake her shock. Even already knowing, it was a punch to the gut that would take time to recover from. Her mouth opened and closed. Her hands twitched.

"Did you kill him?" Maggie asked point-blank, a brutal jab right where the body blow had just landed.

Defensiveness pushed her straight into overacting. "No! You only said he was dead! You didn't say he was murdered!"

She shook her head hard, and it felt as though marbles were pinging around, sparking stars in her vision and bells in her ears. "Oh my God, is that why you asked if anyone else was in the room? Was someone hiding in the room?"

She was hyperventilating, she thought. Panicking. And in that panic, something deep in her lizard brain told her that was good, it was helpful, because this made the performance look real. *Feel* real.

But it didn't feel good. She thought she might pass out and die.

"Mrs. Rye?" Koval said, the words another pealing bell in her ear.

She watched him get up, watched him walk into her kitchen, and she wondered if he was already looking for evidence, searching for a knife or bleach or—a glass of water appeared in her vision. "Take a few sips," he said.

She caught her breath and managed a gulp of the water.

"Better?" he asked.

She nodded and drank a bit more. The water cooled her fevered panic a little. She breathed more naturally.

The murderer would panic too, her anxiety offered in a cruel whisper. *You're not as good as you think you are. You just look more guilty.* But she was able to ignore it. "Can you please just tell me what happened to Brad?" she begged. "I didn't kill him. I didn't hurt him at all. Am I in danger now?"

He watched her for a long time. Maggie scratched at her notepad again. Katherine waited for a response, any response, but Koval only stared. Finally he glanced at Maggie and nodded.

"He was strangled to death," Maggie said.

"Strangled?" Katherine whispered back, looking down at her own hands. They lay on her lap, thin and pale and surely not capable of strangling a grown man.

"Asphyxiation," Maggie clarified as if it meant something important.

Katherine shook her head, true terror beginning to creep along her edges, sending shivers down her nerves. "Do you know who did it? Do you know who it was?"

Detective Koval stood. "As I said, please don't leave town without speaking with us. If you think of anything that could be helpful to the investigation, give me or Detective Hamilton a call. We'd love to chat more." He placed his business card on the coffee table, as if so intent on ignoring her question he didn't even want to hand it to her. Maggie did the same, then stood herself, tucking her notebook away.

"Thank you for your time, Mrs. Rye," she said darkly.

"Should I be scared?" Katherine asked the room. Her first genuine question, but no one responded, and the detectives let themselves out, leaving her alone in suddenly terrifying silence.

Her mind churned and her stomach followed suit. What was going on here? If he'd been murdered, strangled by some crazed person, why hadn't Maggie warned her? Did she really think Katherine might be involved?

If so, it was likely because Katherine had lied to her and left Maggie doubting everything she'd ever said. Then again, maybe Maggie was too busy protecting herself. Or someone else.

"Oh no," she whispered. Strangulation. Asphyxiation. What did that mean? She grabbed her laptop off the table and Googled both terms. Strangulation was only constriction, and it didn't have to be with the hands. Asphyxiation was cutting off the air supply.

After beginning to type "ways to strangle someone," Katherine squeaked and deleted that, then clicked around until she confirmed what she'd been thinking. It could have been done with hands or a ligature. A rope or a garrote, something like that.

Had someone else been there? No. It wasn't possible. But could someone have been *watching*? Watching his room or watching for her? Someone who would've been enraged to see her leaving?

She needed to find out who'd wanted revenge on him, and she couldn't ask Maggie. For the first time, she couldn't trust that Maggie was actually looking out for her. She might be protecting another woman or just her own career. She had a lot to lose, and if someone in the system had killed Brandon Johanssen, Maggie wouldn't want that person caught.

Then again, how had the police found Katherine? How had Detective Koval identified her and tracked her down? Was Maggie preparing to throw Katherine under the bus?

Shit. She could no longer afford to hesitate out of fear of leaving tracks. She'd left a million damn tracks already, and they'd apparently led the police right to her door. A few more weren't going to hurt anything.

There were three main suspects she needed to watch out for. Brandon's wife, the woman in the system who'd targeted him, and Detective Maggie Hamilton. Any one of them could be a danger to her, in one way or another.

When she looked up Nicole Park again on Facebook, trying once more to see if she could read the state of her soul from recent photographs, Katherine added one more possibility to the list: Nicole's husband. If Nicole Park had been the one involved with Brandon, her husband needed to be moved right to the top of the suspect list.

The worst realization of all was that Katherine was on her own. The buffering protection of having a system of other women was now a trap tightening around her. She couldn't lean on anyone unless she eliminated them from the list.

Jesus. She was all alone.

But now that the initial panic had drained out of her, Katherine realized some life-changing truths. She wasn't a victim, she wasn't going down without a fight, and she wasn't getting framed for this either. She refused to be.

After digging into one of the moving boxes, she emerged with a pad of paper and started taking notes, trail of evidence be damned.

CHAPTER 18

GENEVA

"I love you, Ms. Worther!" The tiny girl launched herself at Geneva's legs and squeezed tightly.

Geneva's cheeks already hurt from smiling so much throughout the morning, but she managed another grin. "I'm still walking you out to the pickup line, so we can say goodbye there, sweetie." She hadn't memorized all the kids' names yet, but she was taking home a class photo tonight.

Little kids were just amazing. She'd spent only a few hours with these babies, but she knew the girl giving her one last squeeze wasn't lying about her love. Their hearts were wide open and bursting with emotions they weren't afraid to acknowledge. Of course, those bursting emotions could also be frustration or anger, but those feelings were all valid too. One of her tasks was to help them channel that energy into growth.

She loved them all despite still working on their names. She even loved the quiet, surly one who put his head down on his desk instead of copying out the letter *W* in upper- and lowercase. He might be tired, he might have problems at home, or he might have been born a stubborn curmudgeon from day one. She'd do her best to find out.

God, it felt good to be back.

She was lining up the kids in a snake shape around the big round tables when Jess stuck her head in the room. "I can't stay! How was your first day? Great?"

"It was pretty great," Geneva admitted.

"You owe me dinner, lady. Let's meet up tonight."

"Maybe next week?" she suggested instead. She was already exhausted from putting out a thousand percent more energy than she had in months. It was only Monday morning. She needed to conserve energy to get through her first week.

Jess pulled her head back and winced at something out in the hall- way. "Yeah, good. We'll talk later." She rushed off, calling out instruc- tions to a kid somewhere. Did eighth graders still have to be corralled? Apparently they did.

Geneva reminded the kids to check for any jackets or backpacks they might have left behind; then she marched them out of the class and toward the front doors. This would be the worst part of the day, meeting the parents at the pickup circle, where one of them might recognize her and scream in horror.

But in the end, no one screamed. The moms and dads and nannies were all very kind, most of them effusively thankful to have a teacher in place for the rest of the year. No obvious villains presented themselves, and the one sullen boy perked up when he saw his mom, so maybe he was just a homebody.

Once all eighteen of the kids had been safely handed off, she headed back to her classroom to sanitize the tables for the next day and gather up her things.

The kindergarten lesson plans had been lovingly written out by the permanent teacher already, with little notes everywhere that she'd clearly added from her bed rest. She'd also included an invitation to call that was so desperately friendly Geneva would have to take her up on it. The poor woman was likely going stir-crazy already. But at least she'd have her own little one soon. Geneva would get in touch next week with any questions that developed about the kids or the lesson plans.

Geneva knew she wanted at least one child of her own, maybe two. Over the years, she'd alternately pictured herself with a husband, then a wife, then maybe even a less formal relationship with any one or two people she loved.

Lately she imagined she might just do it alone. Maybe that was easier for her, being free. The next few years would be about establishing a career after that terrible false start. Figuring out where she felt safe enough to settle and put down roots. It would be nice to be within an hour or two of her parents, especially if she really did do it alone. But that was a long way off and still felt impossible. Hell, she didn't even know if she wanted to adopt or give birth.

She finished cleaning up, made one last circuit of the room, then gathered up the lesson plans to take home. She honestly didn't have much work compared to her old classroom duties. All she had to do was follow the plan and maybe come up with an extra craft project or two that had been left open ended.

Then she remembered the assembly scheduled for next week. She had to memorize the song about the history of Colorado the whole school was singing, along with the "Mountain Colors" song the kindergarteners would perform.

She added the lyrics to the stack of lesson plans, then walked out of the classroom, smiling. She couldn't wait. She always cried like a baby when her class performed in an assembly, their adorable little faces intense or scared or theatrically overjoyed. She loved being surprised by the quiet kids who shone onstage and the outgoing kids who refused to open their mouths.

Instead of heading straight for the parking lot, she took a detour to the "tech center," saying a little prayer that it was still some form of library with picture books for her students. Her heart fell when she walked in and rows of printers, scanners, and monitors greeted her. There were even two 3-D printers up against the left wall.

But then she noticed a riot of colors through a doorway on the right and walked through to discover the book room. It wasn't quite as large as the usual school library, but it looked well stocked. She'd try to fit in a visit in the next day or two. Nothing served a child better than an early love affair with books.

Her phone buzzed with a text, and Geneva pulled it free, hoping to God it was Maggie at long last. But when she saw the name, her heart sank. Omi. Her ex. The woman she'd inadvertently violated with that stupid recording. Geneva's private moments had been exposed by the sex tape, but so had Omi's.

Hey, can we grab dinner tonight?

Oh, damn it. She couldn't do this right now. There was way too much going on, and just seeing Omi's name reminded Geneva of the ways her own choices had damaged another person she cared about. She'd made Omi vulnerable and left her hurt too.

On the other hand, Omi had been noble and understanding about the whole thing, and she'd reached out over and over afterward, checking on Geneva after she'd been fired and even sleeping on her couch once or twice in those first weeks. But Geneva had just been too devastated and broken to accept sympathy, especially from someone she felt so awful about involving.

But now that she'd healed a little, she knew she owed Omi some time. Still, all she wanted to do was get Frank off her plate and sink into a good ten hours of sleep.

She texted back with a guilty wince. Tonight? Things are a little crazy.

Next week, next week, next week, she prayed. But not devoutly enough, apparently, because by the time she was back in the hallway, Omi had responded.

Maybe just a drink, then? Please?

Geneva bit back a groan, but guilt got the better of her. She owed Omi, big-time. **Okay. Sure. Can you do early? Five or six? Let me know where.**

It would be good to celebrate, she told her tired body. She could do this. While she was up here, she'd run a few errands, including a trip to her favorite teaching supply store. Then she'd head to the library to find the latest book or two on early childhood education before meeting Omi for a drink.

Surely she could manage one full-length day of activities like a normal person?

The smell of rain greeted her when she finally stepped back outside. The sun was still shining, but huge gray clouds were rolling in over the snow-softened heights of Longs Peak, and the scent warned her that drops were about to fall. She inhaled deeply and felt a little energy rush back into her on the walk across the parking lot. Things had been so hopeless for so long that even the simplest beauty felt invigorating.

She was nearly out of Longmont and approaching the freeway when her phone rang. She tapped the steering wheel to answer it with an extra-cheerful hello, assuming it was her mom or dad checking in.

"Hi, is this Geneva?"

"This is she."

"Hello." The woman sounded hesitant. "I'm sorry to bother you. Can you talk?"

Her cheerfulness was quickly displaced by a caution that crept on spindly legs along her nerves. "Sure?" she said, the word and the tone warring with each other.

"I'm Katherine. I'm from the Hook."

Oh, thank God. Finally! "Okay, did Maggie get my message?"

"No, I mean, I'm from the class. And I need to talk to you about Maggie. About the system."

The first fat drops of rain hit her windshield. Within moments, the sound overwhelmed her hearing, the patter exploding into a roar. Or maybe that was her barreling pulse and screaming brain overtaking all her senses.

Geneva drove past the freeway entrance and pulled into a gas station, her car bouncing and bucking over the curb when she cut it too close.

"Hello?" the woman on the phone said. "Hello? Are you there?"

She turned off the car and put the phone to her ear. "You're her," she bit out, furious or scared, she couldn't tell which. "The woman from the parking lot. I told you not to do this."

"I'm sorry!" She actually did sound sorry, her voice winding up at the end as if she were panicking too.

"I'm hanging up."

"Don't! Please don't hang up! Someone is dead! One of the targets!"

If Geneva thought she was feeling panic before, she'd been wrong. Because now it truly gripped her, squeezing her body until she felt heavy as stone and just as immobile. She didn't respond because she couldn't.

Someone was dead? No, no, no, she couldn't handle that right now. What if—?

"I don't know who else to talk to," the woman whined.

"Talk to fucking Maggie!" Geneva yelled, breaking free of her paralysis. "Not *me!*"

"I can't. I don't know if I can trust her anymore. I don't know what she's hiding or who she's protecting! But I know you weren't involved with my part of the plan. You've been to my home, and she wouldn't have wanted us that close to each other, even if we never met. You don't know who Brad is, right? Or Brandon?"

"No."

"I understand that you think this has nothing to do with you, but everything has gone to complete shit. If any of this comes out, you'll be involved too. Whoever you were targeting and why, that won't be secret anymore."

"Why would you tell anyone? I didn't do anything to you!"

"I'm not threatening you!" Katherine insisted. "It's just reality. If they find out about the system, why any of us were involved . . . I don't want it to come to that. For anyone. We have to take care of each other. That's the whole point, right?"

"Who was it? Who d-died?" She could barely choke the word out because it had only just occurred to her that it could be Frank. She pushed her forehead to the steering wheel, bracing herself. But the woman on the phone said, "Brandon," again, reminding her she'd already tossed that name out there.

It wasn't Frank. It had nothing to do with Geneva or what she'd done. Oh, thank God. The air slowly sighed out of her easing throat.

"Please leave me out of this." She was begging and she didn't even care. She didn't have time to pretend her fear was anger, didn't have time to put up a front. "I can't be involved. I just started . . ." No, she couldn't give any hints like that. "I just can't be involved."

"I only want to know if there's anything you know about Maggie that I don't. Or any of the other women in the system."

The rain roared around her, beating against the car and her mind. She pressed her other hand tight to her ear to block out as much of the storm as she could.

"Okay. All right. But who is this Brandon?" she asked.

"I don't really know enough to explain. I'm not sure who targeted him or why. But I was the one who was supposed to set him up. I mean, I did already, kind of."

Geneva sprang back up straight. "So it could have been *you*? Are you a murder suspect? You're calling me and you're *a murder suspect*?"

"No! I didn't kill him! Why would I seek you out and tell you who I was if I'd killed him? I'd be hiding or running or something."

"Unless you're looking for your next victim."

"Then I could have just followed you home from the Hook!"

Geneva supposed that was true. Unless Katherine was a monster who was toying with her. Regardless, she was a danger to Geneva and to the baby steps she'd managed to make in the past few days.

"I can't help you," she insisted. The only answer that arrived from the other end of the line was a muffled sob. She squeezed her own eyes shut, trying to smother the sympathy uncurling inside her.

"I'm so scared," the woman whispered.

Shit. Geneva was scared too, and she just needed to stop this spiraling plan and turn her back on it forever. And what if this meant Frank was in danger too? Or all of them?

The rain pounded away, cutting her off from the rest of the world, sending her back into the isolation she'd only just escaped. The air in the car grew thick and warm, dragging against her throat when she inhaled. "I can't help you," she repeated.

"You don't know anyone else involved? Not one name?"

Luz, her brain murmured. *Maybe Luz.* But she shook her head. "No. That's the whole point."

"Have you spoken to Maggie? Has she said anything about this?"

"She won't call me back," Geneva said on a rush, the frustration of the past week forcing the words out. "I really need to talk to her, but she doesn't respond."

"God. Do you think we can trust her? Like, *really* trust her? Because she's treating me oddly too."

Geneva said yes immediately, but it was more a wish than an answer, because she had no idea anymore. Yes, they could trust her, because what choice did they have? Maggie was a police detective, for God's sake. She'd been guiding them through this as an experienced authority on what was dangerous or not, what was too legally risky or just edging close to it. That was *why* they could trust her.

But Geneva was in a bad spot, and Maggie was ignoring her, so what did that mean?

"I think I might know one of the other women," Katherine said carefully. Geneva desperately wanted to ask if it was Luz. She thought there was a very good chance Luz was involved based on her reaction to Geneva's mild questioning about Maggie.

"What's her name?" she asked.

"Nicole."

A tiny hint of relief slowed her pulse a bit. "I don't know her."

"She's in my class. I might see if I can get her alone."

"Aren't you scared, though? She might have killed that guy."

"Yeah," she said quietly. "I am scared. I just don't know what else to do. It feels more dangerous for me to wait and hope everyone is being honest. Because if they're not . . . I'm the one who was in touch with this guy."

"I'm sure Maggie is taking care of it," Geneva tried to reassure her. "She'd tell you if you were in danger."

"Yeah," she said, but she clearly didn't believe it and Geneva wasn't sure she did either. "Thanks for answering. I'm just trying to find out as much as I can. I need to be able to protect myself. If you think of anything, will you call me?"

When she hung up, Geneva didn't feel any better. She felt worse.

She had to stop this plan with Frank, because if half of these women were going down, they'd pull her down with them. As of right now, she hadn't hurt anyone. She checked Frank's Instagram religiously, and he was still out there posing and pretending to be cute.

She might just have to contact Luz and politely ask her to drop any plans. She'd say it in a way that was so obscure it would go over Luz's head if she wasn't involved. Either she'd understand or she'd think Geneva was odd. That was a risk she was willing to take.

After not showing up for the Tuesday- or Thursday-night class, Maggie also hadn't been answering her phone, and how was that anything but a terrible sign?

Things were finally going right for Geneva. She had to make sure they didn't start going very, very wrong.

CHAPTER 19

KATHERINE

Ignoring a call from her mom, Katherine tugged the baseball cap lower on her head and blinked her eyes a few times to moisten them. She'd been staring at the front door of HT Realty for so long she felt the vision in her good eye might never recover from the strain.

She didn't even know if Nicole Park was inside, and that only made her tension worse. A white SUV with the office's logo was parked in the lot, but there was every chance in the world it belonged to another employee. Still, only a few of the vehicles sported the logo. The agent with the brand-new cream-colored Lexus clearly didn't want to mar the luxurious look with a stick-on graphic.

Katherine sipped her cappuccino and waited, the headache that swelled behind her forehead finally reaching out to join with the desperate ache at the base of her skull. The pain squeezed, a pincer of misery around her head. She needed a massage or a controlled substance or both, but the only tool she had was lukewarm caffeine.

It had been a whole day since that awful knock on her door, and Maggie still hadn't reached out. Not with an explanation, not with reassurance, not even with a furious accusation. Something was very wrong and getting worse with each second of silence from a woman who was supposed to be on her side.

What the hell was she supposed to do with that uncertainty? Just sit and scream? Well, she'd tried that, and it hadn't worked. She had to take action and get answers or she'd lose her mind.

In the ninety minutes Katherine had been waiting in the HT Realty parking lot, she'd toggled between staring at the glassed-in lobby of the office and staring at her phone, starving for every crumb of information she could scrape together.

Brandon Johanssen's memorial page was finally live, a full week after his death, and Katherine wondered if the delay was related to the police investigation. Or maybe because his wife was too busy covering up her crimes to plan a funeral? Katherine's imagination roiled and spit, throwing out increasingly bizarre fantasies of who had killed him. A hit man? The jealous wife? A serial killer targeting state-level politicians?

His obituary provided clues, but there were so many frenetic details that her idea of him only became more cloudy. Husband, son, father, coach, colleague, politician, and yes, he even owned a water-skiing boat, the shirtless picture of him from just the venue she'd suspected. A larger version of that photo was on his memorial page, him holding a beer on the water, surrounded by three other men, all of them beaming arrogant grins. She ignored the others to focus on him.

A memory flashed through her. Brad's thick waist under her hands, his cologne in her nose as he thrust into her body, a stranger deep inside her. It had all been so surreal and sudden, a rift between the untouched wife she'd been before and a woman clutching a sweating stranger between her legs. She'd experienced it from a distance, a sticky and scandalous procession of sensations.

Even remembering that, the picture of him with his family didn't affect Katherine the way she'd feared it would. That was *Brandon* and had nothing to do with what Brad had been to her for such a brief time.

She didn't even feel particularly guilty looking at his wife. All that arose in her was suspicion.

Like her own husband, Brandon had been faking his way through piousness. An ultraconservative politician who crowed constantly about family values and Christian living while trolling his way through conservative spaces, looking for sex. Someone had finally snapped. But who? God only knew how many people thought he deserved it.

After glancing up at the door, Katherine enlarged the family picture again. Mrs. Johanssen looked a bit sour in the posed photo. Her smile turned down at the edges instead of up, and her eyes didn't crinkle at all, as if she was purposefully using as few muscles as possible. Botox? Or was it only a deep misery that had churned and built until it finally fizzed up into murderous fury on that fateful night?

Katherine had scoured the Hook's Facebook page for any sight of her, but she'd never appeared, and her hair would have stood out in one of the dozens of pictures from the women's nights.

She made the family photo smaller, then larger, but as with Nicole Park's picture, no secret revealed itself. His wife was average weight, average height, average white skin, not pale or particularly tanned. Did that mean she rarely joined him on the water?

Even their two children were hard to decipher, an indeterminate age in the picture that had been posted. The younger might have been five, the older ten, or anywhere in between those ages. The two boys were average, not striking or homely. It was just a regular, forgettable family with a cheating patriarch, a tale as old as time . . . and almost exactly the same as hers.

But Brandon wasn't only a father and husband; he was also a state senator with a passion for judging others. He sponsored bills targeting the vulnerable, sputtering about people whose existence "threatens my family." The same family he continually and joyfully betrayed.

Acid burned in her gut at the hypocrisy of it. Of how he'd thrived on accusing others of his own worst misdeeds. Maybe someone had turned all that hate back on him.

As if summoned by the thought, Nicole Park suddenly appeared in the lobby, reaching to push the door open. She looked better today, or maybe she'd only reapplied her cheerful mask, but her big smile was back, aimed at a man approaching the door from the parking lot.

Katherine grabbed for her door handle, but as she watched, the man turned and began walking with Nicole, deep in discussion, his hands flying with big gestures. Katherine hovered, ready to spring out as soon as he left, but even after Nicole opened the door of her white SUV, she and the man kept talking, their words too far away to hear. Nicole's bright smile remained as she nodded and slipped into her seat, one foot still on the ground.

"Go," Katherine whispered furiously at the man. "Go away."

He didn't move. In fact, he stood there as Nicole finally closed her door, then took only a step back before raising his phone to his ear, already talking again, aiming his big gestures at the person on the call who couldn't see them.

"Crap," she cursed as Nicole began to pull out. Katherine's plan hadn't exactly been airtight, but she'd meant to approach Nicole here in public where it was relatively safe. Now, with no plan at all, she backed out of her own space and followed the white SUV.

For years she'd dreamed of having a different life, of being a different person, and here she was, suddenly a complete stranger to herself as she tailed a possible murder suspect out of the lot and onto a side street. She hung back a bit, frantically recalling everything she'd seen in movies about tailing a car through a city, but when Nicole took a right onto a busier street, Katherine panicked and sped up so she could stick behind her.

When they came to a red light, she was hyperaware that she could see a rectangle of Nicole's face in the SUV's rearview mirror, her smile now replaced by a crumpled frown. If Katherine could see her, that meant if Nicole glanced up, she'd be staring right at Katherine.

She'd been smart enough to wear her prosthetic at least, hoping to draw as little attention as possible. She didn't need her patch to hide from the police anymore. She was fully in their awareness now, a bright spotlight of attention. She'd be in their records forever. She'd be included in any trial.

My God.

The realization would have bowled her over if she'd been standing. There was no way out of this for Katherine. Not anymore. Brandon had been murdered, so she would be part of a trial, the last witness to see him. It would all come out. Peter would know; Charlotte would know; the world would know what she'd done. And that was the *least* worst outcome.

Christ, what if they made a *Dateline* out of this? A good two-hour episode to cover all the strange twists and turns?

When Nicole began to inch forward with the green light, Katherine nearly lurched right into her bumper, her body as clumsy as a windup toy, all jigs and jags. Nicole didn't notice, thank God, and Katherine fell back, putting four car lengths between them.

Finally the white SUV turned into a neighborhood of two-story houses shaded by tall trees. The car slowed, a garage door to the left beginning to rise ahead. Katherine waited, then drove past as Nicole turned and pulled in.

Katherine parked a few houses down. Then she changed her mind and drove around the block, craning her neck for any sign of who might be behind the nondescript beige siding of the home. On her second pass, she saw a young woman leaving, hoisting a backpack over her shoulder. The girl had to step around a tricycle and over a loose pile of sidewalk chalk as she made her way to a beat-up VW bug.

Katherine pulled to the curb so she wouldn't look like she was stalking the teenager. Was the girl a babysitter? There'd been no other car in the two-car garage, so Nicole's husband wasn't there. Maybe they were separated.

Just as the girl opened the door of the VW bug, Nicole Park herself burst out the front door, a little boy hot on her heels. She carried a plastic bag in her hand, waving as she called out.

The girl winced and laughed, then met Nicole behind her battered rear fender to take the bag. The woman Katherine had been following was now standing six feet in front of her car.

She froze like a trapped animal as the two talked, aware any movement could draw Nicole's attention. The boy bounced around their feet, perhaps pretending to be a frog or a rabbit. Nicole patted the girl's arm, looking for all the world like a normal, caring woman as they spoke in friendly tones, the words a bit too muffled for Katherine to make out past the glass and the fear screaming through her mind. The boy darted off, and Nicole gave the girl one more pat before swinging around, her eyes searching for her son.

But instead of finding him, her gaze landed right on Katherine. Suddenly they were looking straight at each other.

Nicole's first response was to tilt her head, one eyebrow tucking down in puzzlement, then she looked briefly friendly, then puzzled again. Katherine's only response was to sit and stare in horror at this possibly dangerous woman.

Yes, she'd wanted to have a conversation at the realty office, but she'd thought it could be casual, a very careful tiptoeing around the subject to see where it led. *Haven't I seen you at the Hook? Have you talked to Maggie lately?* She definitely hadn't meant to very obviously follow her home and start a confrontation.

A loud bang cracked through her head, and Katherine gasped out a scream, slapping a hand to her temple to check for a bullet wound. The world slowed around her as Nicole winced and mouthed a big *Sorry!* as she rushed toward the car. Katherine turned her head on a neck so stiff with tension she could barely move; then she screamed again to see a horrifying face pressed to the glass.

The horrifying face smiled, and it was just the little boy, his nose and lips smashed against the glass, one hand spread wide where he'd slapped the window.

"I'm so sorry!" Nicole said, offering a chagrined smile as she took the boy's hand and tugged him back. She raised her voice to be heard through the window. "Are you here about the painting estimate? Thank you for postponing. I had to drop in to the office."

"I . . ."

"Come on in!"

Katherine didn't remember turning off the car or reaching for the handle. As far as she knew, she'd simply floated out of her seat to stand in the street with Nicole Park. Birds sang above her, impossibly loud, a cacophony filling up her brain.

"Sorry I gave you such short notice," Nicole went on, as friendly as if they'd known each other for years.

Suddenly Katherine was halfway up the woman's driveway, her key fob in her fist, but she had the sense to catch the house key between two fingers like a weapon, as if she were leaving the mall after dark.

This wasn't rational. She knew that. But she rode a wave of madness all the way up the drive and let it sweep her toward the tiny covered porch and the waiting door.

This was a terrible idea. Incredibly stupid. Dangerous.

"I'm Aaron!" the little boy said before racing up the steps and throwing open the door to rush inside.

"Aaron, shoes," Nicole said as she followed him up at a slower pace.

Waves of evil didn't flow off her. The woman seemed totally normal, and no more threatening than she had in class when she'd thrown weak, tepid punches at Katherine's hands. She stepped inside and waved Katherine in.

But Katherine didn't follow. She couldn't. As impetuous as she might be, she wasn't insane. "I'm sorry," she managed to say on a reedy breath. "I'm not here about painting."

"Oh?"

"I'm from . . ."

Despite that they'd worked out together for nearly an hour, Nicole just stared at her, not a hint of recognition in her eyes. Katherine's contact lens was always the perfect disguise.

"I need to ask you about . . ." Katherine glanced past her, toward the sound of kids playing, and dropped her voice to a mere breath. "About Brandon."

Nicole's tanned face went ashen in a split second. Her brown eyes looked suddenly menacing with the whites showing all around the irises like a cornered animal's. She pulled the door tight against her side and moved forward, tugging it shut behind her. There was no denying that she knew exactly who Brandon was.

Nicole glared past her to the street, her gaze racing back and forth before it returned to Katherine. "Who are you? What do you want?"

Katherine took a careful step away. "Did you kill him?" she asked point-blank.

"No!" The horror on her face seemed genuine, a twist of agony and nausea. She shook her head in frantic denial. "No! Of course not! Why are you asking me that?"

"Because you're the one who set him up."

She began to pant, her eyes rolling as she again scanned the street. "Am I under arrest? Please don't do this in front of my children. I can . . . I can come in and talk to you . . ."

Katherine raised her chin and squared her shoulders, aware of the role she was now playing. If Nicole thought she was a cop, she'd be a cop. "When was the last time you saw him?"

"It was months ago! Six months? Maybe seven? I haven't seen him since . . . I had a health thing. He didn't even check on me afterward.

That was over six months ago, so the last time we spoke was before then. He stopped responding to my messages."

The back of her neck tingled. "A health thing?" Her body suddenly crawled with fear. She hadn't demanded he use any protection. Why? Why had she treated it all like a fantasy instead of a very real danger to her?

"I . . . You have all the messages, I suppose. You know what I'm talking about."

Katherine shook her head in confusion, and that was apparently the wrong choice, because Nicole's eyes narrowed in sudden suspicion. "Wait a minute. Are you a detective?"

She couldn't keep up the lie. She'd only stumbled into it, and she had no plan at all. "I'm not a cop," she admitted. "I'm from the Hook. Maggie assigned me to him. To Brandon."

Nicole's mouth closed with a hard click of her teeth, and her whole body pulled in, chin dipping, arms crossing to protect her chest as she stutter-stepped back toward her door. Her hip bumped the wood, and that small contact startled her into a jump. She looked terrified. And if she was terrified of Katherine, that must mean she didn't have any idea who'd hurt Brandon.

Right?

"I didn't do it," Katherine reassured her on a rush. "Maggie knows that." That part was a lie, but she told it with enthusiasm. "You can ask her!"

"Then what the hell are you doing here?"

"I wanted to talk to you outside your office, but I didn't catch you."

"That's not really the point! Why are you *here*?"

"Because I just want to know what's going on! You set him up, right? You wanted revenge."

"Yes, but not like *that*. Please go away. You can't be here." She looked stern and angry, pointing at the road, ordering Katherine away.

But then her finger started to tremble. Her hand dropped. And Nicole began to cry.

"Please," Nicole begged. "He doesn't know."

As wired on fear and adrenaline as she was, Katherine melted a little when Nicole began to sob. She looked utterly defeated, her body a sagging mess of sorrow. Katherine reached out, hesitated, then touched her arm. "Your husband?"

Her head bobbed in a jerky nod. "I just . . ." She inhaled a shuddering breath before sobbing again. "I made a mistake. I get that now. A terrible, selfish mistake. I thought I wanted out of my marriage, but I don't. I don't! Our poor babies . . ."

"Shh," Katherine said, drawing her away from the door. She tugged her down to sit on the first step and even dared to put an arm around her. "I'm sorry. I didn't come here to make trouble for you."

"Why then? *Why?*"

She looked at this broken, weeping woman and chose to tell another lie. "We both had a connection with him, and he's dead, and we can't talk to anyone. I just wanted to talk to someone. That's all."

That tore another sob from Nicole, and she actually turned her face into Katherine's shoulder to weep, though she kept her arms tightly wrapped around her own body.

Katherine felt her own eyes fill with tears at the heartbroken gesture. "You really hadn't talked to him in months?"

"He cut me off completely after the abortion," Nicole finally sobbed.

The *abortion?* Oh my God. Everything went bright in her mind, her questions taking on sharp new edges, and her lingering fear transformed into a painful, digging empathy. She knew what it was like to suffer in silence. To carry it all alone. "I'm so sorry."

"I thought I was in love with him. I thought maybe we'd make it work. How stupid was that? I thought that narcissistic asshole was actually interested in having a life with me!"

"You're not stupid," she whispered. "It's not stupid to love someone."

"I don't think I did. Or maybe I did? I was just so lonely. I was miserable, and I latched on to the attention he poured on me. My husband and I . . . we grew apart." She laughed a little, a quiet, broken chuckle. "He works long shifts. Weekends, nights. During the pandemic he'd stay away to isolate sometimes. And with three kids, we're both exhausted every day, and I just . . . I didn't realize how much I still wanted all this until after."

"After the . . . ?"

"Yeah." Nicole lowered her head into her hands. "I was scared to tell Brandon I was pregnant. Anyone would be. But I was a little excited too. You know? I really thought . . . I really thought it might be a good thing." Her voice quavered with an aching vulnerability.

Katherine smoothed a gentle hand over her shoulder. "What happened?"

"Oh, Brandon immediately said he'd pay for an abortion, and I was completely shocked. That's the stupid part, right? Why did I think he had some kind of core values when we'd both been cheating for months? That doesn't even make sense!"

"We're all stupid about sex and love. We're supposed to be, really; otherwise we wouldn't risk it."

She nodded. "I guess. But I realized who he really was eventually. When I told him I didn't want an abortion, he said I couldn't very well pass off his kid as my husband's, since he's Korean. And again, I could barely process what he meant. I was telling him I wanted to *be* with him, to have a life together, and he was saying such stupid, cruel things."

"I'm sorry."

She calmed a little, pulling back to look at Katherine as she sniffed. "Did you love him too?"

"No. I didn't know him very long. I just recorded us. As proof? That was what you wanted?"

"Yes. That was my revenge. To expose him."

"I understand."

"I was in so much pain. I had to go to the clinic all by myself. I pretended to my husband I was having a really bad period. Then I said I had the flu. I just stayed in bed, crying and pretending I was sick whenever anyone checked on me. I wanted to die. I prayed for it. All Brandon said was 'At least you didn't have to go to another state.' As if he hadn't fought for years to make it illegal here too. As if he would have *cared*."

That awful, broken laugh again. Her body had gone tight with anger. "Then he just cut me off as soon as it was done. He knew I couldn't blow up his life without blowing up my own. And I hated him *so much*. It was eating me alive, these little bleeding holes that felt like they went straight through me. Like there would eventually be so much missing I'd disintegrate."

Katherine knew exactly how that felt. The whole world moving on around you while you bled from a hundred wounds. "I've been through something similar. I get it."

"I needed to wipe that smug, bullshit look off his face for good."

Clearing her throat, Katherine pressed her. "For good?"

Nicole sat straight. "Not like that. Hell, death isn't even good revenge, is it? Now he'll never have to face anything at all. He got to go out on a high, partying with all his friends, and he's an innocent victim."

"So you truly didn't do it?"

She shook her head. She didn't even look concerned by the question. "It's been half a year since I saw him. Maggie knows that."

"And she believes you?"

"We've known each other a long time."

Katherine frowned at that. A long time? Maggie had only started teaching the classes two years before.

"I thought maybe it was his wife," Nicole continued, wrapping her arms around her knees to hold herself in a tight ball. "Maybe someone finally told her."

"Do you know her? Is it possible she found out about the . . ." She gestured toward Nicole's pelvis.

"He would never have told her. Or anyone. He had to protect his fake fucking persona, didn't he? Mr. Sanctity of Life? No, he wanted it all to go away. And me along with it."

Katherine didn't drop her questions. The wife still seemed like a prime possibility. Maybe she was stronger than she looked. "So you don't think she even suspected? You never met her? Never said anything? Or maybe you went to their house?"

"No. Not that he had some moral objection to sleeping with me in his wife's bed, but she's a stay-at-home mom, so his place wasn't available." She shot a hooded glance over her shoulder.

Katherine glanced back at Nicole's front door in surprise. "But here?"

She groaned and admitted, "Once. Just once. But it couldn't really have been any of us, could it? Maggie said he was strangled. Brandon was a pretty strong guy. He'd gained a little weight, but he was an athlete in college. It had to have been a man. Some angry boyfriend or husband."

Katherine was imagining anyone could do something like that with a rope or some other tool, but then her eyes flew wide and her gaze darted to Nicole's door. "A man like your husband?"

She jumped to her feet, lurching from the steps and pulling her body away from Katherine until she stood on the grass of her front lawn. "No. Don't even say that. Ed was working until ten, and then he came straight home."

"Are you sure?"

"Of course I'm sure! You can't just drop into my life and suggest that. He doesn't know anything about any of this. And if he did, he'd kick me out of the house and give me the silent treatment until the day I died. Ed's not violent, but he's undefeated at holding grudges."

"Still, you should verify that he was at work, shouldn't you?"

"Maggie already did that," she said, her mouth stiff and hands clenching.

"Maggie talked to your *husband*?"

"No, she checked on his shift and read his reports from that night to verify. He was actively working. It's documented."

For a moment Katherine didn't see it. She was lost in a blissful bubble of cluelessness, just floating there in confusion. Her gaze focused past Nicole to a spiderweb shimmering between the porch rail and a scraggly bush. A brown-and-yellow spider crouched at the outermost spiral of webbing, waiting.

Then her bubble popped with a wet little shock of fear. *His shift and his reports.* "Nicole," she finally whispered. "Are you saying your husband is a cop too?"

"Yes. That's how we all met."

The spider uncurled itself and disappeared into the bush. Katherine felt all her insides trembling as her body went cold. "You and Maggie and . . . ?"

"Yes. I was an administrative assistant for Denver PD. That's where I met Ed. And Maggie, of course. In fact, I helped her find her current house four years ago."

"I don't understand," Katherine murmured. "She's friends with your husband but you told her about *Brandon*?"

"It wasn't that simple. We're all friends, and Maggie and I got close over the years. She could see I was struggling. I was . . . I was spiraling, after everything. She invited me to try her class, and then she bought me a couple of drinks afterward. I don't know what happened. I broke down and told her. And God, I felt so much better getting it out, just like . . . I shouldn't be telling you any of this either, but like you said, I needed to talk about him to *someone*."

Katherine nodded dumbly.

"He was a big part of my life for months. He was *trauma*. And now he's just dead, and I don't know what to do with the pain. The memories."

Katherine nodded again, but she was barely listening. She'd thought Maggie was being cautious because of the system, but this seemed far deeper than that. She knew Nicole and her husband well. Hell, she might have organized the whole idea of their system around getting revenge on this one man just for Nicole. Or for Ed?

But why? *Why?*

"It wasn't him." Nicole bit out the words with such violence that Katherine blinked back to attention. "So don't ask again. Ed doesn't know anything."

"Sure," Katherine agreed. "Of course." It was the safest thing to say for now, but she didn't believe it for a second.

The front door opened, and Katherine whipped around to see little Aaron grinning. "I clogged the toilet," he said, nearly beaming with pride.

"Oh, great." Nicole sighed. "Okay, I'll be right in to fix it. Close the door."

"I want to come outside."

"It's almost time for dinner. We'll play outside after." When he hesitated, she narrowed her eyes until he slowly shut the door. Seeing him had changed something inside her. She no longer looked sad; she looked furious.

"You need to go," she snapped at Katherine. "And don't come back here, or I'll find you and come to your house too." She looked from Katherine's left eye to her right, and her face went hard. "I remember you now, Katherine. You shouldn't be too hard to track down."

"Are you threatening me?" Katherine asked in a voice gone reedy with alarm. All the mistakes she'd made rushed back at her. How was she supposed to stand up to a conspiracy of police officers?

"Of course I'm threatening you," Nicole said. "You're here accusing me or my husband of something awful. You're disrupting my life. How am I supposed to respond?"

She bit her tongue, afraid to provoke this woman more.

Nicole brushed past her, done with talking, it seemed. But she hesitated at the door before turning slowly back around. "You were supposed to make a tape, right? Post it online? Ruin his career and expose his bullshit?"

Katherine cleared her throat. "Yes."

"Did you do it?"

Blood rushed to her cheeks. "Yes. I made the videos, but I hadn't posted them yet."

Nicole rubbed her face hard with both hands, stretching the skin like she didn't even feel it. "God, I feel *jealous*. How disgusting is that? I feel jealous I wasn't the last woman he met. I wasn't even *that* for him. I was just a tissue he spilled himself into and threw away."

Katherine looked away with a wince. "I know we don't trust each other, but . . ." Stupid sympathy welled up in her again. "You wanted something too. However he used you, you were taking something for yourself. Don't rewrite that part of it with shame. We all *need*, don't we? We're all just so *alone*."

When the lock clicked, she looked up to see the closed door and Nicole gone. But her footsteps didn't move away. She was still standing there. Still listening.

Katherine had an impulse to bang on the door, ring the bell, scream for her to respond. Didn't they all need *more*? Or had Nicole finally found it, satisfied now that she'd almost lost everything?

But what the hell had Katherine found?

She walked to her car, feeling nothing, not the wind on her face, not the grass beneath her shoes, not even her own heart beating. She didn't yet feel the terror, but it loomed, a shadow over her that she couldn't bear to look toward. She didn't want the fear and chaos and danger she'd invited in. She needed to get back to normal . . . but she didn't want her old life either.

Did she?

Had sleeping with Brad been the mistake, or had the mistake been *all* of it? Wanting out, walking away, moving on, needing more? After all, either *she* was wrong or every other person in her life was wrong. Her mom, her daughter, her husband, her priest, her community. Had they known all along that there was nothing out here for her? That she couldn't handle more than what they'd already granted her?

She reached for her car door, her numb fingers fumbling, and then she heard the scuff of a shoe on asphalt, a crunch of sand left over from winter road crews, and she spun to see Maggie standing just beyond her bumper.

"It seems we have quite a bit to talk about, Katherine." When her eyes slid toward the front porch Katherine had just left, her heart sank.

"I guess we do," she whispered.

CHAPTER 20

Luz

"Hi, Mami!" Luz called as she let herself in the front door of the 1920s bungalow her mom shared with Leon. She usually knocked first just in case Leon had a date over, but she'd already been expected for dinner tonight. If Leon had a hot Monday-night date, that was his problem.

"In the kitchen," her mother yelled, as if Luz wasn't already on the way. Ballyhoo raced ahead of her, nails clicking exuberantly on the tile as he whined a little in excitement. His grandmother always gave him a treat before letting him out into the backyard to explore to his heart's content.

"Look at you, sitting so pretty while you wait," her mom was cooing when Luz joined them in the kitchen. "You are so good. Not like those rude dogs. Such a sweet boy."

Her mother wasn't a dog person, but she'd made an exception in her heart for Ballyhoo. Once a huge hunk of carnitas had been offered and enthusiastically gulped down, Ballyhoo trotted to the back and pushed the screen door open to slip outside.

"How's Sveta?" her mom asked immediately.

"She's good. She sends her love."

"Oh, I know. She texted me yesterday. I told her she's not eating enough. They don't have good food over there."

"I'm sure they have food that Russians like, Mom."

She wrinkled her nose in clear disagreement but let it go. "How are you doing all by yourself? Maybe you should move back home."

Luz rolled her eyes, but in all honesty, the thought had crossed her mind. She could save money, have company, and she'd barely have to think about feeding herself. It would be only for a year or two while she saved up to help get Sveta out of Russia. She'd even been searching for software engineering jobs in Europe, eyeing the ones that didn't require her to speak a new language.

But no, she didn't think she could bear to live at home for that long, no matter how much she loved her family.

After popping a slice of green pepper in her mouth, she washed her hands and began unloading the dishwasher.

"Hey, Sis. Here for the free food?" her brother asked as he cruised through the kitchen toward the back door, a pack of Marlboros in his hand.

"You and me both."

"Did Mom tell you?" he called through the screen as it banged closed behind him.

"Tell me what?"

"Oh, stop it," their mom said. "It was nothing."

"Nothing? Fucking feds showed up here."

Luz froze, a bowl half-raised to the cupboard. "The feds? What are you talking about?"

"Immigration," he said.

Luz spun around, the bowl clutched tight to her chest. "What? Why would they come here?"

Her mother tutted. "Just a mistake, mija. It was nothing. Leon, don't worry your sister."

"But what happened? I don't understand." The cold of the glass bowl was seeping into her fingers, her bones.

Her mother shook her head, turning her back on Luz to pour oil into a pan. "They had us mixed up with someone else. Said they'd heard there were undocumented people living here. Asked if I was renting rooms."

No. That wasn't true. It hadn't been a mix-up or an accident. Luz knew that as sure as she knew her own name. Tanner had done it again. She knew it, just as she'd known it with Sveta. He'd been sure to gloat to her after her detainment so Luz would know. *Hey, Luz, did I mention my brother works for ICE???*

Tanner had also known that Luz's father was deported when she was five, because she'd told him that her dad had died in a bus accident in Mexico two years after he'd been sent back. He must have assumed her mother lacked documentation as well. And that heartless, soulless monster had decided to try to take her away. Her *mother*.

My God, he'd tried to steal Luz's whole heart from her, first her girlfriend, and now her mom. The only two loves that kept her going in this world. Why? Why would anyone do that?

"Mamá, did they hurt you?"

She snorted dismissively. "It was fine. I told them to come in and look around, but all they'd find was some dirty laundry on my son's bedroom floor and my certificate of naturalization on the living-room wall."

"Psh," Leon disagreed from outside. "I did my laundry."

"I'm so sorry," Luz whispered.

"It was nothing, and it wasn't your fault."

"It was *him*. I know it was. He still wants to destroy me!"

Leon returned, dragging the smell of cigarettes with him. "He tried it. But that's all he did. Mom offered them lemonade and sent them on their way to bother someone else."

"I didn't have any lemonade, but I was going to make it real sour if they said yes."

She only realized her mom was pulling the bowl from her hands when it was gone and she was in her mother's arms. They were the same height, so Luz could lay her head down on her mother's shoulder and cry.

"Shhh. We're fine, baby. We're fine."

"I'm so sorry. I don't understand why he hates me so much."

"You intimidate him, that's why."

"Don't forget," Leon added, "it's also because he's a goddamn asshole."

It was true and it wasn't. Lots of people were assholes, but most people wouldn't do this. And he wasn't *intimidated* by her. He hated her because she'd taken something he considered his, and he wanted to punish her for it.

Did he know she'd helped get him fired from his new job, or did he just consider her responsible for the entire situation? She almost wanted to try telling him again. Almost wanted to go to his house and spray it on his lawn in herbicide, a secret message that would grow clearer and clearer as each day dawned. *It was Luz.*

"Come on now," her mom said, pressing one more kiss to her hair. "Let's make dinner. You'll feel better after you eat."

She probably would feel better, though her mother's cooking always tasted bittersweet these days, because Sveta wasn't there to join them.

Her mother had nurtured lots of hopes and dreams for Luz that included a wedding in the church and many grandbabies, but when she'd seen her love for Sveta, she'd set all those dreams aside for the sake of happiness.

Luz had been so proud of how easily she'd opened her mind to the relationship and opened her heart to Sveta, with only a few casual mentions of how "lesbians can have babies too" thrown in as a gentle reminder. Luz had done her best to redirect her mom's attention to

Leon, but he'd broken it off with his last long-term girlfriend a year before. There were no children on the horizon there either.

Despite the sadness, they all made dinner together, her mom's chatter filling in for Luz's silence. It was lovely and helped to patch a bit of the hole in her heart, but afterward, her goodbyes were still filled with relief.

She wanted to take her tender feelings back to her quiet condo, where she could snuggle with Ballyhoo and soothe herself with ice cream and a video chat with Sveta. As perfect an evening as she could get these days.

Maybe she'd take one of her drones to the park tonight, try out the low-light settings. Sveta called her "my pretty nerd" when she wanted to fly her drones, but she'd always gone with her, stretching out on a picnic blanket to laugh as Luz hovered the drone above her, recording them as if they were in a movie together.

Luz loved the distance and freedom of the images, the tiny people, the waving treetops. Life was easier up there and so much simpler to understand and map out. Her nerves smoothed out a little just thinking about it.

Ten minutes after she left her mom's, she was unlocking her door when a video call chimed on her phone. Sveta must have sensed that she needed her. "Ballyhoo, it's Sveta!" she said, holding up her phone. She was laughing at his excited bark when she answered.

Her laughter choked into a gasp when Sveta's face filled the screen.

"I'm okay" were her first words, though Luz could barely hear them over her cry of horror. Sveta's right eye was swollen shut, and there was an angry cut along her cheekbone.

"What happened?" Luz cried.

"I'm all right. A bruised rib and this—" She pointed to her face. "But the doctor says my eye is fine, so that's good news."

"Good news?" she screeched, horror seizing her throat and trying to squeeze off her breath. But she refused to collapse. "Your face!" She reached toward the screen as if she could touch her. "What happened?" she demanded again. "A car accident? What?"

Sveta's mouth twisted in a grimace "No. A customer beat me up last night after I told him we were out of his brand of cigarettes."

"Oh my God," Luz wailed. "Why? Why would he do that? Was he drunk? High?"

"I'm sure he was drunk, yes. And angry. He called me an ugly dog, told me I wasn't good for anything except getting him smokes, and if I couldn't do that . . ."

Luz opened her mouth, but no sound emerged.

Sveta's face softened, which only made her swollen eye look more injured, more grotesque. "I am fine, my moon."

"You're not fine! You're hurt!"

"I'll take a few days off, lie low for a while, and it will blow over."

"B-blow over? Isn't he in jail? What's being done?"

Her face was no longer soft. Her mouth tightened into a frighteningly grim smile. "He's a cop. So . . ."

Luz sobbed, not with tears but with enraged disbelief. "I'll kill him," she gasped out. "I will."

"I don't think you can reach him from there."

"No. I mean Tanner. He did this to you. He sent you away and put you in danger, and then he tried to . . ." She chopped her hand through the air, cutting off her own words. "I'll wire you a thousand dollars tonight. I want you to stay home. Stay out of that store. Give your aunt the money and tell her you're taking a month off."

"I can't take your—"

"Yes, you can. And there will be more where that came from. Make whatever inquiries you can. I'm getting you out of there, Sveta. Understand? I'll make this happen."

Sveta smiled sadly at her. "You look so fierce and strong."

"Ha. You might see me punch someone yet."

"I'll be fine. I'll stay home. My face will look better tomorrow."

That was a lie. The bruising would only get worse. But Luz would play along with it, tell her how much better she looked, try to reassure her. "I love you so much," she said.

When they hung up, Luz grabbed Ballyhoo's leash and met him at the door where he was already sitting, bright-eyed and butt wiggling. It was still early, and she was no longer in the mood for ice cream and sympathy. Instead she needed a walk to work off some of her rage. Just enough of it that she could think rationally. If she was being punished for taking something from Tanner, she was going to make damn sure she got payback for all her trouble.

CHAPTER 21

KATHERINE

"There's a high school around the corner," Maggie said. "Why don't you meet me in the back parking lot? It'll be deserted by this time. We can talk there."

Katherine was shaking her head before she realized it. She didn't want isolation with Maggie. Not until she knew what the hell was going on.

Maggie raised one eyebrow. "Oh, I see. You're scared of me now? That's very interesting."

"No! I just . . . I have no idea what's happening. Surely you can understand that. I'm scared. I don't know what to do."

"All right. Fine. Needless to say I can't be seen with you. But there's a park half a mile down Belleview. It should be full of families and evening joggers. I'll park in the shade for privacy. We can talk in my car. Does that work for you?"

Katherine nodded miserably. "Sure."

"Hey," Maggie said. "Don't worry. We'll figure it out."

Katherine wasn't the least bit reassured by that. Maggie's tone had pulled more toward authority than comfort. Still, there was nothing to be done except get in her car and follow her toward the park. She needed answers from her, even if she suspected she wouldn't like them.

This was awful. She couldn't believe Maggie had caught her at Nicole's house. Had she been coming to speak to Nicole? Or had she been following Katherine?

Did the police have her under surveillance?

As the questions screamed through, her stomach turned, so that was apparently her body's top response to stress these days. Katherine clenched her jaw and checked cross traffic before following Maggie across the next street to the block beyond it. They turned right, and she recognized the park when she spotted it. It was ringed by a jogging trail, and just as Maggie had predicted, it was busy with runners moving counterclockwise past parents with strollers.

She pulled in and parked near a huge fir tree, watching as Maggie took a spot beneath the tree that would be harder to see from the blacktop trail. Did Maggie's sedan have those doors she could lock to keep a suspect in? Should Katherine have insisted that they speak in her car instead?

In the end, she calmed herself with the thought that Maggie could hurt her anytime if she wanted to. It didn't matter what decisions Katherine made in this moment. If Maggie had come to her apartment, she would have let her in. And if Katherine wanted any information, she had no choice but to trust her.

But only a little. Before she got out, she tucked her phone under the steering wheel and surreptitiously typed out a quick message to Geneva. One of the women is a friend of Maggie's from the police dept. Nicole Park. Husband is a cop. Feels wrong.

She sent it, aware that she was trying to protect herself from her friend but refusing to think about it too long. After silencing her ringer, she tucked her phone into her purse to hide it, then forced herself to get out and walk to Maggie's car. The air practically crackled with tension when she got inside.

"So you're scared of *me*," Maggie snapped. "Is that what's going on here?"

"No!"

"You're scared of me when you're the person in this car who walked all of us into disaster?"

"I didn't do that. I didn't kill him. This isn't my fault."

"No, it *is* your fault. I can't believe you're even denying it. You went to see that man for no good reason at all, you splashed your face all over every camera in that hotel, and you walked past at least five of them on the way to your own damn car in the parking garage. Do you know what that means? Do you?"

Katherine shook her head, squeezing her purse tight to her chest, aware of a thousand things it could mean, and none of them were good.

"It means because you lied to me, because I wasn't on the lookout for you walking past all those cameras, my partner caught it, and he pulled up your license plate before I even knew he was looking into it. My job is at risk because you lied to me. I'm trying to help you with a problem, and now my entire career is on the line."

"My life is on the line!" she shot back. "Your partner wants to arrest me!"

"He doesn't want to arrest you yet, but that's thanks to my actions, not *yours*. What the hell are you doing, Katherine? Why are you showing up everywhere you shouldn't be? Maybe you *did* kill him. How can I believe anything you say?"

Katherine pressed a hand to her face, tamping down her fear until the guilt rose through like greasy stains of ash. Regardless of whether Maggie knew Nicole or not, Katherine had violated the trust in this relationship. She'd lied and screwed up, and maybe she'd been projecting her guilt onto Maggie because she couldn't handle blaming herself. Maybe this really was all her fault.

"I'm sorry," she said. "I wasn't thinking. I wasn't following the rules."

"So what the hell were you doing?"

"I don't know! I got caught up in it. I was so full of triumph and the joy of . . . of *transgression*. The power of it after all these years. I lost control."

Maggie blew out a hard breath. "So tell me the truth. The real truth this time."

Katherine recognized that Maggie could be a threat to her, a villain. But she couldn't quite believe it. Not after the ways she'd nurtured her, guiding Katherine toward the strength to finally leave Peter. And if she was a villain . . . Katherine couldn't reveal what she knew about Nicole and her husband and their friendship. So she nodded and told only most of the truth.

"I recorded him just as we discussed. Twice. And then he asked me to meet him. That's what happened. I went to that hotel and saw him that one time, and then I left. One stupid thing. I thought it couldn't hurt anything because no one would ever know."

"Christ, you really hung me out to dry. Do you know how blindsided I was when Koval said he had a name and address and it was *you*? We were already in the car. I couldn't stop anything, and I could barely warn you. I just had to hope you didn't throw me under the bus or confess or some other damn disaster."

"I'm so sorry."

"Oh yeah? You're so sorry that you've spent your time since tracking down Nicole?"

Regret flashed through her in a fiery wave. "I'm sorry. I thought I was being set up."

"By me?"

"I didn't know! That's why I went to Nicole's. I thought it could have been her."

"Why? How did you connect this to her?"

She swallowed hard, walking a tightrope of what she should tell and what she shouldn't. "She looked so upset she caught my attention.

It was that night you missed class, and you said I had to go to keep things normal, and she definitely looked like she was forced to be there too. She was really upset and crying, and that was just too much of a coincidence. I assumed she had to be involved one way or another."

She could feel Maggie staring at her for a long, long time, but the only sound in the car was Katherine's pulse, her panic, her breath. This woman—her friend or her enemy?—had a gaze like an x-ray, stripping Katherine down to her bare white bones. What could she see? And how would she interpret it?

When she couldn't take Maggie's silence a moment longer, she blurted out, "I know I shouldn't have tracked her down. I was desperate. I'm scared, Maggie."

Maggie didn't reach out to comfort her, and Katherine blinked back tears as loneliness swept over her.

"And what did you tell her?" she asked coldly instead.

"I asked if she'd murdered Brandon."

Both Maggie's eyebrows flew up at that. "Wow, just like that? And?"

"She said she hasn't seen him in months."

"Did you tell her you'd now dragged her into a murder investigation by creating an interaction between her and the prime suspect?"

Katherine's chin trembled. So did her heart. "Me? I'm the prime suspect?"

Maggie leaned forward, her face drawing within inches before Katherine cowered back. Her head hit the side window with a dull thud.

"Of course you're the prime suspect. But I'm trying to save your ass despite that you are fighting me every inch of the way. Are you going to calm down and act right or not? Because I need to know. I need to be sure. Will you accept the help I'm trying to offer you?"

Katherine nodded, her chin shaking so hard that her teeth chattered. A new suspicion shook itself free of the chaos. "How did you get assigned to his case?"

Maggie drew back, her gaze so intent on Katherine that she could feel it like a touch. The silence dragged on until Katherine thought she meant to ignore the question.

For their entire friendship, she had struggled to picture Maggie at her job. She was tough in boxing class, but she was intensely kind, meeting everyone's gaze with encouragement or sympathy or whatever they needed. But now . . . now Katherine could see the other side. The hard bedrock underneath that withstood liars and violence every day.

Still, when she spoke again, her tone had turned gentle. "I heard his name when another detective caught the case as a possible suicide."

Katherine snapped up straight. "A suicide? You didn't say that. So maybe he just killed himself? Is that what 'suspicious' means?"

"It looked that way at first glance, but only at first glance. We've pretty much ruled that out."

"How? Why?"

"Because when a man strangles himself sitting on the ground with his own tie knotted around a doorknob, he'd normally be able to stop that anytime he wanted instead of clawing at it so desperately he tears up his own throat."

A squeak escaped her at the image of Brad digging at his own skin to try to loosen the fabric cutting off his life.

"So yes, the patrol officers thought he could have been playing a solo sex game that went wrong. It was obviously meant to look that way. The detective was complaining about dealing with another case that would waste his time and manly skills, so I volunteered to grab it for him. I was trying to help you and every other woman in this group."

Katherine swallowed hard and nodded.

"Then you screwed it up by lying to me. This is all worse now. Did you delete everything?"

"Yes."

"I'd never have told you to do that if I'd known you'd been there. You look more guilty because of that. You've really screwed us all, Katherine."

She winced. "I'm so sorry."

"Your bullshit ends this second. You do everything I tell you to from now on. Do you understand?"

"Yes."

"Do *not* contact me. I'll check in with you if I need any information, but you don't get to reach out. And for God's sake, don't make contact with any other women. Am I clear on that? Because that part is very important, which you've known from the start."

"I get it. I'm sorry." A confession hovered on her tongue. That she'd spoken to Geneva too. That she'd called her and texted, leaving yet more clues in the ether. But she couldn't make herself say it. She couldn't make herself trust anymore.

"Come to class," Maggie snapped. "Don't change any routines. And if my partner gets in touch, make every excuse in the world not to speak to him until I can tell you exactly what's happening. Is all of that crystal clear?"

When Katherine nodded, Maggie only stared again. She stared until Katherine swallowed against the desert of her throat and croaked out, "Yes." That seemed to satisfy her.

Her body relaxed a little as if she were as limply tired as Katherine felt. "You have to let me help you," she said. "We're strong together. You know that."

"I do."

"All right. I'll be in touch."

"Wait." Katherine reached toward Maggie's arm as she pushed the car's ignition. She didn't touch her, though. She didn't dare. "Do you believe me? That I didn't do this? Please tell me you believe me."

Maggie turned back toward her, meeting her gaze and holding it for an intense eternity. Her face conveyed so many things. Strength, love, anger, hardness, empathy. Katherine tried to send back honesty and earnestness. If Maggie doubted her, she wouldn't fight for her, wouldn't find the real killer.

Finally, Maggie's mouth relaxed into a sad smile. "Of course I believe you. I know who you are, Katherine. You're not a murderer."

"Thank you."

"We stay strong together," Maggie said in a clear and careful voice. "And we will make this system work for us. I'll fix it."

Those were exactly the reassuring words she'd wanted to hear. But when Katherine got out and closed the door behind her, she didn't feel reassured, because it sounded less like Maggie believed her and more that Maggie was determined to make her own plan work. But what did that mean for Katherine?

Thankfully Maggie pulled out and left her alone, because she didn't think she could drive so soon after that.

Maggie's strength had been her backbone for quite a few months. She'd been immovably determined that Katherine was brave enough to get what she wanted. To fulfill her darkest wishes that others would see her husband as he truly was. Maggie's belief had buoyed Katherine's self-esteem and provided a scaffold for her bravery, allowing Katherine to slowly build it up without fearing a dangerous tumble.

The first time Maggie had proposed that they grab coffee sometime, Katherine had been so flattered she'd floated through her day. Maggie was a force of nature, and everyone needed the beauty of that kind of nature in their lives.

But that strength was an entirely different thing when it was pointed right at Katherine. She was still shaking, sick with regret that she'd disappointed Maggie, and equally sick with the swelling fear that her friend wasn't actually on her side.

Leaning against her car, she watched people jog by, wishing she could get back to that time in her life when she could simply relax with a nice run and think things through. But that wouldn't work anymore.

The things she'd done couldn't be solved with a few moments of calm. One way or another, she'd screwed up everything and pulled other people along with her.

When her phone vibrated, she squeezed her eyes shut, terrified to see what part of her life was cracking apart now. After sending up a quick prayer, she dug out her phone, then frowned at a name she wasn't expecting to see. It was her sister Becca. I talked to Mom. Want to chat?

Did she? She had no idea. Did Becca just want to gloat? It was possible but maybe not probable. She might crow to herself or even her friends, but her sister wasn't cruel enough to rub it directly into Katherine's face.

And honestly, she felt so incredibly alone. Her sister was shining a tiny light into that darkness. That smothering loneliness wasn't because she'd left Peter. She'd felt that way for years.

Who could she talk to when everyone she knew believed divorce was a sin and her husband was a saint? She had no one, and she'd put herself in that place voluntarily by embracing that world.

She looked around at the people running and chatting and playing with kids. She didn't want to go back home to her apartment and worry that her new life would end before it even started. So she walked to a bench and texted back. Sure. Call me?

The bench was hot from the sun, and Katherine melted into it as she set down her bag and waited. The scent of spring flowers swept by in elusive wisps of breeze. Closing her eyes, she felt as if she'd floated back in time to all those years sitting in parks while Charlotte played with other children.

It had been a wound then, the need to leave their home to see other kids. She'd wanted her own gang of running, laughing siblings to fill Charlotte's days. Or maybe she'd never wanted that as much as she'd thought. Maybe it had been a lie she'd told herself, a lie that had poisoned her and turned her body against all those pregnancies.

She didn't know anymore. Couldn't separate her own heart from her desperation to be what others demanded. But the loss had been real, more real to her than to Peter and her mom and their platitudes about finding strength in God and his plan. Peter had lost something he'd *wanted*. She'd lost a part of her.

By the third miscarriage everyone had stopped murmuring their bullshit anyway, and they'd started looking at her as the problem. God might work in mysterious ways, but a woman was probably still to blame. Was she too skinny, too fat, too active, or not active enough? Was she eating too much of the wrong things or not enough of the right things? Was she too stressed and uptight or simply not trying hard enough?

When her phone rang it yanked her back to the park. Disoriented, she looked toward the playground with a frown, momentarily sure she'd lost track of Charlotte.

But no. She'd lost track of a lot recently, but not her daughter.

"Hi," she said stiffly when she answered.

"Hey, Katherine," her sister said. "How are you doing?" Her voice was eerily like their mother's, but her words were so rarely anything their mom would say that the contrast sometimes distracted Katherine. Or it used to. When had they last spoken on the phone? Three years ago? Five?

"I'm good," she said automatically.

"Are you sure? Because from what Mom told me, it sounds like you've been through a lot."

"Yeah. I'm good. Or not really. I'm tired."

"But you moved out, right? Just moving is enough to exhaust anyone, and shit, you're dealing with trauma too."

Trauma. She'd been thinking so much about miscarriage that at first she thought Becca meant that. But no, she meant the trauma of discovering Peter cheating. "I . . . I've known for a long time." And then she admitted the real truth. "Honestly, it was a relief to have it out in the open. I could finally leave."

Tensing, she braced herself for the response she knew was coming from her older sister. *You could have left anytime you wanted. You were a participant, not a victim.* But instead, Becca only said, "I'm really sorry."

Katherine let go of the breath she'd been holding. "I can't imagine what you've heard from Mom."

"Believe me, I took it all with a huge barrel of salt. Want to tell me what really happened?"

So she did, starting with the party, and the apartment, and the divorce lawyer. But then she made a partial confession. "I've been saving for a while. For a few years. I was waiting for . . . I don't know. I was waiting for there to be a real reason. And Charlotte was almost done with high school."

"I had no idea."

"Why would you? We never talk."

"Well," her sister said carefully, "we haven't agreed on much in the last thirty years."

"True. Or maybe it's not true. I have no idea anymore. I don't know what was real and what was just Mom and Peter. How am I supposed to know who I really am when I let them take up all that space inside me for so long? And I did *let* them. I guess that was the easiest thing to do. For almost my entire life, I just let them."

"I can see how that happened. It's hard to break free of inertia."

"Well, you did it. And so did Vivian. You were both stronger than I was."

She could practically hear her sister shrug through the phone. "We were different. We didn't start with inertia. We started with flight. You got stuck in gravity, but we were shot straight out of orbit."

"Does Viv know?"

"She does."

She grimaced, imagining her sisters talking shit about her, laughing at the disintegration of her screwed-up Catholic marriage. "I haven't heard from her."

"I doubt you will. She doesn't like you very much."

Katherine coughed in shock. "Wow. Really? Thanks a lot for just saying it."

Her sister sighed. "Come on. You always sided with Mom. Every time. What did you expect?"

"Jesus, Becca, she was smoking pot, skipping school, and ignoring every curfew. She deliberately provoked Mom constantly. She picked fights every day, and it made my life hell too. There wasn't a moment of peace in that house until Vivian left."

"Did you ever think what it was like for her? Living with a mother who viewed her as the enemy? Telling her she was foul and bad and *wrong*? Can you imagine ever treating your daughter the way Mom treated Viv?"

Katherine had been ready to fight, her shoulders rising in defense against the attack. But now her hand dropped, her mouth fell open. She'd been thinking of Vivian as the bad sister for so long that Becca's words didn't quite penetrate. They were right there, hovering, but Katherine could only *see* them. Could only reach out toward them without quite catching hold.

"I'm sorry," Becca said on a sigh. "I didn't mean to start a fight. I was actually calling to comfort you. Hell of a job I'm doing, huh?"

Katherine managed to close her mouth and swallow down some of her shock. "Yeah."

"How's Charlotte doing with all of this?"

"Um. I guess she seems okay? She's upset, obviously. But she'll be home for spring break, so we'll spend some time together. I thought it would be easier once she was at college and not in the house. But maybe I was wrong?"

"It would be hard no matter when. But you can't sacrifice your happiness for a person who's busy striking out on their own. You've sacrificed enough from what I can tell. How long was it going on?"

"The whole time," she whispered.

"My God, Katherine! You never said anything!"

"If I had, you would have just told me to leave. I could hear it in my head, so I didn't need to hear it from you. I did tell Mom, and she told me to stop being such a bitch to Peter all the time. Ha!"

Becca growled out a curse.

"In the middle of those two options, leaving or staying, it was just me in purgatory. I couldn't figure out what the *right* thing was, and I'd always tried to choose the right thing. But there was no best option, so I just . . . stayed."

"Shit. I'm sorry. I don't really know what to say except that I'm sorry."

"There's nothing to be said. Life is hard. Harder than that for most people. I'm lucky, really, if that's the hardest choice I ever have to make."

"Okay, how about this? How about you come visit me for a week or two? I'm working, so you'd have the place to yourself during the day. There's a trailhead right outside my door. We could get drunk on the weekend. Have a dinner party. Go for walks. Maybe actually get to know one another."

She didn't say no right off the bat. "Without Mom between us," she murmured.

"Exactly."

It was tempting. More than tempting. It seemed like it might be a good idea. Koval had asked her not to leave town, but that was hardly a legal restriction. She could escape to Oregon and get off their radar, let them concentrate on someone who might have actually killed Brandon.

A twig snapped behind her. Gasping, Katherine twisted around to see who it was, but no one was there. No one she could see, anyway.

The bench sat in front of a dense copse of pine trees and bushes, but something had made that noise. She stood up to face the trees.

"Hey, you okay?" her sister asked.

"Yes," she answered, though goose bumps exploded across her skin at the feeling she was being watched. "I'd better go. Give me a few days to think about a trip?"

"Absolutely. Take your time. I've got no plans until the end of the semester."

She hung up, then stared for a long time into the dark-green shadows, thinking of the house she'd just left. Of Nicole. Of her husband.

Could one of them have followed her here? Or was it just an animal in the scrub? "Hello?" she whispered. No one responded.

Just an animal, then. A deer hiding out until dark. A raccoon. Or maybe a killer.

On that note, Katherine grabbed her purse and set off toward the lot. Her pulse ratcheted higher with each step until she was finally locked inside her car and facing the park again. No one had followed her. It wasn't a killer. She was fine. Just the main suspect in a murder investigation.

Great. No big deal.

After pulling out she drove around the one-way loop toward the park's exit, and when she glanced toward the bench where she'd been sitting, she saw a figure. Not a deer or a raccoon, but what looked to be a person, carefully stepping out of the trees. For a moment she second-guessed herself and thought it was just the long angle of an evening shadow, but it was definitely a person, half their body still shielded by fir branches. They wore a knit cap pulled low beneath the hood of a sweatshirt and the kind of face mask a lot of people still wore as protection.

She couldn't make out age or race or even size. It could've been anyone. It could've been Nicole's husband if he'd followed her from his house or if Maggie had told him she was there. Hell, it could have been Nicole herself.

When Katherine stopped to let a group of pedestrians by, one of them was wearing a face mask too, because people still wore them everywhere, even outside. It wasn't sinister.

Shaking her head in an attempt to deny her own panic, Katherine raced to the exit and pulled out. The park was full of normal people. That person could have been chasing a dog or looking for a lost Frisbee. Or maybe they were just a regular old creep of the variety she used to worry about at parks when her daughter was young.

She drove blindly, just wanting to get away. She couldn't trust Nicole about her husband. She couldn't trust Maggie. She was truly all alone in this.

She drove until her body finally calmed and her brain stopped its panic. And when she looked around, she realized she was driving home. Not to her new place but the house she'd shared with her family. Just muscle memory, or was it something deeper? A sign? A wish?

Feeling like a strange tourist, she turned into her neighborhood and wound through the streets of older ranch homes that had been built before land got expensive in Denver. She hadn't been gone long enough for anything to have changed, but she still felt like an interloper as she reached her street and stopped at the curb outside her house.

The sight of her mom's hatchback in the driveway brought a bitter laugh to her lips. Peter was probably home from work by now and being coddled and comforted after tripping over his own dick in public. A yearning rose up in her, so huge and unmanageable that she had no idea what the yearning was for. Her house? Her husband? Or a mother who could love her without countering the goodness with punishment? It hurt so much she had to press her palm hard to her chest to hold it in.

As she watched, a light blinked on in the dining room. A vague shadow moved beyond the wooden blinds. If she walked right up and went inside and announced that she'd come home, would she be greeted with relief or contempt?

"Why not both?" she muttered.

She didn't want to go in. Not really. But she harbored a terrible fear that if Charlotte were there as well, Katherine would be pulled in like a satellite finally losing its hold on the orbit. She'd descend, punished by gravity, yanked down to her destruction, but she'd be where she was meant to be, shattered yet obedient.

Jesus, the drama. Maybe she was getting her period. Her emotions were certainly huge and scattered.

A sudden blare tore her from her overwrought thoughts, and Katherine whipped toward the horn, bracing herself for a crash. What she found was much worse than an out-of-control vehicle. It was her husband glaring at her from the car he'd pulled right beside hers.

"Shit," she said, and he frowned harder as if he'd read her lips. She grimaced in relief when he pulled past and drove up to the garage door that was opening to welcome him in.

She desperately wanted to race away, but she had a bit too much pride for that. So she sat and waited as he emerged from the garage and cut across the lawn to approach her car. "Shit," she said more clearly this time, staring right at him. When he reached her window, she made him stand there for a few long heartbeats until he rolled his eyes and tapped.

She left her car running as a signal that she wasn't staying long but rolled the window down three-quarters of the way. There was no mistaking the pungent scent of whisky on the breeze that slid past Peter's body and into her car. He'd never been a drinker, but apparently her mother hadn't been lying. His short hair stuck up in odd angles, and he wore jeans and an ancient long-sleeved T-shirt that he normally wore to bed.

For one impossible moment, she wondered if he really did love her and miss her. Maybe he'd also realized some hard truths since she'd left him. Maybe he'd realized how good he had it with her.

Then he spoke. "Did you finally decide to come running home?"

Wow. Okay. He definitely wasn't dissolving with regret. "No," she snapped back like the clap of a door shutting.

"Really? That's funny. I thought maybe when the police caught up to you, you'd come to your senses."

All the air seemed to flow right back out the open window, sucking her breath with it. She couldn't protest, couldn't lie or even question. She just stared up at his haggard, ugly expression in utter shock.

He cocked his head, staring her down with a bloodshot gaze.

"W-what . . . ?" she stammered. "What are you talking about?"

He rolled his eyes again, contempt twisting his mouth into a crooked sneer. "A detective came here looking for you, Katherine. I sent him to your new place. Of course I tried to follow up with a call, but you've blocked me. So are you ready to tell me what you did?"

"Nothing!"

"Seems unlikely. I guess I'll have to tell your mother about it and see if she can get it out of you."

"No! I . . . I just witnessed a crime. He wanted a statement. That's all. He interviewed me and then left."

He huffed and shook his head. "You're lying. It's all over your face. What have you been up to out there in the big city all by yourself?"

"I have no idea what you're talking about." Had Koval told him something? Dropped any hints about what he'd seen on surveillance? Her gut rolled in horror of Peter hearing anything about it. It felt like a violation that he might know anything intimate about her now.

"He was very interested in how erratic you've been lately."

When her car jerked forward, she realized she'd never put it in park. She pressed her foot hard to the brake but couldn't help but revel in the way he jumped back in terror that she might run him over.

"What did you say to him?" she demanded.

"I told him the truth. That you've been acting bizarrely for at least two weeks. That you haven't been yourself at all and you'd abruptly moved out and demanded a divorce."

"Why would you do that?"

He shrugged. "Was I wrong? I also let him know that you definitely hadn't been here, so I couldn't be any kind of alibi if you needed one."

"You nasty bastard," she hissed.

"I just hope to God you clean up whatever mess you've made before our daughter gets here."

"Everything's fine," she said stiffly.

"Maybe she should just stay here," he said. "This is her home, after all. Your place is some random flophouse, and your life doesn't sound like a safe space."

"Christ," she cursed, reaching for the window switch to close him out.

He grabbed the glass and held it until she let off the controls, afraid the whirring strain of the motor would give out completely. "Okay, maybe I shouldn't have said that," he conceded. "Why don't you tell me why you came by?"

Was he actually trying for a gentler tone now? What a dick. As if she'd forget the meanness he'd displayed mere seconds ago and show him her honest vulnerability. "I was nearby, and I drove this way on autopilot. That's all."

"And then you sat here staring at the house like you wanted to come in?"

"I didn't," she lied. "I was reflecting on all the crap I'd left behind."

His chin tipped up so he could stare at the clouds for a moment before he shook his head and looked at her again. Now his face seemed all weariness instead of anger.

He softened his tone and tried again, the old manipulation clear in his voice. "Your mom is making dinner. Why don't you come on in? I'm worried about you. That detective seemed serious, you refuse to answer my calls, and clearly your behavior has been completely off these days. What's really going on, Katherine?"

"Nothing."

"Just come in, and we can talk. If there's something wrong . . . I'm here for you."

"Here for me?" she snapped. "When have you ever been here for me? Let go of the window. I'm leaving."

"You'll be back." He frowned with fake concern and tried that same soft tone again. "And I'll be here when you're ready."

"Of course you'll be here. You have a nice house and a free maid."

He shrugged, unashamed.

No, she hadn't been wrong to leave. She hadn't taken anything for granted. A few days away had softened her memories of living here, but they were back in vivid color now. She stared up at his smug face, the arrogant set of his shoulders. "I got an IUD," she said.

"What?" His eyes were still distant and unconcerned.

"After the last miscarriage twelve years ago. I got an IUD. That's why I never got pregnant again."

She could see the moment it hit him, the moment his smugness twisted into betrayal. Good. Let him feel betrayed for once. "What?" he repeated stupidly. She waited, letting it sink all the way in, watching until pain gripped his features. "All those years," he breathed.

"Yes. All those years. Do you remember what you said to me, twelve years ago when we were in the hospital trying to save something that couldn't be saved?"

He stared, silent.

"No, of course you don't. I was on the toilet in my hospital bathroom, bleeding and weeping. I was in so much pain, so sick, that I threw up, and you had to call a nurse to clean the vomit off me while I crouched over the toilet like an animal."

His face scrunched up at the memory, lips contorting.

"And what you said to me, your sick wife . . . what you said in that terrible moment was 'You're disgusting.'" She breathed hard past clenched teeth before she could make herself speak again. "You probably thought I didn't hear you, throwing out such a nasty thing, but I did. I was a wounded animal, still pushing out the last of my child, and you had no sympathy at all. All you felt was disgust. Disgust that I couldn't give you what you wanted."

"I didn't say that," he denied, then immediately moved on. "I was grieving too. *I* was suffering too."

"Sure. But I've decided I don't want a husband who kicks his sick wife because he's in pain. I haven't wanted you at all since then. Not once. And I decided to never, ever give you even a chance for another child."

She lifted her foot from the brake and smashed it to the accelerator to squeal away. As she drove off through the painfully familiar streets of her neighborhood, she knew she had to do everything in her power to make this new life work. No matter what was in her way. Or who.

CHAPTER 22

GENEVA

Geneva didn't know what to do with her tension. That woman had texted her to say more cops were involved than Maggie, and then she hadn't responded to Geneva's exclamation-filled follow-up. Worse yet, she'd already been on her way to meet Omi when the text had arrived, and she couldn't just wait around for an answer.

And my God, she was just exhausted. Weak and achy and ready-to-weep exhausted. She'd spent too many hours in bed over the past months, hiding from the world, and now she desperately wanted to curl up and recover from climbing out of her hole.

The idea of returning to school tomorrow overwhelmed her, as did the constant beat of worry over Frank and the system, but if she could just get a good ten hours of sleep, she'd recover a bit. Maybe twelve hours. Her body sang with weariness.

But her day was almost over. Surely she could handle an early drink with a woman she knew well. It felt like it should be heaven. But then she'd gotten that damn text.

Crap. There was nothing for it. She checked her texts again, took a deep breath, and promised her body it could sleep in a couple of hours at most. Maybe she'd even have dinner after all.

When she walked in and spotted Omi seated at a tiny table at the window, her friend barely managed a halfhearted smile in response to Geneva's wave. Wow. Things weren't good for Omi either.

Geneva braced herself. She could do this. Omi had done her best to comfort Geneva through her crisis. Geneva could do the same for her, even if it took the last little bits of her energy.

Brightening her smile, she leaned in for a tight hug before taking her seat.

"You're dressed up," Omi said, her enviably thick eyebrows drawing together.

"I'm teaching again."

Those seemed to be the magic words that opened up Omi's stern face and even set her shoulders back as if she'd just avoided an attack. Her brown eyes went wide with wonder. With her bleached hair in her favorite hairstyle of high pigtails, she looked the teenager she'd been when they'd met in school. "Really? You got your job back? That's so great!"

Geneva laughed. "No, I definitely did not get that job back, but I got a long-term sub position at a school in Longmont where Jess works. Only half days, but it's something. It's helping pull me out of my darkest days, I think."

"Really?"

"Probably?" Geneva responded with a laugh. "I'm just really worn out. I forgot how much effort it takes to be on for the kids."

Her friend nodded, the trouble slowly leaching back in to cloud her face. Omi had always been a bit all over the place, emotions building and rolling through like summer storms. Her erratic moods were one of the reasons they'd only dated on and off through college.

At first Geneva had liked the way her own steadiness helped even out Omi, but then she'd realized it didn't work that way. She was absorbing Omi's turmoil, helping Omi but hurting herself. Still, they'd stayed friends all these years and scratched that old itch on occasion. A perfect relationship as far as Geneva was concerned. A sweet, safe touchstone.

"How are you doing?" Geneva asked, reaching out to squeeze her hand. She looked thinner. Not exactly skinny, but definitely not her normal chubby self.

"Okay, I guess. I have a new therapist."

"Well, that's fun!" Geneva joked, and Omi smiled briefly, a twisted grimace.

A server brought a cocktail Omi had apparently ordered when she was seated; then he poured water as they looked at their menus, though the bulk of the choices were listed on a chalkboard. This place based their meals on seasonal offerings, but she had no idea what that might mean when their Rocky Mountain spring had barely started. When she glanced over the cocktail menu, she saw that it was longer than the list of food, and took that as a helpful hint. Maybe just a drink, after all.

"What did you get?" she asked, glancing up to find that Omi's martini glass was already nearly empty.

"A rosewater splash."

"Well, damn, if it's that good, I'll have one too."

"Another one for you?" the server asked Omi, then hurried off to make their drinks himself after she nodded emphatically. Omi liked to Uber everywhere, so Geneva just grinned at her clear attempt to get very drunk on a weekday evening.

"Rough day?" Geneva asked.

"Kind of."

"Are you okay?" She reached for Omi's hand again, and her friend curled her fingers tight and squeezed back. She shook her head, then looked up with relief when the server reappeared with the drinks.

Geneva realized Omi's eyes had filled with tears only when the man very gently said, "I'll give you a little time with the menus," and moved gracefully away.

"Hey," Geneva cooed. "What's going on? You want to tell me about it?"

"I really don't," she answered with a dry chuckle.

"Oh? Why not?"

She guessed this was the part where Omi told her she was in a serious relationship and had to cut off contact. A jealous girlfriend, maybe. Her heart fell a little despite that she'd isolated herself for months. The thought that Omi was always there had been a comfort.

Bracing herself, Geneva sipped her own drink while Omi reached for her second. The cool pink taste soothed her a little, but only a little. Something sad was about to happen, and all her senses tingled a warning.

Omi nodded. "All right. Yeah. So I need to tell you something important. I'm sorry." She took a deep breath. "I was in a bad place and acting out, but that isn't an excuse. There is no excuse."

The hair rose on Geneva's arms. "Okay?" she prompted reluctantly. She didn't think it was fair to present someone with bad news and then make them ask for it, but she played along. "What is it?"

Omi folded her hands together, her fingers twisting tightly, the cuticles angry and red against her unpolished nails. "That night. On your birthday. With Frank."

Geneva squinted, waiting for more and refusing to ask again.

"You were drunk, we were both drunk, and you said you loved me."

"All right."

"And I know you've said it before, it just hit me really hard for some reason."

"I do love you, Omi. That didn't end just because we aren't in a relationship."

"I know. I get that. I was in a weird place, like I said. I just thought . . . I don't know. I thought you meant something different, and I built it all up in my head. I came by to talk a couple of nights later, and I was upset you were with that Frank guy again. But then you broke it off with him, and you came to Moab with me for the weekend. Remember?"

"Of course I remember."

"I just . . . I thought we were getting back together. In Moab. You know?"

Geneva gasped as regret clenched a tight hand around her heart. She'd hurt her friend and she hadn't even realized. "Oh no. Omi, I'm sorry. I honestly didn't know. I swear I didn't. I would never have . . ."

Omi laughed, tears in her eyes again. "Please don't apologize. Please. Because it was me, Gennie."

"What was you?"

"I stole the video."

Geneva knew exactly what she was hearing. She knew exactly what it meant. But she shook her head, her mind refusing to process it, shoving it away hard. "No," she murmured. "No."

"It's true."

"No, it's not true." She didn't want it to be true, so it couldn't be. She rejected it completely.

"I'm so sorry. I just . . . I had this weird fantasy in my mind that you'd need me, and I'd be there to take care of you, and then you'd realize how good we were together."

An ocean filled her, an impossible depth of cold and twisting currents. It was all Geneva could feel. The deep, dark pressure of a mile of water pressing down inside her. "You wanted me to *need* you?"

Omi offered a jerky nod.

"You ruined me because you wanted me to *need you*?"

Omi seemed to have gotten control of her tears. Her face looked stiff with discomfort, but when she wiped her cheeks, they stayed dry. She even managed to meet Geneva's gaze. "I know it's terrible."

"You sent it to my *school!* The parents saw it. My . . . my whole family knows!"

"I'm so sorry, Gennie. Clearly, I was out of control. I can't even explain it to myself. I can't re-create my thought process now, because it didn't make any sense."

The ocean inside her churned, chilling every cell of her body as a tidal wave rose up. "You ruined my life. Omi. I'll never . . . Why did you even tell me? I didn't want to know this!"

"I'm sorry. I don't expect you to forgive me. I'm not asking for anything. I just needed to tell you. I'm in therapy twice a week now, and we're making progress, but I couldn't get better without telling you the truth. I had to."

"For you? So *you* could get better?"

"Yes. But you deserved the truth too."

"I didn't ask for it! How am I supposed to process this? How can I trust anyone ever again?" Her heart broke open, spilling blood into the cold tide of her chest. "I loved you, Omi. And you *knew* me. That's the worst part."

Pain stabbed through her as the wounds began to reveal themselves. It was all so much worse than she'd thought it was. "Frank didn't matter. There was only so much some random hookup could hurt me. He was only—" She snapped her mouth closed as her horror doubled and split. "Oh no."

"I'm sorry. I felt like I was drowning, and I latched on to you and pulled you down with me. I can't even explain—"

Geneva surged to her feet, her chair screeching across the painted cement floor. She felt the eyes of the other diners on her and saw their server take a step toward her with a worried frown.

"I have to go," she panted.

"Please—"

"I have to go fix something that you broke. You just . . ." The day after she'd lost her job came flooding back. Omi comforting her. Omi sleeping on her couch to make sure she was okay. Omi holding her while she cried. "I apologized to *you*. You let me weep over how sorry

I was about recording the video. You let me feel like shit for dragging you into it."

Omi's face twisted with a silent sob. "I know."

"My God, if I hadn't pushed you away, would you still be there with me? Pretending? Lying?"

She shook her head, her familiar pigtails bouncing, but Geneva was already turning away, giving Omi her back. "Leave him a good tip," she snapped, and then she was rushing out of the restaurant, racing for her car so she could cry and scream in peace.

Good Lord, Frank had been telling the truth. All his denials had been real. She'd cursed him and sicced the police on him, and then . . . Jesus . . . then she'd set him up to be arrested and thrown in prison.

"Oh shit, oh shit," she chanted past her streaming tears as she slammed her car door. She dragged a sleeve over her wet face and snotty nose, but the tears didn't stop, and then she was bent over the steering wheel and sobbing.

She didn't have time for this new grief, this new horror. When it wouldn't let up, she rocked in her seat, trying to get it all out and control it at the same time.

She had to stop what had been set in motion . . . unless it was already too late. She'd texted Maggie four or five times, and she'd kept checking Frank's Instagram to make sure he was still posting. If he'd been arrested or even pulled over, he wouldn't have stayed quiet about that. It wasn't in his nature.

She drew in a shuddering breath, then managed another. After wiping her face one more time, she opened her phone to check on him again, then immediately opened her contacts and called Maggie. The line rang only once before she heard a message say, "This number is unavailable." She turned her phone to look at the screen. Unavailable? What the hell did that mean? Had Maggie blocked her?

Why? Why would she have done that?

Anger mixed up with her fear and regret and chewed a hole through her heart. She pressed a hand to her chest to stop the sharp stab of pain as she recalled the text from that Katherine woman. Something just wasn't right here. Her broken heart raced. Her breath came faster.

No, she didn't have time for a panic attack. She *couldn't* do this right now.

Closing her eyes, she held her breath and thought of the one comforting thing she could latch on to. She'd done nothing illegal. Not a thing. If drugs had been planted in Frank's car, she had never touched them. If that Brandon guy was dead, she'd never met him.

She was fine. She wasn't going to jail no matter what the hell Maggie Hamilton might be up to. She blew out a breath as slowly as she could; then she breathed in, held it, and repeated the cycle.

An eternity later she tapped the message icon and tried again. This is an emergency. Please call me. I made a mistake about who released the tape. PLEASE CALL NOW.

She hit SEND and . . . nothing happened. Nothing. Until the message changed from blue to green.

Maybe the woman was in a cave. Or her phone was off and had been off for days. Or . . . Maggie really had blocked her.

The thought hurt. Maggie had been a lifeline for her, a shining thread rising out of the dark hole she lived in when she wasn't dragging herself to boxing class. But the pain was like the sting of pinching her skin to distract from a broken leg. Omi's betrayal had exploded inside her, and if Maggie wasn't trustworthy either . . . was that a surprise? Nobody could be trusted, ever.

We have to take care of each other. That was what Katherine had said. Geneva didn't trust these women. She didn't even know them. But somehow that made the idea of reaching out easier. They couldn't hurt her, but maybe, just *maybe* they could help. Whatever happened, they couldn't touch her heart.

Out of an abundance of caution, she hadn't added Luz to her contacts so they wouldn't be easily connected, but she had typed her phone number into Notes. She grabbed it and hesitated only a moment before hitting CALL. Good idea or not, she had no choice. She'd deal with her own worries and grief after she was sure she wasn't sending an innocent man to prison.

"Ballyhoo, no!" she heard over the line as she wiped a few errant tears from her face.

"Hello?" she tried, her voice croaking.

"Hi, sorry about that." An awkward silence fell before Luz spoke again. "My dog," she explained. "Can I help you?"

"Yes, hi, this is Geneva from boxing class?"

"Geneva! Right! What's up?" The dog barked, and the sound went muffled for a few seconds.

"I'm sorry. Are you too busy . . . ?"

"No, we're fine. He just found his bag of treats and decided to help himself. No biggie."

It was now or never. She closed her eyes and spoke. "I'm calling because I think maybe you're part of the system. I think you're *my* part of the system, and I need help."

Silence fell. Even the dog wasn't barking anymore.

Of course she was met with silence, because Luz must be horrified. Geneva had certainly been horrified when that crazy Katherine woman had contacted her. But if Geneva wasn't crazy, maybe that lady wasn't either. And if Maggie had cut them off, they'd have to fix their problems themselves.

The possible danger of it pulled at an already-sore wound, but wasn't that what Maggie had been teaching them from the start? That they were strong together? That they didn't have to be scared?

"Luz?" she tried again. "I'm sorry. I know you're not supposed to know me or talk about any of it, but . . . it was you, right? You got Frank?" A tiny gasp floated over the line at that. She'd been right.

"Why are you calling?" Luz said instead of answering.

"Because I really screwed up, and I need to know if you already . . . did you already do whatever Maggie asked you to do?"

Luz cursed in Spanish, and Geneva dropped her head. It was done. It was too late.

"Why?" Luz asked.

"Somebody did something horrible to me. I lost my job, my future. And I knew it was Frank. I broke it off with him and he acted out afterward, and then someone sent a sex tape to my work. It was him, I had no doubt at all. But it turns out I was wrong. Someone else admitted it to me. Now I need to fix this."

"Call Maggie," she said, the words urgent.

"I tried. She won't respond."

"That doesn't seem like her."

"There's something else going on." Geneva winced, trying to decide how much to say, but the time for discretion had passed when Maggie had abandoned them, and she didn't have time to wallow in the hurt. "One of the other women contacted me. Someone was murdered. One of the men."

Another Spanish curse, this one louder.

"I think Maggie is shutting us out. When was the last time you spoke with her?"

"Shit, I don't know. More than a week ago? I did the thing. With Frank. I haven't talked to her since."

"What thing did you do exactly?" she asked.

"Wait a minute," Luz countered sharply. "Who died? And who killed him? Was it one of *us*?"

"No idea. I didn't know him." It suddenly occurred to Geneva that it could have been Luz's target, the one she'd set up for revenge. "His name was Brandon."

Luz sighed. "Okay. That's not mine either."

"Good. So what happened with Frank? I know we're not supposed to discuss this, but it's an emergency. Please?"

A few heartbeats ticked by in silence, then a few more. "I told her I didn't want anyone hurt," Luz finally said. Her words started slowly but quickly sped up as she spoke. "She said that wouldn't happen. But now apparently someone is dead, so that's completely terrifying and everything has changed!"

"Yeah."

"I don't like this at all. In fact, I hate it. I plan my life out. I'm careful."

"I totally get that, Luz. I swear."

She blew out a frustrated breath. "Okay, I don't want to discuss this anymore. It feels like a setup."

"Luz, *please*. I'm sorry. I swear I'm sorry, but something is *wrong* here. Maggie isn't talking to anyone, and that woman who called me about the dead guy says there are other cops involved in this."

"Maybe because she has something to do with a murder!"

"Maybe. But Maggie cut me off too, and I certainly wasn't involved. I don't even know the man. But I need help. Please. Maybe . . . If you don't want to do it over the phone, maybe we can all meet somewhere and figure out what's happening. A bar or a coffee shop? That way there won't be a record of more calls, but we can help each other and lay everything on the table."

"That's crazy."

"I know it is. And I'm sure your life isn't falling apart like mine is. If you . . . if you got what you needed out of this, you probably just want to move on. It's what we were all supposed to do." The words came out twisted and strangled until she couldn't speak anymore. Not without sobbing.

Omi had been a constant in her life for so long, and maybe Geneva had taken her for granted, but she hadn't deserved *this*. She knew she hadn't. But life was unfair. Frank hadn't deserved all this either. He'd

made bad decisions in his youth, and he could be an overbearing asshole, but—

"I didn't," Luz said.

Geneva pushed a syllable from her tight throat. "What?"

"I didn't get what I needed out of this. So yeah. I'll meet you. Just
don't tell that other woman my name, okay? I don't need any more crazy
in my life. This has all been enough."

Geneva winced, but she nodded. "Okay. I know a good dive bar if
that works for you."

"Sure, I'm pretty low on bar knowledge."

Geneva gave her the address, and they agreed to meet in forty-five
minutes. They'd make this whole plan work for them even without
Maggie.

Geneva groaned in exhaustion. If Maggie was dealing with a murder and trying to cut ties with the women in the system, she probably
wouldn't move forward with the revenge plot against Frank. Whatever
the second step of the plan was, she'd probably drop it. But probably
wasn't good enough.

There were a hundred reasons she couldn't just get in touch with
Frank. She couldn't simply tell him. He'd likely make a point of getting
her in trouble, and she'd just landed a job. When she'd had him dragged
into a police station and questioned, he'd yelled at her that she was
fucking with his life and she'd seriously regret it.

And he'd been absolutely right. She did regret it, deeply.

And Omi . . .

Good God, how was it possible that Omi had done it? Yes, she'd
always been volatile, but she'd never been cruel. Geneva's heart twisted
at the betrayal, the tender fibers tearing open.

They'd loved each other. It hadn't just been sex like it had with
Frank. She'd imagined Omi would be one of those friends she'd know
forever. The pain of it pulled at her, urging her home to her room, to
her bed.

But she couldn't. Not yet.

For a moment she considered forcing the issue with Maggie, going to her station, waiting in the lobby until Maggie agreed to see her. But she couldn't associate herself so closely, couldn't place herself at the station with all those cameras in case all of this came crashing down around the Hook and Detective Maggie Hamilton.

Better to ask for help from the others. Wasn't that the deepest belief that Maggie had instilled in them? That they could help each other without involving any authorities who refused to understand. If Maggie was one of those authorities now, then they'd have to figure it out without her.

She opened her contacts again, touched a name, and waited.

CHAPTER 23

KATHERINE

"Let's help each other."

Katherine gasped into her phone at the woman's words. "Geneva?"

"Yes."

"Are you serious?" Relief twisted up with yet another surge of fear. She needed someone, anyone, on her side, but she knew the safer alternative was to lock herself in a closet and hide.

"As long as it's nothing dangerous, I think we should get together and lay everything out. We each might have information the others need."

She scrubbed a hand over her face, overwhelmed by the idea of getting together, especially after her scare at the park. And her promises to Maggie. "Are you talking about Nicole too?"

"Is that the other cop? Because no."

"She worked for the police, but her husband is the cop."

"I just mean the three of us. Me, you, and the other woman who had nothing to do with Brandon."

"You found her?" Katherine asked, her heart picking up from alert to nearly frantic.

"Yes. Can you meet us in forty-five minutes?"

Katherine didn't even bother to check the clock. Of course she could meet them, but . . . "Where?" she asked warily.

"Mac's bar on Broadway. We all want a public place, and that should be far enough out of our respective circles, I'd think."

It definitely wasn't in Katherine's neighborhood, and as far as she could recall, it was an area that had been up and coming thirty years earlier and had never quite taken off. Not run down but not hip. "Sure. I'll see you there."

Katherine felt oddly excited as she pulled her shoes back on. Her eye was sore from wearing the contact for too long, so she took it out and pulled on her eye patch instead. Better not to look like a crazed red-eyed woman with one wonky pupil. If Geneva was ready to trust her, Katherine was ready to live up to that.

She rushed out early and had already stepped off the elevator into the lobby when she changed her mind and turned toward the back stairwell and the exit there. Just in case. When she got outdoors, she pulled up the hood of her jacket and hurried to her car. The bar was about ten miles away, and she took quite a few wrong turns on purpose, circling around and watching her rearview mirror to see if anyone was following. As far as she could tell, she was on her own.

By the time she got to the intersection, her jaw was screaming with tension, but the sight of the place relaxed her a bit. The name, Mac's, and the bagpiper on the signage indicated some kind of Scottish theme, but the only other decorations in the window were iron bars and two neon beer signs. It looked like the perfect place to not be seen.

Even though she was fifteen minutes early, she pushed open the door carefully, peeking inside for a moment before letting herself in. The theme didn't carry over to the interior. There were no tartans or bagpipes or even plaid wallpaper. It was just a dingy bar with a long oak counter and a few wooden booths toward the back. The crowd was sparse. Maybe the hardest drinkers didn't show up until later.

Katherine ducked her head and aimed for an empty booth. It was uncushioned wood, scarred like the table was, but nothing felt sticky, at least, and no one bothered her. The next booth back was packed full with five men sharing a pitcher, but they weren't rowdy at all. They seemed to be plotting some sort of fantasy game about minotaurs and wizards, and their intense interest in the topic assured Katherine they wouldn't be listening in.

After a few minutes of nervously checking her phone every two seconds, she finally realized there was no server and headed to the bar. Hoping to make a good impression, she bought three glasses of chardonnay and carried them back to the table. If it wasn't the right drink, she'd have them all herself. Maybe she'd have them all herself regardless, because that could be what it took to get past the adrenaline in her bloodstream.

She'd made it only halfway through the first glass when Geneva walked in, the brief flash of outdoor light alerting Katherine. The woman paused for a moment, clearly a bit blind in the dim interior, and God, she looked so young and helpless, standing there wide-eyed. Katherine raised a hand and waved.

"Hi," she said, starting to stand when Geneva approached, then dropping awkwardly back down to the wood. "I got wine. I hope that's okay." She pushed an untouched glass toward the woman as she slid into the booth, then realized her mistake when Geneva frowned at the pale liquid. Katherine squeezed her eyes shut. "I'm sorry. I get it." She started to pull it back toward her, but Geneva shook her head and reached for the glass.

"But to be clear, it's not poisoned, right?"

She didn't know whether to laugh or wince. "I swear it's not. I'll have a sip if you like. Or a gulp."

"It's all good. I'll take it."

"So what's happened?" Katherine pressed.

Geneva sighed and seemed to deflate into the unyielding surface of the booth. "How the hell did this all go so wrong?" She shook her head in weary question. "We should wait for the other woman."

"What's her name? Who is she?"

"She doesn't want to give her name, but I know she was assigned to my target."

"Oh." Katherine blinked several times, imagining them in the same class together, eyeing each other the way Katherine had eyed Nicole. "What did she do for you?"

Geneva groaned and lifted the wine. "I think I know, but I need her to tell me. It got very complicated." After taking a huge gulp of her wine, she put her elbows on the table and met Katherine's gaze. "Someone sent an explicit video of me to my place of work. Revenge porn."

"Holy shit." Katherine covered her mouth in absolute horror. "I'm so sorry." She couldn't imagine it. Couldn't imagine the things she'd done on screen with Brandon sent to people she knew, her neighbors or her associates at the theater. Her face burned at the thought, the skin hot and dry as a rash.

She knew, of course, that she'd been setting Brandon up for exactly that. She knew it, but she didn't *feel* it. The sex itself had been wrong for him. *He'd* been wrong. Wrong for a man who condemned others for their relationships. And especially wrong for a man who wanted to force people to bear unwanted pregnancies when he just tossed his aside and let Nicole deal with any repercussions. She had no doubt Peter would've done exactly the same. In fact, he might have done it in the past.

Jesus. It was the first time that had occurred to her.

Well, if Katherine was a villain too, so be it. Some people deserved a nemesis.

"I blamed it on the wrong person," Geneva said quietly.

"Oh," Katherine said. Then "Oh!" as she realized what Geneva must mean. "You *set up* the wrong person?"

"Exactly." Geneva finished her wine, but she shook her head when Katherine nudged the other one toward her.

"Better not. Apparently my judgment is bad enough as it is." She wiped a tear from her cheek but another one followed.

"I'm sorry," Katherine whispered, wanting to reach out and touch her but afraid closeness wouldn't be welcomed from her.

"I was *so sure*," Geneva said, and the fingers that had just caught her tears clenched into a fist. "I would never have dreamed it was . . . someone who meant something to me."

"Are you okay?"

"No!" But she laughed and the tears stopped.

"Well, at least I can assure you we got the right guy at my house. No question about that one."

"And the dead guy?"

It was Katherine's turn to groan. "Well, considering he was a sup-posedly wholesome, family-values politician who was trolling Christian sites for anonymous sex . . . he seemed right on target."

"That's how you got to him? One of those sites?"

"Yes. I was supposed to have phone sex with him and record it so that he could be exposed."

"Exposed, huh? All right. So what went wrong?"

"I, um, decided to meet him in person instead." At the woman's raised eyebrow, Katherine grimaced. "I know it was a terrible idea, but it wasn't so different from what you did with my husband. It's just sex, right? No big deal."

She felt cool and sophisticated for about two seconds. Until Geneva spoke. "Yeah, I definitely did *not* have sex with your husband."

Katherine's eyes fluttered. So did her heart. "What? But he invited you to his party. You must have . . . I mean, you had a relationship. You were dating."

"We went on one date, but we definitely didn't have sex. No offense, but what is he, sixty?"

"He's fifty!"

"Regardless, I don't know him and he's not my type. I met him for drinks to establish things and get him interested; then I led him on for a couple of weeks, figuring he'd get stupid about it, because I needed to be at that party. That was a pretty tall order, right?" She leaned forward, a twist of pride lifting her mouth. "I said danger was the only thing that turned me on. That I craved it and it got me so, so hot." She lifted both eyebrows and shrugged. "I thought that was a pretty good idea, and it worked. He snuck me in. I just had to get him horny enough to be reckless."

Katherine gaped at her, utterly confused. "You never . . . actually . . . ?"

"No, that night was the first time I ever touched him, and I didn't let it go far."

Katherine's mind reeled. This whole time she'd justified her own risks and sexual daring because others were doing it too. But Geneva, at least, had refused. Now Katherine didn't know if she was horrified or . . . proud?

But when the shock began to fade, she found that she didn't feel either of those things. She just felt an endless twist of hurt.

"What did he say?" she asked, wrapping her hands around the edge of the table. "Peter. When you invited yourself to the party? To our home?"

Geneva's beautiful face fell. "No, don't do that to yourself. Men are pigs. You don't have to try to figure him out."

"I know. I just . . . I've thought about it so many times. Before and after. I suggested the party because I thought he'd find it funny. Hilarious, even. That he could do that right there and no one would know. That *I* wouldn't know. Did he laugh about it?"

She shook her head. "I don't remember. He just said we'd have to make it quick."

But Katherine could read the truth in Geneva's eyes. Of course he'd been amused, imagining the ultimate little gift for his fiftieth birthday.

A sexual tryst right beneath her nose with the stunning young woman he felt he deserved. A beautiful present for himself to service him right there at the party his dull wife had thrown for him.

When had he gotten so arrogant?

Then again, hadn't that been the core of his personality from the start? She'd seen it as confidence and deep belief. The kind of confidence that she was always chasing and could never catch. He'd had it, and she'd wanted it.

But she'd been wrong about Peter. His deepest belief had always been that he was right and everyone else was wrong. That was what drove his righteousness. Not faith, but arrogance. Not good works, but performance.

The church provided the rules by which he could measure himself against others, and it had been an easy win for him. Most of their fellow parishioners didn't believe the rules anymore, much less follow them. He'd lamented the soft social beliefs of Pope Francis and even Father Carlo. The rules were *right there*, and so very few could actually measure up.

"Are you okay?" Geneva asked.

"Yeah. Sorry. You just caught me off guard."

"I'm sorry about your husband."

Katherine laughed, the sound admittedly a bit on the manic side. "Me too." Awkward silence stretched between them like a strained rubber band until Katherine couldn't stand waiting for the snap.

"You want to know something really messed up?" she asked, the question rushing from her mouth. "That guy? My target? He was the only man I've ever had sex with besides my husband. Ever! And then he was immediately murdered. How screwed up is that?"

Geneva's eyes slid to the side, and Katherine, bracing herself, slowly turned her head to find one of the men from the next booth stopped in his tracks next to their table, his pale face quickly going pink.

"Oh," Katherine said, meeting his white-rimmed eyes. "Hi."

Geneva tried to smother a snort of laughter, but it didn't work. Katherine looked from her to the man's dropped jaw then back to Geneva. "Oops," she said, and he immediately scurried away. That only made Geneva laugh harder. Katherine stayed blank with horror for a few more heartbeats until her embarrassment gave way beneath the weight of absurdity, and she began to laugh too.

As tears of amusement streamed from her eyes, Katherine felt as if a thousand pounds were rising off her shoulders, relieving some of the awful strain of isolation and secrets and hurt.

All of this was just so . . . *absurd*. Ridiculous. Awful.

She wiped her eyes just in time to see a woman walk the last few feet to their table and stop. She looked from Geneva to Katherine, her frown deepening as she tossed a long black braid over her shoulder and glared.

"This doesn't look like an emergency to me," she said.

Geneva gasped, and Katherine blinked in shock. At long last, she was meeting the fourth woman.

CHAPTER 24

Luz

Luz couldn't believe she'd broken all the rules just to join some ill-conceived happy hour.

Geneva quickly wiped the smile from her face, but the White woman wearing an eye patch stammered out a cheerful "H-hello!" and sprang to her feet as if she were going to hug Luz. Luz stepped back.

"What's going on?" she asked.

"This is Katherine," Geneva said, gesturing toward the very tall woman, who gave Luz an awkward wave before sliding back into the booth. She looked to be in her forties, lean and pale, and her fingers touched the eye patch as Luz looked at her, as if she were hyperaware of it. Luz wondered if the injury had something to do with her part of the system.

Geneva slid over so Luz could join her, but Luz hesitated for one more moment, wondering if she should just turn around and walk away. Once they exchanged information, there would be no taking it back. But Geneva's words had haunted her for the past forty-five minutes. *If you got what you needed . . .*

No. She seemed to have gotten revenge, but that clearly wasn't what she actually needed. What she needed was some justice, and how the hell was she ever going to get that?

So she slid into the booth. "Hi," she offered the woman across from her. Her brain had been a tornado since she'd spoken to Geneva, torn and spinning, pulling in so many awful thoughts. A dead man, the police involvement, the drugs she'd left in Frank's car, and the horrible, growing rage that she couldn't help Sveta or herself.

The woman, Katherine, eased a glass of golden wine across the table.

Luz shook her head. "I don't drink." With a shrug, the woman slid it back and took a sip.

"So," Luz said. "What in the hell is going on?"

Geneva took a deep breath. "First, will you tell me what happened with Frank?"

She didn't want to. She really didn't want to. As soon as it was done, she'd tried her best to shove it out of her mind and pretend it hadn't happened. But she couldn't resist the pleading sadness in Geneva's fathomless brown eyes.

"Maggie gave me . . ." She glanced toward the tall woman, hesitating to say more, but Geneva touched her arm.

"It's okay. She knows more than both of us."

"Maggie gave me a packet of powder and instructed me on how best to get a ride with Frank. I thought it might take a couple of tries, but it worked. Just as I'd been told, he was distracted by my dog, and I dropped the packet in his glove compartment."

"Shit," Geneva groaned.

Luz held up her hands. "To be clear, I have no idea what it was. I didn't ask, and I didn't want to know."

"But that was all that happened? No cops showed up, you didn't call 911 or anything?"

"No. Nothing. She said she'd take care of the second part later so it wouldn't be associated with my ride."

Geneva looked away, brow tightening with thought. "When was it?"

"Maybe ten days ago? It's been a while. It was a Thursday, I remember that."

"Okay." Geneva pressed her fingertips lightly to her mouth and nodded. "I'm thinking Maggie got distracted by the murder and didn't follow through. So I can still fix this."

Luz held up her hands in a stop motion. "I really need us to pause there. *What* murder? What the hell is happening? And where is Maggie?"

Geneva's eyes shifted to the woman across from them. "Katherine? You want to explain your whole story?"

"Yes," she said. Then "No." She made a strange sound before covering her mouth. "Sorry. It's not funny. It's really not. I'm just . . . very overwhelmed."

Yes, she was laughing again. These women were not okay. Why had she agreed to meet them? Luz wanted to get up and leave, but where would she go? Back to her lonely place and her empty bed so she could go to sleep just to wake up and start a whole new day without Sveta?

"So, um . . ." The woman's right eye shifted quickly back and forth between Luz and Geneva. Luz tried not to stare at the eye patch. She hoped to God this wasn't some bizarre cosplay for her, but she almost thought she could see the tiny point of a pink scar just beneath the top of the patch.

"The man I was assigned to was killed the night I met him." She cleared her throat. "I didn't do it. Obviously."

Luz cocked her head, wondering why it was so obvious.

"Maggie would have arrested me by now!" she insisted. "I was interviewed, but that was almost two days ago. I don't know who did it, or if they know about me or us . . ." She huffed out a big sigh and crossed her arms to hold herself tight. "The woman in our system who wanted revenge on him is in my class. But . . . Can I ask how you both met Maggie?"

"I met her through the Hook," Geneva said.

"Me too," said Luz.

"Okay, that's how I met her too. But the man who died . . . the woman who wanted revenge on him is Nicole. And she's friends with Maggie. Like, actual friends. She has been for years. More important, so is her husband, because he's *also* a police officer and worked with Maggie."

"Wait a minute. Back up. Who's a cop? The dead guy?"

"No. This woman, Nicole, had an affair with a married man, a conservative politician. It ended very badly, and she broke down and told Maggie about it. Because Maggie is her *friend*. So now I'm just wondering . . . was this all about helping her friend? Were we all pulled in as cover for her friend to get revenge? Maybe even for someone to kill him?"

Luz jumped in to defend Maggie. "That doesn't make any sense. Why would we be involved too?"

Katherine leaned forward, fingers spreading wide on the stained wood table. "Who took revenge on your target?"

Drawing in her chin, Luz looked from her to Geneva. "I don't know, actually. I'm not even sure that what happened was part of the system."

"Why?" Geneva asked.

"I wasn't clear on the details Maggie set up. Like I said, I really didn't want to know anything I didn't have to about either plan. I thought that would be safer. Now . . ." Luz scrubbed her hands over her face. "I don't know anymore. But I wanted this man fired from his new job, and he was fired."

Katherine raised her eyebrows, the patch lifting a bit with the movement.

"But it doesn't make any sense," Luz insisted. "Someone sent his employer screenshots of private messages that got super racist. But the conversation was on Nextdoor. You can't just sign up for that! You have to be invited, and your address is verified. Are there so many women in the system that Maggie happened to have someone who lived in his neighborhood?"

Katherine gasped so loudly that Luz jumped, whipping her head toward her. "What?"

"Nicole! Nicole is a real estate agent!"

Luz's jaw dropped, her brain racing to sort through the details and reject them. But it couldn't. A real estate agent could have gotten her hands on a Nextdoor invitation for a certain address, surely. Someone she was selling a house for, or maybe just a house she knew was vacant.

"Maybe I did get him fired, then. Maybe it was our system. But that still doesn't prove anything. Maggie wouldn't have set up this elaborate conspiracy for one person. She could have had you take care of Nicole's problem and Nicole take care of yours! How much easier would that have been?"

Katherine shook her head. "Nicole isn't my husband's type. She has three kids, she's almost my age. No, he wanted . . ." She glanced at Geneva. "Someone young and sexy."

Luz turned to find Geneva wincing and figured the story of their part in the system was pretty straightforward. She winced back in sympathy.

Katherine's sigh turned into a bitter chuckle as she tipped the edge of her wineglass toward them. Her cheeks glowed pink, and Luz noticed the empty glass next to her elbow.

"You know, my bastard husband wanted to wait until marriage to have sex, and I stupidly assumed that meant he believed in something. I even assumed he was a virgin too. It took me years to realize he wanted to *marry* someone pure and innocent, someone untouched enough to

raise his children, but he wanted to *fuck* someone entirely different."
She wrinkled her nose. "Sorry. Excuse my language."

"Madonna-whore complex," Geneva chimed in.

Katherine jerked back a bit in surprise. "What?"

"That's what it's called."

"Oh my God, I heard it once, and I thought it was just a Catholic saying!"

"Nope, it's real, and it is widespread enough to infect the whole world. You're definitely not alone in that."

"And sorry, Geneva," Katherine said softly. "I didn't mean to imply anything."

Geneva grinned. "Yeah, I know, Ms. Wild Thing."

When Katherine covered her pink face with her hands and laughed, Luz figured they'd discussed all this before she arrived. But she'd witnessed enough heterosexual drama to last a lifetime, so she didn't follow up.

"I guess I'm just not understanding any of this," Luz said carefully. "Maggie has been good to me. She has a whole career putting bad guys away. What is it you think she's done?"

Katherine leaned back with a melodramatic groan. "I don't know." She rocked her head back and forth along the wood before popping back up again. "But whatever inspired her, I'm afraid she's dropped us all to cover her own ass. Which . . . fair enough, but what are we supposed to do? I'm terrified. What if Nicole's husband killed that man and Maggie is covering for all of them now? What happens to me?"

Luz shrugged. She didn't have any answers to that, but how was she supposed to help this woman?

"It felt simple before, right?" Katherine said, her voice going soft. "It was such a good idea. But then everything went wrong. Or maybe only I went wrong. This was all my fault, I guess."

Geneva clicked her tongue. "Not unless you murdered that guy."

"And I didn't, to be clear. But I am the one who went off script and messed up the plan." She glanced at Luz. "I met him in person, and I wasn't supposed to. Big mistake. Really big."

"Yikes," Luz muttered, glad she'd stuck to her plan. Mostly. Aside from the time she screamed at Tanner that she'd ruined him. That was quite a mistake too. Had he believed her?

"Yeah, well . . ." Geneva grabbed the wineglass from Katherine's reach and drained it, then held the empty glass up in a sad toast. "I had drugs planted on an innocent man, so let's start a club for assholes, I guess."

Good God, they were both giggling again. Luz huffed in irritation, but her huff somehow turned into a snort of laughter too. "You people are crazy." But she'd turned a little crazy herself, hadn't she? She actually had gotten her revenge, but she still wanted *more*.

"Well, Geneva," Katherine said. "Your problem is actually fixable. So if there's a chance we can't count on Maggie anymore, how do we fix it?"

"I've been trying to figure out a way to get into Frank's car with him, but I can't imagine it. I had him hauled into a police station for questioning, so needless to say, we don't hang out anymore." She turned her brown eyes on Luz, whose heart sank.

"No! I was terrified just dropping that in the glove box! Searching around in there for a tiny packet? How could I do that? What if I got caught?"

Geneva sighed. "I know. It's dangerous."

"Too dangerous!" Luz insisted.

"Maybe Maggie will be at class tomorrow. If she is, I'll talk to her."

"And if she's not?" Katherine pressed. "Are you just supposed to wait and hope?"

Shaking her head, Geneva looked to Luz again.

"No," Luz insisted. "What if Frank called the cops on me or something? What would I say? *Just looking for this pack of drugs right here?* I can't take that chance."

"No," Katherine said, "but I can."

They both turned to look at her.

She shrugged one shoulder. "It's easier for me, right? Middle-aged, middle-class White lady?" When they only stared and didn't respond, she turned up her palms in question. "I watch the news. I get it. If I get caught, I can just cry and say I found the drugs on the sidewalk or I thought it was headache powder or some other dumb lie. Absolutely no one would care or do anything."

"She's got a point," Geneva said. "But do you have a dog?"

"No."

"Well, you can't request a specific driver, so how would you manage to get Frank's car?"

"And why would he have his glove box open?" Luz reminded them. "He has to be going for dog treats."

"Yes!" Katherine said, slapping the table. "So we do it together! Right? It's perfect."

Luz drew her chin in. "How?"

"You and your dog can sit in the back, I'll sit in the front. You distract him, I'll do the dirty work. It'll be easy."

She wanted to say no. She really did. But she'd already felt guilty about planting drugs when Frank had been a bad guy. Now he was just an innocent bystander. How would she sleep at night if she didn't try to make it right?

"Maybe," Luz responded. "Maybe it could work, but it wouldn't be easy. The packet is tiny. No matter how cute my dog is, Frank won't be distracted enough for you to rummage around in his glove compartment for thirty seconds. That's ridiculous."

"Hmm." Katherine tapped her mouth. "Right. I don't suppose your dog would pee on the back seat or something?"

"Ballyhoo? He would never."

They sat in silence for a few long heartbeats before Geneva spoke up. "I could distract Frank."

"You?" Luz sighed and sank down a little. "Like we're all hanging out together and Frank happens to pick us up? I don't think that would make any sense. He'd be on guard, especially around you."

"You're right. But if you call for the car, you two can get in, and I just happen upon you while he's obsessing over your dog, which he will. I knock on his window, demand to talk, make a bit of a scene. Boom. His glove box is already open for the treats. That would give Katherine plenty of time to dig around."

"Yes!" Katherine shouted before covering her mouth and looking around. "Oops. Yes, it's perfect." She turned her gaze on Luz, who tried to think of a good reason not to do it. But Katherine was right. It was perfect, and it didn't really demand any risk of Luz.

"It sounds possible," she agreed.

"But you'd really agree to do that?" Geneva asked. "Both of you?"

Luz hadn't actually agreed yet. She didn't even know why she was here, so why was she considering this? She was done with the system. She could dust her hands and walk away. Surely she'd get over the guilt eventually.

But when she watched Katherine reach out and take Geneva's hand, something in her heart slipped.

"I'll help," Katherine said. "I'd love to."

"Why?" Geneva whispered.

"Well, for me . . ." Her good eye went liquid, the tears brightening the hazel coloring to forest green. "I've been alone. For a long time. And now I feel stronger just sitting here with you. I feel better helping you than I do hiding in my apartment, scared of what happens next. Whether Maggie is on our side or not, I believed what she said. We can help each other. We can at least fix your problem. And we *should*."

The strange feeling in Luz's chest grew, pushing out so quickly it almost hurt. "My target," she suddenly blurted out, "he got my girlfriend deported. And I miss her so much. And even though I got him fired from his job, it's not enough. It's not enough!"

Katherine took her hand too, and Luz knew she squeezed back too hard, but she held tight and didn't let go. "I'll help," she finally said. "Ballyhoo and I are in. I'm Luz, by the way."

"Luz," Katherine repeated softly. "I'm really happy to meet you."

CHAPTER 25

KATHERINE

Katherine didn't bother hiding her movements when she left Mac's. She walked to her car and drove straight home without worrying. She wasn't doing anything wrong. She'd barely done anything wrong to start. If someone had killed that man, they'd find evidence that exonerated her, and this would all go away.

She felt powerful again, the way she'd once felt after spending time with Maggie. An hour with Luz and Geneva had purged her fears that she was hysterical or insane or just a coward. They had each other's backs. If push came to shove and Maggie threw her under the bus, these women would back her up.

Still, tension was dragging her down by the time she got to her building and stepped onto the elevator. She sagged against the wall.

Tomorrow would be a big day, and tonight all she wanted to do was take a bottle of wine to bed and drink until she passed out. But no, her stomach was too sour after days of stress, and she knew she needed to force herself to eat.

Pizza again? she thought as she stepped out of the elevator. Or maybe Chinese. Noodles and rice to soak up the stale acid churning her stomach to a pulp.

She was almost to her apartment when the door across from hers opened. Katherine was already tensing for some kind of conflict with the old lady when she registered that it wasn't that woman in the opening. It was Maggie Hamilton stepping out, her mouth a somber line as the door thudded shut behind her.

Reeling with a sudden, unidentifiable fear, Katherine looked from Maggie to her own apartment, then back again. "What's going on?" she demanded as her mind raced through the possibilities. *Maggie was spying on her by asking the neighbors about her. Maggie was spying on her through the neighbor's peephole. Maggie was spying on her by—*

"She saw someone trying to get into your apartment."

"What?" Katherine wheezed. "What are you talking about? What are you even doing here?"

"Can we go inside, please?"

She looked at her door again, forehead tightening, head aching. She had no idea what Maggie's appearance could mean. Her fear jumped forward, twisting itself into anger. "Wh-what's happening? *What's really happening?*"

"Katherine," she said flatly, and the quiet tone broke through her tumbling emotions. "Let's just talk, all right?"

With no idea how else to respond, she found herself falling silent and doing what Maggie wanted, moving forward with the keys to unlock her place. Maggie moved in quickly behind her and shut the door as soon as they were inside. "I need you to calm down."

It was only then that Katherine realized she was breathing too quickly, her hands shaking and numb. This wasn't normal. It wasn't okay. Maggie was supposed to be her friend, her support system, and now she was lying in wait, watching for her, planning.

But planning what? Nothing good. How could it possibly be anything good?

"Do you know her too?" she asked, panting. "You know my neighbor? She's part of this?"

"No. When Koval and I were here, she poked her head out again when we were leaving. I gave her my card, asked her to call me if she saw anything strange."

"You asked her to watch me."

"No. I'm trying to keep you safe. I've been trying to do that from day one."

"I don't know that!" she shouted. "How am I supposed to know that? All you do is order me around and keep secrets!"

"Katherine, please. Let's just—"

"Did you set me up because you wanted him dead? Brandon? He betrayed your friend, right? Was this all about Nicole from the very start? Oh my God." She was drawing in strained breaths, the air fighting past her swelling throat, whistling and wheezing.

Maggie rushed her, and Katherine could do nothing more than raise her hands in halfhearted defense as her vision went sparkly and warped. "Shh," Maggie said, and Katherine felt warm arms encircling her. "Shh, come on. Let's sit down. Breathe slowly. In and out."

The air strained out, her throat groaning like a sad instrument, but then she was on the couch, Maggie rubbing her back, setting a new rhythm with her quiet orders. "Breathe in for five, then out for ten. In for five . . . that's it. Now out for ten. You've got it. You're okay."

The fireworks in her vision went away, and Maggie's hand was a warm sun on her skin. Katherine came back to her body, back to herself.

"Better?"

She wanted to shake her head no because nothing was better, but she could breathe again. That much was true. Dropping her head, she squeezed her eyes shut.

"All right. The reason I haven't told you anything is that I didn't want you accidentally saying something to Koval," Maggie said. "Okay? But it looks like he's finally accepted that it wasn't you."

Her head popped up. "Really?"

"Yes. There was blood at the scene. I assume you didn't bleed anywhere when you were there?"

"No."

"Well, all right, then. Someone was injured in the struggle. It wasn't Brandon. He didn't have any deep wounds. There were several drops of blood on the carpet under his body and a big drop on his shirt. The DNA should show it wasn't you."

"Oh, thank God!" she cried, her soul lunging toward this get-out-of-jail card with pained relief. And finally, *finally*, Maggie was telling her something. "When?"

"It's not like it is on TV. There's a backlog, and we're working with government funds. It will take weeks."

"Okay. I get that. I can . . . Well, I don't know if I can be patient, but I guess I have no choice. But there must be video? Someone was in there. Someone left."

"Riiight." Maggie drew out the word. "About that."

Katherine pulled her knee up on the couch, twisting around to face Maggie. "What?"

"The data from the room's lock show the door was opened about five minutes after you left. There's a camera at the elevators and a camera at the stairs, and neither recorded someone else arriving or Brandon leaving."

"What does that mean?"

She shrugged. "He could have let in a guest from another room or someone who was already in the hall. We can't know that, but we think that's the entry time."

"There are no cameras in the halls?" When Maggie shook her head, Katherine rushed on. "But someone left at some point!"

"Yes. The lock also shows that someone opened the door about fifty minutes later. But . . ." Maggie slumped back, and for the first time since this whole thing had started, she looked like herself again. Not like an authority figure or a righteous cop, but just a woman. Maybe even a friend. How could Katherine truly know?

"About an hour after you left, the smoke alarm in that hallway was set off by a fire someone started using Kleenex and towels. The entire floor was evacuated."

"Okay?"

"Dozens of people left that floor via the staircase. Then the fire department arrived, and that was about ten more bodies in play, coming and going. It was chaotic."

Katherine gasped. "That's how he got away? He's like some sort of genius serial killer?"

"It wasn't exactly an elaborate scheme. This person killed someone, and they needed a way to evade surveillance. It was a tiny fire that set off the alarms but didn't cause any damage. That was clever, but it was only a temporary evasion with the blood evidence left behind. You're sure it wasn't yours?"

"Yes! We just had regular sex, we didn't—" She flapped her hand awkwardly. "You know. Do weird stuff."

"That's a relief."

"You're telling me." She jumped when she felt Maggie's fingers close over hers; then she turned her hand and held on. She'd been brave with the other women, even proud of herself, but Maggie's touch still felt like the lifeline she'd been chasing for days.

"Koval knows it wasn't you. That's why he didn't arrest you right away. It took him a while to even get back to your portion of the videos. He knows that door opened twice after the camera caught you leaving, and he knows the fire didn't start for nearly an hour."

She squeezed Maggie's hand. "So I'm okay?"

"You're okay. And no, I wasn't setting you up for murder."

"Oh my God. That's good. That's really good."

Maggie leaned back a little to peer at her. "Is that truly what you've been thinking, Katherine? Really?"

She shrugged, embarrassed. "I've been terrified. If there was something I could think, then I thought it. My mind's been racing out of control for a week now."

"I'm sorry. I should have been more sympathetic."

But Katherine's mind had already sprinted ahead to something else. "What happened to the killer?"

"Pardon?"

"He was bleeding? Was it a shooting or a knife . . . ?"

"We're not sure. No weapon was found at the scene, but there were only a few drops of blood. Brandon could have broken this person's nose for all we know. Why? Have you noticed anyone with injuries while you've been running around playing investigator?"

"No. But I haven't been looking for that." Katherine scrubbed her hands over her face. "Remember I told you Brandon opened the door as I was leaving and someone startled him? He closed it again because he wasn't dressed. So whoever was there probably saw me leave. If it was . . . ?"

Maggie gave her a flat stare, clearly aware that Katherine was fishing. And she was. Yes, it was up to the cops to catch the killer, but how the hell was Katherine supposed to rest easy? Maggie wasn't in real danger, but *she* might be. "And now someone is trying to get into my apartment?" she pressed, even though she half assumed it had been her mother again.

"She looked out her peephole and saw someone fiddling with your lock, but that's all she saw. Person was dressed in black, low hat. It could have been anyone."

Jesus, it probably had been her mother. But then she thought of the shadow at the park.

Maggie patted her arm. "By the time I got here, they were long gone, and your door was still locked."

"But *who was it*?"

Maggie cleared her throat. "I'm afraid I don't know. Listen, I wouldn't be surprised if we make an arrest any day now. The halls were crowded after the fire alarm, but we're combing every pixel. Just lie low. Keep your door locked. Be on alert."

"I was thinking of going to my sister's for a few days." Maybe she could even take Charlotte. Instead of spending time here, they could fly to Oregon, and then Katherine could drive her daughter to Spokane. It might actually be a blast. Certainly it would be a relief.

"That's a great idea," Maggie said, probably just hoping she wouldn't have to worry about Katherine's snooping for a while.

"So I officially have your permission to leave the state?"

She rolled her eyes. "There's no legal reason for you to stay."

Katherine opened her mouth to explain about Charlotte's arrival, that she was worried about her daughter too . . . But caution stopped her. Maggie could make every promise about her motivation, but promises weren't truths.

"All right? Are we good?" When Maggie rose, guilt speared Katherine that she hadn't asked for help for Geneva. But she couldn't reveal that either. Couldn't tell Maggie that they were talking and making their own plans. Could she?

Her stomach burned as Maggie moved toward the door and away from accessibility. She could blurt it out right now. *Geneva needs to talk to you!* But their connection was Geneva's secret too. It wasn't only Katherine's to reveal.

So she let Maggie go. Tomorrow they'd take care of Geneva's problem, and if Maggie took care of the murderer, all the good they'd accomplished together might be salvageable. Hope swelled inside her as she picked up the phone to text her daughter.

What would you think about a little road trip?

She'd get this new life back on track, and everything would be better soon.

CHAPTER 26

GENEVA

Her back pressed against the rough brick wall, Geneva glanced around the alley where they'd gathered like some turn-of-the-century gang of female thieves. "We really are crazy," she muttered. She'd spent a full day picking the plan apart, but it seemed as solid as it could get. Worst-case scenario, Katherine wouldn't find the drugs and they'd take an unneeded ride to the airport.

Luz nodded as Ballyhoo wrapped his leash around her legs before she tugged him back the other way. "I think it's a good plan, though. I'm barely even terrified."

"Has he shown up yet?"

Luz checked her phone and shook her head. "Still no takers."

Katherine began to pace. "I hope it's okay I didn't tell Maggie about Frank. I figured it was better to stick with this than stir up any more trouble."

"No, it's good. Better not to let her know you saw us. Just in case."

"Just in case," she agreed. "But everything does seem like it's getting back to normal. Maybe Brandon was just killed by a bookie or something. Or another random husband. I got the impression he did that sort of thing a lot."

"I still think it was his wife," Geneva said. "A woman could kill a man with a tie, I bet. Especially with all that built-up anger."

"True. I bet I could have found the strength to strangle Peter."

Geneva hesitated, thinking of the utterly average man she'd made out with at the birthday party Katherine had thrown for him. "Can I ask you something? Why didn't you just leave him? Now or a long time ago?"

Katherine stopped pacing and tipped her head back to look at the rectangle of sky above them. She stared up at it like she was seeing something up there in the air. "For the longest time, it just didn't seem possible. I don't know why. It's weird now. It feels like that was someone else married to him."

"Well, you do look pretty unrecognizable." She was wearing the contact that disguised her eye injury, slightly tinted sunglasses, red lipstick, and she'd tied a silk scarf over her hair like some old-time movie star.

"Was I supposed to wear a disguise?" Luz asked.

Katherine patted the delicate navy scarf, smoothing the edges. "No, I just really enjoy this. Becoming someone else. Do you think that's a bad sign?"

Geneva laughed. "No, but maybe you should restrict it to cocktail parties and vacations from now on. You know, instead of counterintelligence strikes."

"Maybe."

Her muscles were beginning to ache with nervous energy, so Geneva bounced up and down on her toes a bit, fighting the urge to ask Luz about the rideshare app again.

She knew Frank loved to hang out at a hipster pool hall in central Denver on weekdays, since he posted about it incessantly on social media. But she also knew he always kept an eye out for a good fare even when he was relaxing. He'd once left her place early when he spotted a ride that would net him thirty dollars.

Geneva had called the Hook that afternoon and confirmed that Maggie had once again asked for a substitute instructor. She'd been sure the other women would back out, but they hadn't. Instead they'd both agreed to meet Geneva half a mile from the pool hall and see if Luz could catch him for another pet-friendly ride. If someone else picked it up, they'd cancel and try again every thirty minutes.

So far Luz's request was just hanging out there, waiting for someone to take it. The plan wasn't airtight, but it was better than hoping Maggie would take care of it when she couldn't even be found. This could all be over in half an hour.

Katherine was staring up at the sky again, and when she dropped her face to look at Geneva, her gaze seemed far away.

"When we first got married . . . I'd never lived with a man before, never even had a real boyfriend before him. And we'd argue, of course, like anyone does. But whenever I got upset, whenever I cried, he'd accuse me of being manipulative. 'Stop trying to manipulate me. I see what you're doing.'" She barked out a rough laugh. "I started believing that's actually what I was doing. That crying was my weapon. That my emotions were insulting. But I was just having feelings! I was sad or angry or . . . or *grieving. Jesus.*"

Geneva cringed. Her best friend in high school had dated someone like that. She'd seen it up close.

"So I think . . . ," Katherine continued. "I've asked myself that question too. Why did I stay so long? This isn't the olden days, and lots of other Catholics get divorced. But I'd smothered my own emotions so much I was just filled with cotton. Nothing there to feel, because he didn't want to hear any of that and I didn't want to feel it, anyway. You know?"

"I'm sorry," Geneva said.

Ballyhoo bounced up on his hind legs to lick Katherine's fingers. "Thanks, pup," she said.

"I think I'm going to rescue my girlfriend," Luz said suddenly.

"Oh—" Geneva started, but then Luz jerked her hand up with a gasp to look at the screen.

"It's Frank! He'll be here in three minutes!"

"Oh God," Geneva groaned, her throat burning with acid reflux. She'd never had it before, but she could only assume that was the source of the sour pain.

"So are we going to take the ride?" Luz asked, her words running together. "All the way to the airport?"

"I'll pick you up there," Geneva said. "But hopefully it won't come to that. If I cause enough of a scene here and Katherine manages to find the drugs, you two can just get out and walk away, right? That's what I'd do if there was drama with a driver."

Luz nodded her head in a rapid bob while Katherine grinned with nervous energy. "Ready?" she asked Luz, and they both moved toward the street.

Geneva hung behind, heart pounding and bladder pretending it needed to pee. God, she was scared. Scared to pull this off, but equally scared just to see him. He'd been a bogeyman for months, but now he was a victim. *Her* victim. Resentment and sorrow fought each other in her stomach, churning up more acid.

But she would make this right. She had to.

She eased forward enough that she could see Ballyhoo and just the edge of Luz's shoe as they waited at the curb. A huge thump of bass music suddenly exploded through her chest, and Geneva cried out, swinging around to look behind her. For one moment she thought it was Frank's black car, that he'd somehow clued in to their female gang and its plans and snuck up behind her to ruin it.

But no, it was a black car that had been parked next to a metal door in the alleyway. A man now sat behind the wheel, looking at his phone and smoking a joint.

"Good Lord," she wheezed before turning back toward the mouth of the alley. And then he was there. Frank.

He'd rolled his window down to babytalk to Ballyhoo as Luz opened the back door.

Geneva pressed her spine to the wall and closed her eyes, as if he couldn't see her if she couldn't see him. When she heard the door clap shut, she looked again.

Luz was in the car already, and Katherine was just opening the front door. She glanced over the roof of the car in time to catch Geneva's eye. Geneva nodded.

Frank had already twisted the other way to talk to Ballyhoo in the back seat, so Geneva stepped forward. She couldn't feel her feet, couldn't really feel herself moving at all, but she knew she was closer because she saw Frank pop open the glove compartment as he crowed, "Of course I remember you! What a great dog!"

Ballyhoo barked, then howled, and Frank absolutely cackled with delight as he handed over a treat. Katherine looked from the glove box to Geneva and tipped her chin in a nod.

This was it. She had to do it, so she did.

"Frank," she said, her voice cracking out louder than she'd meant it. Frank's head whipped around.

For a moment he only looked a little lost, but then his eyes widened. "Geneva?"

She tried not to watch Katherine as her hand reached forward. "Hi. What are you doing here?"

"Working," he said, starting to shift his head back toward his passengers, but Geneva lurched forward to put her hands on the edge of the open window.

"Listen. Frank, can we talk for a second? About what happened?"

"No!" He sounded alarmed. Katherine was still hunched forward, searching. "I didn't—"

"Frank, I'm sorry, okay? I wanted to apologize."

That shocked him into freezing. His eyes were locked tight on Geneva now. "What?"

"I'm sorry, Frank. I've finally realized you didn't do it." And then she burst into tears. Not as a ploy or even a manipulation, but because she *was* sorry. Sorry for Frank and her parents and her students. But mostly sorry for herself and the open wound of her heart. Sorry for the way she'd never trust so fully again. Sorry that she'd almost taken Frank down with her.

"Hey, hey," he said, his voice soft and urgent.

He must have gotten out of the car, because he put two awkward hands on her shoulders, clearly at a loss over how to touch her. When she leaned forward, he encircled her in a loose hug. "Hey," he repeated again, the syllable a bit high with panic.

She heard more movement and managed to open her eyes as she drew in a big, stuttering breath. Katherine stood outside the passenger seat, giving Geneva an exaggerated nod and a big thumbs-up. Luz was sliding across the back seat to get out on Katherine's side.

"I'm sorry," Geneva whispered.

"Are you okay?" Frank asked, hands rubbing her back. "Is everything all right?"

"Yeah. I just got overwhelmed when I saw you. I'm sorry that I thought you sent the video. Now I know you didn't. I've been thinking about reaching out, but . . ." She left it at that. "I'm glad I ran into you, though."

"I don't understand. What . . . ?" Frowning, he twisted around to look behind him, but both women had disappeared, vanishing down the street. "Shit. Anyway. What's up with you?"

"I'll just . . . I'll call you sometime, okay?" Geneva offered as she pulled away.

"Sure. Yeah. Hit me up."

She wouldn't. She hoped she never saw him again. But she felt lighter when she leaned in for one last quick hug. "Take care, Frank."

And that was it. It was over. She walked down to the corner, took a right, then nearly jogged two more blocks to the huge paid lot they'd all parked in. Both women were waiting next to Katherine's car. Luz was grinning from ear to ear, and Katherine jumped up and down.

"We did it!" she cried. "Oh my God, we did it! Now what do I do?" She laughed and held out her hand. "I have drugs!"

Geneva waved frantic hands at the little plastic bag. "Good Lord, go throw that in a trash can or something!"

"Okay, okay. Got it." She raced across the lot to a burger place on the corner and pushed open the outdoor garbage bin.

"I think I'm going to throw up," Luz said.

"I actually feel okay after crying."

"Were you really crying? I thought you were acting."

She shrugged. "I freaked out and decided to go with it and let go."

When Katherine returned, her scarf was a little askew, and she'd taken off her glasses to wipe sweat from her brow. "Wow."

"Thank you," Geneva said. "Thank you both so much. I can't believe you did this for me."

They both hugged her and made noise about how it had been nothing, but she knew that wasn't true. They all stood there awkwardly then, coming down from their criminal high, until Ballyhoo barked and tugged at his leash.

Luz sighed. "Well, I guess that's it. I'd better go. Bally is ready for dinner, and I need to start making some plans."

"For how to rescue your girlfriend?" Geneva asked.

"Exactly."

They hugged again, and Luz packed Ballyhoo into her car and drove off with a wave.

All the exhaustion of the past week hit Geneva like a truck, and she let her breath out on a long sigh, half of her strength going with it. "Is there some way I can help you?" she asked Katherine.

"I don't think so. But I'll call if things go sideways. Meeting you has been good for me. Thank you."

"No, thank *you*. That worked out perfectly."

"Hopefully we'll all have happy endings after all!"

"Hopefully."

Katherine got into her car and slipped her sunglasses on, and Geneva waved her off before setting off across the concrete toward the other corner of the lot, already thinking of how early she'd need to be up tomorrow. Class had been great again this morning, despite one potty accident, but—

When she heard a car door open nearby, she pulled her keys out to beep her own lock.

Her fingers were curling around the door handle when something jolted her aside. No, not something. Some*one*. A body shoved her into the next car, spiking pain through her arm and knocking her keys to the ground. Geneva was already turning, ready to scream, when a man spoke in her ear.

"I knew it. I *knew* it."

She couldn't see much of him as she tried to twist away, but she knew it wasn't Frank. His skin was too pale, his shoulders too slight. It was a stranger, a madman, his hands grabbing and pulling her from behind.

Fingers dug cruelly into her arms as she tried to lunge away, and when she finally broke free, she fell, scraping her palms on the ground. Terror swept over her, terror that she was on the ground and vulnerable to anything, hidden by cars from people near the street—

The man grabbed her around the waist and hauled her up so forcefully that all the air left her in a whoosh, stealing the scream she'd been about to unleash. He was pressed against her back, his whole body telling her he was bigger, stronger.

"You're going to tell me everything, understand? Every goddamn thing you two have plotted together."

What was happening? What the fuck was happening? Could it be a friend of Frank's? But why? She tried to force her lungs to expand so she could scream and cry and fight.

When she realized he'd hauled her up and started to carry her across the parking lot, she bucked and twisted, finally getting out a weak yell for help, despite the arm wrapped around her middle.

No. This couldn't be happening. It wasn't real. The sun was still out. There were people inside the restaurant she could see when she lifted her head.

"No!" she screamed, desperately twisting, determined to survive whatever the hell this was. "Stop!"

They reached the next row of cars before the man fumbled his hold. She fell, but she landed with her feet under her and managed to stumble a few steps away, almost making it into the open space past the car bumpers.

Just as she thought she was free, she was jerked to a stop, her sweater pulling against her. She tried to tug it free of his hold, but it didn't budge.

Managing a small cry, she looked down at her fisted hands, and something flashed through her. Anger, strength, or just terror, she wasn't sure. But freedom was right there, and she meant to have it.

She took a deep breath, planted one foot, and turned toward the pull on her body instead of away from it. She let the momentum of his strength add to her speed, and then she swung her fist up as hard as she could just like Maggie had taught her.

The sound hit her first, bone on bone, a crack like stone slightly softened by the yielding layers of skin. Then the pain exploded through her hand as if she'd punched glass and driven the shards into her joints. She cried out at the agony of it, but the pain didn't matter, because the man dropped like a sack of onions, collapsing to the ground with only a soft "Umf!"

Panting and cradling her throbbing hand, Geneva stared down at him for one moment, wondering if she'd hit him so hard she'd killed him, because it certainly felt like she'd broken off a piece of her fist in his face. But his eyes fluttered open, and he looked vaguely up at her.

She didn't recognize him at first. He'd tugged a black beanie low on his head, and the hoodie he wore had ridden almost to the chin he reached up to touch. But a few more seconds of looking into his eyes, and she knew him.

Geneva spun and sprinted to her car to grab her keys from the ground. Without a moment's hesitation, she squealed out of the space, whipped the wheel around, and headed straight for Maggie's police station. She knew where it was. She'd sat outside it a couple of days ago, afraid to go inside. But she wasn't afraid now. She'd walk in and scream until Maggie came out to get her.

This all had to end tonight.

CHAPTER 27

KATHERINE

"Mom, has Dad been in touch?"

She hadn't told Charlotte she'd blocked his calls, so Katherine avoided answering the question. "Why?" Phone pressed to her ear, she glanced at the time on the microwave. It was half past seven. After her adventures with Luz and Geneva, she'd fallen asleep on the couch for a while, and she still felt disoriented from the impromptu nap. "Have you landed?"

"Yes! I'm still on the plane, but Dad hasn't responded to any of my texts, and I'm freaking out. Can you come get me if he doesn't show?"

"Of course." She felt a quick thrill that Peter had dropped the ball and she'd be able to swoop in as the hero. Still, she couldn't help but look toward her door, wondering if anyone might be skulking around out there. "Maybe he's just driving?" she suggested.

"Maybe. We're still taxiing, and I have to wait for my bag."

"I'll call Grandma and see if she knows anything. Don't stress about it; just text me your flight info. I might be a little late. Or maybe he's already there and his phone died."

"Yeah, maybe. I'll text if I see him. Thanks, Mom."

Frowning, Katherine walked out onto her patio, unable to shake a feeling of strangeness. It was Tuesday, so maybe he was stuck in a late work meeting?

Hesitant to call him, she tried her mom. The phone rang for a long time before she finally answered, her voice frazzled and short. "What is it?"

"Have you seen Peter?"

"Not for a couple of days. Our palm order went missing, and I've been running around gathering up extras."

"Your what?"

"It's Palm Sunday in a few days, Katherine! My word, you've really lost your way."

"Oh, palm leaves. I see."

"The post office must have stashed it God knows where, and now I'm begging for palms from other parishes like a pauper. I can't believe how stingy some of these churches are."

"Got it. Well, I'm heading out to pick up Charlotte. I guess Peter forgot about her flight."

Her mother snorted. "That doesn't seem likely. It was all he could talk about when I last saw him. He kept saying everything would be fine. I think he's ashamed of how awful the whole situation has become."

She could tell by her dark scorn that "the whole situation" was Katherine leaving, not Peter cheating. Or maybe it was both. Maybe she was finally coming to the belated realization that her son-in-law wasn't the perfect boy she'd needed him to be. Katherine let herself feel a moment of hope.

"Wherever he is, he's not answering his phone. I'm heading out to the airport now. Worst case, we both show up and have to pretend to be civil. Good luck with the palms, Mom."

She didn't tell her she and Charlotte were going to visit Becca. She hoped she could put off the discussion until after she returned. Better to experience a reunion without even a hint of their mother between them.

Rushing, she brushed her hair and pulled on a bra and a clean shirt to look fresh for her daughter. After she snapped her eye patch into place, she was out the door and nearly jogging to the elevator.

Joy bubbled up in her as she drove toward the freeway. Not only was she in the clear about Brandon's murder, but now she'd get to see her daughter early and spend at least a few minutes with her. Despite all her mistakes, everything was working out.

She was halfway there when Charlotte texted to say she was at the baggage carousel and her dad was nowhere to be found. If she still loved him, Katherine would be frantic, calling every friend, checking in with Father Carlo. But he didn't belong to her anymore. She'd let him go, so she felt only a mild concern for Charlotte's peace of mind and very little worry about what could have happened to Peter.

Was it possible his drinking had gotten so bad he'd spent the day on a bender and passed out? If that was the case, Charlotte could stay with her. They could even leave early for Oregon. Whatever she wanted to do.

She spent the rest of the drive waiting for another text or a call telling her to turn around, and she found herself speeding faster and faster toward the white peaks of Denver International, determined to beat the clock so she wouldn't miss the chance to see her daughter, however briefly.

But then she was gliding up to the pickup area, and Charlotte was right there waving, a slightly strained smile on her face. She looked the same, tall and slim like Katherine, but carrying herself with absolute confidence, as if she wanted to be even taller. Katherine fought tears as she pulled to a stop and leapt from the car to hug her girl tightly.

"Were you waiting long?" she asked before she breathed in the scent of her daughter's skin.

"Not long."

Charlotte squeezed her back in a way she hadn't in a long time, and Katherine's heart opened up from years of hibernation. She'd wanted this closeness back, but she'd had no idea how to get it. It was likely her own fault. Without even realizing it, she'd closed herself off to survive, and who wanted to hold on to someone who was barely there?

She grabbed the suitcase as soon as Charlotte let her go and hauled it into the trunk. "Dirty clothes?" she asked.

"Maybe!"

"Well, let's get going. I'll take you to the house, and we'll make sure everything's okay."

Charlotte's nervousness about the late pickup bubbled up into chattiness, and she told a dozen stories in quick succession about her roommate, her favorite professor, the professor she despised, and her new group of friends from a campus wilderness group. She'd tried rock climbing, which Katherine wanted to know nothing about. She made her daughter promise not to tell her about those trips until she returned from them.

"I won't sleep a wink, and you'll emerge from the woods to fifty-five missed calls from your mom. Nobody wants that."

Charlotte laughed. "I'm not your baby anymore, Mom."

"I know that, because babies don't climb cliffs. In fact, you're allowed to lock them in tiny cages to keep them from wandering off and doing dangerous things like that."

"Fair point. I won't give you any details. So what have you been up to?" she asked, and Katherine choked on a horrified laugh, because she would never, ever tell Charlotte what she'd been up to. Though she supposed that at some point in her old age she might confess to having been a murder suspect for a few days. But that was a very long way off.

"You know . . . I've been unpacking. Making plans. I'm thinking about going back to school."

"Really?"

"Should I apply to Gonzaga?"

"Mom. That's not even funny."

"It's kind of funny," she said. "Admit it."

Charlotte giggled, and Katherine's grin was so wide it hurt her cheeks.

"We could room together."

"Stop, Mom."

Things still felt light even when they turned onto her old street, but when they both saw how dark the house was, silence fell between them.

"Do you think he's okay?" Charlotte asked, her tone so hushed it was nearly a whisper. It was the first time it hit Katherine that he might truly be in danger. He was fifty and under a lot of stress. It wouldn't be unheard-of for a man like that to have a heart attack.

"Maybe you should wait in the car."

"Don't say that, Mom."

Nodding, she turned off the car and stepped out onto the driveway. She desperately wanted to order Charlotte not to come in, but it wasn't even her home anymore. She was here only because her daughter was staying here.

She took Charlotte's key from her and reluctantly unlocked the front door. "Peter?" she called out; then she yelled his name more loudly, reaching for the entry light to chase away the threatening shadows. "Peter?"

The place seemed shut down and deserted, as if no one had opened a window or door in days. Her mother had kept the house clean, but it still felt . . . stale. She crept farther in, Charlotte silent at her side.

The moment she turned on a light in the family room, Katherine spotted an empty whisky bottle. "Peter?" she called again as she crossed into the kitchen. The sink held a few dirty dishes, mostly glass tumblers.

"I'll check the bedroom," she said. "You wait here."

This time Charlotte agreed, her face pale and eyes roaming over every surface.

The hallway light didn't respond when she flipped the switch, though she tried three times just in case, her skin crawling at the dimness. She could still see; she just didn't like the feeling of gloom reaching out toward her.

The master-bedroom door was closed, and Katherine found herself nearly tiptoeing down the hall, which made no sense at all. "Peter?" she tried again. "I'm here with Charlotte! I picked her up at the airport!"

Nothing. She snapped on the bathroom switch just to reassure herself. The light barely penetrated the hall.

"Charlotte, check the garage. See if his car is there."

No sound, no movement, no light beneath the bedroom door. It seemed to draw farther away from her, a fun-house nightmare effect as every worst possibility jittered through her head.

She heard Charlotte move into the kitchen, heard the sharp squeak of that one floorboard that needed repair, a sound she couldn't have named before that felt like intimacy now. She wasn't supposed to be here anymore, inside this house, playing at being his concerned wife.

"His car is here!" Charlotte called.

She knew he wouldn't kill himself over her. She simply wasn't worth that much to this man who believed suicide to be a mortal sin. But did he really believe in mortal sin, or had every moment of it been a game? A way to best others?

Regardless, she'd half expected him to have settled into relief by now. Relief that he could trade up and move on without his disappointment of a wife. She couldn't wrap her head around his sudden descent into drinking and rage.

Despite her slow steps, she'd finally reached the bedroom door, and she had no excuse to hesitate, so she forced herself to raise a hand and knock. The first effort was laughably weak, an ignorable tapping. She knocked more firmly, holding her breath.

No response came. If Charlotte hadn't been there, she knew full well that she would have turned and left, unwilling to brave the space beyond the door. She even looked back wistfully at the bright entry, only to find her daughter there waiting, her arms crossed tight, her teeth worrying at her lip.

This was one of those terrifying moments of parenthood when you couldn't ignore that you were the big, brave grown-up. You were the only one who could chase away the monsters, and there was no one else to call.

So she turned the knob. "I'm coming in!" she tried, hoping for a groan of hungover misery in response.

The door swung in on thick grayness, revealing only a lighter rectangle of reflected light on the carpet. The room smelled awful. Body odor and booze and vomit. Katherine whispered his name one more time as her hand slid over the wall, searching for the switch. It had to be there, right there where she'd reached for it a million times, but she found only smoothness. It had disappeared, another victim of this terrible fun house. It was gone.

But then she brushed hard plastic with her pinky, took a breath, and caught the switch.

Peter was dead. He was lying on the bed, so pale he looked nearly blue, a pool of vomit near his head, his hands loosely curled at his sides. There was a glass on the side table and a plastic bottle of some medication next to a notepad.

And he was *dead*.

She almost backed out and closed the door, almost shut out everything so she could flee. But then she thought she saw the barest rise of his vomit-stained chest. "Peter?"

Rushing forward, she reached out to touch his shoulder, his mouth. His skin felt clammy and cool, but she felt the shush of breath across her palm. Katherine snapped out his name one more time, but he didn't flinch or respond in any way.

"Charlotte!" she screamed. "Call 911!"

"What's wrong?" her daughter wailed, suddenly ten years younger, a scared child again.

"He needs an ambulance!"

She tapped his face with a few slaps, trying to jar him awake, but he still didn't respond. She glanced at the nightstand and saw that the bottle was an over-the-counter sleep aid, and the notebook next to it was scrawled with his familiar, spiky handwriting, as if he'd tried to cut the page with his words.

I'm sorry. It wasn't my fault.

Was he trying for absolution from the sin of suicide? Did he think that would be enough?

She shook the thought from her mind and pulled the pillow from beneath his head to straighten his airway. He was still breathing and didn't need CPR, but she grabbed a wad of tissues to swipe at his mouth and clear it of vomit.

Beneath the sickness, his chin was swollen and bleeding from a cut along the edge, though she had no idea what could have caused it. Perhaps he'd stumbled from bed at some point and fallen.

The sound of her daughter's voice reached her, warbling with fear as she spoke, but Katherine's pulse was hammering too loudly for her to make out the words. Then another thundering began, drowning out her heart, and Charlotte was yelling, "He's in there! Please help him! He's in the bedroom!"

How? How had help arrived so quickly? Had Katherine lost time? Had she passed out in shock and just come to? The ambulance couldn't possibly be here. Unless Peter had managed to call for himself in the minutes before she arrived.

Oh God, that must have been it. He'd regretted this awful act and reached out for help.

"I think he took sleeping pills," she said, glancing up at the sound of people stepping through the doorway.

But they weren't paramedics at all. Maggie was first inside the room, then Koval, then two uniformed officers.

She felt only fear for herself in that moment. The horrified realization that they meant to arrest her after all. That they'd chased her here to drag her away in front of her daughter. "No," she murmured. "You can't. He's not okay."

But only Maggie looked at her. Koval rushed forward, checking for Peter's pulse as Katherine pushed off the bed and stepped away from one of the other police officers, her hands up in surrender.

"Mrs. Rye," Maggie said.

Katherine glanced toward her in confusion.

"Come over here while they check him out."

"We called for an ambulance," she whispered.

"Okay, we'll take care of him. He'll be placed under arrest once he's awake and aware."

Yes, she'd obviously passed out and lost time and her hold on reality, because none of this made any sense. "What are you talking about?"

"Your husband is being arrested for the murder of Brandon Johanssen."

"No. Maggie, that's not right."

Maggie's eyes slid toward her partner, then back to Katherine. She shook her head in the sparest of movements, but Katherine didn't care if she somehow revealed they were on a first-name basis. "My husband didn't know I was with Brandon. And if he did, he wouldn't give a damn. He doesn't care about me. You've got the wrong person. Peter has nothing to do with this."

"He's on tape at the hotel. I saw him with my own eyes. He got off the elevator on the sixth floor about five minutes after you did."

She shook her head, her ears ringing so loudly it sounded like sirens.

"Mom?" Charlotte asked, her voice choked with tears.

Katherine spun toward her daughter, poised in the doorway, both slender hands raised to her mouth. "Oh, baby," she said, rushing forward to gather her up in her arms. "He's going to be okay. It was just an accident." A lie, but she'd tell it for as long as she could.

292

"What happened?"

A clatter of footsteps and equipment sounded from the entry, cutting off any explanation she could think to give. The actual paramedics hurried down the hallway, and Katherine pulled her daughter out of the way toward the master bath. "They're here. He'll be fine. He'll be okay. They'll take good care of him."

Another lie perhaps, but she'd gladly tell it over and over.

Koval looked up and dipped his chin in a nod at Maggie; then he pointed at his arm.

"What?" Katherine demanded. Maggie turned toward her. "What's he saying?"

"That Peter has a wound on his arm, and I imagine we'll discover that the blood at the scene is a DNA match."

"Mom? What is she talking about?"

"Nothing, baby. Just a mix-up." She glared at Maggie until the detective finally moved back toward the gaggle of first responders preparing to load Peter onto a gurney. An oxygen mask covered his face, and as she watched, the female paramedic took his pulse and then gave him an injection. No one was pounding on his chest or reaching for paddles, so she loosened her hold on Charlotte by a tiny degree.

"We'll follow him to the hospital," she said.

"Can I ride with him?" When Katherine didn't answer, Charlotte repeated the question more loudly. "Can I ride with my dad?"

Without looking up, the paramedic said, "If you're over eighteen, you can ride in the front."

Katherine wanted to say no; she wanted to keep Charlotte here and hide the painful truth from their daughter for as long as she could. But Charlotte was an adult now, and she was already rushing forward to follow the crowd, and no one could stop her, not even her mom.

In truth, cowardly as it was, Katherine felt relieved that she wouldn't have to be the one to say the words *overdose* or *suicide* aloud to their little girl . . . much less *under arrest*.

"I'll see you as soon as we get there!" she called instead. And yet she hung back as they strapped Peter onto the gurney and began to rush him from the room. She hung back because Maggie did, and Katherine was caught up in staring wide-eyed at her friend or enemy or whatever she was, waiting for any of this to make sense.

Maggie's voice dropped to a bare rumble of a whisper. "I shouldn't tell you any of this after the chaotic hell you've created, but yes, it was Peter. He's on the surveillance video, his arm is injured, and he was following you today."

"What?" she breathed.

"You know how I know?"

She shook her head, assuming from her tone that the answer wasn't a simple sighting by the cops.

"I know because he spotted Geneva there, snuck up on her after you and Luz left, and tried to force her into his car."

A hail of shocks seemed to hit her at once, the realization of what that all must mean. That Maggie knew the women had been colluding. That Katherine had lied to her about everything once again . . . and worse, the sickening, churning realization that there was only one reason Peter would be at the same random location as Katherine.

He'd been following her. For how long? She thought of the person at the park. Then she thought of meeting Brad at the hotel.

But it made no sense.

"Is Geneva okay?" she managed to ask.

"She's fine. She knocked him on his ass, apparently."

Katherine touched her face, remembering Peter's swollen chin and jaw. "So he knows? About all of us?"

"He certainly doesn't know enough. She said he was growling something about a conspiracy, but no one will want to hear that from him now. It'll just be the ravings of a man who went over the edge and is desperate to avoid blame."

For a fleeting moment she felt relief. It was over. Peter didn't know about the system, and the killer had been caught. But that was just a flash of blue sky as her mind tumbled. And tumbled. And then she hit the ground again. The killer was Peter. Her husband. Which meant the murder was her fault. And it meant that Charlotte's whole world was about to explode into deadly little bits that might cut right through her. Her baby was about to lose her father in one of the worst possible ways.

"I need to go," she mumbled, lurching for the bedroom door.

"We have questions, Mrs. Rye," Maggie called after her, still invested in the cover-up when all Katherine could imagine was the aftermath.

"I need to go," she said again, stumbling down the hall to push her way past Koval in the entry.

"Let her," she heard him say as she burst outside.

The moon was just rising, glowing against the mountains. It was still the same day, when she felt like she'd been stuck in that dark bedroom forever. The sirens hadn't even completely escaped the neighborhood when she pulled out and began tracing their route. She passed another patrol car and several neighbors standing in groups in their driveways. A woman she'd known for fifteen years met Katherine's gaze as she passed. Neither of them raised a hand.

"God, please keep my Charlotte safe," she prayed, her belief rushing back to her as pure desperation. "Please let her get through this without scars." Impossible, of course, and why would God grant her, of all people, a miracle? He wouldn't. Either because Katherine didn't deserve it or he didn't exist, and she didn't care which. All she knew was that her daughter would suffer.

The hospital was only four miles away. When they'd first moved in, Katherine had been comforted, imagining all the times she'd go into labor, how fast things might move by the third or fourth birth. Years later, she'd only thought of it as the place she'd gone for the D and C to remove one dead child from her womb. And then that last terrible stay when Peter had destroyed what was left of her love. Now it would be the place her husband died or was arrested. Either way, his life would end there, and there was nothing she could do to save him.

Heart pulling toward her poor, breaking daughter, Katherine turned onto the road to the hospital and hit the gas.

CHAPTER 28

Luz

Dependable, punctual, perfectionist Luz hadn't sprung fully formed that way from the body of her mother. Her assets were strengths, but they were also tools for chipping through her rough beginning, coping mechanisms she'd learned over years of uncertainty and scarcity.

Life had never been easy for the Molina family, but Luz's first memory was of the crying and chaos of her father's deportation when she was five. They'd been making ends meet, and then suddenly they hadn't, and Luz and her older brother had been far too young to contribute to the family budget.

Her mother had been a constant loving presence in her life, but sometimes her mom had felt more like an idea than an actual person, because she'd worked constantly to support them. At age seven, her brother had begun looking after Luz, walking her to and from school and learning to cook simple meals. Leon had been a good big brother, protective, but he certainly hadn't been immune from the rebellion of adolescence, and he'd started getting into trouble when Luz had still been young, nine or ten.

When Leon and his friends had taken to stealing small bills and spare change from nearby homes, Luz had been dragged along on their after-school forays to act as lookout. His new hobby had lasted only about six months before he'd been caught by a homeowner asleep in a back bedroom, and Leon had lost a tooth in the resulting beating.

He'd lost a hell of a lot more than that when their mother had found out. He'd been sent to his uncle in California to work in vineyards for two months *to learn about hard work*. He'd returned taller, stronger, and more responsible, though he'd never quite been her mischievous brother again. But he'd settled down and now managed an HVAC business and had helped pay off the house he and their mom lived in.

But in those wild and wicked six months of being professional child thieves, Luz had learned a lot. The signs that a house was occupied, which entry points were likely to be unlocked or poorly maintained, and the best way to get in if all else failed.

Luz thought about all those things as she watched on her phone screen as Tanner's garage door opened, exposing the ass end of his black pickup.

Safely around the corner, she immediately popped the trunk of her car so she could pull out the doggy stroller Sveta had purchased for Ballyhoo when he was a puppy. He hadn't used it since—too undignified and confining—but she unfolded it, clicked the hood into place, and zipped the weatherproof covering around the seat. Wearing sunglasses, a medical mask, and a huge sun hat she'd stuffed her hair under, Luz kept her head tucked as she walked down the sidewalk, her eyes on her phone, watching the feed from the drone hovering high above his house.

Tanner reversed out, and Luz turned the corner and headed toward his house as if she belonged there. When he roared off down the street, his garage door was on the descent. She moved calmly up his driveway, shoved the doggy carrier ahead, and watched it fly past the safety sensors that stopped the door in its tracks.

Once she'd ducked under, she stepped immediately to the garage controller and hit the button twice, taking a deep, shaky breath as the door finally finished its descent.

Even in bad neighborhoods most people didn't lock the interior door of the garage, too irritated by the inconvenience of digging for keys when they were carrying groceries or toddlers. It was 9:00 a.m. on a weekday, Tanner's daughter was at school, and Luz had the house to herself for at least a few minutes, so she let herself in.

Tanner didn't believe in "babying" dogs, which was especially hilarious considering how Luz had gotten in, but she knew he insisted his dog stay outside during the day, even in winter. *Dogs are pets, not children,* he'd said more than once.

Still, she made a kissing noise and waited a few moments just in case. Nothing. No dog, no cat, no unexpected family members.

Her own calmness surprised her as she walked straight into the kitchen, her eyes on the prize. Big, tough Tanner had the same terrible habit of many men of his type: he bragged. He fancied himself an instructor in the school of life, passing on a constant stream of helpful tidbits. The best way to lace tennis shoes. The ideal time of day to take a flight. Exactly the right amount of lawn watering during a drought. And just how much cash you should have on hand for a worldwide emergency . . . and, of course, the safest spot to keep that stash.

Luz hadn't asked, but he'd happily supplied the answers: twenty thousand dollars was just the right amount for buying your way out of a global food shortage or escaping a country tumbling into civil war or some other unforeseen calamity. And Tanner kept his bundle of cash frozen in a block of ice and wrapped in foil and plastic wrap labeled *Stew Meat. No one wants ancient stew meat,* he'd laughed.

Better to mark it tripas, she'd said, but he hadn't gotten the joke.

He might have moved it. He might have remembered that he'd told Luz, his mortal enemy, where he kept twenty grand hidden in his house.

Then again, she doubted he saw her as any kind of threat at all, despite his alarm when she'd confronted him.

When the floor creaked beneath her foot, Luz froze, shot through with her first spike of real fear. But it faded quickly, gobbled up by the anger that had lived in her boiling blood for days.

None of this was fair. And if it wasn't fair for her, it didn't need to be fair for him either. He'd made her into this, his enemy, the thief of his livelihood. He'd tried to destroy everything she loved, so he deserved this small revenge. Someday he would need that money, and someday he'd be very surprised to find it gone.

Luz opened the freezer door of the stainless-steel refrigerator with a gloved hand. Like everyone else's freezer, it was packed. Ice cream cartons, frozen microwavable meals, packs of veggies, and wrapped leftovers all stuffed into too little space. Heart sinking, she resigned herself to unloading each shelf in the search.

Five minutes later, fingers icy despite her gloves, her heart was in free fall. It wasn't there. There wasn't even anything close to it. She'd unwrapped a piece of cake and a lump of something that looked like meatloaf even though she knew they weren't the right size.

It was hopeless. There was no money. No money to help Luz relocate to Europe. No money to get Sveta out of Russia. She'd have to wait and save and find a way to make it work in a year or two. She could move in with her mom and brother. Send Sveta money so she could get a safer job that didn't require her to be out at midnight. She could manage it in six months if she tried hard.

The anger boiled up again, and she cried out, a ragged scream of rage that made the dog in the backyard start barking. Resigned, she packed everything carefully back where it belonged.

Luz turned to go, stomping toward the garage door set between the kitchen and the family room. Pictures hung on the walls, pictures of Tanner and his daughter, a beautiful girl despite her reluctant half smiles. Tanner's family was safe. No one could take that away from him the way he'd taken it away from Luz. But she'd done all she could to hurt him, and now she had to admit defeat. It wasn't enough. It would never be enough.

But then she noticed the dark line of a partly open door to her right and, just beyond it, a step descending to another level. Tanner had a basement.

Heart hammering, she hurried toward the door to fling it open and hit the light switch. A straight set of white wooden stairs led down to an unknown space below. With a worried glance at the display on her phone, she said a quick prayer and pulled the drone control from her pack to fly it a bit higher. Now she could see down the street to the next block over. No vehicles moved. He wasn't returning yet.

Luz dared to dart down the stairs and turn on the light switch at the bottom. The left side of the basement was roughly finished, the wall graced with a huge television. A sectional leather sofa sat in front of it, with several gaming systems on the carpeted floor.

But to the right, the floor was cement, and from the bottom of the stairs, she spotted a water heater, a furnace, and a huge white deep freezer.

"Yes!" she hissed, and sprinted toward it, her ears burning with a premonition that she would hear the garage door rise at any moment. If it did . . . She should have brought the doggy stroller inside, if only to have the chance to escape out the back door. But it was too late. She'd made that mistake, but it would be worth it if . . .

A puff of cold air rose to greet her when she opened the top of the freezer. Luz dug her hands right into the assortment of bagged and boxed foods, haphazardly sliding things aside before digging deeper boxes out. When the pile collapsed in, she finally started tossing things out two by two, desperate to reach the bottom.

And suddenly, there it was. A perfectly wrapped rectangle marked *Stew Meat 2017*. "Fucking bingo," she growled.

After tucking the heavy block into her pack, she put everything she'd tossed out back into the freezer, did her best to smooth out the pile of packages, then shut the top. The block was a cold lump against the skin of her back, but the rest of her burned hot as fire. Her heart felt as if it might explode from her chest.

She took a deep breath and raced up the stairs, barely feeling any strain on her thighs, the adrenaline was so thick in her blood. She turned off the lights, then checked the drone again, carefully touching her gaze on every intersection of every road she could see. A red SUV drove down the next street over, but it stayed straight and didn't veer toward Tanner's. She was in the clear.

Luz walked out, opened the garage door, and grabbed Ballyhoo's stroller. She was already outside when she realized the problem. She couldn't close the door from here. If he found his garage door open when he got home, he might shrug it off as some malfunction, but he might also look far too closely for any clues. She didn't want him to have an inkling, not until he really needed that money and couldn't have it.

After parking the stroller on the grass, Luz ran back into the garage, punched the button, and sprinted for the closing door. She high-stepped over the sensors at the base of the opening, ducked below the descending metal, and slid her body outside. The door thunked closed behind her, and she was clear.

This time she didn't bother hurrying away. Instead she sashayed down the driveway, grabbed the stroller, and pushed it idly toward the corner, a satisfied smile on her face and a block of ice cooling her heart.

She'd start applying for an overseas job tomorrow and figure out who they needed to bribe at the border, and she and Sveta would be free.

CHAPTER 29

KATHERINE

It still felt so strange to be in the house, even though it had been six months since she'd left her apartment and returned to her old home. It seemed as if she were house sitting her own bad dreams.

Katherine wanted to put it on the market—she desperately needed to be anywhere else—but selling the only home Charlotte had ever known felt like yet another violation of her daughter's life. Katherine hated every moment of being there, but she couldn't pull that security out from under Charlotte. She'd lost too much already.

At first she'd been so consumed with her father surviving and recovering that she'd failed to recognize even the idea that he was accused of a terrible crime. Then she'd refused to believe any of the facts or evidence, no matter who presented it. Instead, she'd listened to her father, who didn't deny his own guilt to her, but rambled on and on about a conspiracy. It was all a setup, he'd claimed. A deliberate campaign by Katherine to ruin his life.

It didn't even matter that he'd since pled guilty, bargaining down to a charge of second-degree murder of the lowest class. A crime of passion, basically. The plea bargain meant a sentence of only twelve years. With good behavior, he would be out well before his sixtieth birthday.

She shook her head in disgust. The judge apparently accepted that sometimes men like Peter just had violent outbursts that couldn't be contained. An unfortunate fact of life.

Peter hadn't had much choice but to plead guilty. The evidence had been overwhelming. But at first . . . at first even Katherine hadn't believed it. How in the world would Peter have found her at that hotel, and why would he have cared what she was doing there? He didn't love her. She knew he didn't.

The answers had come slowly, but they'd been indisputable. First, they'd found a tracking app on his phone that had been paired to a tag hidden in Katherine's purse. Based on the history in the app, he'd activated it two days before she'd moved out of their home and had been monitoring her every movement since.

Then they'd found a detailed file he'd been keeping, beginning with his suspicion that his wife had set him up to get caught cheating. He'd had no saved pictures of the woman he'd met online and no proof of who she really was since she'd deleted her account after their encounter. But he'd written up an elaborate description of her and saved every message they'd exchanged.

She'd been coy and mysterious. Eager yet evasive. His wife must have hired this person, he'd insisted to anyone who would listen. Why else would she have deleted her every track after his party?

No one believed him about Geneva, of course. She was a random hookup who'd been caught in Peter's arms by his wife. Obviously the woman had wiped her account after that. It wasn't hard to figure out.

Even his lawyer had asked him to shut up about spotting someone who looked like his lover with Katherine in a Denver parking lot. The best his little conspiratorial fantasy would get him was a charge of assault and attempted kidnapping. It wasn't going to do him any good to claim he'd tried to drag a woman into his car, no matter who she was. And if his wife had set him up for cheating, that certainly didn't absolve him of murder.

Of course, none of his claims had mattered once the DNA was confirmed to be his. His lawyer had negotiated a deal, and two months after Peter's arrest, he'd confessed . . . but even then, Katherine's original suspicions had been validated.

He had never been jealous. He hadn't followed her to a hotel and lost his mind over his wife sleeping with another man. No, he hadn't given one moment of thought about that. Instead, he'd been convinced that she had set him up, and he'd been trying to prove it. Trying to best her one more time.

Katherine felt simultaneously vindicated and broken by that. The emotion in her husband's so-called crime of passion had been bitter contempt, not love, not jealousy. He'd tracked her to the hotel, gotten there just in time to see her paying the bartender, and followed her up to the sixth floor. He'd lurked there in the hallway for an hour, shielding himself in a recessed doorway after Brandon had opened his door. Once she'd left, he'd knocked, then shoved his way in, demanding to know what Brandon and Katherine had *clearly* planned together.

He'd been convinced they were lovers, scheming a way to get as much of Peter's hard-earned assets and swollen retirement accounts as they could, all while overseeing the ruin of the life he'd so carefully cultivated.

Brandon had denied it and resisted, shoving Peter into a wall, and they'd wrestled. Peter remembered getting his arm under Brandon's neck, but Brandon had strained for a hotel pen lying on the nightstand, and he'd stabbed Peter in the arm.

After that injury, Peter claimed to remember nothing; he'd blacked out from pain and panic. He wasn't even sure he'd killed Brandon.

Katherine could imagine the part he didn't want to discuss, didn't want to remember. How Brandon had been half-dressed in a dress shirt and underwear, how Peter must have wrapped the unknotted tie around his neck and squeezed for long, long minutes. How he'd then looped the other end around the closet doorknob in an attempt to make it look like some sort of sex game gone wrong.

All of it just to refuse Katherine any type of victory.

He'd been caught up by the conspiracy then, determined to prove that he'd been right, that he wasn't a violent person, just a man pushed to the edge by a bitch with an elaborate scheme.

And he'd been right, almost. Not about Brandon, but about Geneva. About Katherine. She knew she wasn't responsible for his violent reaction, but . . . still. Still, the guilt hung from her, pulling her body down if she let herself think about that awful time too much. So she did her best not to.

When a knock snapped her from that heavy weight, Katherine looked up from her packing with a sigh. She recognized the racket as her mother's insistent tapping. She hadn't agreed to stop walking in unannounced, but Katherine had started bolting the door to give her no choice.

It had been a couple of weeks since her last visit, and Katherine figured she'd better answer it since she was leaving for a trip in the morning. Still, she didn't hurry, idly hoping her mom would give up and go away.

When Katherine opened the front door, there she was, arms crossed and mouth frowning. "Charlotte told me you're going to Rebecca's again."

Her heart almost broke apart at that, a sharp pain ripping open the tender wound for another round of hurt. She'd texted Charlotte that she'd be out of town and where she was going, but Charlotte hadn't responded. She never did.

Without any discussion with Katherine, Charlotte had taken a job in Seattle for the summer, and when she came to Denver to visit her father in prison, she stayed with her grandmother instead of at home.

"Yes," Katherine said wearily, "I'm going to Rebecca's."

"Why can't she come here to visit? I'm her mother."

"I don't know, Mom." But she did know. Vivian was coming too, a tentative reunion, an attempt to heal the rift that Katherine had helped her mother create.

She'd caused so much pain in her life, and she just wanted to try to fix one thing at a time. Becca had been kind enough to orchestrate the reunion and play referee.

Katherine realized now that she'd been so stuck in her role as Peter's wife and Mary's daughter that she'd still been playing by their rules. She'd embraced those rules even as she'd crowed about being free. That had been her worst mistake. If she'd really been strong and past Peter's reach, she would have simply walked away and dealt with the consequences.

Instead of being truly brave and stepping into a new life on her terms, she'd wanted to change *his* narrative in *his* world. She'd still been filthy from all those years steeped in him, and her actions had contaminated Charlotte forever.

Turning her back on her mom, Katherine headed to the kitchen to take an Advil for the headache that had sprung into immediate, pulsing life.

"I wish you'd sell this place," her mom said from behind her. "It just reminds me of everything you lost."

Katherine nearly spit out her water. *She* didn't want to be reminded of Katherine's loss. She was the ultimate victim.

She inhaled, practicing the deep-breathing techniques she'd learned through meditation. "I want Charlotte to know she has a home she can come back to anytime. It won't be forever, but I feel it's the right thing for now. It's paid off. I'll save on rent money when I start school."

"School," her mother scoffed. "It's nothing but cheap trade work."

Ignoring her, Katherine sipped from her water and stared through the patio doors to the trembling leaves of an aspen tree.

She'd finally made a decision. Not dental work, but something that called to her new life, her new interests. Katherine was going to be a private investigator.

The thought made her smile to herself.

She had no plans to get a gun or work with the police. God no. But she already had a prospective career path with an insurance company investigating property fraud. She was going to get revenge on arrogant liars every day, and she'd get paid for it. Maybe she'd even get to wear disguises sometimes.

After the case had closed, Maggie had recommended Katherine to a contact. Said she had an eye for detail. That part always cracked Katherine up.

"It hardly matters," her mother said, her tone miffed at being ignored. "Charlotte can stay at my place. She'll always have a home there."

"A home?" Katherine snapped without even thinking. "With *you*?"

"I raised you three girls, didn't I?"

She turned to gape at her mother. "You provided us shelter and food, yes, but a home? A home is refuge, Mom. It's safety and love and a soft place to land. Have Becca and Vivian ever treated you like you were *home*?"

"The melodrama again," her mom said, completely stiff in the face of pain.

Katherine took another deep breath. She held it, then let it out so softly that it calmed her. "Right," she whispered. "That's fine. But you should go. I have a lot of packing to do. Will you tell Charlotte that I love her?"

"She's still not speaking to you, hm?"

Ignoring that, Katherine turned away, but she froze then, blew out one more breath, and realized she was playing by her mom's rules again, a mistake she'd promised herself she wouldn't continue to make.

Katherine turned back and reached out to wrap her arms around her mom and hold her the way she wished she'd been held. Her body didn't relax, but Katherine held on. "Just tell my daughter I love her, all right? I love her so much."

What she didn't say was that after her visit with her sisters, she was going to drive to Gonzaga and leave a note on her daughter's door: *I love you. I'm sorry. I'm in the church if you want to talk.*

Katherine's life was broken. It was a pile of shattered pieces too small to hide behind. But the good news was that she couldn't hide anymore. She had to stand there and feel every moment of her life now.

She didn't speak to Geneva regularly, because it felt too risky, but she knew she was teaching full time and loving it. And Luz had apparently moved to the Czech Republic, of all places. Everyone was moving on, and Katherine had to move on too.

But she wasn't scared. All she could do was be strong and brave and wait for her daughter to come around. On her own terms. It was what they all deserved.

CHAPTER 30

MAGGIE

Maggie knew what she'd done wrong. But she knew what she'd done right too.

As she sat in the office of the Hook, sorting through a list of women who'd called to inquire about the class, she bit down hard on the end of her pencil, the wood yielding beneath her teeth in a way that both satisfied and invited her to bite harder.

There was no real justice in this world, and if she'd had any naïveté about that in her youth, it was long gone now. But she could still expect a little redemption, couldn't she? She could expect some payback, especially if she orchestrated it herself.

There were things in this country that were illegal and things that were wrong, and then there were things that were prosecutable. In her career, she'd discovered that those circles very rarely overlapped.

White-collar crimes were hard to prove, and so they were usually ignored. The criminals who stole millions walked away with far less punishment than those who stole shitty cars. In fact, the biggest thieves often got elected to public office, or at least promoted to CEO.

The same too-hard-to-prove immunity applied to sexual assault, of course. It was most often he said–she said, and God only knew what women might say and why. Who could understand such inscrutable creatures? They couldn't even be trusted to be witnesses to their own assaults.

And of course drug offenses most often hurt no one at all but were the easiest to prosecute. If you're holding, you're guilty. And if it's planted on you, you're still guilty.

But it was deeper than that, wasn't it? Because there were countless wrongs that were no crime at all. Racism, sexism, discrimination, and all the other meanness out there thriving in everyday lives. No one did a thing about those. We're powerless as individuals in the face of the daily wrongs that slash at us as we move through our worlds.

Who the hell could you call for help when someone muttered a slur as they passed by? There was nothing you could do but absorb it and get through the rest of your day.

She'd experienced it herself over and over. Middle school racism. High school grabbing. Parties at college with poisonously strong drinks pushed on every girl out in the open, the leering looks and winks flying between the boys as if it were all fun and games.

And of course, every nasty joke told about Maggie by her fellow officers once she'd joined the force. Every flavor of banal ugliness thrown at her with *Lighten up!* floating behind it like a sparkling tail. She'd lightened up until she'd practically disappeared into mist. Lightened up until she couldn't feel her own heart.

Still, she hadn't expected it in her own home. She should have, but she hadn't.

Her ex-husband was a cop too. They'd been equals in every way. They had the same friends, same background, same beliefs, same workplace, same religion. Safe in his keeping, secure in their partnership, Maggie had let her guard down and left her most delicate vulnerabilities exposed. She'd loved him fully and had completely immersed herself in that perfect union, because she needed to be soft sometimes or she'd turn to stone.

The stone that she was now. The rock that wanted to smash the world to bits.

When she discovered that he was sleeping with a new trainee, she was no longer considered a partner. No longer protected. Instead she became the enemy, and their friends circled him to form a shield.

Maggie, you should forgive him. You shouldn't hurt his career. It was only a mistake, Maggie. No husband is perfect. He's a good man, it's a stressful job, can't you just . . . Can't you just lighten up?

Her softness began to callus over even before her husband, her love, her *man* started his campaign to discredit her and render her voiceless and choiceless.

They'd all known her for years, but suddenly, out of the blue, she was no longer a fellow officer. Instead she was a crazy bitch, a bad cop, a frigid broad, and a vengeful ex all at once. She was reduced to just another object as he flashed topless pictures of her to the other guys in the station to prove she was just like every other female. Weak and wild. Worthy of scorn. Nothing special.

She'd lost out on one promotion before the divorce was final. Then another after. She was defeated. She couldn't fight back without proving him right. So she finally gave up. She moved from Dallas to Denver, just to have a goddamn chance.

Nothing he did was illegal, not back then, but all of it deserved a revenge that she would never get. The system wasn't designed to work for her. She might have known that on some level for most of her life, but by God, she knew it in her bones then.

She'd tried to leave it behind by walking away. And Denver had been good to her. She rose through the ranks. Became a detective. Kept her head down and tried to ignore the darkness that didn't lurk through life so much as strut, safe from consequence. Then she'd started giving classes at the Hook, hoping to help a few women along the way.

But it hadn't been enough, not after Nicole had confessed to her and brought Maggie's rage to the surface. She couldn't really say why.

Nicole had told her what happened, and she didn't judge her. She was a woman who'd made mistakes and tried to correct them. She was working to keep her family together, to come back from the depths.

But then Maggie had looked up the man who'd nearly destroyed Nicole. She'd watched his smarmy videos, read the legislation he'd sponsored. And all of it, *all of it*, was a tool to punish others. A weapon to turn on people who didn't comply.

Another cruelty to keep *his* system in power and on top.

That was the moment she decided she needed to create her own. And so she did. Something she could be in charge of, a lever she could pull.

Turned out to be nearly as flawed as any other system, but . . . she'd learned some things. She knew what she'd done wrong, and she could fix that.

It had been a mistake to move so quickly. To bring in any woman willing to give it a shot. Not everyone was strong enough to build a brand-new structure on a fresh foundation. Not everyone could handle the pressure. She'd settled for enthusiasm when she should have demanded reliability.

And perhaps she'd let it get too complicated, feeding elaborate schemes into issues that could have been resolved with a simple picture or a drunken confession. But each circumstance demanded the right cure, didn't it? Creating something like that took careful contemplation, careful planning, pieces fitting together with no gaps at all. Recklessness needed to be avoided at all costs.

She'd left too many crumbs to follow. There should have been no texts or traceable phone calls, and absolutely no friends involved. It would have been better to let Nicole work out her pain with her therapist. To keep her at a distance instead of letting her in. Maggie had allowed her heartache for her friends' marriage, for two people who truly loved each other, cloud her own judgment and lead her astray. A mistake and a misstep.

But mistakes could be corrected, and people could always find their way back to the right path. Next time she'd be more careful. She'd take time. Months of planning and space to cut out any woman who gave a hint of instability. Three women this time instead of four. Risks seemed to multiply exponentially like rabbits.

When the studio door opened with a rush of traffic noise, Maggie looked up from her email to see a woman walking in, a bit uncertain. She was medium height and appealingly round, with a cute angular bob and huge brown eyes. Though she looked young enough to be a student, she was actually a college English professor Maggie had met after giving a talk at a divorce support group.

"Deepti!" she called, waving her hand to draw her attention back to the tiny office. "You came!"

"Oh," she yelped, touching her neck with a nervous hand. "Hi, Maggie! Yes, I'm here. For what that's worth."

"Come on back."

Her gaze darted around at the boxing equipment as she approached, clearly terrified by the idea of trying out this new thing. But she'd come, just as Maggie had thought she would.

Though Deepti was soft-spoken and held her body as if someone might reach out and startle her at any moment, she always met Maggie's gaze with unflinching strength. She struck her as a smart woman who knew how to observe and take everything in without drawing notice to herself. Exactly the kind of woman Maggie could help. And trust.

She gestured toward the one chair wedged into the tight space of the office that smelled of tape and old sweat. "No pressure. You can just observe today and see what you think! I bet you'll get hooked. No pun intended."

"That sounds great," she answered with a laugh, though she clutched her purse in a tight embrace as she perched at the edge of the chair.

"As you watch, keep in mind that I've only ever had one or two clients who've done this before. Everyone is new when they start. So if you're impressed by what you see, don't forget that will be you in just a few weeks of trying. I believe this will be great for you."

Nodding, Deepti relaxed a little. "Me too. I'm good at jump rope, anyway! So that won't be new."

Maggie laughed, thinking of her own girlhood, jump roping her way through the neighborhood with friends. They'd been fast and free and daring, climbing trees and leaping the creeks that had been tucked beneath roadways in their crowded neighborhood.

Funny how much girls believed in their own bodies before being told they shouldn't. "Good. I'm glad. You hang out and observe the class, and then maybe we can grab a bite, if you want to."

"Oh, that would be lovely. Thank you!"

"Don't thank me. Your story really inspired me." Maggie glanced up as the first two clients of the evening walked in, chatting as they dropped bags on the ground. "I can't wait to hear more."

She looked back to Deepti and met her eyes, holding her liquid brown gaze as Maggie let her face glow with confidence in her. The depth of the look she returned belied her passive pose. Deepti was strong and used to hiding it. But she'd be so much stronger with the right support. Maggie could feel that potential in her, silent and waiting.

"And, Deepti . . . ," she said finally, leaning forward. Deepti inched forward a little as well, waiting for a secret, joining in. "If you're comfortable . . . we really need to talk more about that ex-husband of yours. I have some thoughts."

ABOUT THE AUTHOR

Victoria Helen Stone is the Amazon Charts bestselling author of *Jane Doe* and *Problem Child* in the Jane Doe series; *At the Quiet Edge*; *The Last One Home*; *Half Past*; *False Step*; and *Evelyn, After*. She is also the author of twenty-nine books as *USA Today* bestselling author Victoria Dahl and the recipient of the prestigious American Library Association Reading List award for best genre fiction. Published in more than a dozen languages, Victoria writes in her home office high in the Wasatch Mountains of Utah, far from her origins in the flattest plains of Minnesota, Texas, and Oklahoma. She enjoys summer trail hikes in the mountains almost as much as she enjoys staying inside by the fire during winter. Victoria is passionate about dessert, true crime, and her terror of mosquitoes. For more information, visit www.victoriahelenstone.com.